Henry Thoreau

The Writings of Henry Thoreau
Volume VI

Outlook

Henry Thoreau

The Writings of Henry Thoreau
Volume VI

1. Auflage | ISBN: 978-3-73263-036-3

Erscheinungsort: Frankfurt am Main, Deutschland

Erscheinungsjahr: 2018

Outlook Verlag GmbH, Frankfurt.

THE WRITINGS OF HENRY DAVID THOREAU

IN TWENTY VOLUMES

VOLUME VI

MANUSCRIPT EDITION
LIMITED TO SIX HUNDRED COPIES
NUMBER 65 ——

Sabbatia ***(page 264)***

Thoreau's Boat-landing, Concord River

THE WRITINGS OF

HENRY DAVID THOREAU

FAMILIAR LETTERS

EDITED BY F. B. SANBORN

ENLARGED EDITION

BOSTON AND NEW YORK
HOUGHTON MIFFLIN ANDCOMPANY
MDCCCCVI

INTRODUCTION

The fortune of Henry Thoreau as an author of books has been peculiar, and such as to indicate more permanence of his name and fame than could be predicted of many of his contemporaries. In the years of his literary activity (twenty-five in all), from 1837 to 1862,—when he died, not quite forty-five years old,—he published but two volumes, and those with much delay and difficulty in finding a publisher. But in the thirty-two years after his death, nine volumes were published from his manuscripts and fugitive pieces,—the present being the tenth. Besides these, two biographies of Thoreau had appeared in America, and two others in England, with numerous reviews and sketches of the man and his writings,—enough to make several volumes more. Since 1894 other biographies and other volumes have appeared, and now his writings in twenty volumes are coming from the press. The sale of his books and the interest in his life are greater than ever; and he seems to have grown early into an American classic, like his Concord neighbors, Emerson and Hawthorne. Pilgrimages are made to his grave and his daily haunts, as to theirs,—and those who come find it to be true, as was said by an accomplished woman (Miss Elizabeth Hoar) soon after his death, that "Concord is Henry's monument, adorned with suitable inscriptions by his own hand."

When Horace wrote of a noble Roman family,—

Crescit occulto velut arbor aevo

Fama Marcelli,"—

he pointed in felicitous phrase to the only fame that posterity has much regarded,—the slow-growing, deep-rooted laurel of renown. And Shakespeare, citing the old English rhyming saw,—

Small herbs have grace,

Great weeds do grow apace,"—

signified the same thing in a parable,—the popularity and suddenness of transient things, contrasted with the usefully permanent. There were plenty of authors in Thoreau's time (of whom Willis may be taken as the type) who would have smiled loftily to think that a rustic from the Shawsheen and Assabet could compete with the traveled scholar or elegant versifier who commanded the homage of drawing-rooms and magazines, for the prize of lasting remembrance; yet who now are forgotten, or live a shadowy life in the alcoves of libraries, piping forth an ineffective voice, like the shades in Virgil's Tartarus. But Thoreau was wiser when he wrote at the end of his poem, "Inspiration,"—

Fame cannot tempt the bard

Who's famous with his God;

Nor laurel him reward

Who has his Maker's nod."

He strove but little for glory, either immediate or posthumous, well knowing that it is the inevitable and unpursued result of what men do or say,—

"Our fatal shadow that walks by us still."

The Letters of Thoreau, though not less remarkable in some aspects than what he wrote carefully for publication, have thus far scarcely had justice done them. The selection made for a small volume in 1865 was designedly done to exhibit one phase of his character,—the most striking, if you will, but not the most native or attractive. "In his own home," says Ellery Channing, who knew him more inwardly than any other, "he was one of those characters who may be called 'household treasures;' always on the spot, with skillful eye and hand, to raise the best melons in the garden, plant the orchard with choicest trees, or act as extempore mechanic; fond of the pets, his sister's flowers, or sacred Tabby; kittens were his favorites,—he would play with them by the half-hour. No whim or coldness, no absorption of his time by public or private business, deprived those to whom he belonged of his kindness and affection. He did the duties that lay nearest, and satisfied those in his immediate circle; and whatever the impressions from the theoretical part of his writings, when the matter is probed to the bottom, good sense and good feeling will be detected in it." This is preëminently true; and the affectionate conviction of this made his sister Sophia dissatisfied with Emerson's rule of selection among the letters. This she confided to me, and this determined me, should occasion offer, to give the world some day a fuller and more familiar view of our friend.

For this purpose I have chosen many letters and mere notes, illustrating his domestic and gossipy moods,—for that element was in his mixed nature, inherited from the lively maternal side,—and even the colloquial vulgarity (using the word in the strict sense of "popular speech") that he sometimes allowed himself. In his last years he revolted a little at this turn of his thoughts, and, as Channing relates, "rubbed out the more humorous parts of his essays, originally a relief to their sterner features, saying, 'I cannot bear the levity I find;'" to which Channing replied that he ought to spare it, even to the puns, in which he abounded almost as much as Shakespeare. His friend was right,—the obvious incongruity was as natural to Thoreau as the grace and French elegance of his best sentences. In the dozen letters newly added to this edition, these contrasted qualities hardly appear so striking as in the longer, earlier ones; but they all illustrate events of his life or points in his character which are essential for fully understanding this most original of all American authors. The present volume is enlarged by some thirty pages, chiefly by additional letters to Ricketson, and all those to C. H. Greene. The modesty and self-deprecation in the Michigan correspondence will attract notice.

I have not rejected the common and trivial in these letters; being well assured that what the increasing number of Thoreau's readers desire is to see this piquant original just as he was,—not arrayed in the paradoxical cloak of the Stoic sage, nor sitting complacent in the cynic earthenware cave of Diogenes, and bidding Alexander stand out of his sunshine. He did those acts also; but they were not the whole man. He was far more poet than cynic or stoic; he had the proud humility of those sects, but still more largely that unconscious pride which comes to the poet when he sees that his pursuits are those of the few and not of the multitude. This perception came early to Thoreau, and was expressed in some unpublished verses dating from his long, solitary rambles, by night and day, on the seashore at Staten Island, where he first learned the sombre magnificence of Ocean. He feigns himself the son of what might well be one of Homer's fishermen, or the shipwrecked seaman of Lucretius,—

"Saevis projectus ab undis
Cui tantum in vita restet transire malorum,"—

and then goes on thus with his parable:—

Within a humble cot that looks to sea,

Daily I breathe this curious warm life;

Beneath a friendly haven's sheltering lee

My noiseless day with mystery still is rife.

'T is here, they say, my simple life began,—

And easy credence to the tale I lend,

For well I know 't is here I am a man,—

But who will simply tell me of the end?

These eyes, fresh-opened, spied the far-off Sea,

That like a silent godfather did stand,

Nor uttered one explaining word to me,

While introducing straight godmother Land.
And yonder still stretches that silent Main,
With many glancing ships besprinkled o'er;
And earnest still I gaze and gaze again
Upon the selfsame waves and friendly shore.
Infinite work my hands find there to do,
Gathering the relics which the waves upcast:
Each storm doth scour the sea for something new,
And every time the strangest is the last.
My neighbors sometimes come with lumbering carts.
As if they wished my pleasant toil to share;
But straight they go again to distant marts,
For only weeds and ballast are their care."

"Only weeds and ballast?" that is exactly what Thoreau's neighbors would have said he was gathering, for the most of his days; yet now he is seen to have collected something more durable and precious than they with their implements and market-carts. If they viewed him with a kind of scorn and pity, it must be said that he returned the affront; only time seems to have sided with the poet in the controversy that he maintained against his busy age.

Superiority,—moral elevation, without peevishness or condescension,—this was Thoreau's distinguishing quality. He softened it with humor, and sometimes sharpened it with indignation; but he directed his satire and his censure as often against himself as against mankind; men he truly loved,—if they would not obstruct his humble and strictly chosen path. The letters here printed show this, if I mistake not,—and the many other epistles of his, still uncollected, would hardly vary the picture he has sketched of himself, though they would add new facts. Those most to be sought for are his replies to the generous letters of his one English correspondent.[1]

The profile portrait reproduced in photogravure for this volume is less known than it should be,—for it alone of the four likenesses extant shows the aquiline features as his comrades of the wood and mountain saw them,—not weakened by any effort to bring him to the standard of other men in garb or expression. The artist, Mr. Walton Ricketson, knew and admired him. To him and to his sister Anna I am indebted for the letters and other material found in their volume "Daniel Ricketson and His Friends."

F. B. S.

CONCORD MASS., March 1, 1906.

FAMILIAR LETTERS OF THOREAU

Henry D. Thoreau, from the Ricketson Medallion
(page 263)

I
YEARS OF DISCIPLINE

It was a happy thought of Thoreau's friend Ellery Channing, himself a poet, to style our Concord hermit the "poet-naturalist;" for there seemed to be no year of his life and no hour of his day when Nature did not whisper some secret in his ear,—so intimate was he with her from childhood. In another connection, speaking of natural beauty, Channing said, "There is Thoreau,—he knows about it; give him sunshine and a handful of nuts, and he has enough." He was also a naturalist in the more customary sense,—one who studied and arranged methodically in his mind the facts of outward nature; a good botanist and ornithologist, a wise student of insects and fishes; an observer of the winds, the clouds, the seasons, and all that goes to make up what we call "weather" and "climate." Yet he was in heart a poet, and held all the accumulated knowledge of more than forty years not so much for use as for delight. As Gray's poor friend West said of himself, "like a clear-flowing stream, he reflected the beauteous prospect around;" and Mother Nature had given Thoreau for his prospect the meandering Indian river of Concord, the woodland pastures and fair lakes by which he dwelt or rambled most of his life. Born in the East Quarter of Concord, July 12, 1817, he died in the village, May 6, 1862; he was there fitted for Harvard College, which he entered in 1833, graduating in 1837; and for the rest of his life was hardly away from the town for more than a year in all. Consequently his letters to his family are few, for he was usually among them; but when separated from his elder brother John, or his sisters Helen and Sophia, he wrote to them, and these are the earliest of his letters which have been preserved. Always thoughtful for others, he has left a few facts to aid his biographer, respecting his birth and early years. In his Journal of December 27, 1855, he wrote:—

"Recalled this evening, with the aid of Mother, the various houses (and towns) in which I have lived, and some events of my life. Born … in the Minott house on the Virginia Road, where Father occupied Grandmother's 'thirds,' carrying on the farm. The Catherines [had] the other half of the house,—Bob Catherine and [brother] John threw up the turkeys. Lived there about eight months; Si Merriam the next neighbor. Uncle David [Dunbar] died when I was six weeks old.[2] I was baptized in the old meeting-house, by Dr. Ripley, when I was three months, and did not cry. [In] the Red House, where Grandmother lived, we [had] the west side till October, 1818,—hiring of Josiah Davis, agent for the Woodwards; there were Cousin Charles and Uncle Charles [Dunbar], more or less. According to the day-book first used by Grandfather [Thoreau],[3] dated 1797 (his part cut out and [then] usedby

Father in Concord in 1808-9, and in Chelmsford in 1818-21), Father hired of Proctor [in Chelmsford], and shop of Spaulding. Chelmsford till March, 1821; last charge in Chelmsford about middle of March, 1821. Aunt Sarah taught me to walk there, when fourteen months old. Lived next the meeting-house, where they kept the powder in the garret. Father kept shop and painted signs, etc.

“Pope’s house, at South End in Boston (a ten-footer) five or six months,—moved from Chelmsford through Concord, and may have tarried in Concord a little while.

“Day-book says, ‘Moved to Pinkney Street [Boston], September 10, 1821, on Monday;’ Whitwell’s house, Pinckney Street, to March, 1823; brick house, Concord, to spring of 1826; Davis house (next to Samuel Hoar’s) to May 7, 1827; Shattuck house (now Wm. Munroe’s) to spring of 1835; Hollis Hall, Cambridge, 1833; Aunts’ house to spring of 1837. [This was what is now the inn called ‘Thoreau House.’] At Brownson’s [Canton] while teaching in winter of 1835. Went to New York with Father peddling in 1836.”

This brings the date down to the year in which Henry Thoreau left college, and when the family letters begin. The notes continue, and now begin to have a literary value.

“Parkman house to fall of 1844; was graduated in 1837; kept town school a fortnight in 1837; began the big Red Journal, October, 1837; found my first arrowheads, fall of 1837; wrote a lecture (my first) on Society, March 14, 1838, and read it before the Lyceum, in the Masons’ Hall, April 11, 1838; went to Maine for a school in May, 1838; commenced school [in the Parkman house[4]] in the summer of 1838; wrote an essay on ‘Sound and Silence’ December, 1838; fall of 1839 up the Merrimack to White Mountains; ‘Aulus Persius Flaccus’ (first printed paper of consequence), February 10, 1840; the Red Journal of 546 pages ended June, 1840; Journal of 396 pages ended January 31, 1841.

“Went to R. W. Emerson’s in spring of 1841 [about April 25], and stayed there to summer of 1843; went to [William Emerson’s], Staten Island, May, 1843, and returned in December, or to Thanksgiving, 1843; made pencils in 1844; Texas house to August 29, 1850; at Walden, July, 1845, to fall of 1847; then at R. W. Emerson’s to fall of 1848, or while he was in Europe; Yellow House (reformed) till the present.”

As may be inferred from this simple record of the many mansions, chiefly small ones, in which he had spent his first thirty-eight years, there was nothing distinguished in the fortunes of Thoreau’s family, who were small merchants, artisans, or farmers mostly. On the father’s side they were from the isle of Jersey, where a French strain mingled with his English or Scandinavian blood; on the other side he was of Scotch and English descent, counting Jones, Dunbar, and Burns among his feminine ancestors. Liveliness and humor came to him from his Scotch connection; from father and grandfather he inherited a grave steadiness of mind rather at variance with his mother's vivacity. Manual dexterity was also inherited; so that he practiced the simpler mechanic arts with ease and skill; his mathematical training and his outdoor habits fitted him for a land-surveyor; and by that art, as well as by pencil-making, lecturing, and writing, he paid his way in the world, and left a small income from his writings to those who survived him. He taught pupils also, as did his brother and sisters; but it was not an occupation that he long followed after John's death in 1842. With these introductory statements we may proceed to Thoreau's first correspondence with his brother and sisters.

As an introduction to the correspondence, and a key to the young man's view of life, a passage may be taken from Thoreau's "part" at his college commencement, August 16, 1837. He was one of two to hold what was called a "Conference" on "The Commercial Spirit,"—his alternative or opponent in the dispute being Henry Vose, also of Concord, who, in later years, was a Massachusetts judge. Henry Thoreau,[5] then just twenty, said:—

"The characteristic of our epoch is perfect freedom,—freedom of thought and action. The indignant Greek, the oppressed Pole, the jealous American assert it. The skeptic no less than the believer, the heretic no less than the faithful child of the church, have begun to enjoy it. It has generated an unusual degree of energy and activity; it has generated the *commercial spirit*. Man thinks faster and freer than ever before. He, moreover, moves faster and freer. He is more restless, because he is more independent than ever. The winds and the waves are not enough for him; he must needs ransack the bowels of the earth, that he may make for himself a highway of iron over its surface.

"Indeed, could one examine this beehive of ours from an observatory among the stars, he would perceive an unwonted degree of bustle in these later ages. There would be hammering and chipping in one quarter; baking and brewing, buying and selling, money-changing and speechmaking in another. What impression would he receive from so general and impartial a survey. Would it appear to him that mankind used this world as not abusing it? Doubtless he would first be struck with the profuse beauty of our orb; he would never tire of admiring its varied zones and seasons, with their changes of living. He could not but notice that restless animal for whose sake it was contrived; but where he found one man to admire with him his fair dwelling-place, the ninety and nine would be scraping together a little of the gilded dust upon its surface.... We are to look chiefly for the origin of the commercial spirit, and the power that still cherishes and sustains it, in a blind and unmanly love of wealth. Wherever this exists, it is too sure to become the ruling spirit; and, as a natural consequence, it infuses into all our thoughts and affections a degree of its own selfishness; we become selfish in our patriotism, selfish in our domestic relations, selfish in our religion.

"Let men, true to their natures, cultivate the moral affections, lead manly and independent lives; let them make riches the means and not the end of existence, and we shall hear no more of the commercial spirit. The sea will not stagnate, the earth will be as green as ever, and the air as pure. This curious world which we inhabit is more wonderful than it is convenient; more beautiful than it is useful; it is more to be admired and enjoyed than used. The order of things should be somewhat reversed; the seventh should be man's day of toil, wherein to earn his living by the sweat of his brow; and the other six his Sabbath of the affections and the soul,—in which to range this widespread garden, and drink in the soft influences and sublime revelations of Nature.... The spirit we are considering is not altogether and without exception bad. We rejoice in it as one more indication of the entire and universal freedom that characterizes the age in which we live,—as an indication that the human race is making one more advance in that infinite series of progressions which awaits it. We glory in those very excesses which are a source of anxiety to the wise and good; as an evidence that man will not always be the slave of matter,—but ere long, casting off those earth-born desires which identify him with the brute, shall pass the days of his sojourn in this his nether paradise, as becomes the Lord of Creation."[6]

This passage is noteworthy as showing how early the philosophic mind was developed in Thoreau, and how much his thought and expression were influenced by Emerson's first book,—"Nature." But the soil in which that germinating seed fell was naturally prepared to receive it; and the wide diversity between the master and the disciple soon began to appear. In 1863, reviewing Thoreau's work, Emerson said, "That oaken strength which I noted whenever he walked or worked, or surveyed wood-lots,—the same unhesitating hand with which a field-laborer accosts a piece of work which I should shun as a waste of strength, Henry shows in his literary task. He has muscle, and ventures on and performs feats which I am forced to decline. In reading him I find the same thoughts, the same spirit that is in me; but he takes a step beyond, and illustrates by excellent images that which I should have conveyed in a sleepy generalization." True as this is, it omits one point of difference only too well known to Emerson,—the controversial turn of Thoreau's mind, in which he was so unlike Emerson and Alcott, and which must have given to his youthful utterances in company the air of something requiring an apology.

This, at all events, seems to have been the feeling of Helen Thoreau,[7] whose pride in her brother was such that she did not wish to see him misunderstood. A pleasing indication of both these traits is seen in the first extant letter of Thoreau to this sister. I have this in an autograph copy made by Mr. Emerson, when he was preparing the letters for partial publication, soon after Henry's death. For some reason he did not insert it in his volume; but it quite deserves to be printed, as indicating the period when it was clear to Thoreau that he must think for himself, whatever those around him might think.

TO HELEN THOREAU (AT TAUNTON).

Concord, October 27, 1837.

Dear Helen,—Please you, let the defendant say a few words in defense of his long silence. You know we have hardly done our own deeds, thought our own thoughts, or lived our own lives hitherto. For a man to act himself, he must be perfectly free; otherwise he is in danger of losing all sense of responsibility or of self-respect. Now when such a state of things exists, that the sacred opinions one advances in argument are apologized for by his friends, before his face, lest his hearers receive a wrong impression of the man,—when such gross injustice is of frequent occurrence, where shall we look, and not look in vain, for men, deeds, thoughts? As well apologize for the grape that it is sour, or the thunder that it is noisy, or the lightning that it tarries not.

Further, letter-writing too often degenerates into a communicating of facts, and not of truths; of other men's deeds and not our thoughts. What are the convulsions of a planet, compared with the emotions of the soul? or the rising of a thousand suns, if that is not enlightened by a ray?

Your affectionate brother,
Henry.

It is presumed the tender sister did not need a second lesson; and equally that Henry did not see fit always to write such letters as he praised above,—for he was quite ready to give his correspondents facts, no less than thoughts, especially in his family letters.

Next to this epistle, chronologically, comes one in the conventional dialect of the American Indian, as handed down by travelers and romancers, by Jefferson, Chateaubriand, Lewis, Clarke, and Fenimore Cooper. John Thoreau, Henry's brother, was born in 1815 and died January 11, 1842. He was teaching at Taunton in 1837.

TO JOHN THOREAU (AT TAUNTON).

(Written as from one Indian to another.)

Musketaquid, 202 Summers, two Moons, eleven Suns,

since the coming of the Pale Faces.
(November 11, 1837.)

TAHATAWAN, Sachimaussan, to his brother sachem, Hopeful of Hopewell,—hoping that he is well:—

Brother: It is many suns that I have not seen the print of thy moccasins by our council-fire; the Great Spirit has blown more leaves from the trees, and many clouds from the land of snows have visited our lodge; the earth has become hard, like a frozen buffalo-skin, so that the trampling of many herds is like the Great Spirit's thunder; the grass on the great fields is like the old man of many winters, and the small song sparrow prepares for his flight to the land whence the summer comes.

Brother: I write these things because I know that thou lovest the Great Spirit's creatures, and wast wont to sit at thy lodge-door, when the maize was green, to hear the bluebird's song. So shalt thou, in the land of spirits, not only find good hunting-grounds and sharp arrowheads, but much music of birds.

Brother: I have been thinking how the Pale-Faces have taken away our lands,—and was a woman. You are fortunate to have pitched your wigwam nearer to the great salt lake, where the Pale-Face can never plant corn.

Brother: I need not tell thee how we hunted on the lands of the Dundees,—a great war-chief never forgets the bitter taunts of his enemies. Our young men called for strong water; they painted their faces and dug up the hatchet. But their enemies, the Dundees, were women; they hastened to cover their hatchets with wampum. Our braves are not many; our enemies took a few strings from the heap their fathers left them, and our hatchets are buried. But not Tahatawan's; his heart is of rock when the Dundees sing,—his hatchet cuts deep into the Dundee braves.

Brother: There is dust on my moccasins; I have journeyed to the White Lake, in the country of the Ninares.[8] The Long-Knife has been there,—like a woman I paddled his war-canoe. But the spirits of my fathers were angered; the waters were ruffled, and the Bad Spirit troubled the air.

The hearts of the Lee-vites are gladdened; the young Peacock has returned to his lodge at Naushawtuck. He is the Medicine of his tribe, but his heart is like the dry leaves when the whirlwind breathes. He has come to help choose new chiefs for the tribe, in the great council-house, when two suns are past.—There is no seat for Tahatawan in the council-house. He lets the squaws talk,—his voice is heard above the war-whoop of his tribe, piercing the hearts of his foes; his legs are stiff, he cannot sit.

Brother: Art thou waiting for the spring, that the geese may fly low over thy wigwam? Thy arrows are sharp, thy bow is strong. Has Anawan killed all the eagles? The crows fear not the winter. Tahatawan's eyes are sharp,—he can track a snake in the grass, he knows a friend from a foe; he welcomes a friend to his lodge though the ravens croak.

Brother: Hast thou studied much in the medicine-books of the Pale-Faces? Dost thou understand the long talk of the Medicine whose words are like the music of the mockingbird? But our chiefs have not ears to hear him; they listen like squaws to the council of old men,—they understand not his words. But, Brother, he never danced the war-dance, nor heard the war-whoop of his enemies. He was a squaw; he stayed by the wigwam when the braves were out, and tended the tame buffaloes.

Fear not; the Dundees have faint hearts and much wampum. When the grass is green on the Great Fields, and the small titmouse returns again, we will hunt the buffalo together.

Our old men say they will send the young chief of the Karlisles, who lives in the green wigwam and is a great Medicine, that his word may be heard in the long talk which the wise men are going to hold at Shawmut, by the salt lake. He is a great talk, and will not forget the enemies of his tribe.

14th Sun. The fire has gone out in the council-house. The words of our old men have been like the vaunts of the Dundees. The Eagle-Beak was moved to talk like a silly Pale-Face, and not as becomes a great war-chief in a council of braves. The young Peacock is a woman among braves; he heard not the words of the old men,—like a squaw he looked at his medicine-paper.[9] The young chief of the green wigwam has hung up his moccasins; he will not leave his tribe till after the buffalo have come down on to the plains.

Brother: This is a long talk, but there is much meaning to my words; they are not like the thunder of canes when the lightning smites them. Brother, I have just heard *thy talk* and am well pleased; thou art getting to be a great Medicine. The Great Spirit confound the enemies of thy tribe.

TAHATAWAN.
His mark [a bow and arrow].

This singular letter was addressed to John Thoreau at Taunton, and was so carefully preserved in the family that it must have had value in their eyes, as recalling traits of the two Thoreau brothers, and also events in the village life of Concord, more interesting to the young people of 1837 than to the present generation. Some of its parables are easy to read, others quite obscure. The annual State election was an important event to Henry Thoreau then,—more so than it afterwards appeared; and he was certainly on the Whig side in politics, like most of the educated youths of Concord. His "young chief of the Karlisles" was Albert Nelson, son of a Carlisle physician, who began to practice law in Concord in 1836, and was afterwards chief justice of the Superior Court of the County of Suffolk. He was defeated at the election of 1837, as a Whig candidate for the legislature, by a Democrat. Henry Vose, above named, writing from "Butternuts," in New York, three hundred miles west of Concord, October 22, 1837, said to Thoreau: "You envy my happy situation, and mourn over your fate, which condemns you to loiter about Concord and grub among clamshells [for Indian relics]. If this were your only source of enjoyment while in Concord,—but I know that it is not. I well remember that 'antique and fish-like' office of *Major* Nelson (to whom, and to Mr. Dennis, and Bemis, and John Thoreau, I wish to be remembered); and still more vividly do I remember the fairer portion of the community in C." This indicates a social habit in Henry and John Thoreau, which the Indian "talk" also implies. Tahatawan, whom Henry here impersonated, was the mythical Sachem of Musketaquid (the Algonquin name for Concord River and region), whose fishing and hunting lodge was on the hill Naushawtuck, between the two rivers so much navigated by the Thoreaus. In 1837 the two brothers were sportsmen, and went shooting over the Concord meadows and moors, but of course the "buffalo" was a figure of speech; they never shot anything larger than a raccoon. A few years later they gave up killing the game.

TO JOHN THOREAU (AT TAUNTON).

Concord, February 10, 1838.

Dear John,—Dost expect to elicit a spark from so dull a steel as myself, by that flinty subject of thine? Truly, one of your copper percussion caps would have fitted this nail-head better.

Unfortunately, the "Americana"[10] has hardly two words on the subject. The process is very simple. The stone is struck with a mallet so as to produce pieces sharp at one end, and blunt at the other. These are laid upon a steel line (probably a chisel's edge), and again struck with the mallet, and flints of the required size are broken off. A skillful workman may make a thousand in a day.

So much for the "Americana." Dr. Jacob Bigelow in his "Technology," says, "Gunflints are formed by a skillful workman, who breaks them out with a hammer, a roller, and steel chisel, with small, repeated strokes."

Your ornithological commission shall be executed. When are you coming home?

Your affectionate brother,

HENRY D. THOREAU.

TO JOHN THOREAU (AT TAUNTON).

CONCORD, March 17, 1838.

DEAR JOHN,—Your box of relics came safe to hand, but was speedily deposited on the carpet, I assure you. What could it be? Some declared it must be Taunton herrings: "Just nose it, sir!" So down we went on to our knees, and commenced smelling in good earnest,—now horizontally from this corner to that, now perpendicularly from the carpet up, now diagonally,—and finally with a sweeping movement describing the circumference. But it availed not. Taunton herring would not be smelled. So we e'en proceeded to open it *vi et chisel*. What an array of nails! Four nails make a quarter, four quarters a yard, —i' faith, this is n't cloth measure! Blaze away, old boy! Clap in another wedge, then! There, softly! she begins to gape. Just give that old stickler, with a black hat on, another hoist. Aye, we'll pare his nails for him! Well done, old fellow, there's a breathing-hole for you. "Drive it in!" cries one; "Nip it off!" cries another. Be easy, I say. What's done may be undone. Your richest veins don't lie nearest the surface. Suppose we sit down and enjoy the prospect, for who knows but we may be disappointed? When they opened Pandora's box, all the contents escaped except Hope, but in this case hope is uppermost, and will be the first to escape when the box is opened. However, the general voice was for kicking the coverlid off.

The relics have been arranged numerically on a table. When shall we set up housekeeping? Miss Ward thanks you for her share of the spoils; also accept many thanks from your humble servant "for yourself."

I have a proposal to make. Suppose by the time you are released we should start in company for the West, and there either establish a school jointly, or procure ourselves separate situations. Suppose, moreover, you should get ready to start previous to leaving Taunton, to save time. Go *I* must, at all events. Dr. Jarvis enumerates nearly a dozen schools which I could have,—all such as would suit you equally well.[11] I wish you would write soon about this. It is high season to start. The canals are now open, and traveling comparatively cheap. I think I can borrow the cash in this town. There's nothing like trying.

Brigham wrote you a few words on the 8th, which father took the liberty to read, with the advice and consent of the family. He wishes you to send him those [numbers] of the "Library of Health" received since 1838, if you are in Concord; otherwise, he says you need not trouble yourself about it at present. He is in C., and enjoying better health than usual. But one number, and that you have, has been received.

The bluebirds made their appearance the 14th day of March; robins and pigeons have also been seen. Mr. Emerson has put up the bluebird-box in due form. All send their love.

From your aff. br.
H. D. Thoreau.

[Postscript by Helen Thoreau.]

Dear John,—Will you have the kindness to inquire at Mr. Marston's for an old singing-book I left there,—the "Handel and Haydn Collection," without a cover? Have you ever got those red handkerchiefs? Much love to the Marstons, Crockers, and Muenschers. Mr. Josiah Davis has failed. Mr. and Mrs. Howe have both written again, urging my going to Roxbury; which I suppose I shall do. What day of the month shall you return?

Helen.

One remark in this letter calls for attention,—that concerning the "bluebird-box" for Mr. Emerson. In 1853 Emerson wrote in his journal: "Long ago I wrote of Gifts, and neglected a capital example. John Thoreau, Jr., one day put a bluebird's box on my barn,—fifteen years ago it must be,—and there it still is, with every summer a melodious family in it, adorning the place and singing his praises. There's a gift for you,—which cost the giver no money, but nothing which he bought could have been so good. I think of another, quite inestimable. John Thoreau knew how much I should value a head of little Waldo, then five years old. He came to me and offered to take him to a daguerreotypist who was then in town, and he (Thoreau) would see it well done. He did it, and brought me the daguerre, which I thankfully paid for. A few months after, my boy died; and I have since to thank John Thoreau for that wise and gentle piece of friendship."

Little Waldo Emerson died January 27, 1842, and John Thoreau the same month; so that this taking of the portrait must have been but a few months before his own death, January 11. Henry Thoreau was then living in the Emerson family.

TO JOHN THOREAU (AT WEST ROXBURY).

Concord, July 8, 1838.

Dear John,—We heard from Helen to-day, and she informs us that you are coming home by the first of August. Now I wish you to write and let me know exactly when your vacation takes place, that I may take one at the same time. I am in school from 8 to 12 in the morning, and from 2 to 4 in the afternoon. After that I read a little Greek or English, or, for variety, take a stroll in the fields. We have not had such a year for berries this long time,—

the earth is actually blue with them. High blueberries, three kinds of low, thimble- and raspberries constitute my diet at present. (Take notice,—I only diet between meals.) Among my deeds of charity, I may reckon the picking of a cherry tree for two helpless single ladies, who live under the hill; but i' faith, it was robbing Peter to pay Paul,—for while I was exalted in charity towards them, I had no mercy on my own stomach. Be advised, my love for currants continues.

The only addition that I have made to my stock of ornithological information is in the shape not of a *Fring. melod.*,—but surely a melodious Fringilla,—the *F. juncorum*, or rush-sparrow. I had long known him by note, but never by name.

Report says that Elijah Stearns is going to take the town school. I have four scholars, and one more engaged. Mr. Fenner left town yesterday. Among occurrences of ill omen may be mentioned the falling out and cracking of the inscription stone of Concord Monument.[12] Mrs. Lowell and children are at Aunts'. Peabody [a college classmate] walked up last Wednesday, spent the night, and took a stroll in the woods.

Sophia says I must leave off and pen a few lines for her to Helen: so good-by. Love from all, and among them your aff. brother,

H. D. T.

The school above mentioned as begun by Henry Thoreau in this summer of 1838 was joined in by John, after finishing his teaching at West Roxbury, and was continued for several years. It was in this school that Louisa Alcott and her sister received some instruction, after their father removed from Boston to Concord, in the spring of 1840. It was opened in the Parkman house, where the family then lived, and soon after was transferred to the building of the Concord Academy,[13] not far off. John Thoreau taught the English branches and mathematics; Henry taught Latin and Greek and the higher mathematics, —and it was the custom of both brothers to go walking with their pupils one afternoon each week. It is as a professional schoolmaster that Henry thus writes to his sister Helen, then teaching at Roxbury, after a like experience in Taunton.

Concord Battle-Ground

TO HELEN THOREAU (AT ROXBURY).

CONCORD, October 6, 1838.

DEAR HELEN,—I dropped Sophia's letter into the box immediately on taking yours out, else the tone of the former had been changed.

I have no acquaintance with "Cleaveland's First Lessons," though I have peeped into his abridged grammar, which I should think very well calculated for beginners,—at least for such as would be likely to wear out one book before they would be prepared for the abstruser parts of grammar. Ahem!

As no one can tell what was the Roman pronunciation, each nation makes the Latin conform, for the most part, to the rules of its own language; so that with us of the vowels only A has a peculiar sound. In the end of a word of more than one syllable it is sounded like "ah," as *pennah*, *Lydiah*, *Hannah*, etc., without regard to case; but "*da*" is never sounded "*dah*," because it is a monosyllable. All terminations in *es*, and plural cases in *os*, as you know, are pronounced long,—as *homines* (hominese), *dominos* (dominose), or, in English, *Johnny Vose*. For information, see Adams' "Latin Grammar," before the Rudiments.

This is all law and gospel in the eyes of the world; but remember I am speaking, as it were, in the third person, and should sing quite a different tune if it were I that had made the quire. However, one must occasionally hang his harp on the willows, and play on the Jew's harp, in such a strange country as this.

One of your young ladies wishes to study mental philosophy, hey? Well, tell her that she has the very best text-book that I know of in her possession already. If she do not believe it, then she should have bespoken another better in another world, and not have expected to find one at "Little & Wilkins." But if she wishes to know how poor an apology for a mental philosophy men have tacked together, synthetically or analytically, in these latter days,—how they have squeezed the infinite mind into a compass that would not nonplus a surveyor of Eastern Lands—making Imagination and Memory to lie still in their respective apartments like ink-stand and wafers in a lady's escritoire,—why let her read Locke, or Stewart, or Brown. The fact is, mental philosophy is very like Poverty, which, you know, begins at home; and indeed, when it goes abroad, it is poverty itself.

Chorus. I should think an abridgment of one of the above authors, or of Ambercrombie, would answer her purpose. It may set her a-thinking. Probably there are many systems in the market of which I am ignorant.

As for themes, say first "Miscellaneous Thoughts." Set one up to a window, to note what passes in the street, and make her comments thereon; or let her gaze in the fire, or into a corner where there is a spider's web, and philosophize, moralize, theorize, or what not. What their hands find to putter about, or their minds to think about, that let them write about. To say nothing of advantage or disadvantage of this, that, or the other, let them set down their ideas at any given season, preserving the chain of thought as complete as may be.

This is the style pedagogical. I am much obliged to you for your piece of information. Knowing your dislike to a sentimental letter, I remain

Your affectionate brother,
H. D. T.

The next letter to Helen carries this pedagogical style a little farther, for it is in Latin, addressed "Ad Helenam L. Thoreau, Roxbury, Mass.," and postmarked "Concord, Jan. 25" (1840).

TO HELEN THOREAU (AT ROXBURY).

CONCORDIAE, Dec. Kal. Feb. A. D. MDCCCXL.

CARA SOROR,—Est magnus acervus nivis ad limina, et frigus intolerabile intus. Coelum ipsum ruit, credo, et terram operit. Sero stratum linquo et mature repeto; in fenestris multa pruina prospectum absumit; et hic miser scribo, non currente calamo, nam digiti mentesque torpescunt. Canerem cum Horatio, si vox non faucibus haeserit,—

Vides ut alta stet nive candidum
Nawshawtuct, nec jam sustineant onus
  Silvae laborantes, geluque
  Flumina constiterint acuto?
Dissolve frigus, ligna super foco
Large reponens, etc.

Sed olim, Musa mutata, et laetiore plectro,
Neque jam stabulis gaudet pecus, aut arator igne,
      Nec prata canis albicant pruinis;
Jam Cytherea choros ducit Venus imminente luna.

Quam turdus ferrugineus ver reduxerit, tu, spero, linques curas scholasticas, et, negotio religato, desipere in loco audebis; aut mecum inter sylvas, aut super scopulos Pulchri-Portus, aut in cymba super lacum Waldensem, mulcens fluctus manu, aut speciem miratus sub undas.

Bulwerius est mihi nomen incognitum,—unus ex ignobile vulgo, nec refutandus nec laudandus. Certe alicui nonnullam honorem habeo qui insanabili cacoethe scribendi teneatur.

Specie flagrantis Lexingtonis non somnia deturbat? At non Vulcanum Neptunumque culpemus, cum superstitioso grege. Natura curat animalculis aeque ac hominibus; cum serena, tum procellosa, amica est.

Si amas historiam et fortia facta heroum, non depone Rollin, precor; ne Clio offendas nunc, nec illa det veniam olim. Quos libros Latinos legis? legis, inquam, non studes. Beatus qui potest suos libellos tractare, et saepe perlegere, sine metu domini urgentis! ab otio injurioso procul est: suos amicos et vocare et dimittere quandocunque velit, potest. Bonus liber opus nobilissimum hominis. Hinc ratio non modo cur legeres, sed cur tu quoque scriberes; nec lectores carent; ego sum. Si non librum meditaris, libellum certe. Nihil posteris proderit te spirasse, et vitam nunc leniter nunc aspere egisse; sed cogitasse praecipue et scripsisse. Vereor ne tibi pertaesum hujus epistolae sit; necnon alma lux caret,

  Majoresque cadunt altis de montibus umbrae.

Quamobrem vale,—imo valete, et requiescatis placide, Sorores.

H. D. Thoreaus.

Memento scribere!

Cara Sophia,—Samuel Niger crebris aegrotationibus, quae agilitatem et aequum animum abstulere, obnoxius est; iis temporibus ad cellam descendit, et multas horas (ibi) manet.

Flores, ah crudelis pruina! parvo leti discrimine sunt. Cactus frigore ustus est, gerania vero adhuc vigent.

Conventus sociabiles hac hieme reinstituti fuere. Conveniunt (?) ad meum domum mense quarto vel quinto, ut tu hic esse possis. Matertera Sophia cum nobis remanet; quando urbem revertet non scio. Gravedine etiamnum, sed non tam aegre, laboramus.

Adolescentula E. White apud pagum paulisper moratur. Memento scribere intra duas hebdomedas.

Te valere desiderium est

Tui Matris,
C. Thoreaus.

P. S. Epistolam die solis proxima expectamus. (Amanuense, H. D. T.)

Barring a few slips, this is a good and lively piece of Latin, and noticeable for its thought as well as its learning and humor. The poets were evidently his favorites among Latin authors. Shall we attempt a free translation, such as Thoreau would give?

VERNACULAR VERSION.

Concord, January 23, 1840.

Dear Sister,—There is a huge snow-drift at the door, and the cold inside is intolerable. The very sky is coming down, I guess, and covering up the ground. I turn out late in the morning, and go to bed early; there is thick frost on the windows, shutting out the view; and here I write in pain, for fingers and brains are numb. I would chant with Horace, if my voice did not stick in my throat,—

See how Naushawtuct, deep in snow,

Stands glittering, while the bendingwoods

Scarce bear their burden, and the floods

Feel arctic winter stay their flow.

Pile on the firewood, melt the cold,

Spare nothing, etc.

But soon, changing my tune, and with a cheerfuller note, I'll say,—

No longer the flock huddles up in the stall, the plowman bends over the fire,

No longer frost whitens the meadow;

But the goddess of love, while the moon shines above,

Sets us dancing in light and in shadow.

When Robin Redbreast brings back the springtime, I trust that you will lay your school duties aside, cast off care, and venture to be gay now and then; roaming with me in the woods, or climbing the Fair Haven cliffs,—or else, in my boat on Walden, let the water kiss your hand, or gaze at your image in the wave.

Bulwer is to me a name unknown,—one of the unnoticed crowd, attracting neither blame nor praise. To be sure, I hold any one in some esteem who is helpless in the grasp of the writing demon.

Does not the image of the Lexington afire trouble your dreams?[14] But we may not, like the superstitious mob, blame Vulcan or Neptune,—neither fire nor water was in fault. Nature takes as much care for midgets as for mankind; she is our friend in storm and in calm.

If you like history, and the exploits of the brave, don't give up Rollin, I beg; thus would you displease Clio, who might not forgive you hereafter. What Latin are you reading? I mean *reading*, not studying. Blessed is the man who can have his library at hand, and oft peruse the books, without the fear of a taskmaster! he is far enough from harmful idleness, who can call in and dismiss these friends when he pleases. An honest book's the noblest work of man. There's a reason, now, not only for your reading, but for writing something, too. You will not lack readers,—here am I, for one. If you cannot compose a volume, then try a tract. It will do the world no good, hereafter, if you merely exist, and pass life smoothly or roughly; but to have thoughts, and write them down, that helps greatly.

I fear you will tire of this epistle; the light of day is dwindling, too,—

And longer fall the shadows of the hills.

Therefore, good-by; fare ye well, and sleep in quiet, both my sisters! Don't forget to write.

H. D. Thoreau.

POSTSCRIPT. (BY MRS. THOREAU.)

Dear Sophia,—Sam Black [the cat] is liable to frequent attacks that impair his agility and good-nature; at such times he goes down cellar, and stays many hours. Your flowers—O, the cruel frost!—are all but dead; the cactus is withered by cold, but the geraniums yet flourish. The Sewing Circle has been revived this winter; they meet at our house in April or May, so that you may then be here. Your Aunt Sophia remains with us,—when she will return to the city I don't know. We still suffer from heavy colds, but not so much. Young Miss E. White is staying in the village a little while (is making a little visit in town). Don't forget to write within two weeks. We expect a letter next Sunday.

That you may enjoy good health is the prayer of

Your mother,
C. Thoreau.

(H. D. T. was the scribe.)

Cats were always an important branch of the Thoreaus' domestic economy, and Henry was more tolerant of them than men are wont to be. Flowers were the specialty of Sophia, who, when I knew her, from 1855 to 1876, usually had a small conservatory in a recess of the dining-room. At this time (1840) she seems to have been aiding Helen in her school. The next letter, to Helen, is of a graver tone:—

TO HELEN THOREAU (AT ROXBURY).

Concord, June 13, 1840.

Dear Helen,—That letter to John, for which you had an opportunity doubtless to substitute a more perfect communication, fell, as was natural, into the hands of his "transcendental brother," who is his proxy in such cases, having been commissioned to acknowledge and receipt all bills that may be presented. But what's in a name? Perhaps it does not matter whether it be John or Henry. Nor will those same six months have to be altered, I fear, to suit his case as well. But methinks they have not passed entirely without intercourse, provided we have been sincere though humble worshipers of the same virtue in the mean time. Certainly it is better that we should make ourselves quite sure of such a communion as this by the only course which is completely free from suspicion,—the coincidence of two earnest and aspiring lives,—than run the risk of a disappointment by relying wholly or chiefly on so meagre and uncertain a means as speech, whether written or spoken, affords. How often, when we have been nearest each other bodily, have we really been farthest off! Our tongues were the witty foils with which we fenced each other off. Not that we have not met heartily and with profit as members of one family, but it was a small one surely, and not that other human family. We have met frankly and without concealment ever, as befits those who have an instinctive trust in one another, and the scenery of whose outward lives has been the same, but never as prompted by an earnest and affectionate desire to probe deeper our mutual natures. Such intercourse, at least, if it has ever been, has not condescended to the vulgarities of oral communication, for the ears are provided with no lid as the eye is, and would not have been deaf to it in sleep. And now glad am I, if I am not mistaken in imagining that some such transcendental inquisitiveness has traveled post *thither*,—for, as I observed before, where the bolt hits, thither was it aimed,—any arbitrary direction notwithstanding.

Thus much, at least, our *kindred* temperament of mind and body—and long *family*-arity—have done for us, that we already find ourselves standing on a solid and natural footing with respect to one another, and shall not have to waste time in the so often unavailing endeavor to arrive fairly at this simple ground.

Let us leave trifles, then, to accident; and politics, and finance, and such gossip, to the moments when diet and exercise are cared for, and speak to each other deliberately as out of one infinity into another,—you there in time and space, and I here. For beside this relation, all books and doctrines are no better than gossip or the turning of a spit.

Equally to you and Sophia, from

Your affectionate brother,
H. D. THOREAU.

We come now to the period when Thoreau entered on more intimate relations with Emerson. There was a difference of fourteen years in their ages, which had hitherto separated them intellectually; but now the young scholar, thinker, and naturalist had so fast advanced that he could meet his senior on more equal terms, and each became essential to the other. With all his prudence and common sense, in which he surpassed most men, Emerson was yet lacking in some practical faculties; while Thoreau was the most practical and handy person in all matters of every-day life,—a good mechanic and gardener, methodical in his habits, observant and kindly in the domestic world, and attractive to children, who now were important members of the Emerson household. He was therefore invited by Emerson to make his house a home,—looking after the garden, the business affairs, and performing the office of a younger brother or a grown-up son. The invitation was accepted in April, 1841, and Thoreau remained in the family, with frequent absences, until he went in May, 1843, to reside with Mr. William Emerson, near New York, as the tutor of his sons. During these two years much occurred of deep moment to the two friends. Young Waldo Emerson, the beautiful boy, died, and just before, John Thoreau, the sunny and hopeful brother, whom Henry seems to have loved more than any human being. These tragedies brought the bereaved nearer together, and gave to Mrs. Emerson in particular an affection for Thoreau and a trust in him which made the intimate life of the household move harmoniously, notwithstanding the independent and eccentric genius of Thoreau.

TO MRS. LUCY BROWN[15] (AT PLYMOUTH).

CONCORD, July 21, 1841.

DEAR FRIEND,—Don't think I need any prompting to write to you; but what tough earthenware shall I put into my packet to travel over so many hills, and thrid so many woods, as lie between Concord and Plymouth? Thank fortune it is all the way down hill, so they will get safely carried; and yet it seems as if it were writing against time and the sun to send a letter east, for no natural force forwards it. You should go dwell in the West, and then I would deluge you with letters, as boys throw feathers into the air to see the wind take them. I should rather fancy you at evening dwelling far away behind the serene curtain of the West,—the home of fair weather,—than over by the chilly sources of the east wind.

What quiet thoughts have you nowadays which will float on that east wind to west, for so we may make our worst servants our carriers,—what progress made from *can't* to *can*, in practice and theory? Under this category, you remember, we used to place all our philosophy. Do you have any still, startling, well moments, in which you think grandly, and speak with emphasis? Don't take this for sarcasm, for not in a year of the gods, I fear, will such a golden approach to plain speaking revolve again. But away with such fears; by a few miles of travel we have not distanced each other's sincerity.

I grow savager and savager every day, as if fed on raw meat, and my tameness is only the repose of untamableness. I dream of looking abroad summer and winter, with free gaze, from some mountain-side, while my eyes revolve in an Egyptian slime of health,—I to be nature looking into nature with such easy sympathy as the blue-eyed grass in the meadow looks in the face of the sky. From some such recess I would put forth sublime thoughts daily, as the plant puts forth leaves. Now-a-nights I go on to the hill to see the sun set, as one would go home at evening; the bustle of the village has run on all day, and left me quite in the rear; but I see the sunset, and find that it can wait for my slow virtue.

But I forget that you think more of this human nature than of this nature I praise. Why won't you believe that mine is more human than any single man or woman can be? that in it, in the sunset there, are all the qualities that can adorn a household, and that sometimes, in a fluttering leaf, one may hear all your Christianity preached.

You see how unskillful a letter-writer I am, thus to have come to the end of my sheet when hardly arrived at the beginning of my story. I was going to be soberer, I assure you, but now have only room to add, that if the fates allot you a serene hour, don't fail to communicate some of its serenity to your friend,

HENRY D. THOREAU.

No, no. Improve so rare a gift for yourself, and send me of your leisure.

TO MRS. LUCY BROWN (AT PLYMOUTH).

CONCORD, Wednesday evening,
September 8, [1841.]

DEAR FRIEND,—Your note came wafted to my hand like the first leaf of the fall on the September wind, and I put only another interpretation upon its lines than upon the veins of those which are soon to be strewed around me. It is nothing but Indian summer here at present. I mean that any weather seems reserved expressly for our late purposes whenever we happen to be fulfilling them. I do not know what right I have to so much happiness, but rather hold it in reserve till the time of my desert.

What with the crickets and the crowing of cocks, and the lowing of kine, our Concord life is sonorous enough. Sometimes I hear the cock bestir himself on his perch under my feet, and crow shrilly before dawn; and I think I might have been born any year for all the phenomena I know. We count sixteen eggs daily now, when arithmetic will only fetch the hens up to thirteen; but the world is young, and we wait to see this eccentricity complete its period.

My verses on Friendship are already printed in the *Dial*; not expanded, but reduced to completeness by leaving out the long lines, which always have, or should have, a longer or at least another sense than short ones.

Just now I am in the mid-sea of verses, and they actually rustle around me as the leaves would round the head of Autumnus himself should he thrust it up through some vales which I know; but, alas! many of them are but crisped and yellow leaves like his, I fear, and will deserve no better fate than to make mould for new harvests. I see the stanzas rise around me, verse upon verse, far and near, like the mountains from Agiocochook, not all having a terrestrial existence as yet, even as some of them may be clouds; but I fancy I see the gleam of some Sebago Lake and Silver Cascade, at whose well I may drink one day. I am as unfit for any practical purpose—I mean for the furtherance of the world's ends—as gossamer for ship-timber; and I, who am going to be a pencil-maker to-morrow,[16] can sympathize with God Apollo, who served

King Admetus for a while on earth. But I believe he found it for his advantage at last,—as I am sure I shall, though I shall hold the nobler part at least out of the service.

Don't attach any undue seriousness to this threnody, for I love my fate to the very core and rind, and could swallow it without paring it, I think. You ask if I have written any more poems? Excepting those which Vulcan is now forging, I have only discharged a few more bolts into the horizon,—in all, three hundred verses—and sent them, as I may say, over the mountains to Miss Fuller, who may have occasion to remember the old rhyme:—

Three scipen gode

Comen mid than flode

Three hundred cnihten."

But these are far more Vandalic than they. In this narrow sheet there is not room even for one thought to root itself. But you must consider this an odd leaf of a volume, and that volume

Your friend,
HENRY D. THOREAU.

TO MRS. LUCY BROWN (AT PLYMOUTH).

CONCORD, October 5, 1841.

DEAR FRIEND,—I send you Williams's[17] letter as the last remembrancer to one of those "whose acquaintance he had the pleasure to form while in Concord." It came quite unexpectedly to me, but I was very glad to receive it, though I hardly know whether my utmost sincerity and interest can inspire a sufficient answer to it. I should like to have you send it back by some convenient opportunity.

Pray let me know what you are thinking about any day,—what most nearly concerns you. Last winter, you know, you did more than your share of the talking, and I did not complain for want of an opportunity. Imagine your stove-door out of order, at least, and then while I am fixing it you will think of enough things to say.

What makes the value of your life at present? what dreams have you, and what realizations? You know there is a high table-land which not even the east wind reaches. Now can't we walk and chat upon its plane still, as if there were no lower latitudes? Surely our two destinies are topics interesting and grand enough for any occasion.

I hope you have many gleams of serenity and health, or, if your body will grant you no positive respite, that you may, at any rate, enjoy your sickness occasionally, as much as I used to tell of. But here is the bundle going to be done up, so accept a "good-night" from

HENRY D. THOREAU.

TO MRS. LUCY BROWN (AT PLYMOUTH).

CONCORD, March 2, 1842.

DEAR FRIEND,—I believe I have nothing new to tell you, for what was news you have learned from other sources. I am much the same person that I was, who should be so much better; yet when I realize what has transpired, and the greatness of the part I am unconsciously acting, I am thrilled, and it seems as if there were none in history to match it.

Soon after John's death I listened to a music-box, and if, at any time, that event had seemed inconsistent with the beauty and harmony of the universe, it was then gently constrained into the placid course of nature by those steady notes, in mild and unoffended tone echoing far and wide under the heavens. But I find these things more strange than sad to me. What right have I to grieve, who have not ceased to wonder? We feel at first as if some opportunities of kindness and sympathy were lost, but learn afterward that any *pure grief* is ample recompense for all. That is, if we are faithful; for a great grief is but sympathy with the soul that disposes events, and is as natural as the resin on Arabian trees. Only Nature has a right to grieve perpetually, for she only is innocent. Soon the ice will melt, and the blackbirds sing along the river which he frequented, as pleasantly as ever. The same everlasting serenity will appear in this face of God, and we will not be sorrowful if he is not.

We are made happy when reason can discover no occasion for it. The memory of some past moments is more persuasive than the experience of present ones. There have been visions of such breadth and brightness that these motes were invisible in their light.

I do not wish to see John ever again,—I mean him who is dead,—but that other, whom only he would have wished to see, or to be, of whom he was the imperfect representative. For we are not what we are, nor do we treat or esteem each other for such, but for what we are capable of being.

As for Waldo, he died as the mist rises from the brook, which the sun will soon dart his rays through. Do not the flowers die every autumn? He had not even taken root here. I was not startled to hear that he was dead; it seemed the most natural event that could happen. His fine organization demanded it, and nature gently yielded its request. It would have been strange if he had lived. Neither will nature manifest any sorrow at his death, but soon the note of the lark will be heard down in the meadow, and fresh dandelions will spring from the old stocks where he plucked them last summer.

I have been living ill of late, but am now doing better. How do you live in that Plymouth world, nowadays?[18] Please remember me to Mary Russell. You must not blame me if I do *talk to the clouds*, for I remain

Your friend,
HENRY D. THOREAU.

TO MRS. LUCY BROWN (AT PLYMOUTH).

CONCORD, January 24, 1843.

DEAR FRIEND,—The other day I wrote you a letter to go in Mrs. Emerson's bundle, but, as it seemed unworthy, I did not send it, and now, to atone for that, I am going to send this, whether it be worthy or not. I will not venture upon news, for, as all the household are gone to bed, I cannot learn what has been told you. Do you read any noble verses nowadays? or do not verses still seem noble? For my own part, they have been the only things I remembered, or that which occasioned them, when all things else were blurred and defaced. All things have put on mourning but they; for the elegy itself is some victorious melody or joy escaping from the wreck.

It is a relief to read some true book, wherein all are equally dead,—equally alive. I think the best parts of Shakespeare would only be enchanced by the most thrilling and affecting events. I have found it so. And so much the more, as they are not intended for consolation.

Do you think of coming to Concord again? I shall be glad to see you. I should be glad to know that I could see you when I would.

We always seem to be living just on the brink of a pure and lofty intercourse, which would make the ills and trivialness of life ridiculous. After each little interval, though it be but for the night, we are prepared to meet each other as gods and goddesses.

I seem to have dodged all my days with one or two persons, and lived upon expectation,—as if the bud would surely blossom; and so I am content to live.

What means the fact—which is so common, so universal—that some soul that has lost all hope for itself can inspire in another listening soul an infinite confidence in it, even while it is expressing its despair?

I am very happy in my present environment, though actually mean enough myself, and so, of course, all around me; yet, I am sure, we for the most part are transfigured to one another, and are that to the other which we aspire to be ourselves. The longest course of mean and trivial intercourse may not prevent my practicing this divine courtesy to my companion. Notwithstanding all I hear about brooms, and scouring, and taxes, and housekeeping, I am constrained to live a strangely mixed life,—as if even Valhalla might have its kitchen. We are all of us Apollos serving some Admetus.

I think I must have some Muses in my pay that I know not of, for certain musical wishes of mine are answered as soon as entertained. Last summer I went to Hawthorne's suddenly for the express purpose of borrowing his music-box, and almost immediately Mrs. Hawthorne proposed to lend it to me. The other day I said I must go to Mrs. Barrett's to hear hers, and lo! straightway Richard Fuller sent me one for a present from Cambridge. It is a very good one. I should like to have you hear it. I shall not have to employ you to borrow for me now. Good-night.

From your affectionate friend,
H. D. T.

TO RICHARD F. FULLER (AT CAMBRIDGE).

CONCORD, January 16, 1843.

DEAR RICHARD,—I need not thank you for your present, for I hear its music, which seems to be playing just for us two pilgrims marching over hill and dale of a summer afternoon, up those long Bolton hills and by those bright Harvard lakes, such as I see in the placid Lucerne on the lid; and whenever I hear it, it will recall happy hours passed with its donor.

When did mankind make that foray into nature and bring off this booty? For certainly it is but history that some rare virtue in remote times plundered these strains from above and communicated them to men. Whatever we may think of it, it is a part of the harmony of the spheres you have sent me; which has condescended to serve us Admetuses, and I hope I may so behave that this may always be the tenor of your thought for me.

If you have any strains, the conquest of your own spear or quill, to accompany these, let the winds waft them also to me.

I write this with one of the "primaries" of my osprey's wings, which I have preserved over my glass for some state occasion, and now it offers.

Mrs. Emerson sends her love.

TO MRS. LUCY BROWN (AT PLYMOUTH).

CONCORD, Friday evening, January 25, 1843.

DEAR FRIEND,—Mrs. Emerson asks me to write you a letter, which she will put into her bundle to-morrow along with the "Tribunes" and "Standards," and miscellanies, and what not, to make an assortment. But what shall I write?

You live a good way off, and I don't know that I have anything which will bear sending so far. But I am mistaken, or rather impatient when I say this,—for we all have a gift to send, not only when the year begins, but as long as interest and memory last. I don't know whether you have got the many I have sent you, or rather whether you were quite sure where they came from. I mean the letters I have sometimes launched off eastward in my thought; but if you have been happier at one time than another, think that then you received them. But this that I now send you is of another sort. It will go slowly, drawn by horses over muddy roads, and lose much of its little value by the way. You may have to pay for it, and it may not make you happy after all. But what shall be my new-year's gift, then? Why, I will send you my still fresh remembrance of the hours I have passed with you here, for I find in the remembrance of them the best gift you have left to me. We are poor and sick creatures at best; but we can have well memories, and sound and healthy thoughts of one another still, and an intercourse may be remembered which was without blur, and above us both.

Perhaps you may like to know of my estate nowadays. As usual, I find it harder to account for the happiness I enjoy, than for the sadness which instructs me occasionally. If the little of this last which visits me would only be sadder, it would be happier. One while I am vexed by a sense of meanness; one while I simply wonder at the mystery of life; and at another, and at another, seem to rest on my oars, as if propelled by propitious breezes from I know not what quarter. But for the most part I am an idle, inefficient, lingering (one term will do as well as another, where all are true and none true enough) member of the great commonwealth, who have most need of my own charity,—if I could not be charitable and indulgent to myself, perhaps as good a subject for my own satire as any. You see how, when I come to talk of myself, I soon run dry, for I would fain make that a subject which can be no subject for me, at least not till I have the grace to rule myself.

I do not venture to say anything about your griefs, for it would be unnatural for me to speak as if I grieved with you, when I think I do not. If I were to see you, it might be otherwise. But I know you will pardon the trivialness of this letter; and I only hope—as I know that you have reason to be so—that you are still happier than you are sad, and that you remember that the smallest seed of faith is of more worth than the largest fruit of happiness. I have no doubt that out of S——'s death you sometimes draw sweet consolation, not only for that, but for long-standing griefs, and may find some things made smooth by it, which before were rough.

I wish you would communicate with me, and not think me unworthy to know any of your thoughts. Don't think me unkind because I have not written to you. I confess it was for so poor a reason as that you almost made a principle of not answering. I could not speak truly with this ugly fact in the way; and perhaps I wished to be assured, by such evidence as you could not voluntarily give, that it was a kindness. For every glance at the moon, does she not send me an answering ray? Noah would hardly have done himself the pleasure to release his dove, if she had not been about to come back to him with tidings of green islands amid the waste.

But these are far-fetched reasons. I am not speaking directly enough to yourself now; so let me say *directly*

From your friend,
HENRY D. THOREAU.

Exactly when correspondence began between Emerson and Thoreau is not now to be ascertained, since all the letters do not seem to have been preserved. Their acquaintance opened while Thoreau was in college, although Emerson may have seen the studious boy at the town school in Concord, or at the "Academy" there, while fitting for college. But they only came to know each other as sharers of the same thoughts and aspirations in the autumn of 1837, when, on hearing a new lecture of Emerson's, Helen Thoreau said to Mrs. Brown, then living or visiting in the Thoreau family, "Henry has a thought very like that in his journal" (which he had newly begun to keep). Mrs. Brown desired to see the passage, and soon bore it to her sister, Mrs. Emerson, whose husband saw it, and asked Mrs. Brown to bring her young friend to see him. By 1838 their new relation of respect was established, and Emerson wrote to a correspondent, "I delight much in my young friend, who seems to have as free and erect a mind as any I have ever met." A year later (Aug. 9, 1839), he wrote to Carlyle, "I have a young poet in this village, named Thoreau, who writes the truest verses." Indeed, it was in the years 1839-40 that he seems to have written the poems by which he is best remembered. Thoreau told me in his last illness that he had written many verses and destroyed many,—this fact he then regretted, although he had done it at the instance of Emerson, who did not praise them. "But," said he, "they may have been better than we thought them, twenty years ago."

The earliest note which I find from Emerson to Thoreau bears no date, but must have been written before 1842, for at no later time could the persons named in it have visited Concord together. Most likely it was in the summer of 1840, and to the same date do I assign a note asking Henry to join the Emersons in a party to the Cliffs (*scopuli Pulchri-Portus*), and to bring his flute,—for on that pastoral reed Thoreau played sweetly. The first series of letters from Thoreau to Emerson begins early in 1843, about the time the letters just given were written to Mrs. Brown. In the first he gives thanks to

Emerson for the hospitality of his house in the two preceding years; a theme to which he returned a few months later,—for I doubt not the lovely sad poem called "The Departure" was written at Staten Island soon after his leaving the Emerson house in Concord for the more stately but less congenial residence of William Emerson at Staten Island, whither he betook himself in May, 1843. This first letter, however, was sent from the Concord home to Waldo Emerson at Staten Island, or perhaps in New York, where he was that winter giving a course of lectures.

In explanation of the passages concerning Bronson Alcott, in this letter, it should be said that he was then living at the Hosmer Cottage, in Concord, with his English friends, Charles Lane and Henry Wright, and that he had refused to pay a tax in support of what he considered an unjust government, and was arrested by the constable, Sam Staples, in consequence.

TO R. W. EMERSON (AT NEW YORK).

Concord, January 24, 1843.

Dear Friend,—The best way to correct a mistake is to make it right. I had not spoken of writing to you, but as you say you are about to write to me when you get my letter, I make haste on my part in order to get yours the sooner. I don't well know what to say to earn the forthcoming epistle, unless that Edith takes rapid strides in the arts and sciences—or music and natural history—as well as over the carpet; that she says "papa" less and less abstractedly every day, looking in *my* face,—which may sound like a *Ranz des Vaches* to yourself. And Ellen declares every morning that "papa *may* come home to-night;" and by and by it will have changed to such positive statement as that "papa came home *larks* night."

Elizabeth Hoar still flits about these clearings, and I meet her here and there, and in all houses but her own, but as if I were not the less of her family for all that. I have made slight acquaintance also with one Mrs. Lidian Emerson, who almost persuades me to be a Christian, but I fear I as often lapse into heathenism. Mr. O'Sullivan[19] was here three days. I met him at the Atheneum [Concord], and went to Hawthorne's [at the Old Manse] to tea with him. He expressed a great deal of interest in your poems, and wished me to give him a list of them, which I did; he saying he did not know but he should notice them. He is a rather puny-looking man, and did not strike me. We had nothing to say to one another, and therefore we said a great deal! He, however, made a point of asking me to write for his Review, which I shall be glad to do. He is, at any rate, one of the not-bad, but does not by any means take you by storm,—no, nor by calm, which is the best way. He expects to see you in New York. After tea I carried him and Hawthorne to the Lyceum.

Mr. Alcott has not altered much since you left. I think you will find him much the same sort of person. With Mr. Lane I have had one regular chat *à la* George Minott, which of course was greatly to our mutual grati- and edification; and, as two or three as regular conversations have taken place since, I fear there may have been a precession of the equinoxes. Mr. Wright, according to the last accounts, is in Lynn, with uncertain aims and prospects, —maturing slowly, perhaps, as indeed are all of us. I suppose they have told you how near Mr. Alcott went to the jail, but I can add a good anecdote to the rest. When Staples came to collect Mrs. Ward's taxes, my sister Helen asked him what he thought Mr. Alcott meant,—what his idea was,—and he answered, "I vum, I believe it was nothing but principle, for I never heerd a man talk honester."

There was a lecture on Peace by a Mr. Spear (ought he not to be beaten into a plowshare?), the same evening, and, as the gentlemen, Lane and Alcott, dined at our house while the matter was in suspense,—that is, while the constable was waiting for his receipt from the jailer,—we there settled it that we, that is, Lane and myself, perhaps, should agitate the State while Winkelried lay in durance. But when, over the audience, I saw our hero's head moving in the free air of the Universalist church, my fire all went out, and the State was safe as far as I was concerned. But Lane, it seems, had cogitated and even written on the matter, in the afternoon, and so, out of courtesy, taking his point of departure from the Spear-man's lecture, he drove gracefully *in medias res*, and gave the affair a very good setting out; but, to spoil all, our martyr very characteristically, but, as artists would say, in bad taste, brought up the rear with a "My Prisons," which made us forget Silvio Pellico himself.

Mr. Lane wishes me to ask you to see if there is anything for him in the New York office, and pay the charges. Will you tell me what to do with Mr. [Theodore] Parker, who was to lecture February 15th? Mrs. Emerson says my letter is written instead of one from her.

At the end of this strange letter I will not write—what alone I had to say—to thank you and Mrs. Emerson for your long kindness to me. It would be more ungrateful than my constant thought. I have been your pensioner for nearly two years, and still left free as under the sky. It has been as free a gift as the sun or the summer, though I have sometimes molested you with my mean acceptance of it,—I who have failed to render even those slight services of the *hand* which would have been for a sign at least; and, by the fault of my nature, have failed of many better and higher services. But I will not trouble you with this, but for once thank you as well as Heaven.

Your friend, H. D. T.

Mrs. Lidian Emerson, the wife of R. W. Emerson, and her two daughters,

Ellen and Edith, are named in this first letter, and will be frequently mentioned in the correspondence. At this date, Edith, now Mrs. W. H. Forbes, was fourteen months old. Mr. Emerson's mother, Madam Ruth Emerson, was also one of the household, which had for a little more than seven years occupied the well-known house under the trees, east of the village.

TO R. W. EMERSON (AT NEW YORK).

Concord, February 10, 1843.

Dear Friend,—I have stolen one of your own sheets to write you a letter upon, and I hope, with two layers of ink, to turn it into a comforter. If you like to receive a letter from me, too, I am glad, for it gives me pleasure to write. But don't let it come amiss; it must fall as harmlessly as leaves settle on the landscape. I will tell you what we are doing this now. Supper is done, and Edith—the dessert, perhaps more than the dessert—is brought in, or even comes in *per se*; and round she goes, now to this altar, and then to that, with her monosyllabic invocation of "oc," "oc." It makes me think of "Langue d'oc." She must belong to that province. And like the gypsies she talks a language of her own while she understands ours. While she jabbers Sanskrit, Parsee, Pehlvi, say "Edith go bah!" and "bah" it is. No intelligence passes between us. She knows. It is a capital joke,—that is the reason she smiles so. How well the secret is kept! she never descends to explanation. It is not buried liked a common secret, bolstered up on two sides, but by an eternal silence on the one side, at least. It has been long kept, and comes in from the unexplored horizon, like a blue mountain range, to end abruptly at our door one day. (Don't stumble at this steep simile.) And now she studies the heights and depths of nature

On shoulders whirled in some eccentric orbit

Just by old Pæstum's temples and the perch

Where Time doth plume his wings.

And now she runs the race over the carpet, while all Olympia applauds,—mamma, grandma, and uncle, good Grecians all,—and that dark-hued barbarian, Partheanna Parker, whose shafts go through and through, not backward! Grandmamma smiles over all, and mamma is wondering what papa would say, should she descend on Carlton House some day. "Larks night" 's abed, dreaming of "pleased faces" far away. But now the trumpet sounds, the games are over; some Hebe comes, and Edith is translated. I don't know where; it must be to some cloud, for I never was there.

Query: what becomes of the answers Edith thinks, but cannot express? She really gives you glances which are before this world was. You can't feel any difference of age, except that you have longer legs and arms.

Mrs. Emerson said I must tell you about domestic affairs, when I mentioned that I was going to write. Perhaps it will inform you of the state of all if I only say that I am well and happy in your house here in Concord.

Your friend,
HENRY.

Don't forget to tell us what to do with Mr. Parker when you write next. I lectured this week. It was as bright a night as you could wish. I hope there were no stars thrown away on the occasion.

[A part of the same letter, though bearing a date two days later, and written in a wholly different style, as from one sage to another, is this postscript:]

February 12, 1843.

DEAR FRIEND,—As the packet still tarries, I will send you some thoughts, which I have lately relearned, as the latest public and private news.

How mean are our relations to one another! Let us pause till they are nobler. A little silence, a little rest, is good. It would be sufficient employment only to cultivate true ones.

The richest gifts we can bestow are the least marketable. We hate the kindness which we understand. A noble person confers no such gift as his whole confidence: none so exalts the giver and the receiver; it produces the truest gratitude. Perhaps it is only essential to friendship that some vital trust should have been reposed by the one in the other. I feel addressed and probed even to the remote parts of my being when one nobly shows, even in trivial things, an implicit faith in me. When such divine commodities are so near and cheap, how strange that it should have to be each day's discovery! A threat or a curse may be forgotten, but this mild trust translates me. I am no more of this earth; it acts dynamically; it changes my very substance. I cannot do what before I did. I cannot be what before I was. Other chains may be broken, but in the darkest night, in the remotest place, I trail this thread. Then things cannot *happen*. What if God were to confide in us for a moment! Should we not then be gods?

How subtle a thing is this confidence! Nothing sensible passes between; never any consequences are to be apprehended should it be misplaced. Yet something has transpired. A new behavior springs; the ship carries new ballast in her hold. A sufficiently great and generous trust could never be abused. It should be cause to lay down one's life,—which would not be to lose it. Can there be any mistake up there? Don't the gods know where to invest their wealth? Such confidence, too, would be reciprocal. When one confides greatly in you, he will feel the roots of an equal trust fastening themselves in him. When such trust has been received or reposed, we dare not speak, hardly to see each other; our voices sound harsh and untrustworthy. We are as instruments which the Powers have dealt with. Through what straits would we not carry this little burden of a magnanimous trust! Yet no harm could possibly come, but simply faithlessness. Not a feather, not a straw, is intrusted; that packet is empty. It is only *committed* to us, and, as it were, all things are committed to us.

The kindness I have longest remembered has been of this sort,—the sort unsaid; so far behind the speaker's lips that almost it already lay in my heart. It did not have far to go to be communicated. The gods cannot misunderstand, man cannot explain. We communicate like the burrows of foxes, in silence and darkness, under ground. We are undermined by faith and love. How much more full is Nature where we think the empty space is than where we place the solids!—full of fluid influences. Should we ever communicate but by these? The spirit abhors a vacuum more than Nature. There is a tide which pierces the pores of the air. These aerial rivers, let us not pollute their currents. What meadows do they course through? How many fine mails there are which traverse their routes! He is privileged who gets his letter franked by them.

I believe these things.

HENRY D. THOREAU.

Emerson replied to these letters in two epistles of dates from February 4 to 12, 1843,—in the latter asking Thoreau to aid him in editing the April number of the *Dial* of which he had taken charge. Among other things, Emerson desired a manuscript of Charles Lane, Alcott's English friend, to be sent to him in New York, where he was detained several weeks by his lectures. He added: "Have we no news from Wheeler? Has Bartlett none?" Of these persons, the first, Charles Stearns Wheeler, a college classmate of Thoreau, and later Greek tutor in the college, had gone to Germany,—where he died the next summer,—and was contributing to the quarterly *Dial*. Robert Bartlett, of Plymouth, a townsman of Mrs. Emerson, was Wheeler's intimate friend, with whom he corresponded.[20] To this editorial request Thoreau, who was punctuality itself, replied at once.

TO R. W. EMERSON (AT NEW YORK).

Concord, February 15, 1843.

My dear Friend,—I got your letters, one yesterday and the other to-day, and they have made me quite happy. As a packet is to go in the morning, I will give you a hasty account of the *Dial*. I called on Mr. Lane this afternoon, and brought away, together with an abundance of good-will, first, a bulky catalogue of books without commentary,—some eight hundred, I think he told me, with an introduction filling one sheet,—ten or a dozen pages, say, though I have only glanced at them; second, a review—twenty-five or thirty printed pages—of Conversations on the Gospels, Record of a School, and Spiritual Culture, with rather copious extracts. However, it is a good subject, and Lane says it gives him satisfaction. I will give it a faithful reading directly. [These were Alcott's publications, reviewed by Lane.] And now I come to the little end of the horn; for myself, I have brought along the Minor Greek Poets, and will mine there for a scrap or two, at least. As for Etzler, I don't remember any "rude and snappish speech" that you made, and if you did it must have been longer than anything I had written; however, here is the book still, and I will try. Perhaps I have some few scraps in my Journal which you may choose to print. The translation of the Æschylus I should like very well to continue anon, if it should be worth the while. As for poetry, I have not remembered to write any for some time; it has quite slipped my mind; but sometimes I think I hear the mutterings of the thunder. Don't you remember that last summer we heard a low, tremulous sound in the woods and over the hills, and thought it was partridges or rocks, and it proved to be thunder gone down the river? But sometimes it was over Wayland way, and at last burst over our heads. So we'll not despair by reason of the drought. You see it takes a good many words to supply the place of one deed; a hundred lines to a cobweb, and but one cable to a man-of-war. The *Dial* case needs to be reformed in manyparticulars. There is no news from Wheeler, none from Bartlett.

They all look well and happy in this house, where it gives me much pleasure to dwell.

Yours in haste, HENRY.

P. S.

Wednesday evening, February 16.

DEAR FRIEND,—I have time to write a few words about the *Dial*. I have just received the three first signatures, which do not yet complete Lane's piece. He will place five hundred copies for sale at Munroe's bookstore. Wheeler has sent you two full sheets—more about the German universities—and proper names, which will have to be printed in alphabetical order for convenience; what this one has done, that one is doing, and the other intends to do. Hammer-Purgstall (Von Hammer) may be one, for aught I know. However, there are two or three *things* in it, as well as names. One of the books of Herodotus is discovered to be out of place. He says something about having sent Lowell, by the last steamer, a budget of literary news, which he will have communicated to you ere this. Mr. Alcott has a letter from Heraud,[21] and a book written by him,—the Life of Savonarola,—which he wishes to have republished here. Mr. Lane will write a notice of it. (The latter says that what is in the New York post-office *may* be directed to Mr. Alcott.) Miss [Elizabeth] Peabody has sent a "Notice to the readers of the *Dial*" which is not good.

Mr. Chapin lectured this evening, and so rhetorically that I forgot my duty and heard very little. I find myself better than I have been, and am meditating some other method of paying debts than by lectures and writing,—which will only do to talk about. If anything of that "other" sort should come to your ears in New York, will you remember it for me?

Excuse this scrawl, which I have written over the embers in the dining-room. I hope that you live on good terms with yourself and the gods.

Yours in haste, HENRY.

Mr. Lane and his lucubrations proved to be tough subjects, and the next letter has more to say about them and the *Dial*. Lane had undertaken to do justice to Mr. Alcott and his books, as may still be read in the pages of that April number of the Transcendentalist quarterly.

TO R. W. EMERSON (AT NEW YORK).

CONCORD, February 20, 1843.

MY DEAR FRIEND,—I have read Mr. Lane's review, and *can* say, speaking for this world and for fallen man, that "it is good for us." As they say in geology, time never fails, there is always enough of it, so I may say, criticism never fails; but if I go and read elsewhere, I say it is good,—far better than any notice Mr. Alcott has received, or is likely to receive from another quarter. It is at any rate "the other side" which Boston needs to hear. I do not send it to you, because time is precious, and because I think you would accept it, after all. After speaking briefly of the fate of Goethe and Carlyle in their own countries, he says, "To Emerson in his own circle is but slowly accorded a worthy response; and Alcott, almost utterly neglected," etc. I will strike out what relates to yourself, and correcting some verbal faults, send the rest to the printer with Lane's initials.

The catalogue needs amendment, I think. It wants completeness now. It should consist of such books only as they would tell Mr. [F. H.] Hedge and [Theodore] Parker they had got; omitting the Bible, the classics, and much besides,—for there the incompleteness begins. But you will be here in season for this.

It is frequently easy to make Mr. Lane more universal and attractive; to write, for instance, "universal ends" instead of "the universal end," just as we pull open the petals of a flower with our fingers where they are confined by its own sweets. Also he had better not say "books designed for the nucleus of a *Home* University," until he makes that word "home" ring solid and universal too. This is that abominable dialect. He had just given me a notice of George Bradford's Fénelon for the Record of the Months, and speaks of extras of the Review and Catalogue, if they are printed,—even a hundred, or thereabouts. How shall this be arranged? Also he wishes to use some manuscripts of his which are in your possession, if you do not. Can I get them?

I think of no news to tell you. It is a serene summer day here, all above the snow. The hens steal their nests, and I steal their eggs still, as formerly. This is what I do with the hands. Ah, labor,—it is a divine institution, and conversation with many men and hens.

Do not think that my letters require as many special answers. I get one as often as you write to Concord. Concord inquires for you daily, as do all the members of this house. You must make haste home before we have settled all the great questions, for they are fast being disposed of. But I must leave room for Mrs. Emerson.

Mrs. Emerson's letter, after speaking of other matters, gave a lively sketch of Thoreau at one of Alcott's Conversations in her house, which may be quoted as illustrating the young Nature-worshiper's position at the time, and the more humane and socialistic spirit of Alcott and Lane, who were soon to leave Concord for their experiment of communistic life at "Fruitlands," in the rural town of Harvard.

"Last evening we had the 'Conversation,' though, owing to the bad weather, but few attended. The subjects were: What is Prophecy? Who is a Prophet?

and The Love of Nature. Mr. Lane decided, as for all time and the race, that this same love of nature—of which Henry [Thoreau] was the champion, and Elizabeth Hoar and Lidian (though L. disclaimed possessing it herself) his faithful squiresses—that this love was the most subtle and dangerous of sins; a refined idolatry, much more to be dreaded than gross wickednesses, because the gross sinner would be alarmed by the depth of his degradation, and come up from it in terror, but the unhappy idolaters of Nature were deceived by the refined quality of their sin, and would be the last to enter the kingdom. Henry frankly affirmed to both the wise men that they were wholly deficient in the faculty in question, and therefore could not judge of it. And Mr. Alcott as frankly answered that it was because they went beyond the mere material objects, and were filled with spiritual love and perception (as Mr. T. was not), that they seemed to Mr. Thoreau not to appreciate outward nature. I am very heavy, and have spoiled a most excellent story. I have given you no idea of the scene, which was ineffably comic, though it made no laugh at the time; I scarcely laughed at it myself,—too deeply amused to give the usual sign. Henry was brave and noble; well as I have always liked him, he still grows upon me."

Before going to Staten Island in May, 1843, Thoreau answered a letter from the same Richard Fuller who had made him the musical gift in the previous winter. He was at Harvard College, and desired to know something of Thoreau's pursuits there,—concerning which Channing says in his Life,[22] "He was a respectable student, having done there a bold reading in English poetry,—even to some portions or the whole of Davenant's 'Gondibert.'" This, Thoreau does not mention in his letter, but it was one of the things that attracted Emerson's notice, since he also had the same taste for the Elizabethan and Jacobean English poets. An English youth, Henry Headley, pupil of Dr. Parr, and graduate of Oxford in 1786, had preceded Thoreau in this study of poets that had become obsolete; and it was perhaps Headley's volume, "Select Beauties of Ancient English Poetry, with Remarks by the late Henry Headley," published long after his death,[23] that served Thoreau as a guide to Quarles and the Fletchers, Daniel, Drummond, Drayton, Habington, and Raleigh,—poets that few Americans had heard of in 1833.

TO RICHARD F. FULLER (AT CAMBRIDGE).

Concord, April 2, 1843.

Dear Richard,—I was glad to receive a letter from you so bright and cheery. You speak of not having made any conquests with your own spear or quill as yet; but if you are tempering your spear-head during these days, and fitting a straight and tough shaft thereto, will not that suffice? We are more pleased to consider the hero in the forest cutting cornel or ash for his spear, than marching in triumph with his trophies. The present hour is always wealthiest when it is poorer than the future ones, as that is the pleasantest site which affords the pleasantest prospects.

What you say about your studies furnishing you with a "mimic idiom" only, reminds me that we shall all do well if we learn so much as to talk,—to speak truth. The only fruit which even much living yields seems to be often only some trivial success,—the ability to do some slight thing better. We make conquest only of husks and shells for the most part,—at least apparently,—but sometimes these are cinnamon and spices, you know. Even the grown hunter you speak of slays a thousand buffaloes, and brings off only their hides and tongues. What immense sacrifices, what hecatombs and holocausts, the gods exact for very slight favors! How much sincere life before we can even utter one sincere word.

What I was learning in college was chiefly, I think, to express myself, and I see now, that as the old orator prescribed, 1st, action; 2d, action; 3d, action; my teachers should have prescribed to me, 1st, sincerity; 2d, sincerity; 3d, sincerity. The old mythology is incomplete without a god or goddess of sincerity, on whose altars we might offer up all the products of our farms, our workshops, and our studies. It should be our Lar when we sit on the hearth, and our Tutelar Genius when we walk abroad. This is the only panacea. I mean sincerity in our dealings with ourselves mainly; any other is comparatively easy. But I must stop before I get to 17thly. I believe I have but one text and one sermon.

Your rural adventures beyond the West Cambridge hills have probably lost nothing by distance of time or space. I used to hear only the sough of the wind in the woods of Concord, when I was striving to give my attention to a page of calculus. But, depend upon it, you will love your native hills the better for being separated from them.

I expect to leave Concord, which is my Rome, and its people, who are my Romans, in May, and go to New York, to be a tutor in Mr. William Emerson's family. So I will bid you good-by till I see you or hear from you again.

Going to Staten Island, early in May, 1843, Thoreau's first care was to write to his "Romans, countrymen, and lovers by the banks of the Musketaquid,"—beginning with his mother, his sisters, and Mrs. Emerson. To Sophia and Mrs. E. he wrote May 22,—to Helen, with a few touching verses on his brother John, the next day; and then he resumed the correspondence with Emerson. It seems that one of his errands near New York was to make the acquaintance of literary men and journalists in the city, in order to find a vehicle for publication, such as his neighbor Hawthorne had finally found in the pages of the *Democratic Review*. For this purpose Thoreau made himself known to

Henry James, and other friends of Emerson, and to Horace Greeley, then in the first freshness of his success with the *Tribune*,—a newspaper hardly more than two years old then, but destined to a great career, in which several of the early Transcendentalists took some part.

TO HIS FATHER AND MOTHER (AT CONCORD).

CASTLETON, STATEN ISLAND, May 11, 1843.

DEAR MOTHER AND FRIENDS AT HOME,—We arrived here safely at ten o'clock on Sunday morning, having had as good a passage as usual, though we ran aground and were detained a couple of hours in the Thames River, till the tide came to our relief. At length we curtseyed up to a wharf just the other side of their Castle Garden,—very incurious about them and their city. I believe my vacant looks, absolutely inaccessible to questions, did at length satisfy an army of starving cabmen that I did not want a hack, cab, or anything of that sort as yet. It was the only demand the city made on us; as if a wheeled vehicle of some sort were the sum and summit of a reasonable man's wants. "Having tried the water," they seemed to say, "will you not return to the pleasant securities of land carriage? Else why your boat's prow turned toward the shore at last?" They are a sad-looking set of fellows, not permitted to come on board, and I pitied them. They had been expecting me, it would seem, and did really wish that I should take a cab; though they did not seem rich enough to supply me with one.

It was a confused jumble of heads and soiled coats, dangling from flesh-colored faces,—all swaying to and fro, as by a sort of undertow, while each whipstick, true as the needle to the pole, still preserved that level and direction in which its proprietor had dismissed his forlorn interrogatory. They took sight from them,—the lash being wound up thereon, to prevent your attention from wandering, or to make it concentre upon its object by the spiral line. They began at first, perhaps, with the modest, but rather confident inquiry, "Want a cab, sir?" but as their despair increased, it took the affirmative tone, as the disheartened and irresolute are apt to do: "You want a cab, sir," or even, "You want a nice cab, sir, to take you to Fourth Street." The question which one had bravely and hopefully begun to put, another had the tact to take up and conclude with fresh emphasis,—twirling it from his particular whipstick as if it had emanated from his lips,—as the sentiment did from his heart. Each one could truly say, "Them 's my sentiments." But it was a sad sight.

I am seven and a half miles from New York, and, as it would take half a day at least, have not been there yet. I have already run over no small part of the island, to the highest hill, and some way along the shore. From the hill directly behind the house I can see New York, Brooklyn, Long Island, the Narrows, through which vessels bound to and from all parts of the world chiefly pass,—Sandy Hook and the Highlands of Neversink (part of the coast of New Jersey),—and, by going still farther up the hill, the Kill van Kull, and Newark Bay. From the pinnacle of one Madame Grimes's house, the other night at sunset, I could see almost round the island. Far in the horizon there was a fleet of sloops bound up the Hudson, which seemed to be going over the edge of the earth; and in view of these trading ships commerce seems quite imposing.

But it is rather derogatory that your dwelling-place should be only a neighborhood to a great city,—to live on an inclined plane. I do not like their cities and forts, with their morning and evening guns, and sails flapping in one's eye. I want a whole continent to breathe in, and a good deal of solitude and silence, such as all Wall Street cannot buy,—nor Broadway with its wooden pavement. I must live along the beach, on the southern shore, which looks directly out to sea,—and see what that great parade of water means, that dashes and roars, and has not yet wet me, as long as I have lived.

I must not know anything about my condition and relations here till what is not permanent is worn off. I have not yet subsided. Give me time enough, and I may like it. All my inner man heretofore has been a Concord impression; and here come these Sandy Hook and Coney Island breakers to meet and modify the former; but it will be long before I can make nature look as innocently grand and inspiring as in Concord.

Your affectionate son,
Henry D. Thoreau.

TO SOPHIA THOREAU (AT CONCORD).

Castleton, Staten Island, May 22, 1843.

Dear Sophia,—I have had a severe cold ever since I came here, and have been confined to the house for the last week with bronchitis, though I am now getting out, so I have not seen much in the botanical way. The cedar seems to be one of the most common trees here, and the fields are very fragrant with it. There are also the gum and tulip trees. The latter is not very common, but is very large and beautiful, having flowers as large as tulips, and as handsome. It is not time for it yet.

The woods are now full of a large honeysuckle in full bloom, which differs from ours in being red instead of white, so that at first I did not know its genus. The painted-cup is very common in the meadows here. Peaches, and especially cherries, seem to grow by all the fences. Things are very forward here compared with Concord. The apricots growing out-of-doors are already as large as plums. The apple, pear, peach, cherry, and plum trees have shed their blossoms. The whole island is like a garden, and affords very fine scenery.

In front of the house is a very extensive wood, beyond which is the sea, whose roar I can hear all night long, when there is a wind; if easterly winds have prevailed on the Atlantic. There are always some vessels in sight,—ten, twenty, or thirty miles off,—and Sunday before last there were hundreds in long procession, stretching from New York to Sandy Hook, and far beyond, for Sunday is a lucky day.

I went to New York Saturday before last. A walk of half an hour, by half a dozen houses, along the Richmond road—that is the road that leads to Richmond, on which we live—brings me to the village of Stapleton, in Southfield, where is the lower dock; but if I prefer I can walk along the shore three quarters of a mile farther toward New York to the quarantine village of Castleton, to the upper dock, which the boat leaves five or six times every day, a quarter of an hour later than the former place. Farther on is the village of New Brighton, and farther still Port Richmond, which villages another steamboat visits.

In New York I saw George Ward, and also Giles Waldo and William Tappan, whom I can describe better when I have seen them more. They are young friends of Mr. Emerson. Waldo came down to the island to see me the next day. I also saw the Great Western, the Croton water-works, and the picture-gallery of the National Academy of Design. But I have not had time to see or do much yet.

Tell Miss Ward I shall try to put my microscope to a good use, and if I find any new and preservable flower, will throw it into my commonplace-book. Garlic, the original of the common onion, grows here all over the fields, and during its season spoils the cream and butter for the market, as the cows like it very much.

Tell Helen there are two schools of late established in the neighborhood, with large prospects, or rather designs, one for boys and another for girls. The latter by a Miss Errington, and though it is only small as yet, I will keep my ears open for her in such directions. The encouragement is very slight.

I hope you will not be washed away by the Irish sea.

Tell Mother I think my cold was not wholly owing to imprudence. Perhaps I was being acclimated.

Tell Father that Mr. Tappan, whose son I know,—and whose clerks young

Tappan and Waldo are,—has invented and established a new and very important business, which Waldo thinks would allow them to burn ninety-nine out of one hundred of the stores in New York, which now only offset and cancel one another. It is a kind of intelligence office for the whole country, with branches in the principal cities, giving information with regard to the credit and affairs of every man of business of the country. Of course it is not popular at the South and West. It is an extensive business and will employ a great many clerks.

Love to all—not forgetting Aunt and Aunts—and Miss and Mrs. Ward.

On the 23d of May he wrote from Castleton to his sister Helen thus:—

Dear Helen,—In place of something fresher, I send you the following verses from my Journal, written some time ago:—

Brother, where dost thou dwell?
   What sun shines for thee now?
Dost thou indeed fare well
   As we wished here below?
What season didst thou find?
   'T was winter here.
Are not the Fates more kind
   Than they appear?
Is thy brow clear again,
   As in thy youthful years?
And was that ugly pain
   The summit of thy fears?[24]
Yet thou wast cheery still;
   They could not quench thy fire;
Thou didst abide their will,
   And then retire.
Where chiefly shall I look
   To feel thy presence near?
Along the neighboring brook
   May I thy voice still hear?

Dost thou still haunt the brink
  Of yonder river's tide?
And may I ever think
  That thou art by my side?
What bird wilt thou employ
  To bring me word of thee?
For it would give them joy,—
  'T would give them liberty,
To serve their former lord
  With wing and minstrelsy.
A sadder strain mixed with their song,
  They've slowlier built their nests;
Since thou art gone
  Their lively labor rests.
Where is the finch, the thrush
  I used to hear?
Ah, they could well abide
  The dying year.
Now they no more return,
  I hear them not;
They have remained to mourn,
  Or else forgot.

As the first letter of Thoreau to Emerson was to thank him for his lofty friendship, so now the first letter to Mrs. Emerson, after leaving her house, was to say similar things, with a passing allusion to her love of flowers and of gardening, in which she surpassed all his acquaintance in Concord, then and afterward. A letter to Emerson followed, touching on the *Dial* and on several of his new and old acquaintance. "Rockwood Hoar" is the person since known as judge and cabinet officer,—the brother of Senator Hoar, and of Thoreau's special friends Elizabeth and Edward Hoar. Channing is the poet, who had lately printed his first volume, without finding many readers.

TO MRS. EMERSON (AT CONCORD).

Castleton, Staten Island, May 22, 1843.

My Dear Friend,—I believe a good many conversations with you were left in an unfinished state, and now indeed I don't know where to take them up. But I will resume some of the unfinished silence. I shall not hesitate to know you. I think of you as some elder sister of mine, whom I could not have avoided,—a sort of lunar influence,—only of such age as the moon, whose time is measured by her light. You must know that you represent to me woman, for I have not traveled very far or wide,—and what if I had? I like to deal with you, for I believe you do not lie or steal, and these are very rare virtues. I thank you for your influence for two years. I was fortunate to be subjected to it, and am now to remember it. It is the noblest gift we can make; what signify all others that can be bestowed? You have helped to keep my life "on loft," as Chaucer says of Griselda, and in a better sense. You always seemed to look down at me as from some elevation,—some of your high humilities,—and I was the better for having to look up. I felt taxed not to disappoint your expectation; for could there be any accident so sad as to be respected for something better than we are? It was a pleasure even to go away from you, as it is not to meet some, as it apprised me of my high relations; and such a departure is a sort of further introduction and meeting. Nothing makes the earth seem so spacious as to have friends at a distance; they make the latitudes and longitudes.

You must not think that fate is so dark there, for even here I can see a faint reflected light over Concord, and I think that at this distance I can better weigh the value of a doubt there. Your moonlight, as I have told you, though it is a reflection of the sun, allows of bats and owls and other twilight birds to flit therein. But I am very glad that you can elevate your life with a doubt, for I am sure that it is nothing but an insatiable faith after all that deepens and darkens its current. And your doubt and my confidence are only a difference of expression.

I have hardly begun to live on Staten Island yet; but, like the man who, when forbidden to tread on English ground, carried Scottish ground in his boots, I carry Concord ground in my boots and in my hat,—and am I not made of Concord dust? I cannot realize that it is the roar of the sea I hear now, and not the wind in Walden woods. I find more of Concord, after all, in the prospect of the sea, beyond Sandy Hook, than in the fields and woods.

If you were to have this Hugh the gardener for your man, you would think a new dispensation had commenced. He might put a fairer aspect on the natural world for you, or at any rate a screen between you and the almshouse. There is a beautiful red honeysuckle now in blossom in the woods here, which should be transplanted to Concord; and if what they tell me about the tulip tree be true, you should have that also. I have not seen Mrs. Black yet, but I intend to call on her soon. Have you established those simpler modes of living yet?—"In the full tide of successful operation?"

Tell Mrs. Brown that I hope she is anchored in a secure haven and derives much pleasure still from reading the poets, and that her constellation is not quite set from my sight, though it is sunk so low in that northern horizon. Tell Elizabeth Hoar that her bright present did "carry ink safely to Staten Island," and was a conspicuous object in Master Haven's inventory of my effects. Give my respects to Madam Emerson, whose Concord face I should be glad to see here this summer; and remember me to the rest of the household who have had vision of me. Shake a day-day to Edith, and say good-night to Ellen for me. Farewell.

TO R. W. EMERSON (AT CONCORD).

CASTLETON, STATEN ISLAND, May 23.

MY DEAR FRIEND,—I was just going to write to you when I received your letter. I was waiting till I had got away from Concord. I should have sent you something for the *Dial* before, but I have been sick ever since I came here, rather unaccountably,—what with a cold, bronchitis, acclimation, etc., still unaccountably. I send you some verses from my Journal which will help make a packet. I have not time to correct them, if this goes by Rockwood Hoar. If I can finish an account of a winter's walk in Concord, in the midst of a Staten Island summer,—not so wise as true, I trust,—I will send it to you soon.

I have had no later experiences yet. You must not count much upon what I can do or learn in New York. I feel a good way off here; and it is not to be visited, but seen and dwelt in. I have been there but once, and have been confined to the house since. Everything there disappoints me but the crowd; rather, I was disappointed with the rest before I came. I have no eyes for their churches, and what else they find to brag of. Though I know but little about Boston, yet what attracts me, in a quiet way, seems much meaner and more pretending than there,—libraries, pictures, and faces in the street. You don't know where any respectability inhabits. It is in the crowd in Chatham Street. The crowd is something new, and to be attended to. It is worth a thousand Trinity Churches and Exchanges while it is looking at them, and will run over them and trample them under foot one day. There are two things I hear and am aware I live in the neighborhood of,—the roar of the sea and the hum of the city. I have just come from the beach (to find your letter), and I like it much. Everything there is on a grand and generous scale,—seaweed, water, and sand; and even the dead fishes, horses, and hogs have a rank, luxuriant odor; great shad-nets spread to dry; crabs and horseshoes crawling over the sand; clumsy boats, only for service, dancing like sea-fowl over the surf, and ships afar off going about their business.

Waldo and Tappan carried me to their English alehouse the first Saturday, and Waldo spent two hours here the next day. But Tappan I have only seen. I like his looks and the sound of his silence. They are confined every day but Sunday, and then Tappan is obliged to observe the demeanor of a church-goer to prevent open war with his father.

I am glad that Channing has got settled, and that, too, before the inroad of the Irish. I have read his poems two or three times over, and partially through and under, with new and increased interest and appreciation. Tell him I saw a man buy a copy at Little & Brown's. He may have been a virtuoso, but we will give him the credit. What with Alcott and Lane and Hawthorne, too, you look strong enough to take New York by storm. Will you tell L., if he asks, that I have been able to do nothing about the books yet?

Believe that I have something better to write you than this. It would be unkind to thank you for particular deeds.

TO R. W. EMERSON (AT CONCORD).

Staten Island, June 8, 1843.

Dear Friend,—I have been to see Henry James, and like him very much. It was a great pleasure to meet him. It makes humanity seem more erect and respectable. I never was more kindly and faithfully catechised. It made me respect myself more to be thought worthy of such wise questions. He is a man, and takes his own way, or stands still in his own place. I know of no one so patient and determined to have the good of you. It is almost friendship, such plain and human dealing. I think that he will not write or speak inspiringly; but he is a refreshing, forward-looking and forward-moving man, and he has naturalized and humanized New York for me. He actually reproaches you by his respect for your poor words. I had three hours' solid talk with him, and he asks me to make free use of his house. He wants an expression of your faith, or to be sure that it is faith, and confesses that his own treads fast upon the neck of his understanding. He exclaimed, at some careless answer of mine: "Well, you Transcendentalists are wonderfully consistent. I must get hold of this somehow!" He likes Carlyle's book,[25] but says that it leaves him in an excited and unprofitable state, and that Carlyle is so ready to obey his humor that he makes the least vestige of truth the foundation of any superstructure, not keeping faith with his better genius nor truest readers.

I met Wright on the stairs of the Society Library, and W. H. Channing and Brisbane on the steps. The former (Channing) is a concave man, and you see by his attitude and the lines of his face that he is retreating from himself and from yourself, with sad doubts. It is like a fair mask swaying from the drooping boughs of some tree whose stem is not seen. He would break with a conchoidal fracture. You feel as if you would like to see him when he has made up his mind to run all the risks. To be sure, he doubts because he has a great hope to be disappointed, but he makes the possible disappointment of too much consequence. Brisbane, with whom I did not converse, did not impress me favorably. He looks like a man who has lived in a cellar, far gone in consumption. I barely saw him, but he did not look as if he could let Fourier go, in any case, and throw up his hat. But I need not have come to New York to write this.

I have seen Tappan for two or three hours, and like both him and Waldo; but I always see those of whom I have heard well with a slight disappointment. They are so much better than the great herd, and yet the heavens are not shivered into diamonds over their heads. Persons and things flit so rapidly through my brain nowadays that I can hardly remember them. They seem to be lying in the stream, stemming the tide, ready to go to sea, as steamboats when they leave the dock go off in the opposite direction first, until they are headed right, and then begins the steady revolution of the paddle-wheels; and *they* are not quite cheerily headed anywhither yet, nor singing amid the shrouds as they bound over the billows. There is a certain youthfulness and generosity about them, very attractive; and Tappan's more reserved and solitary thought commands respect.

After some ado, I discovered the residence of Mrs. Black, but there was palmed off on me, in her stead, a Mrs. Grey (quite an inferior color), who told me at last that she was not Mrs. Black, but her mother, and was just as glad to see me as Mrs. Black would have been, and so, forsooth, would answer just as well. Mrs. Black had gone with Edward Palmer to New Jersey, and would return on the morrow.

I don't like the city better, the more I see it, but worse. I am ashamed of my eyes that behold it. It is a thousand times meaner than I could have imagined. It will be something to hate,—that's the advantage it will be to me; and even the best people in it are a part of it, and talk coolly about it. The pigs in the street are the most respectable part of the population. When will the world learn that a million men are of no importance compared with *one* man? But I must wait for a shower of shillings, or at least a slight dew or mizzling of sixpences, before I explore New York very far.

The sea-beach is the best thing I have seen. It is very solitary and remote, and you only remember New York occasionally. The distances, too, along the shore, and inland in sight of it, are unaccountably great and startling. The sea seems very near from the hills, but it proves a long way over the plain, and yet you may be wet with the spray before you can believe that you are there. The far seems near, and the near far. Many rods from the beach, I step aside for the Atlantic, and I see men drag up their boats on to the sand, with oxen, stepping about amid the surf, as if it were possible they might draw up Sandy Hook.

I do not feel myself especially serviceable to the good people with whom I live, except as inflictions are sanctified to the righteous. And so, too, must I serve the boy. I can look to the Latin and mathematics sharply, and for the rest behave myself. But I cannot be in his neighborhood hereafter as his Educator, of course, but as the hawks fly over my own head. I am not attracted toward him but as to youth generally. He shall frequent me, however, as much as he can, and I'll be I.

Bradbury[26] told me, when I passed through Boston, that he was coming to New York the following Saturday, and would then settle with me, but he has not made his appearance yet. Will you, the next time you go to Boston, present that order for me which I left with you?

If I say less about Waldo and Tappan now, it is, perhaps, because I may have more to say by and by. Remember me to your mother and Mrs. Emerson, who, I hope, is quite well. I shall be very glad to hear from her, as well as from you. I have very hastily written out something for the *Dial*, and send it only because you are expecting something,—though something better. It seems idle and Howittish, but it may be of more worth in Concord, where it belongs. In great haste. Farewell.

TO HIS FATHER AND MOTHER (AT CONCORD).

Castleton, June 8, 1843.

Dear Parents,—I have got quite well now, and like the lay of the land and the look of the sea very much,—only the country is so fair that it seems rather too much as if it were made to be looked at. I have been to New York four or five times, and have run about the island a good deal.

George Ward, when I last saw him, which was at his house in Brooklyn, was studying the daguerreotype process, preparing to set up in that line. The boats run now almost every hour from 8 A. M. to 7 P. M., back and forth, so that I can get to the city much more easily than before. I have seen there one Henry James, a lame man, of whom I had heard before, whom I like very much; and he asks me to make free use of his house, which is situated in a pleasant part of the city, adjoining the University. I have met several people whom I knew before, and among the rest Mr. Wright, who was on his way to Niagara.

I feel already about as well acquainted with New York as with Boston,—that is, about as little, perhaps. It is large enough now, and they intend it shall be larger still. Fifteenth Street, where some of my new acquaintance live, is two or three miles from the Battery, where the boat touches,—clear brick and stone, and no "give" to the foot; and they have laid out, though not built, up to the 149th street above. I had rather see a brick for a specimen, for my part, such as they exhibited in old times. You see it is "quite a day's training" to make a few calls in different parts of the city (to say nothing of twelve miles by water and land,—*i. e.*, not brick and stone), especially if it does not rain shillings, which might interest omnibuses in your behalf. Some omnibuses are marked "Broadway—Fourth Street," and they go no farther; others "Eighth Street," and so on,—and so of the other principal streets. (This letter will be circumstantial enough for Helen.)

This is in all respects a very pleasant residence,—much more rural than you would expect of the vicinity of New York. There are woods all around. We breakfast at half past six, lunch, if we will, at twelve, and dine or sup at five; thus is the day partitioned off. From nine to two, or thereabouts, I am the schoolmaster, and at other times as much the pupil as I can be. Mr. and Mrs. Emerson are not indeed of my kith or kin in any sense; but they are irreproachable and kind. I have met no one yet *on the island* whose acquaintance I shall cultivate,—or hoe round,—unless it be our neighbor Captain Smith, an old fisherman, who catches the fish called "moss-bonkers"—so it sounds—and invites me to come to the beach, where he spends the week, and see him and his fish.

Farms are for sale all around here, and so, I suppose men are for purchase. North of us live Peter Wandell, Mr. Mell, and Mr. Disosway (don't mind the spelling), as far as the Clove road; and south, John Britton, Van Pelt, and Captain Smith, as far as the Fingerboard road. Behind is the hill, some 250 feet high, on the side of which we live; and in front the forest and the sea,—the latter at the distance of a mile and a half.

Tell Helen that Miss Errington is provided with assistance. This were a good place as any to establish a school, if one could wait a little. Families come down here to board in the summer, and three or four have been already established this season.

As for money matters, I have not set my traps yet, but I am getting my bait ready. Pray, how does the garden thrive, and what improvements in the pencil line? I miss you all very much. Write soon, and send a Concord paper to

Your affectionate son,
HENRY D. THOREAU.

The traps of this sportsman were magazine articles,—but the magazines that would pay much for papers were very few in 1843. One such had existed in Boston for a short time,—the *Miscellany,*—and it printed a good paper of Thoreau's, but the pay was not forthcoming. His efforts to find publishers more liberal in New York were not successful. But he continued to write for fame in the *Dial*, and helped to edit that.

TO MRS. EMERSON.

Staten Island, June 20, 1843.

My very dear Friend,—I have only read a page of your letter, and have come out to the top of the hill at sunset, where I can see the ocean, to prepare to read the rest. It is fitter that it should hear it than the walls of my chamber. The very crickets here seem to chirp around me as they did not before. I feel as if it were a great daring to go on and read the rest, and then to live accordingly. There are more than thirty vessels in sight going to sea. I am almost afraid to look at your letter. I see that it will make my life very steep, but it may lead to fairer prospects than this.

You seem to me to speak out of a very clear and high heaven, where any one may be who stands so high. Your voice seems not a voice, but comes as much from the blue heavens as from the paper.

My dear friend, it was very noble in you to write me so trustful an answer. It will do as well for another world as for this; such a voice is for no particular time nor person, but it makes him who may hear it stand for all that is lofty and true in humanity. The thought of you will constantly elevate my life; it will be something always above the horizon to behold, as when I look up at the evening star. I think I know your thoughts without seeing you, and as well here as in Concord. You are not at all strange to me.

I could hardly believe, after the lapse of one night, that I had such a noble letter still at hand to read,—that it was not some fine dream. I looked at midnight to be sure that it was real. I feel that I am unworthy to know you, and yet they will not permit it wrongfully.

I, perhaps, am more willing to deceive by appearances than you say you are; it would not be worth the while to tell how willing; but I have the power perhaps too much to forget my meanness as soon as seen, and not be incited by permanent sorrow. My actual life is unspeakably mean compared with what I know and see that it might be. Yet the ground from which I see and say this is some part of it. It ranges from heaven to earth, and is all things in an hour. The experience of every past moment but belies the faith of each present. We never conceive the greatness of our fates. Are not these faint flashes of light which sometimes obscure the sun their certain dawn?

My friend, I have read your letter as if I was not reading it. After each pause I could defer the rest forever. The thought of you will be a new motive for every right action. You are another human being whom I know, and might not our topic be as broad as the universe? What have we to do with petty rumbling news? We have our own great affairs. Sometimes in Concord I found my actions dictated, as it were, by your influence, and though it led almost to trivial Hindoo observances, yet it was good and elevating. To hear that you have sad hours is not sad to me. I rather rejoice at the richness of your experience. Only think of some sadness away in Pekin,—unseen and unknown there. What a mine it is! Would it not weigh down the Celestial Empire, with all its gay Chinese? Our sadness is not sad, but our cheap joys. Let us be sad about all we see and are, for so we demand and pray for better. It is the constant prayer and whole Christian religion. I could hope that you would get well soon, and have a healthy body for this world, but I know this cannot be; and the Fates, after all, are the accomplishers of our hopes. Yet I do hope that you may find it a worthy struggle, and life seem grand still through the clouds.

What wealth is it to have such friends that we cannot think of them without elevation! And we can think of them any time and anywhere, and it costs nothing but the lofty disposition. I cannot tell you the joy your letter gives me, which will not quite cease till the latest time. Let me accompany your finest thought.

I send my love to my other friend and brother, whose nobleness I slowly recognize.

Henry.

TO MRS. THOREAU (AT CONCORD).

Staten Island, July 7, 1843.

Dear Mother,—I was very glad to get your letter and papers. Tell Father that circumstantial letters make very substantial reading, at any rate. I like to know even how the sun shines and garden grows with you. I did not get my money in Boston, and probably shall not at all. Tell Sophia that I have pressed some blossoms of the tulip tree for her. They look somewhat like white lilies. The magnolia, too, is in blossom here.

Pray, have you the seventeen-year locust in Concord? The air here is filled with their din. They come out of the ground at first in an imperfect state, and, crawling up the shrubs and plants, the perfect insect bursts out through the back. They are doing great damage to the fruit and forest trees. The latter are covered with dead twigs, which in the distance look like the blossoms of the chestnut. They bore every twig of last year's growth in order to deposit their eggs in it. In a few weeks the eggs will be hatched, and the worms fall to the ground and enter it, and in 1860 make their appearance again. I conversed about their coming this season before they arrived. They do no injury to the leaves, but, beside boring the twigs, suck their sap for sustenance. Their din is heard by those who sail along the shore from the distant woods,—Phar-r-r-aoh. Phar-r-r-aoh. They are departing now. Dogs, cats, and chickens subsist mainly upon them in some places.

I have not been to New York for more than three weeks. I have had an interesting letter from Mr. Lane,[27] describing their new prospects. My pupil and I are getting on apace. He is remarkably well advanced in Latin, and is well advancing.

Your letter has just arrived. I was not aware that it was so long since I wrote home; I only knew that I had sent five or six letters to the town. It is very refreshing to hear from you, though it is not all good news. But I trust that Stearns Wheeler is not dead. I should be slow to believe it. He was made to work very well in this world. There need be no tragedy in his death.

The demon which is said to haunt the Jones family, hovering over their eyelids with wings steeped in juice of poppies, has commenced another campaign against me. I am "clear Jones" in this respect at least. But he finds little encouragement in my atmosphere, I assure you, for I do not once fairly lose myself, except in those hours of truce allotted to rest by immemorial custom. However, this skirmishing interferes sadly with my literary projects, and I am apt to think it a good day's work if I maintain a soldier's eye till nightfall. Very well, it does not matter much in what wars we serve, whether in the Highlands or the Lowlands. Everywhere we get soldiers' pay still.

Give my love to Aunt Louisa, whose benignant face I sometimes see right in the wall, as naturally and necessarily shining on my path as some star of unaccountably greater age and higher orbit than myself. Let it be inquired by her of George Minott, as from me,—for she sees him,—if he has seen any pigeons yet, and tell him there are plenty of jack snipes here. As for William P., the "worthy young man,"—as I live, my eyes have not fallen on him yet.

I have not had the influenza, though here are its headquarters,—unless my first week's cold was it. Tell Helen I shall write to her soon. I have heard Lucretia Mott. This is badly written; but the worse the writing the sooner you get it this time from

Your affectionate son,
H. D. T.

TO R. W. EMERSON (AT CONCORD).

Staten Island, July 8, 1843.

Dear Friends,—I was very glad to hear your voices from so far. I do not believe there are eight hundred human beings on the globe. It is all a fable, and I cannot but think that you speak with a slight outrage and disrespect of Concord when you talk of fifty of them. There are not so many. Yet think not that I have left all behind, for already I begin to track my way over the earth, and find the cope of heaven extending beyond its horizon,—forsooth, like the roofs of these Dutch houses. My thoughts revert to those dear hills and that *river* which so fills up the world to its brim,—worthy to be named with Mincius and Alpheus,—still drinking its meadows while I am far away. How can it run heedless to the sea, as if I were there to countenance it? George Minott, too, looms up considerably,—and many another old familiar face. These things all look sober and respectable. They are better than the environs of New York, I assure you.

I am pleased to think of Channing as an inhabitant of the gray town. Seven cities contended for Homer dead. Tell him to remain at least long enough to establish Concord's right and interest in him. I was beginning to know the man. In imagination I see you pilgrims taking your way by the red lodge and the cabin of the brave farmer man, so youthful and hale, to the still cheerful woods. And Hawthorne, too, I remember as one with whom I sauntered, in old heroic times, along the banks of the Scamander, amid the ruins of chariots and heroes. Tell him not to desert, even after the tenth year. Others may say, "Are there not the cities of Asia?" But what are they? Staying at home is the heavenly way.

And Elizabeth Hoar, my brave townswoman, to be sung of poets,—if I may speak of her whom I do not know. Tell Mrs. Brown that I do not forget her, going her way under the stars through this chilly world,—I did *not* think of the wind,—and that I went a little way with her. Tell her not to despair. Concord's little arch does not span all our fate, nor is what transpires under it law for the universe.

And least of all are forgotten those walks in the woods in ancient days,—too sacred to be idly remembered,—when their aisles were pervaded as by a fragrant atmosphere. They still seem youthful and cheery to my imagination as Sherwood and Barnsdale,—and of far purer fame. Those afternoons when we wandered o'er Olympus,—and those hills, from which the sun was seen to set, while still our day held on its way.

At last he rose and twitched his mantle blue;

To-morrow to fresh woods, and pastures new."

I remember these things at midnight, at rare intervals. But know, my friends, that I a good deal hate you all in my most private thoughts, as the substratum of the little love I bear you. Though you are a rare band, and do not make half use enough of one another.

I think this is a noble number of the *Dial*.[28] It perspires thought and feeling. I can speak of it now a little like a foreigner. Be assured that it is not written in vain,—it is not for me. I hear its prose and its verse. They provoke and inspire me, and they have my sympathy. I hear the sober and the earnest, the sad and the cheery voices of my friends, and to me it is a long letter of encouragement and reproof; and no doubt so it is to many another in the land. So don't give up the ship. Methinks the verse is hardly enough better than the prose. I give my vote for the "Notes from the Journal of a Scholar," and wonder you don't print them faster. I want, too, to read the rest of the "Poet and the Painter." Miss Fuller's is a noble piece,—rich, extempore writing, talking with pen in hand. It is too good not to be better, even. In writing, conversation should be folded many times thick. It is the height of art that, on the first perusal, plain common sense should appear; on the second, severe truth; and on a third, beauty; and, having these warrants for its depth and reality, we may then enjoy the beauty for evermore. The sea-piece is of the best that is going, if not of the best that is staying. You have spoken a good word for Carlyle. As for the "Winter's Walk," I should be glad to have it printed in the *Dial* if you think it good enough, and will criticise it; otherwise send it to me, and I will dispose of it.

I have not been to New York for a month, and so have not seen Waldo and Tappan. James has been at Albany meanwhile. You will know that I only describe my personal adventures with people; but I hope to see more of them, and *judge* them too. I am sorry to learn that Mrs. Emerson is no better. But let her know that the Fates pay a compliment to those whom they make sick, and they have not to ask, "What have I done?"

Remember me to your mother, and remember me yourself as you are remembered by

H. D. T.

I had a friendly and cheery letter from Lane a month ago.

TO HELEN THOREAU (AT ROXBURY).

Staten Island, July 21, 1843.

Dear Helen,—I am not in such haste to write home when I remember that I make my readers pay the postage. But I believe I have not taxed you before.

I have pretty much explored this island, inland and along the shore, finding my health inclined me to the peripatetic philosophy. I have visited telegraph stations, Sailors' Snug Harbors, Seaman's Retreats, Old Elm Trees, where the Huguenots landed, Britton's Mills, and all the villages on the island. Last Sunday I walked over to Lake Island Farm, eight or nine miles from here, where Moses Prichard lived, and found the present occupant, one Mr. Davenport, formerly from Massachusetts, with three or four men to help him, raising sweet potatoes and tomatoes by the acre. It seemed a cool and pleasant retreat, but a hungry soil. As I was coming away, I took my toll out of the soil in the shape of arrowheads, which may after all be the surest crop, certainly not affected by drought.

I am well enough situated here to observe one aspect of the modern world at least. I mean the migratory,—the western movement. Sixteen hundred immigrants arrived at quarantine ground on the 4th of July, and more or less every day since I have been here. I see them occasionally washing their persons and clothes: or men, women, and children gathered on an isolated quay near the shore, stretching their limbs and taking the air; the children running races and swinging on this artificial piece of the land of liberty, while their vessels are undergoing purification. They are detained but a day or two, and then go up to the city, for the most part without having *landed*here.

In the city, I have seen, since I wrote last, W. H. Channing, at whose home, in Fifteenth Street, I spent a few pleasant hours, discussing the all-absorbing question "what to do for the race." (He is sadly in earnest about going up the river to rusticate for six weeks, and issues a new periodical called *The Present* in September.) Also Horace Greeley, editor of the *Tribune*, who is cheerfully in earnest, at his office of all work, a hearty New Hampshire boy as one would wish to meet, and says, "Now be neighborly," and believes only, or mainly, first, in the Sylvania Association, somewhere in Pennsylvania; and, secondly, and most of all, in a new association to go into operation soon in New Jersey, with which he is connected. Edward Palmer came down to see me Sunday before last. As for Waldo and Tappan, we have strangely dodged one another, and have not met for some weeks.

I believe I have not told you anything about Lucretia Mott. It was a good while ago that I heard her at the Quaker Church in Hester Street. She is a preacher, and it was advertised that she would be present on that day. I liked all the proceedings very well, their plainly greater harmony and sincerity than elsewhere. They do nothing in a hurry. Every one that walks up the aisle in his square coat and expansive hat has a history, and comes from a house to a house. The women come in one after another in their Quaker bonnets and handkerchiefs, looking all like sisters or so many chickadees. At length, after a long silence,—waiting for the Spirit,—Mrs. Mott rose, took off her bonnet, and began to utter very deliberately what the Spirit suggested. Her self-possession was something to see, if all else failed; but it did not. Her subject was, "The Abuse of the Bible," and thence she straightway digressed to slavery and the degradation of woman. It was a good speech,—Transcendentalism in its mildest form. She sat down at length, and, after a long and decorous silence, in which some seemed to be really digesting her words, the elders shook hands, and the meeting dispersed. On the whole, I liked their ways and the plainness of their meeting-house. It looked as if it was indeed made for service.

I think that Stearns Wheeler has left a gap in the community not easy to be filled. Though he did not exhibit the highest qualities of the scholar, he promised, in a remarkable degree, many of the essential and rarer ones; and his patient industry and energy, his reverent love of letters, and his proverbial accuracy, will cause him to be associated in my memory even with many venerable names of former days. It was not wholly unfit that so pure a lover of books should have ended his pilgrimage at the great book-mart of the world. I think of him as healthy and brave, and am confident that if he had lived he would have proved useful in more ways than I can describe. He would have been authority on all matters of fact, and a sort of connecting link between men and scholars of different walks and tastes. The literary enterprises he was planning for himself and friends remind me of an older and more studious time. So much, then, remains for us to do who survive. Love to all. Tell all my friends in Concord that I do not send my love, but retain it still.

Your affectionate brother.

TO MRS. THOREAU (AT CONCORD).

Staten Island, August 6, 1843.

Dear Mother,—As Mr. William Emerson is going to Concord on Tuesday, I must not omit sending a line by him,—though I wish I had something more weighty for so direct a post. I believe I directed my last letter to you by mistake; but it must have appeared that it was addressed to Helen. At any rate, this is to you without mistake.

I am chiefly indebted to your letters for what I have learned of Concord and family news, and am very glad when I get one. I should have liked to be in Walden woods with you, but not with the railroad. I think of you all very often, and wonder if you are still separated from me only by so many miles of earth, or so many miles of memory. This life we live is a strange dream, and I don't believe at all any account men give of it. Methinks I should be content to sit at the back door in Concord, under the poplar tree, henceforth forever. Not that I am homesick at all,—for places are strangely indifferent to me,—but Concord is still a cynosure to my eyes, and I find it hard to attach it, even in imagination, to the rest of the globe, and tell where the seam is.

I fancy that this Sunday evening you are pouring over some select book, almost transcendental perchance, or else "Burgh's Dignity," or Massillon, or the *Christian Examiner*. Father has just taken one more look at the garden, and is now absorbed in Chaptelle, or reading the newspaper quite abstractedly, only looking up occasionally over his spectacles to see how the rest are engaged, and not to miss any newer news that may not be in the paper. Helen has slipped in for the fourth time to learn the very latest item. Sophia, I suppose, is at Bangor; but Aunt Louisa, without doubt, is just flitting away to some good meeting, to save the credit of you all.

It is still a cardinal virtue with me to keep awake. I find it impossible to write or read except at rare intervals, but am, generally speaking, tougher than formerly. I could make a pedestrian tour round the world, and sometimes think it would perhaps be better to do at once the things I *can*, rather than be trying to do what at present I cannot do well. However, I shall awake sooner or later.

I have been translating some Greek, and reading English poetry, and a month ago sent a paper to the *Democratic Review*, which, at length, they were sorry they could not accept; but they could not adopt the sentiments. However, they were very polite, and earnest that I should send them something else, or reform that.

I go moping about the fields and woods here as I did in Concord, and, it seems, am thought to be a surveyor,—an Eastern man inquiring narrowly into the condition and value of land, etc., here, preparatory to an extensive speculation. One neighbor observed to me, in a mysterious and half-inquisitive way, that he supposed I must be pretty well acquainted with the state of things; that I kept pretty close; he did n't see any surveying instruments, but perhaps I had them in my pocket.

I have received Helen's note, but have not heard of Frisbie Hoar yet.[29] She is a faint-hearted writer, who could not take the responsibility of blotting one sheet alone. However, I like very well the blottings I get. Tell her I have not seen Mrs. Child nor Mrs. Sedgwick.

Love to all from your affectionate son.

TO R. W. EMERSON (AT CONCORD).

STATEN ISLAND, August 7, 1843.

MY DEAR FRIEND,—I fear I have nothing to send you worthy of so good an opportunity. Of New York I still know but little, though out of so many thousands there are no doubt many units whom it would be worth my while to know. Mr. James[30] talks of going to Germany soon with his wife to learn the language. He says he must know it; can never learn it here; there he may absorb it; and is very anxious to learn beforehand where he had best locate himself to enjoy the advantage of the highest culture, learn the language in its purity, and not exceed his limited means. I referred him to Longfellow. Perhaps you can help him.

I have had a pleasant talk with Channing; and Greeley, too, it was refreshing to meet. They were both much pleased with your criticism on Carlyle, but thought that you had overlooked what chiefly concerned them in the book,—its practical aim and merits.

I have also spent some pleasant hours with Waldo and Tappan at their counting-room, or rather intelligence office.

I must still reckon myself with the innumerable army of invalids,—undoubtedly in a fair field they would rout the well,—though I am tougher than formerly. Methinks I could paint the sleepy god more truly than the poets have done, from more intimate experience. Indeed, I have not kept my eyes very steadily open to the things of this world of late, and hence have little to report concerning them. However, I trust the awakening will come before the last trump,—and then perhaps I may remember some of my dreams.

I study the aspects of commerce at its Narrows here, where it passes in review before me, and this seems to be beginning at the right end to understand this Babylon. I have made a very rude translation of the Seven against Thebes, and Pindar too I have looked at, and wish he was better worth translating. I believe even the best things are not equal to their fame. Perhaps it would be better to translate fame itself,—or is not that what the poets themselves do? However, I have not done with Pindar yet. I sent a long article on Etzler's book to the *Democratic Review* six weeks ago, which at length they have determined not to accept, as they could not subscribe to all the opinions, but asked for other matter,—purely literary, I suppose. O'Sullivan wrote me that articles of this kind have to be referred to the circle who, it seems, are represented by this journal, and said something about "collective we" and "homogeneity."

Pray don't think of Bradbury & Soden[31] any more,—

For good deed done through praiere

Is sold and bought too dear, I wis,

To herte that of great valor is."

I see that they have given up their shop here.

Say to Mrs. Emerson that I am glad to remember how she too dwells there in Concord, and shall send her anon some of the thoughts that belong to her. As for Edith, I seem to see a star in the east over where the young child is. Remember me to Mrs. Brown.

These letters for the most part explain themselves, with the aid of several to Thoreau's family, which the purpose of Emerson, in 1865, to present his friend in a stoical character, had excluded from the collection then printed. Mention of C. S. Wheeler and his sad death in Germany had come to him from Emerson, as well as from his own family at Concord,—of whose occupations Thoreau gives so genial a picture in the letter of August 6 to his mother. Emerson wrote: "You will have read and heard the sad news to the little village of Lincoln, of Stearns Wheeler's death. Such an overthrow to the hopes of his parents made me think more of them than of the loss the community will suffer in his kindness, diligence, and ingenuous mind." He died at Leipsic, in the midst of Greek studies which have since been taken up and carried farther by a child of Concord, Professor Goodwin of the same university. Henry James, several times mentioned in the correspondence, was the moral and theological essayist (father of the novelist Henry James, and the distinguished Professor James of Harvard), who was so striking a personality in Concord and Cambridge circles for many years. W. H. Channing was a Christian Socialist fifty years ago,—cousin of Ellery Channing, and nephew and biographer of Dr. Channing. Both he and Horace Greeley were then deeply interested in the Fourierist scheme of association, one development of which was going on at Brook Farm, under direction of George Ripley, and another, differing in design, at Fruitlands, under Bronson Alcott and Charles Lane. The jocose allusions of Thoreau to his Jones ancestors (the descendants of the Tory Colonel Jones of Weston) had this foundation in fact,—that his uncle, Charles Dunbar, soon to be named in connection with Daniel Webster, suffered from a sort of lethargy, which would put him to sleep in the midst of conversation. Webster had been retained in the once famous "Wyman case," of a bank officer charged with fraud, and had exerted his great forensic talent for a few days in the Concord court-house. Emerson wrote Thoreau: "You will have heard of the Wyman trial, and the stir it made in the village. But the Cliff and Walden knew nothing of that."

TO MRS. THOREAU (AT CONCORD).

Castleton, Tuesday, August 29, 1843.

DEAR MOTHER,—Mr. Emerson has just given me warning that he is about to send to Concord, which I will endeavor to improve. I am a great deal more wakeful than I was, and growing stout in other respects,—so that I may yet accomplish something in the literary way; indeed, I should have done so before now but for the slowness and poverty of the "Reviews" themselves. I have tried sundry methods of earning money in the city, of late, but without success: have rambled into every bookseller's or publisher's house, and discussed their affairs with them. Some propose to me to do what an honest man cannot. Among others, I conversed with the Harpers—to see if they might not find me useful to them; but they say that they are making $50,000 annually, and their motto is to let well alone. I find that I talk with these poor men as if I were over head and ears in business, and a few thousands were no consideration with me. I almost reproach myself for bothering them so to no purpose; but it is a very valuable experience, and the best introduction I could have.

We have had a tremendous rain here last Monday night and Tuesday morning. I was in the city at Giles Waldo's, and the streets at daybreak were absolutely impassable for the water. Yet the accounts of the storm that you may have seen are exaggerated, as indeed are all such things, to my imagination. On Sunday I heard Mr. Bellows preach here on the island; but the fine prospect over the Bay and Narrows, from where I sat, preached louder than he,—though he did far better than the average, if I remember aright. I should have liked to see Daniel Webster walking about Concord; I suppose the town shook, every step he took. But I trust there were some sturdy Concordians who were not tumbled down by the jar, but represented still the upright town. Where was George Minott? he would not have gone far to see him. Uncle Charles should have been there,—he might as well have been catching cat naps in Concord as anywhere.

And then, what a whetter-up of his memory this event would have been! You'd have had all the classmates again in alphabetical order reversed,—"and Seth Hunt and Bob Smith—and he was a student of my father's,—and where's Put now? and I wonder—you—if Henry's been to see George Jones yet! A little account with Stow,—Balcom,—Bigelow, poor miserable t-o-a-d, —(sound asleep.) I vow, you,—what noise was that?—saving grace—and few there be—That's clear as preaching,—Easter Brooks,—morally deprived,—How charming is divine philosophy,—some wise and some otherwise,—Heighho! (sound asleep again) Webster's a smart fellow—bears his age well, —how old should you think he was? you—does he look as if he were ten years younger than I?"

I met, or rather, was overtaken by Fuller, who tended for Mr. How, the other day, in Broadway. He dislikes New York very much. The Mercantile Library, —that is, its Librarian, presented me with a stranger's ticket, for a month, and I was glad to read the Reviews there, and Carlyle's last article. I have bought some pantaloons; stockings show no holes yet. These pantaloons cost $2.25 ready made.

In haste.

TO R. W. EMERSON (AT CONCORD).

STATEN ISLAND, September 14, 1843.

DEAR FRIEND,—Miss Fuller will tell you the news from these parts, so I will only devote these few moments to what she does n't know as well. I was absent only one day and night from the island, the family expecting me back immediately. I was to earn a certain sum before winter, and thought it worth the while to try various experiments. I carried *The Agriculturist* about the city, and up as far as Manhattanville, and called at the Croton Reservoir, where, indeed, they did not want any Agriculturists, but paid well enough in their way.

Literature comes to a poor market here; and even the little that I write is more than will sell. I have tried *The Dem. Review*, *The New Mirror*, and *Brother Jonathan*.[32] The last two, as well as the *New World*, are overwhelmed with contributions which cost nothing, and are worth no more. *The Knickerbocker* is too poor, and only *The Ladies' Companion* pays. O'Sullivan is printing the manuscript I sent him some time ago, having objected only to my want of sympathy with the Committee.

I doubt if you have made more corrections in my manuscript than I should have done ere this, though they may be better; but I am glad you have taken any pains with it. I have not prepared any translations for the *Dial*, supposing there would be no room, though it is the only place for them.

I have been seeing men during these days, and trying experiments upon trees; have inserted three or four hundred buds (quite a Buddhist, one might say). Books I have access to through your brother and Mr. McKean, and have read a good deal. Quarles's "Divine Poems" as well as "Emblems" are quite a discovery.

I am very sorry Mrs. Emerson is so sick. Remember me to her and to your mother. I like to think of your living on the banks of the Mill Brook, in the midst of the garden with all its weeds; for what are botanical distinctions at this distance?

TO HIS MOTHER (AT CONCORD).

STATEN ISLAND, October 1, 1843.

Dear Mother,—I hold together remarkably well as yet,—speaking of my outward linen and woolen man; no holes more than I brought away, and no stitches needed yet. It is marvelous. I think the Fates must be on my side, for there is less than a plank between me and—Time, to say the least. As for Eldorado, that is far off yet. My bait will not tempt the rats,—they are too well fed. The *Democratic Review* is poor, and can only afford half or quarter pay, which it *will* do; and they say there is a *Ladies' Companion* that pays,—but I could not write anything companionable. However, speculate as we will, it is quite gratuitous; for life, nevertheless and never the more, goes steadily on, well or ill-fed, and clothed somehow, and "honor bright" withal. It is very gratifying to live in the prospect of great successes always; and for that purpose we must leave a sufficient foreground to see them through. All the painters prefer distant prospects for the greater breadth of view and delicacy of tint. But this is no news, and describes no new conditions.

Meanwhile I am somnambulic at least,—stirring in my sleep; indeed, quite awake. I read a good deal, and am pretty well known in the libraries of New York. Am in with the librarian (one Dr. Forbes) of the Society Library, who has lately been to Cambridge to learn liberality, and has come back to let me take out some un-take-out-able books, which I was threatening to read on the spot. And Mr. McKean, of the Mercantile Library, is a true gentleman (a former tutor of mine), and offers me every privilege there. I have from him a perpetual stranger's ticket, and a citizen's rights besides,—all which privileges I pay handsomely for by improving.

A canoe race "came off" on the Hudson the other day, between Chippeways and New Yorkers, which must have been as moving a sight as the buffalo hunt which I witnessed. But canoes and buffaloes are all lost, as is everything here, in the mob. It is only the people have come to see one another. Let them advertise that there will be a gathering at Hoboken,—having bargained with the ferryboats,—and there will be, and they need not throw in the buffaloes.

I have crossed the bay twenty or thirty times, and have seen a great many immigrants going up to the city for the first time: Norwegians, who carry their old-fashioned farming-tools to the West with them, and will buy nothing here for fear of being cheated; English operatives, known by their pale faces and stained hands, who will recover their birthright in a little cheap sun and wind; English travelers on their way to the Astor House, to whom I have done the honors of the city; whole families of emigrants cooking their dinner upon the pavement,—all sunburnt, so that you are in doubt where the foreigner's face of flesh begins; their tidy clothes laid on, and then tied to their swathed bodies, which move about like a bandaged finger,—caps set on the head as if woven of the hair, which is still growing at the roots,—each and all busily cooking, stooping from time to time over the pot, and having something to drop in it, that so they may be entitled to take something out, forsooth. They look like respectable but straitened people, who may turn out to be Counts when they get to Wisconsin, and will have this experience to relate to their children.

Seeing so many people from day to day, one comes to have less respect for flesh and bones, and thinks they must be more loosely joined, of less firm fibre, than the few he had known. It must have a very bad influence on children to see so many human beings at once,—mere herds of men.

I came across Henry Bigelow a week ago, sitting in front of a hotel in Broadway, very much as if he were under his father's stoop. He is seeking to be admitted into the bar in New York, but as yet had not succeeded. I directed him to Fuller's store, which he had not found, and invited him to come and see me if he came to the island. Tell Mrs. and Miss Ward that I have not forgotten them, and was glad to hear from George—with whom I spent last night—that they had returned to C. Tell Mrs. Brown that it gives me as much pleasure to know that she thinks of me and my writing as if I had been the author of the piece in question,—but I did not even read over the papers I sent. The *Mirror* is really the most readable journal here. I see that they have printed a short piece that I wrote to sell, in the *Dem. Review*, and still keep the review of "Paradise," that I may include in it a notice of another book by the same author, which they have found, and are going to send me.

I don't know when I shall come home; I like to keep that feast in store. Tell Helen that I do not see any advertisement for her, and I am looking for myself. If I could find a rare opening, I might be tempted to try with her for a year, till I had paid my debts, but for such I am sure it is not well to go out of New England. Teachers are but poorly recompensed, even here. Tell her and Sophia (if she is not gone) to write to me. Father will know that this letter is to him as well as to you. I send him a paper which usually contains the news, —if not all that is stirring, all that has stirred,—and even draws a little on the future. I wish he would send me, by and by, the paper which contains the results of the Cattle-Show. You must get Helen's eyes to read this, though she is a scoffer at honest penmanship.

TO MRS. EMERSON (AT CONCORD).

STATEN ISLAND, October 16, 1843.

MY DEAR FRIEND,—I promised you some thoughts long ago, but it would be hard to tell whether these are the ones. I suppose that the great questions of "Fate, Freewill, Foreknowledge absolute," which used to be discussed at Concord, are still unsettled. And here comes [W. H.] Channing, with his

Present to vex the world again,—a rather galvanic movement, I think. However, I like the man all the better, though his schemes the less. I am sorry for his confessions. Faith never makes a confession.

Have you had the annual berrying party, or sat on the Cliffs a whole day this summer? I suppose the flowers have fared quite as well since I was not there to scoff at them; and the hens, without doubt, keep up their reputation.

I have been reading lately what of Quarles's poetry I could get. He was a contemporary of Herbert, and a kindred spirit. I think you would like him. It is rare to find one who was so much of a poet and so little of an artist. He wrote long poems, almost epics for length, about Jonah, Esther, Job, Samson, and Solomon, interspersed with meditations after a quite original plan,—Shepherd's Oracles, Comedies, Romances, Fancies, and Meditations,—the quintessence of meditation,—and Enchiridions of Meditation all divine,—and what he calls his Morning Muse; besides prose works as curious as the rest. He was an unwearied Christian, and a reformer of some old school withal. Hopelessly quaint, as if he lived all alone and knew nobody but his wife, who appears to have reverenced him. He never doubts his genius; it is only he and his God in all the world. He uses language sometimes as greatly as Shakespeare; and though there is not much straight grain in him, there is plenty of tough, crooked timber. In an age when Herbert is revived, Quarles surely ought not to be forgotten.

I will copy a few such sentences as I should read to you if there. Mrs. Brown, too, may find some nutriment in them.

How does the Saxon Edith do? Can you tell yet to which school of philosophy she belongs,—whether she will be a fair saint of some Christian order, or a follower of Plato and the heathen? Bid Ellen a good-night or good-morning from me, and see if she will remember where it comes from; and remember me to Mrs. Brown, and your mother, and Elizabeth Hoar.

TO R. W. EMERSON (AT CONCORD).

Staten Island, October 17, 1843.

My dear Friend,—I went with my pupil to the Fair of the American Institute, and so lost a visit from Tappan, whom I met returning from the Island. I should have liked to hear more news from his lips, though he had left me a letter and the *Dial*, which is a sort of circular letter itself. I find Channing's[33] letters full of life, and I enjoy their wit highly. Lane writes straight and solid, like a guide-board, but I find that I put off the "social tendencies" to a future day, which may never come. He is always Shaker fare, quite as luxurious as his principles will allow. I feel as if I were ready to be appointed a committee on poetry, I have got my eyes so whetted and proved of late, like the knife-sharpener I saw at the Fair, certified to have been "in constant use in a gentleman's family for more than two years." Yes, I ride along the ranks of the English poets, casting terrible glances, and some I blot out, and some I spare. McKean has imported, within the year, several new editions and collections of old poetry, of which I have the reading, but there is a good deal of chaff to a little meal,—hardly worth bolting. I have just opened Bacon's "Advancement of Learning" for the first time, which I read with great delight. It is more like what Scott's novels *were* than anything.

I see that I was very blind to send you my manuscript in such a state; but I have a good *second* sight, at least. I could still shake it in the wind to some advantage, if it would hold together. There are some sad mistakes in the printing. It is a little unfortunate that the "Ethnical Scriptures" should hold out so well, though it does really hold out. The Bible ought not to be very large. Is it not singular that, while the religious world is gradually picking to pieces its old testaments, here are some coming slowly after, on the seashore, picking up the durable relics of perhaps older books, and putting them together again?

Your Letter to Contributors is excellent, and hits the nail on the head. It will taste sour to their palates at first, no doubt, but it will bear a sweet fruit at last. I like the poetry, especially the Autumn verses. They ring true. Though I am quite weather-beaten with poetry, having weathered so many epics of late. The "Sweep Ho!" sounds well this way. But I have a good deal of fault to find with your "Ode to Beauty." The tune is altogether unworthy of the thoughts. You slope too quickly to the rhyme, as if that trick had better be performed as soon as possible, or as if you stood over the line with a hatchet, and chopped off the verses as they came out, some short and some long. But give us a long reel, and we'll cut it up to suit ourselves. It sounds like parody. "Thee knew I of old," "Remediless thirst," are some of those stereotyped lines. I am frequently reminded, I believe, of Jane Taylor's "Philosopher's Scales," and how the world

"Flew out with a bounce,"

which

"Yerked the philosopher out of his cell;"

or else of

"From the climes of the sun all war-worn and weary."

I had rather have the thought come ushered with a flourish of oaths and curses. Yet I love your poetry as I do little else that is near and recent, especially when you get fairly round the end of the line, and are not thrown back upon the rocks. To read the lecture on "The Comic" is as good as to be in our town meeting or Lyceum once more.

I am glad that the Concord farmers plowed well this year; it promises that something will be done these summers. But I am suspicious of that *Brittonner*, who advertises so many cords of *good* oak, chestnut, and maple wood for sale. *Good!* ay, good for what? And there shall not be left a stone upon a stone. But no matter,—let them hack away. The sturdy Irish arms that do the work are of more worth than oak or maple. Methinks I could look with equanimity upon a long street of Irish cabins, and pigs and children reveling in the genial Concord dirt; and I should still find my Walden Wood and Fair Haven in their tanned and happy faces.

I write this in the corn-field—it being washing-day—with the inkstand Elizabeth Hoar gave me;[34] though it is not redolent of corn-stalks, I fear. Let me not be forgotten by Channing and Hawthorne, nor our gray-suited neighbor under the hill [Edmund Hosmer].

This letter will be best explained by a reference to the *Dial* for October, 1843. The "Ethnical Scriptures" were selections from the Brahminical books, from Confucius, etc., such as we have since seen in great abundance. The Autumn verses are by Channing; "Sweep Ho!" by Ellen Sturgis, afterwards Mrs. Hooper; the "Youth of the Poet and Painter" also by Channing. The Letter to Contributors, which is headed simply "A Letter," is by Emerson, and has been much overlooked by his later readers; his "Ode to Beauty" is very well known, and does not deserve the slashing censure of Thoreau, though, as it now stands, it is better than first printed. Instead of

Love drinks at thy banquet

Remediless thirst,"

we now have the perfect phrase,

Love drinks at thy *fountain*

False waters of thirst."

"The Comic" is also Emerson's. There is a poem, "The Sail," by William Tappan, so often named in these letters, and a sonnet by Charles A. Dana, afterwards of the *New York Sun*.

TO HELEN THOREAU (AT CONCORD).

STATEN ISLAND, October 18, 1843.

Dear Helen,—What do you mean by saying that "*we* have written eight times by private opportunity"? Is n't it the more the better? And am I not glad of it? But people have a habit of not letting me know it when they go to Concord from New York. I endeavored to get you *The Present* when I was last in the city, but they were all sold; and now another is out, which I will send, if I get it. I did not send the *Democratic Review*, because I had no copy, and my piece was not worth fifty cents. You think that Channing's words would apply to me too, as living more in the natural than the moral world; but I think that you mean the world of men and women rather, and reformers generally. My objection to Channing and all that fraternity is that they need and deserve sympathy themselves rather than are able to render it to others. They want faith, and mistake their private ail for an infected atmosphere; but let any one of them recover hope for a moment, and right his *particular* grievance, and he will no longer train in that company. To speak or do anything that shall concern mankind, one must speak and act as if well, or from that grain of health which he has left. This *Present* book indeed is blue, but the hue of its thoughts is yellow. I say these things with the less hesitation, because I have the jaundice myself; but I also know what it is to be well. But do not think that one can escape from mankind who is one of them, and is so constantly dealing with them.

I could not undertake to form a nucleus of an institution for the development of infant minds, where none already existed. It would be too cruel. And then, as if looking all this while one way with benevolence, to walk off another about one's own affairs suddenly! Something of this kind is an unavoidable objection to that.

I am very sorry to hear such bad news about Aunt Maria; but I think that the worst is always the least to be apprehended, for nature is averse to it as well as we. I trust to hear that she is quite well soon. I send love to her and Aunt Jane. For three months I have not known whether to think of Sophia as in Bangor or Concord, and now you say that she is going directly. Tell her to write to me, and establish her whereabouts, and also to get well directly. And see that she has something worthy to do when she gets down there, for that's the best remedy for disease.

Your affectionate brother,
H. D. THOREAU.

II
GOLDEN AGE OF ACHIEVEMENT

This was the golden age of hope and achievement for the Concord poets and philosophers. Their ranks were not yet broken by death (for Stearns Wheeler was hardly one of them), their spirits were high, and their faith in each other unbounded. Emerson wrote thus from Concord, while Thoreau was perambulating Staten Island and calling on "the false booksellers:" "Ellery Channing is excellent company, and we walk in all directions. He remembers you with great faith and hope; thinks you ought not to see Concord again these ten years—that you ought to grind up fifty Concords in your mill—and much other opinion and counsel he holds in store on this topic. Hawthorne walked with me yesterday afternoon, and not until after our return did I read his 'Celestial Railroad,' which has a serene strength which we cannot afford not to praise, in this low life."

The Transcendentalists had their quarterly, and even their daily organ, for Mr. Greeley put the *Tribune* at their service, and gave places on its staff to Margaret Fuller and her brother-in-law Channing, and would gladly have made room for Emerson in its columns, if the swift utterance of a morning paper had suited his habit of publication. While in the *Tribune* office, Ellery Channing thus wrote to Thoreau, after he had returned home, disappointed with New York, to make lead pencils in his father's shop at Concord.

ELLERY CHANNING TO THOREAU (AT CONCORD).

March 5, 1845.

My dear Thoreau,—The handwriting of your letter is so miserable that I am not sure I have made it out. If I have, it seems to me you are the same old sixpence you used to be, rather rusty, but a genuine piece. I see nothing for you in this earth but that field which I once christened "Briars;" go out upon that, build yourself a hut, and there begin the grand process of devouring yourself alive. I see no alternative, no other hope for you. Eat yourself up; you will eat nobody else, nor anything else. Concord is just as good a place as any other; there are, indeed, more people in the streets of that village than in the streets of this. This is a singularly muddy town; muddy, solitary, and silent.

In your line, I have not done a great deal since I arrived here; I do not mean the Pencil line, but the Staten Island line, having been there once, to walk on a beach by the telegraph, but did not visit the scene of your dominical duties. Staten Island is very distant from No. 30 Ann Street. I saw polite William Emerson in November last, but have not caught any glimpse of him since then. I am as usual suffering the various alternations from agony to despair, from hope to fear, from pain to pleasure. Such wretched one-sided productions as you know nothing of the universal man; you may think yourself well off.

That baker, Hecker, who used to live on two crackers a day, I have not seen; nor Black, nor Vethake, nor Danesaz, nor Rynders, nor any of Emerson's old cronies, excepting James, a little fat, rosy Swedenborgian amateur with the look of a broker and the brains and heart of a Pascal. William Channing, I see nothing of him; he is the dupe of good feelings, and I have all-too-many of these now. I have seen something of your friends, Waldo and Tappan, and have also seen our good man McKean, the keeper of that stupid place, the Mercantile Library.

Acting on Channing's hint, and an old fancy of his own, Thoreau, in the summer of 1845, built his cabin at Walden and retired there; while Hawthorne entered the Salem custom-house, and Alcott, returning defeated from his Fruitlands paradise, was struggling with poverty and discouragement at Concord. Charles Lane, his English comrade, withdrew to New York or its vicinity, and in 1846 to London, whence he had come in 1842, full of hope and enthusiasm. A few notes of his, or about him, may here find place. They were sent to Thoreau at Concord, and show that Lane continued to value his candid friend. The first, written after leaving Fruitlands, introduces the late Father Hecker, who had been one of the family there, to Thoreau. The second and third relate to the sale of the Alcott-Lane Library, and other matters.

Walden Woods

CHARLES LANE TO THOREAU (AT CONCORD).

BOSTON, December 3, 1843.

DEAR FRIEND,—As well as my wounded hands permit, I have scribbled something for friend Hecker, which if agreeable may be the opportunity for entering into closer relations with him; a course I think likely to be mutually encouraging, as well as beneficial to all men. But let it reach him in the manner most conformable to your own feelings. That from all perils of a false position you may shortly be relieved, and landed in the position where you feel "at home," is the sincere wish of yours most friendly,

CHARLES LANE.

MR. HENRY THOREAU,
Earl House, Coach Office.

NEW YORK, February 17, 1846.

DEAR FRIEND,—The books you were so kind as to deposit about two years and a half ago with Messrs. Wiley & Putnam have all been sold, but as they were left in your name it is needful, in strict business, that you should send an order to them to pay to me the amount due. I will therefore thank you to inclose me such an order at your earliest convenience in a letter addressed to your admiring friend,

CHARLES LANE,
Post Office, New York City.

BOONTON, N. J., March 30, 1846.

DEAR FRIEND,—If the human nature participates of the elemental I am no longer in danger of becoming suburban, or super-urban, that is to say, too urbane. I am now more likely to be converted into a petrifaction, for slabs of rock and foaming waters never so abounded in my neighborhood. A very Peter I shall become: on this rock *He* has built *his church*. You would find much joy in these eminences and in the views therefrom.

My pen has been necessarily unproductive in the continued motion of the sphere in which I have lately been moved. You, I suppose, have not passed the winter to the world's unprofit.

You never have seen, as I have, the book with a preface of 450 pages and a text of 60. My letter is like unto it.

I have only to add that your letter of the 26th February did its work, and that I submit to you cordial thanks for the same. Yours truly,

CHAS. LANE.

I hope to hear occasionally of your doings and those of your compeers in your classic plowings and diggings.

TO HENRY D. THOREAU,
Concord Woods.

Thoreau's letters to Lane have not come into any editor's hands. In England, before Lane's discovery by Alcott, in 1842, he had been the editor of the *Mark-Lane Gazette* (or something similar), which gave the price-current of wheat, etc., in the English markets. Emerson found him in Hampstead, London, in February, 1848, and wrote to Thoreau: "I went last Sunday, for the first time, to see Lane at Hampstead, and dined with him. He was full of friendliness and hospitality; has a school of sixteen children, one lady as matron, then Oldham. That is all the household. They looked just comfortable."

"Lane instructed me to ask you to forward his *Dials* to him, which must be done, if you can find them. Three bound volumes are among his books in my library. The fourth volume is in unbound numbers at J. Munroe & Co.'s shop, received there in a parcel to my address, a day or two before I sailed, and which I forgot to carry to Concord. It must be claimed without delay. It is certainly there,—was opened by me and left; and they can inclose all four volumes to Chapman for me."

This would indicate that he had not lost interest in the days and events of his American sojourn,—unpleasant as some of these must have been to the methodical, prosaic Englishman.

While at Walden, Thoreau wrote but few letters; there is, however, a brief correspondence with Mr. J. E. Cabot, then an active naturalist, coöperating with Agassiz in his work on the American fishes, who had requested Thoreau to procure certain species from Concord. The letters were written from the cabin at Walden, and it is this same structure that figures in the letters from Thoreau to Emerson in England, as the proposed nucleus of the cottage of poor Hugh the gardener, before he ran away from Concord, as there narrated, on a subsequent page. The first sending of river-fish was in the end of April, 1847. Then followed this letter:—

TO ELLIOT CABOT (AT BOSTON).

CONCORD, May 8, 1847.

DEAR SIR,—I believe that I have not yet acknowledged the receipt of your notes, and a five-dollar bill. I am very glad that the fishes afforded Mr. Agassiz so much pleasure. I could easily have obtained more specimens of the *Sternothærus odoratus*; they are quite numerous here. I will send more of them ere long. Snapping turtles are perhaps as frequently met with in our muddy river as anything, but they are not always to be had when wanted. It is now rather late in the season for them. As no one makes a business of seeking them, and they are valued for soups, science may be forestalled by appetite in this market, and it will be necessary to bid pretty high to induce persons to obtain or preserve them. I think that from seventy-five cents to a dollar apiece would secure all that are in any case to be had, and will set this price upon their heads, if the treasury of science is full enough to warrant it.

You will excuse me for taking toll in the shape of some, it may be, impertinent and unscientific inquiries. There are found in the waters of the Concord, so far as I know, the following kinds of fishes:—

Pickerel. Besides the common, fishermen distinguish the brook, or grass pickerel, which bites differently, and has a shorter snout. Those caught in Walden, hard by my house, are easily distinguished from those caught in the river, being much heavier in proportion to their size, stouter, firmer-fleshed, and lighter-colored. The little pickerel which I sent last, jumped into the boat in its fright.

Pouts. Those in the pond are of different appearance from those that I have sent.

Breams. Some more green, others more brown.

Suckers. The horned, which I sent first, and the black. I am not sure whether the common or Boston sucker is found here. Are the three which I sent last, which were speared in the river, identical with the three black suckers, taken by hand in the brook, which I sent before? I have never examined them minutely.

Perch. The river perch, of which I sent five specimens in the box, are darker-colored than those found in the pond. There are myriads of small ones in the latter place, and but few large ones. I have counted ten transverse bands on some of the smaller.

Lampreys. Very scarce since the dams at Lowell and Billerica were built.

Shiners. Leuciscus chrysoleucus, silver and golden. What is the difference?

Roach or *Chiverin* (*Leuciscus pulchellus*, *argenteus*, or what not). The *white* and the *red.* The former described by Storer, but the latter, which deserves distinct notice, not described, to my knowledge. Are the minnows (called here dace), of which I sent three live specimens, I believe, one larger and two smaller, the young of this species?

Trout. Of different appearance in different brooks in this neighborhood.

Eels.

Red-finned Minnows, of which I sent you a dozen alive. I have never recognized them in any books. Have they any scientific name?

If convenient, will you let Dr. Storer see these brook minnows? There is also a kind of dace or fresh-water smelt in the pond, which is, perhaps, distinct from any of the above. What of the above does M. Agassiz particularly wish to see? Does he want more specimens of kinds which I have already sent? There are also minks, muskrats, frogs, lizards, tortoises, snakes, caddice-worms, leeches, muscles, etc., or rather, *here they are.* The funds which you sent me are nearly exhausted. Most fishes can now be taken with the hook, and it will cost but little trouble or money to obtain them. The snapping turtles will be the main expense. I should think that five dollars more, at least, might be profitably expended.

TO ELLIOT CABOT (AT BOSTON).

CONCORD, June 1, 1847.

Dear Sir,—I send you 15 pouts, 17 perch, 13 shiners, 1 larger land tortoise, and 5 muddy tortoises, all from the pond by my house. Also 7 perch, 5 shiners, 8 breams, 4 dace(?), 2 muddy tortoises, 5 painted do., and 3 land do., all from the river. One black snake, alive, and one dormouse(?) caught last night in my cellar. The tortoises were all put in alive; the fishes were alive yesterday, *i. e.*, Monday, and some this morning. Observe the difference between those from the pond, which is pure water, and those from the river.

I will send the light-colored trout and the pickerel with the longer snout, which is our large one, when I meet with them. I have set a price upon the heads of snapping turtles, though it is late in the season to get them.

If I wrote red-finned eel, it was a slip of the pen; I meant red-finned minnow. This is their name here; though smaller specimens have but a slight reddish tinge at the base of the pectorals.

Will you, at your leisure, answer these queries?

Do you mean to say that the twelve banded minnows which I sent are undescribed, or only one? What are the scientific names of those minnows which have any? Are the four dace I send to-day identical with one of the former, and what are they called? Is there such a fish as the black sucker described,—distinct from the common?

AGASSIZ TO THOREAU (AT CONCORD).

In October, 1849, Agassiz, in reply to a request from Thoreau that he would lecture in Bangor, sent this characteristic letter:—

"I remember with much pleasure the time when you used to send me specimens from your vicinity, and also our short interview in the Marlborough Chapel.[35] I am under too many obligations of your kindness to forget it. I am very sorry that I missed your visit in Boston; but for eighteen months I have now been settled in Cambridge. It would give me great pleasure to engage for the lectures you ask from me for the Bangor Lyceum; but I find it has been last winter such a heavy tax upon my health, that I wish for the present to make no engagements; as I have some hope of making my living this year by other efforts,—and beyond the necessity of my wants, both domestic and scientific, I am determined not to exert myself; as all the time I can thus secure to myself must be exclusively devoted to science. My only business is my intercourse with nature; and could I do without draughtsmen, lithographers, etc., I would live still more retired. This will satisfy you that whenever you come this way I shall be delighted to see you,—since I have also heard something of your mode of living."

Agassiz had reason indeed to remember the collections made by Thoreau, since (from the letters of Mr. Cabot) they aided him much in his comparison of the American with the European fishes. When the first firkin of Concord fish arrived in Boston, where Agassiz was then working, "he was highly delighted, and began immediately to spread them out and arrange them for his draughtsman. Some of the species he had seen before, but never in so fresh condition; others, as the breams and the pout, he had seen only in spirits, and the little tortoise he knew only from the books. I am sure you would have felt fully repaid for your trouble," adds Mr. Cabot, "if you could have seen the eager satisfaction with which he surveyed each fin and scale." Agassiz himself wrote the same day: "I have been highly pleased to find that the small mud turtle was really the *Sternothærus odoratus*, as I suspected,—a very rare species, quite distinct from the snapping turtle. The suckers were all of one and the same species (*Catastomus tuberculatus*); the female has the tubercles. As I am very anxious to send some snapping turtles home with my first boxes, I would thank Mr. T. very much if he could have some taken for me."

Mr. Cabot goes on: "Of the perch Agassiz remarked that it was almost identical with that of Europe, but distinguishable, on close examination, by the tubercles on the sub-operculum.... More of the painted tortoises would be acceptable. The snapping turtles are very interesting to him as forming a transition from the turtles proper to the alligator and crocodile.... We have received three boxes from you since the first." (May 27.) "Agassiz was much surprised and pleased at the extent of the collections you sent during his absence in New York. Among the fishes there is one, and probably two, new species. The fresh-water smelt he does not know. He is very anxious to see the pickerel with the long snout, which he suspects may be the *Esox estor*, or Maskalongé; he has seen this at Albany.... As to the minks, etc., I know they would all be very acceptable to him. When I asked him about these, and more specimens of what you have sent, he said, 'I dare not make any request, for I do not know how much trouble I may be giving to Mr. Thoreau; but my method of examination requires many more specimens than most naturalists would care for.'" (June 1.) "Agassiz is delighted to find one, and he thinks two, more new species; one is a Pomotis,—the bream without the red spot in the operculum, and with a red belly and fins. The other is the shallower and lighter colored shiner. The four dace you sent last are *Leuciscus argenteus*. They are different from that you sent before under this name, but which was a new species. Of the four kinds of minnow, two are new. There is a black sucker (*Catastomus nigricans*), but there has been no specimen among those you have sent, and A. has never seen a specimen. He seemed to know your mouse, and called it the white-bellied mouse. It was the first specimen he had seen. I am in hopes to bring or send him to Concord, to look after new *Leucisci*, etc." Agassiz did afterwards come, more than once, and examined turtles with Thoreau.

Soon after this scientific correspondence, Thoreau left his retreat by Walden to take the place of Emerson in his household, while his friend went to visit Carlyle and give lectures in England. The letters that follow are among the longest Thoreau ever composed, and will give a new conception of the writer to those who may have figured him as a cold, stoical, or selfish person, withdrawn from society and its duties. The first describes the setting out of Emerson for Europe.

TO SOPHIA THOREAU (AT BANGOR).

Concord, October 24, 1847.

Dear Sophia,—I thank you for those letters about Ktaadn, and hope you will save and send me the rest, and anything else you may meet with relating to the Maine woods. That Dr. Young is both young and green too at traveling in the woods. However, I hope he got "yarbs" enough to satisfy him. I went to Boston the 5th of this month to see Mr. Emerson off to Europe. He sailed in the Washington Irving packet-ship; the same in which Mr. [F. H.] Hedge went before him. Up to this trip the first mate aboard this ship was, as I hear, one Stephens, a Concord boy, son of Stephens the carpenter, who used to live above Mr. Dennis's. Mr. Emerson's stateroom was like a carpeted dark closet, about six feet square, with a large keyhole for a window. The window was about as big as a saucer, and the glass two inches thick, not to mention another skylight overhead in the deck, the size of an oblong doughnut, and about as opaque. Of course it would be in vain to look up, if any contemplative promenader put his foot upon it. Such will be his lodgings for two or three weeks; and instead of a walk in Walden woods he will take a promenade on deck, where the few trees, you know, are stripped of their bark. The steam-tug carried the ship to sea against a head wind without a rag of sail being raised.

I don't remember whether you have heard of the new telescope at Cambridge or not. They think it is the best one in the world, and have already seen more than Lord Rosse or Herschel. I went to see Perez Blood's, some time ago, with Mr. Emerson. He had not gone to bed, but was sitting in the wood-shed, in the dark, alone, in his astronomical chair, which is all legs and rounds, with a seat which can be inserted at any height. We saw Saturn's rings, and the mountains in the moon, and the shadows in their craters, and the sunlight on the spurs of the mountains in the dark portion, etc., etc. When I asked him the power of his glass, he said it was 85. But what is the power of the Cambridge glass? 2000!!! The last is about twenty-three feet long.

I think you may have a grand time this winter pursuing some study,—keeping a journal, or the like,—while the snow lies deep without. Winter is the time for study, you know, and the colder it is the more studious we are. Give my respects to the whole Penobscot tribe, and tell them that I trust we are good brothers still, and endeavor to keep the chain of friendship bright, though I do dig up a hatchet now and then. I trust you will not stir from your comfortable winter quarters, Miss Bruin, or even put your head out of your hollow tree, till the sun has melted the snow in the spring, and "the green buds, they are a-swellin'."

From your Brother Henry.

This letter will explain some of the allusions in the first letter to Emerson in England. Perez Blood was a rural astronomer living in the extreme north quarter of Concord, next to Carlisle, with his two maiden sisters, in the midst of a fine oak wood; their cottage being one of the points in view when Thoreau and his friends took their afternoon rambles. Sophia Thoreau, the younger and soon the only surviving sister, was visiting her cousins in Maine, the "Penobscot tribe" of whom the letter makes mention, with an allusion to the Indians of that name near Bangor. His letter to her and those which follow were written from Emerson's house, where Thoreau lived during the master's absence across the ocean. It was in the orchard of this house that Alcott was building that summer-house at which Thoreau, with his geometrical eye, makes merry in the next letter.

TO R. W. EMERSON (IN ENGLAND).

Concord, November 14, 1847.

Dear Friend,—I am but a poor neighbor to you here,—a very poor companion am I. I understand that very well, but that need not prevent my *writing* to you now. I have almost never written letters in my life, yet I think I can write as good ones as I frequently see, so I shall not hesitate to write this, such as it may be, knowing that you will welcome anything that reminds you of Concord.

I have banked up the young trees against the winter and the mice, and I will look out, in my careless way, to see when a pale is loose or a nail drops out of its place. The broad gaps, at least, I will occupy. I heartily wish I could be of good service to this household. But I, who have only used these ten digits so long to solve the problem of a living, how can I? The world is a cow that is hard to milk,—life does not come so easy,—and oh, how thinly it is watered ere we get it! But the young bunting calf, he will get at it. There is no way so direct. This is to earn one's living by the sweat of his brow. It is a little like joining a community, this life, to such a hermit as I am; and as I don't keep the accounts, I don't know whether the experiment will succeed or fail finally.

At any rate, it is good for society, so I do not regret my transient nor my permanent share in it.

Lidian [Mrs. Emerson] and I make very good housekeepers. She is a very dear sister to me. Ellen and Edith and Eddy and Aunty Brown keep up the tragedy and comedy and tragic-comedy of life as usual. The two former have not forgotten their old acquaintance; even Edith carries a young memory in her head, I find. Eddy can teach us all how to pronounce. If you should discover any rare hoard of wooden or pewter horses, I have no doubt he will know how to appreciate it. He occasionally surveys mankind from my shoulders as wisely as ever Johnson did. I respect him not a little, though it is I that lift him up so unceremoniously. And sometimes I have to set him down again in a hurry, according to his "mere will and good pleasure." He very seriously asked me, the other day, "Mr. Thoreau, will you be my father?" I am occasionally Mr. Rough-and-tumble with him that I may not miss *him*, and lest he should miss *you* too much. So you must come back soon, or you will be superseded.

Alcott has heard that I laughed, and so set the people laughing, at his arbor, though I never laughed louder than when I was on the ridge-pole. But now I have not laughed for a long time, it is so serious. He is very grave to look at. But, not knowing all this, I strove innocently enough, the other day, to engage his attention to my mathematics. "Did you ever study geometry, the relation of straight lines to curves, the transition from the finite to the infinite? Fine things about it in Newton and Leibnitz." But he would hear none of it,—men of taste preferred the natural curve. Ah, he is a crooked stick himself. He is getting on now so many *knots* an hour. There is one knot at present occupying the point of highest elevation,—the present highest point; and as many knots as are not handsome, I presume, are thrown down and cast into the pines. Pray show him this if you meet him anywhere in London, for I cannot make him hear much plainer words here. He forgets that I am neither old nor young, nor anything in particular, and behaves as if I had still some of the animal heat in me. As for the building, I feel a little oppressed when I come near it. It has no great disposition to be beautiful; it is certainly a wonderful structure, on the whole, and the fame of the architect will endure as long as it shall stand. I should not show you this side alone, if I did not suspect that Lidian had done complete justice to the other.

Mr. [Edmund] Hosmer has been working at a tannery in Stow for a fortnight, though he has just now come home sick. It seems that he was a tanner in his youth, and so he has made up his mind a little at last. This comes of reading the New Testament. Was n't one of the Apostles a tanner? Mrs. Hosmer remains here, and John looks stout enough to fill his own shoes and his father's too.

Mr. Blood and his company have at length seen the stars through the great telescope, and he told me that he thought it was worth the while. Mr. Peirce made him wait till the crowd had dispersed (it was a Saturday evening), and then was quite polite,—conversed with him, and showed him the micrometer, etc.; and he said Mr. Blood's glass was large enough for all ordinary astronomical work. [Rev.] Mr. Frost and Dr. [Josiah] Bartlett seemed disappointed that there was no greater difference between the Cambridge glass and the Concord one. They used only a power of 400. Mr. Blood tells me that he is too old to study the calculus or higher mathematics. At Cambridge they think that they have discovered traces of another satellite to Neptune. They have been obliged to exclude the public altogether, at last. The very dust which they raised, "which is filled with minute crystals," etc., as professors declare, having to be wiped off the glasses, would ere long wear them away. It is true enough, Cambridge college is really beginning to wake up and redeem its character and overtake the age. I see by the catalogue that they are about establishing a scientific school in connection with the university, at which any one above eighteen, on paying one hundred dollars annually (Mr. Lawrence's fifty thousand dollars will probably diminish this sum), may be instructed in the highest branches of science,—in astronomy, "theoretical and practical, with the use of the instruments" (so the great Yankee astronomer may be born without delay), in mechanics and engineering to the last degree. Agassiz will ere long commence his lectures in the zoölogical department. A chemistry class has already been formed under the direction of Professor Horsford. A new and adequate building for the purpose is already being erected. They have been foolish enough to put at the end of all this earnest the old joke of a diploma. Let every sheep keep but his own skin, I say.

I have had a tragic correspondence, for the most part all on one side, with Miss ——. She did really wish to—I hesitate to write—marry me. That is the way they spell it. Of course I did not write a deliberate answer. How could I deliberate upon it? I sent back as distinct a *no* as I have learned to pronounce after considerable practice, and I trust that this *no* has succeeded. Indeed, I wished that it might burst, like hollow shot, after it had struck and buried itself and made itself felt there. *There was no other way.* I really had anticipated no such foe as this in my career.

I suppose you will like to hear of my book, though I have nothing worth writing about it. Indeed, for the last month or two I have forgotten it, but shall certainly remember it again. Wiley & Putnam, Munroe, the Harpers, and Crosby & Nichols have all declined printing it with the least risk to themselves; but Wiley & Putnam will print it in their series, and any of them anywhere, at *my* risk. If I liked the book well enough, I should not delay; but for the present I am indifferent. I believe this is, after all, the course you advised,—to let it lie.

I do not know what to say of myself. I sit before my green desk, in the chamber at the head of the stairs, and attend to my thinking, sometimes more, sometimes less distinctly. I am not unwilling to think great thoughts if there are any in the wind, but what they are I am not sure. They suffice to keep me awake while the day lasts, at any rate. Perhaps they will redeem some portion of the night ere long.

I can imagine you astonishing, bewildering, confounding, and sometimes delighting John Bull with your Yankee notions, and that he begins to take a pride in the relationship at last; introduced to all the stars of England in succession, after the lecture, until you pine to thrust your head once more into a genuine and unquestionable nebula, if there be any left. I trust a common man will be the most uncommon to you before you return to these parts. I have thought there was some advantage even in death, by which we "mingle with the herd of common men."

Hugh [the gardener] still has his eye on the Walden *agellum*, and orchards are waving there in the windy future for him. That's the where-I'll-go-next, thinks he; but no important steps are yet taken. He reminds me occasionally of this open secret of his, with which the very season seems to labor, and affirms seriously that as to his wants—wood, stone, or timber—I know better than he. That is a clincher which I shall have to avoid to some extent; but I fear that it is a wrought nail and will not break. Unfortunately, the day after cattle-show —the day after small beer—he was among the missing, but not long this time. The Ethiopian cannot change his skin nor the leopard his spots, nor indeed Hugh—his Hugh.

As I walked over Conantum, the other afternoon, I saw a fair column of smoke rising from the woods directly over my house that was (as I judged), and already began to conjecture if my deed of sale would not be made invalid by this. But it turned out to be John Richardson's young wood, on the southeast of your field. It was burnt nearly all over, and up to the rails and the road. It was set on fire, no doubt, by the same Lucifer that lighted Brooks's lot before. So you see that your small lot is comparatively safe for this season, the back fire having been already set for you.

They have been choosing between John Keyes and Sam Staples, if the world wants to know it, as representative of this town, and Staples is chosen. The candidates for governor—think of my writing this to you!—were Governor Briggs and General Cushing, and Briggs is elected, though the Democrats have gained. Ain't I a brave boy to know so much of politics for the nonce? But I should n't have known it if Coombs had n't told me. They have had a peace meeting here,—I should n't think of telling you if I did n't know anything would do for the English market,—and some men, Deacon Brown at the head, have signed a long pledge, swearing that they will "treat all mankind as brothers henceforth." I think I shall wait and see how they treat me first. I think that Nature meant kindly when she made our brothers few. However, my voice is still for peace. So good-by, and a truce to all joking, my dear friend, from

H. D. T.

Upon this letter some annotations are to be made. "Eddy" was Emerson's youngest child, Edward Waldo, then three years old and upward,—of late years his father's biographer. Hugh, the gardener, of whom more anon, bargained for the house of Thoreau on Emerson's land at Walden, and for a field to go with it; but the bargain came to naught, and the cabin was removed three or four miles to the northwest, where it became a granary for Farmer Clark and his squirrels, near the entrance to the park known as Estabrook's. Edmund Hosmer was the farming friend and neighbor with whom, at one time, G. W. Curtis and his brother took lodgings, and at another time the Alcott family. The book in question was "A Week on the Concord and Merrimack Rivers."

To these letters Emerson replied from England:—

Dear Henry,—Very welcome in the parcel was your letter, very precious your thoughts and tidings. It is one of the best things connected with my coming hither that you could and would keep the homestead; that fireplace shines all the brighter, and has a certain permanent glimmer therefor. Thanks, ever more thanks for the kindness which I well discern to the youth of the house: to my darling little horseman of pewter, wooden, rocking, and what other breeds,—destined, I hope, to ride Pegasus yet, and, I hope, not destined to be thrown; to Edith, who long ago drew from you verses which I carefully preserve; and to Ellen, whom by speech, and now by letter, I find old enough to be companionable, and to choose and reward her own friends in her own fashions. She sends me a poem to-day, which I have read three times!

TO R. W. EMERSON (IN ENGLAND).

Concord, December 15, 1847.

Dear Friend,—You are not so far off but the affairs of *this* world still attract you. Perhaps it will be so when we are dead. Then look out. Joshua R. Holman, of Harvard, who says he lived a month with [Charles] Lane at Fruitlands, wishes to *hire* said Lane's farm for one or more years, and will pay

$125 rent, taking out of the same a half, if necessary, for repairs,—as for a new bank-wall to the barn cellar, which he says is indispensable. Palmer is gone, Mrs. Palmer is going. This is all that is known or that is worth knowing. Yes or no? What to do?

Hugh's plot begins to thicken. He starts thus: eighty dollars on one side; Walden, field and house, on the other. How to bring these together so as to make a garden and a palace?

	$80		
1st,	$10	go over to unite the two lots.	Field House
let	———		
	$70		
	$6	for Wetherbee's rocks to found your palace on.	
	$64	—so far, indeed, we have already got.	
	$4	to bring the rocks to the field.	
	$60		
Save	$20	by all means, to measure the field, and you have left	
	$40	to complete the palace, build cellar, and dig well. Build the cellar yourself, and let *well* alone,—and now how does it stand?	
	$40	to complete the palace somewhat like this.	

For when one asks, "Why do you want twice as much room more?" the reply is, "Parlor, kitchen, and bedroom,—these make the palace."

"Well, Hugh, what will you do? Here are forty dollars to buy a new house, twelve feet by twenty-five, and add it to the old."

"Well, Mr. Thoreau, as I tell you, I know no more than a child about it. It shall be just as you say."

"Then build it yourself, get it roofed, and get in.

Commence at one end and leave it half done,

And let time finish what money's begun."

So you see we have forty dollars for a nest egg; sitting on which, Hugh and I alternately and simultaneously, there may in course of time be hatched a house that will long stand, and perchance even lay fresh eggs one day for its owner; that is, if, when he returns, he gives the young chick twenty dollars or more in addition, by way of "swichin," to give it a start in the world.

The *Massachusetts Quarterly Review* came out the 1st of December, but it does not seem to be making a sensation, at least not hereabouts. I know of none in Concord who take or have seen it yet.

We wish to get by all possible means some notion of your success or failure in England,—more than your two letters have furnished. Can't you send a fair sample both of young and of old England's criticism, if there is any printed? Alcott and [Ellery] Channing are equally greedy with myself.

HENRY THOREAU.

C. T. Jackson takes the *Quarterly* (new one), and will lend it to us. Are you not going to send your wife some news of your good or ill success by the newspapers?

TO R. W. EMERSON (IN ENGLAND).

CONCORD, December 29, 1847.

MY DEAR FRIEND,—I thank you for your letter. I was very glad to get it; and I am glad again to write to you. However slow the steamer, no time intervenes between the writing and the reading of thoughts, but they come freshly to the most distant port. I am here still, and very glad to be here, and shall not trouble you with any complaints because I do not fill my place better. I have had many good hours in the chamber at the head of the stairs,—a solid time, it seems to me. Next week I am going to give an account to the Lyceum of my expedition to Maine. Theodore Parker lectures to-night. We have had Whipple on Genius,—too weighty a subject for him, with his antithetical definitions new-vamped,—what it *is*, what it is *not*, but altogether what it is *not*; cuffing it this way and cuffing it that, as if it were an India-rubber ball. Really, it is a subject which should expand, expand, accumulate itself before the speaker's eyes as he goes on, like the snowballs which the boys roll in the street; and when it stops, it should be so large that he cannot start it, but must leave it there. [H. N.] Hudson, too, has been here, with a dark shadow in the core of him, and his desperate wit, so much indebted to the surface of him,—wringing out his words and snapping them off like a dish-cloth; very remarkable, but not memorable. Singular that these two best lecturers should have so much "wave" in their timber,—their solid parts to be made and kept solid by shrinkage and contraction of the whole, with consequent checks and fissures.

Ellen and I have a good understanding. I appreciate her genuineness. Edith tells me after her fashion: "By and by I shall grow up and be a woman, and then I shall remember how you exercised me." Eddy has been to Boston to Christmas, but can remember nothing but the coaches, all Kendall's coaches. There is no variety of that vehicle that he is not familiar with. He *did* try twice to tell us something else, but, after thinking and stuttering a long time, said, "I don't know what the word is,"—the *one* word, forsooth, that would have disposed of all that Boston phenomenon. If you did not know him better than I, I could tell you more. He is a good companion for me, and I am glad that we are all natives of Concord. It is *young Concord*. Look out, World!

Mr. Alcott seems to have sat down for the winter. He has got Plato and other books to read. He is as large-featured and hospitable to traveling thoughts and thinkers as ever; but with the same Connecticut philosophy as ever, mingled with what is better. If he would only stand upright and toe the line!—though he were to put off several degrees of largeness, and put on a considerable degree of littleness. After all, I think we must call him particularly *your* man.

I have pleasant walks and talks with Channing. James Clark—the Swedenborgian that was—is at the poorhouse, insane with too large views, so that he cannot support himself. I see him working with Fred and the rest. Better than be there and not insane. It is strange that they will make ado when a man's body is buried, but not when he thus really and tragically dies, or seems to die. Away with your funeral processions,—into the ballroom with them! I hear the bell toll hourly over there.[36]

Lidian and I have a standing quarrel as to what is a suitable state of preparedness for a traveling professor's visit, or for whomsoever else; but further than this we are not at war. We have made up a dinner, we have made up a bed, we have made up a party, and our own minds and mouths, three several times for your professor, and he came not. Three several turkeys have died the death, which I myself carved, just as if he had been there; and the company, too, convened and demeaned themselves accordingly. Everything was done up in good style, I assure you, with only the part of the professor omitted. To have seen the preparation (though Lidian says it was nothing extraordinary) I should certainly have said he was a-coming, but he did not. He must have found out some shorter way to Turkey,—some overland route, I think. By the way, he was complimented, at the conclusion of his course in Boston, by the mayor moving the appointment of a committee to draw up resolutions expressive, etc., which was done.

I have made a few verses lately. Here are some, though perhaps not the best, —at any rate they are the shortest,—on that universal theme, yours as well as mine, and several other people's:—

The good how can we trust!

Only the wise are just.

The good, we use,

The wise we cannot choose;

These there are none above.

The good, they know and love,

But are not known again

By those of lesser ken.

They do not charm us with their eyes,

But they transfix with their advice;

No partial sympathy they feel

With private woe or private weal,

But with the universe joy and sigh,

Whose knowledge is their sympathy.

Good-night. HENRY THOREAU.

P. S.—I am sorry to send such a medley as this to you. I have forwarded Lane's *Dial* to Munroe, and he tells the expressman that all isright.

TO R. W. EMERSON (IN ENGLAND).

CONCORD, January 12, 1848.

It is hard to believe that England is so near as from your letters it appears; and that this identical piece of paper has lately come all the way from there hither, begrimed with the English dust which made you hesitate to use it; from England, which is only historical fairyland to me, to America, which I have put my spade into, and about which there is no doubt.

I thought that you needed to be informed of Hugh's progress. He has moved his house, as I told you, and dug his cellar, and purchased stone of Sol Wetherbee for the last, though he has not hauled it; all which has cost sixteen dollars, which I have paid. He has also, as next in order, run away from Concord without a penny in his pocket, "crying" by the way,—having had another long difference with strong beer, and a first one, I suppose, with his wife, who seems to have complained that he sought other society; the one difference leading to the other, perhaps, but I don't know which was the leader. He writes back to his wife from Sterling, near Worcester, where he is chopping wood, his distantly kind reproaches to her, which I read straight through to her (not to his bottle, which he has with him, and no doubt addresses orally). He says that he will go on to the South in the spring, and will never return to Concord. Perhaps he will not. Life is not tragic enough for him, and he must try to cook up a more highly seasoned dish for himself. Towns which keep a barroom and a gun-house and a reading-room, should also keep a steep precipice whereoff impatient soldiers may jump. His sun went down, *to me*, bright and steady enough in the west, but it never came up in the east. Night intervened. He departed, as when a man dies suddenly; and perhaps wisely, if he was to go, without settling his affairs. They knew that that was a thin soil and not well calculated for pears. Nature is rare and sensitive on the score of nurseries. You may cut down orchards and grow forests at your pleasure. Sand watered with strong beer, though stirred with industry, will not produce grapes. He dug his cellar for the new part too near the old house, Irish like, though I warned him, and it has caved and let one end of the house down. Such is the state of his domestic affairs. I laugh with the Parcæ only. He had got the upland and the orchard and a part of the meadow plowed by Warren, at an expense of eight dollars, still unpaid, which of course is no affair of yours.

I think that if an honest and small-familied man, who has no affinity for moisture in him, but who has an affinity for sand, can be found, it would be safe to rent him the shanty as it is, and the land; or you can very easily and simply let nature keep them still, without great loss. It may be so managed, perhaps, as to be a home for somebody, who shall in return serve you as fencing stuff, and to fix and locate your lot, as we plant a tree in the sand or on the edge of a stream; without expense to you in the meanwhile, and without disturbing its possible future value.

I read a part of the story of my excursion to Ktaadn to quite a large audience of men and boys, the other night, whom it interested. It contains many facts and some poetry. I have also written what will do for a lecture on "Friendship."

I think that the article on you in *Blackwood's* is a good deal to get from the reviewers,—the first purely literary notice, as I remember. The writer is far enough off, in every sense, to speak with a certain authority. It is a better judgment of posterity than the public had. It is singular how sure he is to be mystified by any uncommon sense. But it was generous to put Plato into the list of mystics. His confessions on this subject suggest several thoughts, which I have not room to express here. The old word *seer*,—I wonder what the reviewer thinks that means; whether that *he* was a man who could *see more than himself*.

I was struck by Ellen's asking me, yesterday, while I was talking with Mrs. Brown, if I did not use "*colored* words." She said that she could tell the color of a great many words, and amused the children at school by so doing. Eddy climbed up the sofa, the other day, *of his own accord*, and kissed the picture of his father,—"right on his shirt, I did."

I had a good talk with Alcott this afternoon. He is certainly the youngest man of his age we have seen,—just on the threshold of life. When I looked at his gray hairs, his conversation sounded pathetic; but I looked again, and they reminded me of the gray dawn. He is getting better acquainted with Channing, though he says that, if they were to live in the same house, they would soon sit with their backs to each other.[37]

You must excuse me if I do not write with sufficient directness to yourself, who are a far-off traveler. It is a little like shooting on the wing, I confess.

Farewell. HENRY THOREAU.

TO R. W. EMERSON (IN ENGLAND).

CONCORD, February 23, 1848.

DEAR WALDO,—For I think I have heard that that is your name,—my letter which was put last into the leathern bag arrived first. Whatever I may *call* you, I know you better than I know your name, and what becomes of the fittest name if in any sense you are here with him who *calls*, and not there simply to be called?

I believe I never thanked you for your lectures, one and all, which I heard formerly read here in Concord. I *know* I never have. There was some excellent reason each time why I did not; but it will never be too late. I have that advantage, at least, over you in my education.

Lidian is too unwell to write to you; so I must tell you what I can about the children and herself. I am afraid she has not told you how unwell she is,—or to-day perhaps we may say has been. She has been confined to her chamber four or five weeks, and three or four weeks, at least, to her bed, with the jaundice. The doctor, who comes once a day, does not let her read (nor can she now) nor *hear* much reading. She has written her letters to you, till recently, sitting up in bed, but he said he would not come again if she did so. She has Abby and Almira to take care of her, and Mrs. Brown to read to her; and I also, occasionally, have something to read or to say. The doctor says she must not expect to "take any comfort of her life" for a week or two yet. She wishes me to say that she has written two long and full letters to you about the household economies, etc., which she hopes have not been delayed. The children are quite well and full of spirits, and are going through a regular course of picture-seeing, with commentary by me, every evening, for Eddy's behoof. All the Annuals and "Diadems" are in requisition, and Eddy is forward to exclaim, when the hour arrives, "Now for the demdems!" I overheard this dialogue when Frank [Brown] came down to breakfast the other morning.

Eddy. "Why, Frank, I am astonished that you should leave your boots in the dining-room."

Frank. "I guess you mean *surprised*, don't you?"

Eddy. "No, boots!"

"If Waldo were here," said he, the other night, at bedtime, "we'd be four going upstairs." Would he like to tell papa anything? No, not anything; but finally, yes, he would,—that one of the white horses in his new barouche is broken! Ellen and Edith will perhaps speak for themselves, as I hear something about letters to be written by them.

Mr. Alcott seems to be reading well this winter: Plato, Montaigne, Ben Jonson, Beaumont and Fletcher, Sir Thomas Browne, etc., etc. "I believe I have read them all now, or nearly all,"—those English authors. He is rallying for another foray with his pen, in his latter years, not discouraged by the past, into that crowd of unexpressed ideas of his, that undisciplined Parthian army, which, as soon as a Roman soldier would face, retreats on all hands, occasionally firing backwards; easily routed, not easily subdued, hovering on the skirts of society. Another summer shall not be devoted to the raising of vegetables (Arbors?) which rot in the cellar for want of consumers; but perchance to the arrangement of the material, the brain-crop which the winter has furnished. I have good talks with him. His respect for Carlyle has been steadily increasing for some time. He has read him with new sympathy and appreciation.

I see Channing often. He also goes often to Alcott's, and confesses that he has made a discovery in him, and gives vent to his admiration or his confusion in characteristic exaggeration; but between this extreme and that you may get a fair report, and draw an inference if you can. Sometimes he will ride a broomstick still, though there is nothing to keep him, or it, up but a certain centrifugal force of whim, which is soon spent, and there lies your stick, not worth picking up to sweep an oven with now. His accustomed path is strewn with them. But then again, and perhaps for the most part, he sits on the Cliffs amid the lichens, or flits past on noiseless pinion, like the barred owl in the daytime, as wise and unobserved. He brought me a poem the other day, for me, on Walden Hermitage: not remarkable.[38]

Lectures begin to multiply on my desk. I have one on Friendship which is new, and the materials of some others. I read one last week to the Lyceum, on The Rights and Duties of the Individual in Relation to Government,—much to Mr. Alcott's satisfaction.

Joel Britton has failed and gone into chancery, but the woods continue to fall before the axes of other men. Neighbor Coombs[39] was lately found dead in the woods near Goose Pond, with his half-empty jug, after he had been rioting a week. Hugh, by the last accounts, was still in Worcester County. Mr. Hosmer, who is himself again, and living in Concord, has just hauled the rest of your wood, amounting to about ten and a half cords.

The newspapers say that they have printed a pirated edition of your Essays in England. Is it as bad as they say, and undisguised and unmitigated piracy? I thought that the printed scrap would entertain Carlyle, notwithstanding its history. If this generation will see out of its hind-head, why then you may turn your back on its forehead. Will you forward it to him for me?

The Hosmer House

This stands written in your day-book: "September 3d. Received of Boston Savings Bank, on account of Charles Lane, his deposit with interest, $131.33. 16th. Received of Joseph Palmer, on account of Charles Lane, three hundred twenty-three 36/100 dollars, being the balance of a note on demand for four hundred dollars, with interest, $323.36."

If you have any directions to give about the trees, you must not forget that spring will soon be upon us.

Farewell. From your friend,

HENRY THOREAU.

Before a reply came to this letter, Thoreau had occasion to write to Mr. Elliot Cabot again. The allusions to the "Week" and to the Walden house are interesting.

TO ELLIOT CABOT.

CONCORD, March 8, 1848.

DEAR SIR,—Mr. Emerson's address is as yet, "R. W. Emerson, care of Alexander Ireland, Esq., Examiner Office, Manchester, England." We had a letter from him on Monday, dated at Manchester, February 10, and he was then preparing to go to Edinburgh the next day, where he was to lecture. He thought that he should get through his northern journeying by the 25th of February, and go to London to spend March and April, and if he did not go to Paris in May, then come home. He has been eminently successful, though the papers this side of the water have been so silent about his adventures.

My book,[40] fortunately, did not find a publisher ready to undertake it, and you can imagine the effect of delay on an author's estimate of his own work. However, I like it well enough to mend it, and shall look at it again directly when I have dispatched some other things.

I have been writing lectures for our own Lyceum this winter, mainly for my own pleasure and advantage. I esteem it a rare happiness to be able to *write* anything, but there (if I ever get there) my concern for it is apt to end. Time & Co. are, after all, the only quite honest and trustworthy publishers that we know. I can sympathize, perhaps, with the barberry bush, whose business it is solely to *ripen* its fruit (though that may not be to sweeten it) and to protect it with thorns, so that it holds on all winter, even, unless some hungry crows come to pluck it. But I see that I must get a few dollars together presently to manure my roots. Is your journal able to pay anything, provided it likes an article well enough? I do not promise one. At any rate, I mean always to spend only words enough to purchase silence with; and I have found that this, which is so valuable, though many writers do not prize it, does not cost much, after all.

I have not obtained any more of the mice which I told you were so numerous in my cellar, as my house was removed immediately after I saw you, and I have been living in the village since.

However, if I should happen to meet with anything rare, I will forward it to you. I thank you for your kind offers, and will avail myself of them so far as to ask if you can anywhere borrow for me for a short time the copy of the *Revue des Deux Mondes* containing a notice of Mr. Emerson. I should like well to read it, and to read it to Mrs. Emerson and others. If this book is not easy to be obtained, do not by any means trouble yourself about it.

TO R. W. EMERSON.[41]

Concord, March 23, 1848.

Dear Friend,—Lidian says I must write a sentence about the children. Eddy says he cannot sing,—"not till mother is a-going to be well." We shall hear his voice very soon, in that case, I trust. Ellen is already thinking what will be done when you come home; but then she thinks it will be some loss that I shall go away. Edith says that I shall come and see them, and always at tea-time, so that I can play with her. Ellen thinks she likes father best because he jumps her sometimes. This is the latest news from

Yours, etc., Henry.

P. S.—I have received three newspapers from you duly which I have not acknowledged. There is an anti-Sabbath convention held in Boston to-day, to which Alcott has gone.

That friend to whom Thoreau wrote most constantly and fully, on all topics, was Mr. Harrison Blake of Worcester, a graduate of Harvard two years earlier than Thoreau, in the same class with two other young men from Concord,—E. R. Hoar and H. B. Dennis. This circumstance may have led to Mr. Blake's visiting the town occasionally, before his intimacy with its poet-naturalist began, in the year 1848. At that time, as Thoreau wrote to Horace Greeley, he had been supporting himself for five years wholly by the labor of his hands; his Walden hermit life was over, yet neither its record nor the first book had been published, and Thoreau was known in literature chiefly by his papers in the *Dial*, which had then ceased for four years. In March, 1848, Mr. Blake read Thoreau's chapter on Persius in the *Dial* for July, 1840,—and though he had read it before without being much impressed by it, he now found in it "pure depth and solidity of thought." "It has revived in me," he wrote to Thoreau, "a haunting impression of you, which I carried away from some spoken words of yours.… When I was last in Concord, you spoke of retiring farther from our civilization. I asked you if you would feel no longings for the society of your friends. Your reply was in substance, 'No, I am nothing.' That reply was memorable to me. It indicated a depth of resources, a completeness of renunciation, a poise and repose in the universe, which to me is almost inconceivable; which in you seemed domesticated, and to which I look up with veneration. I would know of that soul which can say 'I am nothing.' I would be roused by its words to a truer and purer life. Upon me seems to be dawning with new significance the idea that God is here; that we have but to bow before Him in profound submission at every moment, and He will fill our souls with his presence. In this opening of the soul to God, all duties seem to centre; what else have we to do?… If I understand rightly the significance of your life, this is it: You would sunder yourself from society, from the spell of institutions, customs, conventionalities, that you may lead a fresh, simple life with God. Instead of breathing a new life into the old forms, you would have a new life without and within. There is something sublime to me in this attitude,—far as I may be from it myself.… Speak to me in this hour as you are prompted.… I honor you because you abstain from action, and open your soul that you may *be* somewhat. Amid a world of noisy, shallow actors it is noble to stand aside and say, 'I will simply *be*.' Could I plant myself at once upon the truth, reducing my wants to their minimum, … I should at once be brought nearer to nature, nearer to my fellow-men,—and life would be infinitely richer. But, alas! I shiver on the brink."

Thus appealed to by one who had so well attained the true Transcendental shibboleth,—"God working in us, both to will and to do,"—Thoreau could not fail to make answer, as he did at once, and thus:—

TO HARRISON BLAKE (AT WORCESTER).

[The first of many letters.]

Concord, March 27, 1848.

I am glad to hear that any words of mine, though spoken so long ago that I can hardly claim identity with their author, have reached you. It gives me pleasure, because I have therefore reason to suppose that I have uttered what concerns men, and that it is not in vain that man speaks to man. This is the value of literature. Yet those days are so distant, in every sense, that I have had to look at that page again, to learn what was the tenor of my thoughts then. I should value that article, however, if only because it was the occasion of your letter.

I do believe that the outward and the inward life correspond; that if any should succeed to live a higher life, others would not know of it; that difference and distance are one. To set about living a true life is to go a journey to a distant country, gradually to find ourselves surrounded by new scenes and men; and as long as the old are around me, I know that I am not in any true sense living a new or a better life. The outward is only the outside of that which is within. Men are not concealed under habits, but are revealed by them; they are their true clothes. I care not how curious a reason they may give for their abiding by them. Circumstances are not rigid and unyielding, but our habits are rigid. We are apt to speak vaguely sometimes, as if a divine life were to be grafted on to or built over this present as a suitable foundation. This might do if we could so build over our old life as to exclude from it all the warmth of our affection, and addle it, as the thrush builds over the cuckoo's egg, and lays her own atop, and hatches that only; but the fact is, we —so thin is the partition—hatch them both, and the cuckoo's always by a day first, and that young bird crowds the young thrushes out of the nest. No. Destroy the cuckoo's egg, or build a new nest.

Change is change. No new life occupies the old bodies;—they decay. *It* is born, and grows, and flourishes. Men very pathetically inform the old, accept and wear it. Why put up with the almshouse when you may go to heaven? It is embalming,—no more. Let alone your ointments and your linen swathes, and go into an infant's body. You see in the catacombs of Egypt the result of that experiment,—that is the end of it.

I do believe in simplicity. It is astonishing as well as sad, how many trivial affairs even the wisest man thinks he must attend to in a day; how singular an affair he thinks he must omit. When the mathematician would solve a difficult problem, he first frees the equation of all incumbrances, and reduces it to its simplest terms. So simplify the problem of life, distinguish the necessary and the real. Probe the earth to see where your main roots run. I would stand upon facts. Why not see,—use our eyes? Do men know nothing? I know many men who, in common things, are not to be deceived; who trust no moonshine; who count their money correctly, and know how to invest it; who are said to be prudent and knowing, who yet will stand at a desk the greater part of their lives, as cashiers in banks, and glimmer and rust and finally go out there. If they *know* anything, what under the sun do they do that for? Do they know what *bread* is? or what it is for? Do they know what life is? If they *knew* something, the places which know them now would know them no more forever.

This, our respectable daily life, on which the man of common sense, the Englishman of the world, stands so squarely, and on which our institutions are founded, is in fact the veriest illusion, and will vanish like the baseless fabric of a vision; but that faint glimmer of reality which sometimes illuminates the darkness of daylight for all men, reveals something more solid and enduring than adamant, which is in fact the cornerstone of the world.

Men cannot conceive of a state of things so fair that it cannot be realized. Can any man honestly consult his experience and say that it is so? Have we any facts to appeal to when we say that our dreams are premature? Did you ever hear of a man who had striven all his life faithfully and singly toward an object and in no measure obtained it? If a man constantly aspires, is he not elevated? Did ever a man try heroism, magnanimity, truth, sincerity, and find that there was no advantage in them? that it was a vain endeavor? Of course we do not expect that our paradise will be a garden. We know not what we ask. To look at literature;—how many fine thoughts has every man had! how few fine thoughts are expressed! Yet we never have a fantasy so subtle and ethereal, but that *talent merely*, with more resolution and faithful persistency, after a thousand failures, might fix and engrave it in distinct and enduring words, and we should see that our dreams are the solidest facts that we know. But I speak not of dreams.

What can be expressed in words can be expressed in life.

My actual life is a fact, in view of which I have no occasion to congratulate myself; but for my faith and aspiration I have respect. It is from these that I speak. Every man's position is in fact too simple to be described. I have sworn no oath. I have no designs on society, or nature, or God. I am simply what I am, or I begin to be that. I *live* in the *present*. I only remember the past, and anticipate the future. I love to live. I love reform better than its modes. There is no history of how bad became better. I believe something, and there is nothing else but that. I know that I am. I know that another is who knows more than I, who takes interest in me, whose creature, and yet whose kindred, in one sense, am I. I know that the enterprise is worthy. I know that things work well. I have heard no bad news.

As for positions, combinations, and details,—what are they? In clear weather, when we look into the heavens, what do we see but the sky and the sun?

If you would convince a man that he does wrong, do right. But do not care to convince him. Men will believe what they see. Let them see.

Pursue, keep up with, circle round and round your life, as a dog does his master's chaise. Do what you love. Know your own bone; gnaw at it, bury it, unearth it, and gnaw it still. Do not be too moral. You may cheat yourself out of much life so. Aim above morality. Be not simply good; be good for something. All fables, indeed, have their morals; but the innocent enjoy the story. Let nothing come between you and the light. Respect men and brothers only. When you travel to the Celestial City, carry no letter of introduction. When you knock, ask to see God,—none of the servants. In what concerns you much, do not think that you have companions: know that you are alone in the world.

Thus I write at random. I need to see you, and I trust I shall, to correct my mistakes. Perhaps you have some oracles for me.

HENRY THOREAU.

TO HARRISON BLAKE (AT WORCESTER).

CONCORD, May 2, 1848

"We must have our bread." But what is our bread? Is it baker's bread? Methinks it should be very *home-made* bread. What is our meat? Is it butcher's meat? What is that which we *must* have? Is that bread which we are now earning sweet? Is it not bread which has been suffered to sour, and then been sweetened with an alkali, which has undergone the vinous, the acetous, and sometimes the putrid fermentation, and then been whitened with vitriol? Is this the bread which we must have? Man must earn his bread by the sweat of his brow, truly, but also by the sweat of his brain within his brow. The body can feed the body only. I have tasted but little bread in my life. It has been mere grub and provender for the most part. Of bread that nourished the brain and the heart, scarcely any. There is absolutely none on the tables even of the rich.

There is not one kind of food for all men. You must and you will feed those faculties which you exercise. The laborer whose body is weary does not require the same food with the scholar whose brain is weary. Men should not labor foolishly like brutes, but the brain and the body should always, or as much as possible, work and rest together, and then the work will be of such a kind that when the body is hungry the brain will be hungry also, and the same food will suffice for both; otherwise the food which repairs the waste energy of the overwrought body will oppress the sedentary brain, and the degenerate scholar will come to esteem all food vulgar, and all getting a living drudgery.

How shall we earn our bread is a grave question; yet it is a sweet and inviting question. Let us not shirk it, as is usually done. It is the most important and practical question which is put to man. Let us not answer it hastily. Let us not be content to get our bread in some gross, careless, and hasty manner. Some men go a-hunting, some a-fishing, some a-gaming, some to war; but none have so pleasant a time as they who in earnest seek to earn their bread. It is true actually as it is true really; it is true materially as it is true spiritually, that they who seek honestly and sincerely, with all their hearts and lives and strength, to earn their bread, do earn it, and it is sure to be very sweet to them. A very little bread,—a very few crumbs are enough, if it be of the right quality, for it is infinitely nutritious. Let each man, then, earn at least a crumb of bread for his body before he dies, and know the taste of it,—that it is identical with the bread of life, and that they both go down at one swallow.

Our bread need not ever be sour or hard to digest. What Nature is to the mind she is also to the body. As she feeds my imagination, she will feed my body; for what she says she means, and is ready to do. She is not simply beautiful to the poet's eye. Not only the rainbow and sunset are beautiful, but to be fed and clothed, sheltered and warmed aright, are equally beautiful and inspiring. There is not necessarily any gross and ugly fact which may not be eradicated from the life of man. We should endeavor practically in our lives to correct all the defects which our imagination detects. The heavens are as deep as our aspirations are high. So high as a tree aspires to grow, so high it will find an atmosphere suited to it. Every man should stand for a force which is perfectly irresistible. How can any man be weak who dares *to be* at all? Even the tenderest plants force their way up through the hardest earth and the crevices of rocks; but a man no material power can resist. What a wedge, what a beetle, what a catapult, is an *earnest* man! What can resist him?

It is a momentous fact that a man may be *good*, or he may be *bad*; his life may be *true*, or it may be *false*; it may be either a shame or a glory to him. The good man builds himself up; the bad man destroys himself.

But whatever we do we must do confidently (if we are timid, let us, then, act timidly), not expecting more light, but having light enough. If we confidently expect more, then let us wait for it. But what is this which we have? Have we not already waited? Is this the beginning of time? Is there a man who does not see clearly beyond, though only a hair's breadth beyond where he at any time stands?

If one hesitates in his path, let him not proceed. Let him respect his doubts, for doubts, too, may have some divinity in them, That we have but little faith is not sad, but that we have but little faithfulness. By faithfulness faith is earned. When, in the progress of a life, a man swerves, though only by an angle infinitely small, from his proper and allotted path (and this is never done quite unconsciously even at first; in fact, that was his broad and scarlet sin,—ah, he knew of it more than he can tell), then the drama of his life turns to tragedy, and makes haste to its fifth act. When once we thus fall behind ourselves, there is no accounting for the obstacles which rise up in our path, and no one is so wise as to advise, and no one so powerful as to aid us while we abide on that ground. Such are cursed with *duties*, and the *neglect of their duties*. For such the decalogue was made, and other far more voluminous and terrible codes.

These departures,—who have not made them?—for they are as faint as the parallax of a fixed star, and at the commencement we say they are nothing,—that is, they originate in a kind of sleep and forgetfulness of the soul when it is naught. A man cannot be too circumspect in order to keep in the straight road, and be sure that he sees all that he may at any time see, that so he may distinguish his true path.

You ask if there is no doctrine of sorrow in my philosophy. Of acute sorrow I suppose that I know comparatively little. My saddest and most genuine sorrows are apt to be but transient regrets. The place of sorrow is supplied, perchance, by a certain hard and proportionately barren indifference. I am of kin to the sod, and partake largely of its dull patience,—in winter expecting the sun of spring. In my cheapest moments I am apt to think that it is n't my business to be "seeking the spirit," but as much its business to be seeking me. I know very well what Goethe meant when he said that he never had a chagrin but he made a poem out of it. I have altogether too much patience of this kind. I am too easily contented with a slight and almost animal happiness. My happiness is a good deal like that of the woodchucks.

Methinks I am never quite committed, never wholly the creature of my moods, but always to some extent their critic. My only integral experience is in my vision. I see, perchance, with more integrity than I feel.

But I need not tell you what manner of man I am,—my virtues or my vices. You can guess if it is worth the while; and I do not discriminate them well.

I do not write this at my hut in the woods. I am at present living with Mrs. Emerson, whose house is an old home of mine, for company during Mr. Emerson's absence.

You will perceive that I am as often talking to myself, perhaps, as speaking to you.

Here is a confession of faith, and a bit of self-portraiture worth having; for there is little except faithful statement of the fact. Its sentences are based on the questions and experiences of his correspondent; yet they diverge into that atmosphere of humor and hyperbole so native to Thoreau; in whom was the oddest mixture of the serious and the comic, the literal and the romantic. He addressed himself also, so far as his unbending personality would allow, to the mood or the need of his correspondent; and he had great skill in fathoming character and describing in a few touches the persons he encountered; as may be seen in his letters to Emerson, especially, who also had, and in still greater measure, this "fatal gift of penetration," as he once termed it. This will be seen in the contrast of Thoreau's correspondence with Mr. Blake, and that he was holding at the same time with Horace Greeley,—persons radically unlike.

In August, 1846, Thoreau sent to Greeley his essay on Carlyle, asking him to find a place for it in some magazine. Greeley sent it to R. W. Griswold, then editing *Graham's Magazine* in Philadelphia, who accepted it and promised to pay for it, but did not publish it till March and April, 1847; even then the promised payment was not forthcoming. On the 31st of March, 1848, a year and a half after it had been put in Griswold's possession, Thoreau wrote again to Greeley, saying that no money had come to hand. At once, and at the very time when Mr. Blake was opening his spiritual state to Thoreau (April 3, 1848), the busy editor of the *Tribune* replied: "It saddens and surprises me to know that your article was not paid for by Graham; and, since my honor is involved, I will see that you are paid, and that at no distant day." Accordingly, on May 17, he adds: "To-day I have been able to lay my hand on the money due you. I made out a regular bill for the contribution, drew a draft on G. R. Graham for the amount, gave it to his brother in New York for collection, and received the money. I have made Graham pay you seventy-five dollars, but I only send you fifty dollars," having deducted twenty-five dollars for the advance of that sum he had made a month before to Thoreau for his "Ktaadn and the Maine Woods," which finally came out in *Sartain's Union Magazine* of Philadelphia, late in 1848. To this letter and remittance of fifty dollars Thoreau replied, May 19, 1848, substantially thus:—

TO HORACE GREELEY (AT NEW YORK).

CONCORD, May 19, 1848.

MY FRIEND GREELEY,—I have to-day received from you fifty dollars. It is five years that I have been maintaining myself entirely by manual labor,—not getting a cent from any other quarter or employment. Now this toil has occupied so few days,—perhaps a single month, spring and fall each,—that I must have had more leisure than any of my brethren for study and literature. I have done rude work of all kinds. From July, 1845, to September, 1847, I lived by myself in the forest, in a fairly good cabin, plastered and warmly covered, which I built myself. There I earned all I needed, and kept to my own affairs. During that time my weekly outlay was but seven and twenty cents; and I had an abundance of all sorts. Unless the human race perspire more than I do, there is no occasion to live by the sweat of their brow. If men cannot get on without money (the smallest amount will suffice), the truest method of earning it is by working as a laborer at one dollar per day. You are least dependent so; I speak as an expert, having used several kinds of labor.

Why should the scholar make a constant complaint that his fate is specially hard? We are too often told of "the pursuit of knowledge under difficulties,"—how poets depend on patrons and starve in garrets, or at last go mad and die. Let us hear the other side of the story. Why should not the scholar, if he is really wiser than the multitude, do coarse work now and then? Why not let his greater wisdom enable him to do without things? If you say the wise man is unlucky, how could you distinguish him from the foolishly unfortunate?

My friend, how can I thank you for your kindness? Perhaps there is a better way,—I will convince you that it is felt and appreciated. Here have I been sitting idle, as it were, while you have been busy in my cause, and have done so much for me. I wish you had had a better subject; but good deeds are no less good because their object is unworthy.

Yours was the best way to collect money,—but I should never have thought of it; I might have waylaid the debtor perchance. Even a business man might not have thought of it,—and I cannot be called that, as business is understood usually,—not being familiar with the routine. But your way has this to commend it also,—if you make the draft, you decide how much to draw. You drew just the sum suitable.

The Ktaadn paper can be put in the guise of letters, if it runs best so; dating each part on the day it describes. Twenty-five dollars more for it will satisfy me; I expected no more, and do not hold you to pay that,—for you asked for something else, and there was delay in sending. So, if you use it, send me twenty-five dollars now or after you sell it, as is most convenient; but take out the expenses that I see you must have had. In such cases carriers generally get the most; but you, as carrier here, get no money, but risk losing some, besides much of your time; while I go away, as I must, giving you unprofitable thanks. Yet trust me, my pleasure in your letter is not wholly a selfish one. May my good genius still watch over me and my added wealth!

P. S.—My book grows in bulk as I work on it; but soon I shall get leisure for those shorter articles you want,—then look out.

The "book," of course, was the "Week," then about to go through the press; the shorter articles were some that Greeley suggested for the Philadelphia magazines. Nothing came of this, but the correspondence was kept up until 1854, and led to the partial publication of "Cape Cod" and "The Yankee in Canada" in the newly launched *Putnam's Magazine*, of which G. W. Curtis was editor. But he differed with Thoreau on a matter of style or opinion (the articles appearing as anonymous, or editorial), and the author withdrew his MS. The letters of Greeley in this entertaining series are all preserved; but Greeley seems to have given Thoreau's away for autographs; and the only one accessible as yet is that just paraphrased.

TO HARRISON BLAKE (AT MILTON).

Concord, August 10, 1849.

Mr. Blake,—I write now chiefly to say, before it is too late, that I shall be glad to see you in Concord, and will give you a chamber, etc., in my father's house, and as much of my poor company as you can bear.

I am in too great haste this time to speak to your, or out of my, condition. I might say,—you might say,—comparatively speaking, be not anxious to avoid poverty. In this way the wealth of the universe may be securely invested. What a pity if we do not live this short time according to the laws of the long time,—the eternal laws! Let us see that we stand erect here, and do not lie along by our *whole length* in the dirt. Let our meanness be our footstool, not our cushion. In the midst of this labyrinth let us live a *thread* of life. We must act with so rapid and resistless a purpose in *one* direction, that our vices will necessarily trail behind. The nucleus of a comet is almost a star. Was there ever a genuine dilemma? The laws of earth are for the feet, or inferior man; the laws of heaven are for the head, or superior man; the latter are the former sublimed and expanded, even as radii from the earth's centre go on diverging into space. Happy the man who observes the heavenly and the terrestrial law in just proportion; whose every faculty, from the soles of his feet to the crown of his head, obeys the law of its level; who neither stoops nor goes on tiptoe, but lives a balanced life, acceptable to nature and to God.

These things I say; other things I do.

I am sorry to hear that you did not receive my book earlier. I directed it and left it in Munroe's shop to be sent to you immediately, on the twenty-sixth of May, before a copy had been sold.

Will you remember me to Mr. Brown, when you see him next: he is well remembered by

HENRY THOREAU.

I still owe you a worthy answer.

TO HARRISON BLAKE.

CONCORD, November 20, 1849.

MR. BLAKE,—I have not forgotten that I am your debtor. When I read over your letters, as I have just done, I feel that I am unworthy to have received or to answer them, though they are addressed, as I would have them, to the ideal of me. It behooves me, if I would reply, to speak out of the rarest part of myself.

At present I am subsisting on certain wild flavors which nature wafts to me, which unaccountably sustain me, and make my apparently poor life rich. Within a year my walks have extended themselves, and almost every afternoon (I read, or write, or make pencils in the forenoon, and by the last means get a living for my body) I visit some new hill, or pond, or wood, many miles distant. I am astonished at the wonderful retirement through which I move, rarely meeting a man in these excursions, never seeing one similarly engaged, unless it be my companion, when I have one. I cannot help feeling that of all the human inhabitants of nature hereabouts, only we two have leisure to admire and enjoy our inheritance.

"Free in this world as the birds in the air, disengaged from every kind of chains, those who have practiced the *yoga* gather in Brahma the certain fruit of their works."

Depend upon it that, rude and careless as I am, I would fain practice the *yoga* faithfully.

"The yogi, absorbed in contemplation, contributes in his degree to creation: he breathes a divine perfume, he hears wonderful things. Divine forms traverse him without tearing him, and, united to the nature which is proper to him, he goes, he acts as animating original matter."

To some extent, and at rare intervals, even I am a yogi.

I know little about the affairs of Turkey, but I am sure that I know something about barberries and chestnuts, of which I have collected a store this fall. When I go to see my neighbor, he will formally communicate to me the latest news from Turkey, which he read in yesterday's mail,—"Now Turkey by this time looks determined, and Lord Palmerston"—Why, I would rather talk of the bran, which, unfortunately, was sifted out of my bread this morning, and thrown away. It is a fact which lies nearer to me. The newspaper gossip with which our hosts abuse our ears is as far from a true hospitality as the viands which they set before us. We did not need them to feed our bodies, and the news can be bought for a penny. We want the inevitable news, be it sad or cheering, wherefore and by what means they are extant this *new* day. If they are well, let them whistle and dance; if they are dyspeptic, it is their duty to complain, that so they may in any case be *entertaining*. If words were invented to conceal thought, I think that newspapers are a great improvement on a bad invention. Do not suffer your life to be taken by newspapers.

I thank you for your hearty appreciation of my book. I am glad to have had such a long talk with you, and that you had patience to listen to me to the end. I think that I had the advantage of you, for I chose my own mood, and in one sense your mood too,—that is, a quiet and attentive reading mood. Such advantage has the writer over the talker. I am sorry that you did not come to Concord in your vacation. Is it not time for another vacation? I am here yet, and Concord is here.

You will have found out by this time who it is that writes this, and will be glad to have you write to him, without his subscribing himself

HENRY D. THOREAU.

P. S.—It is so long since I have seen you, that, as you will perceive, I have to speak, as it were, *in vacuo*, as if I were sounding hollowly for an echo, and it did not make much odds what kind of a sound I made. But the gods do not hear any rude or discordant sound, as we learn from the echo; and I know that the nature toward which I launch these sounds is so rich that it will modulate anew and wonderfully improve my rudest strain.

TO HARRISON BLAKE (AT MILTON).

CONCORD, April 3, 1850.

MR. BLAKE,—I thank you for your letter, and I will endeavor to record some of the thoughts which it suggests, whether pertinent or not. You speak of poverty and dependence. Who are poor and dependent? Who are rich and independent? When was it that men agreed to respect the appearance and not the reality? Why should the appearance *appear*? Are we well acquainted, then, with the reality? There is none who does not lie hourly in the respect he pays to false appearance. How sweet it would be to treat men and things, for an hour, for just what they are! We wonder that the sinner does not confess his sin. When we are weary with travel, we lay down our load and rest by the wayside. So, when we are weary with the burden of life, why do we not lay down this load of falsehoods which we have volunteered to sustain, and be refreshed as never mortal was? Let the beautiful laws prevail. Let us not weary ourselves by resisting them. When we would rest our bodies we cease to support them; we recline on the lap of earth. So, when we would rest our spirits, we must recline on the Great Spirit. Let things alone; let them weigh what they will; let them soar or fall. To succeed in letting only one thing alone in a winter morning, if it be only one poor frozen-thawed apple that hangs on a tree, what a glorious achievement! Methinks it lightens through the dusky universe. What an infinite wealth we have discovered! God reigns, *i. e.*, when we take a liberal view,—when a liberal view is presented us.

Let God alone if need be. Methinks, if I loved him more, I should keep him—I should keep myself rather—at a more respectful distance. It is not when I am going to meet him, but when I am just turning away and leaving him alone, that I discover that God is. I say, God. I am not sure that that is the name. You will know whom I mean.

If for a moment we make way with our petty selves, wish no ill to anything, apprehend no ill, cease to be but as the crystal which reflects a ray,—what shall we not reflect! What a universe will appear crystallized and radiant around us!

I should say, let the Muse lead the Muse,—let the understanding lead the understanding, though in any case it is the farthest forward which leads them both. If the Muse accompany, she is no muse, but an amusement. The Muse should lead like a star which is very far off; but that does not imply that we are to follow foolishly, falling into sloughs and over precipices, for it is not foolishness, but understanding, which is to follow, which the Muse is appointed to lead, as a fit guide of a fit follower?

Will you live? or will you be embalmed? Will you live, though it be astride of a sunbeam; or will you repose safely in the catacombs for a thousand years? In the former case, the worst accident that can happen is that you may break your neck. Will you break your heart, your soul, to save your neck? Necks and pipe-stems are fated to be broken. Men make a great ado about the folly of demanding too much of life (or of eternity?), and of endeavoring to live according to that demand. It is much ado about nothing. No harm ever came from that quarter. I am not afraid that I shall exaggerate the value and significance of life, but that I shall not be up to the occasion which it is. I shall be sorry to remember that I was there, but noticed nothing remarkable,—not so much as a prince in disguise; lived in the golden age a hired man; visited Olympus even, but fell asleep after dinner, and did not hear the conversation of the gods. I lived in Judæa eighteen hundred years ago, but I never knew that there was such a one as Christ among my contemporaries! If there is anything more glorious than a congress of men a-framing or amending of a constitution going on, which I suspect there is, I desire to see the morning papers. I am greedy of the faintest rumor, though it were got by listening at the keyhole. I will dissipate myself in that direction.

I am glad to know that you find what I have said on Friendship worthy of attention. I wish that I could have the benefit of your criticism; it would be a rare help to me. Will you not communicate it?

TO HARRISON BLAKE (AT MILTON).

CONCORD, May 28, 1850.

MR. BLAKE,—"I never found any contentment in the life which the newspapers record,"—anything of more value than the cent which they cost. Contentment in being covered with dust an inch deep! We who walk the streets, and hold time together, are but the refuse of ourselves, and that life is for the shells of us,—of our body and our mind,—for our scurf,—a thoroughly *scurvy* life. It is coffee made of coffee-grounds the twentieth time, which was only coffee the first time,—while the living water leaps and sparkles by our doors. I know some who, in their charity, give their coffee-grounds to the poor! We, demanding news, and putting up with *such* news! Is it a new convenience, or a new accident, or, rather, a new perception of the truth that we want!

You say that "the serene hours in which friendship, books, nature, thought, seem alone primary considerations, visit you but faintly." Is not the attitude of expectation somewhat divine?—a sort of home-made divineness? Does it not compel a kind of sphere-music to attend on it? And do not its satisfactions merge at length, by insensible degrees, in the enjoyment of the thing expected?

What if I should forget to write about my not writing? It is not worth the while to make that a theme. It is as if I had written every day. It is as if I had never written before. I wonder that you think so much about it, for not writing is the most like writing, in my case, of anything I know.

Why will you not relate to me your dream? That would be to realize it somewhat. You tell me that you dream, but not what you dream. I can *guess* what comes to pass. So do the frogs dream. Would that I knew what. I have never found out whether they are awake or asleep,—whether it is day or night with them.

I am preaching, mind you, to bare walls, that is, to myself; and if you have chanced to come in and occupy a pew, do not think that my remarks are directed at you particularly, and so slam the seat in disgust. This discourse was written long before these exciting times.

Some absorbing employment on your higher ground,—your upland farm,—whither no cart-path leads, but where you mount alone with your hoe,—where the life everlasting grows; there you raise a crop which needs not to be brought down into the valley to a market; which you barter for heavenly products.

Do you separate distinctly enough the support of your body from that of your essence? By how distinct a course commonly are these two ends attained! Not that they should not be attained by one and the same means,—that, indeed, is the rarest success,—but there is no half and half about it.

I shall be glad to read my lecture to a small audience in Worcester such as you describe, and will only require that my expenses be paid. If only the parlor be large enough for an echo, and the audience will embarrass themselves with hearing as much as the lecturer would otherwise embarrass himself with reading. But I warn you that this is no better calculated for a promiscuous audience than the last two which I read to you. It requires, in every sense, a concordant audience.

I will come on next Saturday and spend Sunday with you if you wish it. Say so if you do.

"Drink deep, or taste not the Pierian spring."

Be not deterred by melancholy on the path which leads to immortal health and joy. When they tasted of the water of the river over which they were to go, they thought it tasted a little bitterish to the palate, but it proved sweeter when it was down.

H. D. T.

NOTE.—The "companion" of his walks, mentioned by Thoreau in November, 1849, was Ellery Channing; the neighbor who insisted on talking of Turkey was perhaps Emerson, who, after his visit to Europe in 1848, was more interested in its politics than before. Pencil-making was Thoreau's manual work for many years; and it must have been about this time (1849-53) that he "had occasion to go to New York to peddle some pencils," as he says in his journal for November 20, 1853. He adds, "I was obliged to manufacture one thousand dollars' worth of pencils, and slowly dispose of, and finally sacrifice them, in order to pay an assumed debt of one hundred dollars." This debt was for the printing of the *Week*, published in 1849, and finally paid for in 1855. Thoreau's pencils have sold (in 1893) for 25 cents each. For other facts concerning his debt to James Munroe, see Sanborn's *Thoreau*, pp. 230, 235.

III
FRIENDS AND FOLLOWERS

TO R. W. EMERSON[42] (AT CONCORD).

FIRE ISLAND BEACH, Thursday
morning, July 25, 1850.

DEAR FRIEND,—I am writing this at the house of Smith Oakes, within one mile of the wreck. He is the one who rendered most assistance, William H. Channing came down with me, but I have not seen Arthur Fuller, nor Greeley, nor Marcus Spring. Spring and Charles Sumner were here yesterday, but left soon. Mr. Oakes and wife tell me (all the survivors came, or were brought, directly to their house) that the ship struck at ten minutes after four A. M., and all hands, being mostly in their nightclothes, made haste to the forecastle, the water coming in at once. There they remained; the passengers *in* the forecastle, the crew above it, doing what they could. Every wave lifted the forecastle roof and washed over those within. The first man got ashore at nine; many from nine to noon. At flood-tide, about half past three o'clock, when the ship broke up entirely, they came out of the forecastle, and Margaret sat with her back to the foremast, with her hands on her knees, her husband and child already drowned. A great wave came and washed her aft. The steward (?) had just before taken her child and started for shore. Both were drowned.

The broken desk, in a bag, containing no very valuable papers; a large black leather trunk, with an upper and under compartment, the upper holding books and papers; a carpetbag, probably Ossoli's, and one of his shoes (?) are all the Ossoli effects known to have been found. Four bodies remain to be found: the two Ossolis, Horace Sumner, and a sailor. I have visited the child's grave. Its body will probably be taken away to-day. The wreck is to be sold at auction, excepting the hull, to-day.

The mortar would not go off. Mrs. Hasty, the captain's wife, told Mrs. Oakes that she and Margaret divided their money, and tied up the halves in handkerchiefs around their persons; that Margaret took sixty or seventy dollars. Mrs. Hasty, who can tell all about Margaret up to eleven o'clock on Friday, is said to be going to Portland, New England, to-day. She and Mrs. Fuller must, and probably will, come together. The cook, the last to leave, and the steward (?) will know the rest. I shall try to see them. In the meanwhile I shall do what I can to recover property and obtain particulars hereabouts. William H. Channing—did I write it?—has come with me. Arthur Fuller[43] has this moment reached the house. He reached the beach last night. We got here yesterday noon. A good part of the wreck still holds together where she struck, and something may come ashore with her fragments. The last body was found on Tuesday, three miles west. Mrs. Oakes dried the papers which were in the trunk, and she says they appeared to be of various kinds. "Would they cover that table?" (a small round one). "They would if spread out. Some were tied up." There were twenty or thirty books "in the same half of the trunk. Another smaller trunk, empty, came ashore, but there was no mark on it." She speaks of Paulina as if she might have been a sort of nurse to the child. I expect to go to Patchogue, whence the pilferers must have chiefly come, and advertise, etc.

TO HARRISON BLAKE (IN MILTON).

Concord August 9, 1850.

Mr. Blake,—I received your letter just as I was rushing to Fire Island beach to recover what remained of Margaret Fuller, and read it on the way. That event and its train, as much as anything, have prevented my answering it before. It is wisest to speak when you are spoken to. I will now endeavor to reply, at the risk of having nothing to say.

I find that actual events, notwithstanding the singular prominence which we all allow them, are far less real than the creations of my imagination. They are truly visionary and insignificant,—all that we commonly call life and death,—and affect me less than my dreams. This petty stream which from time to time swells and carries away the mills and bridges of our habitual life, and that mightier stream or ocean on which we securely float,—what makes the difference between them? I have in my pocket a button which I ripped off the coat of the Marquis of Ossoli, on the seashore, the other day. Held up, it intercepts the light,—an actual button,—and yet all the life it is connected with is less substantial to me, and interests me less, than my faintest dream. Our thoughts are the epochs in our lives: all else is but as a journal of the winds that blew while we were here.

I say to myself, Do a little more of that work which you have confessed to be good. You are neither satisfied nor dissatisfied with yourself, without reason. Have you not a thinking faculty of inestimable value? If there is an experiment which you would like to try, try it. Do not entertain doubts if they are not agreeable to you. Remember that you need not eat unless you are hungry. Do not read the newspapers. Improve every opportunity to be melancholy. As for health, consider yourself well. Do not engage to find things as you think they are. Do what nobody else can do for you. Omit to do anything else. It is not easy to make our lives respectable by any course of activity. We must repeatedly withdraw into our shells of thought, like the tortoise, somewhat helplessly; yet there is more than philosophy in that.

Do not waste any reverence on my attitude. I merely manage to sit up where I have dropped. I am sure that my acquaintances mistake me. They ask my advice on high matters, but they do not know even how poorly on 't I am for hats and shoes. I have hardly a shift. Just as shabby as I am in my outward apparel, ay, and more lamentably shabby, am I in my inward substance. If I should turn myself inside out, my rags and meanness would indeed appear. I am something to him that made me, undoubtedly, but not much to any other that he has made.

Would it not be worth while to discover nature in Milton? be native to the universe? I, too, love Concord best, but I am glad when I discover, in oceans and wildernesses far away, the material of a million Concords: indeed, I am lost, unless I discover them. I see less difference between a city and a swamp than formerly. It is a swamp, however, too dismal and dreary even for me, and I should be glad if there were fewer owls, and frogs, and mosquitoes in it. I prefer ever a more cultivated place, free from miasma and crocodiles. I am so sophisticated, and I will take my choice.

As for missing friends,—what if we do miss one another? have we not agreed on a rendezvous? While each wanders his own way through the wood, without anxiety, ay, with serene joy, though it be on his hands and knees, over rocks and fallen trees, he cannot but be in the right way. There is no wrong way to him. How can he be said to miss his friend, whom the fruits still nourish and the elements sustain? A man who missed his friend at a turn, went on buoyantly, dividing the friendly air, and humming a tune to himself, ever and anon kneeling with delight to study each little lichen in his path, and scarcely made three miles a day for friendship. As for conforming outwardly, and living your own life inwardly, I do not think much of that. Let not your right hand know what your left hand does in that line of business. It will prove a failure. Just as successfully can you walk against a sharp steel edge which divides you cleanly right and left. Do you wish to try your ability to resist distension? It is a greater strain than any soul can long endure. When you get God to pulling one way, and the devil the other, each having his feet well braced,—to say nothing of the conscience sawing transversely,—almost any timber will give way.

I do not dare invite you earnestly to come to Concord, because I know too well that the berries are not thick in my fields, and we should have to take it out in viewing the landscape. But come, on every account, and we will see—one another.

No letters of the year 1851 have been found by me. On the 27th of December, 1850, Mr. Cabot wrote to say that the Boston Society of Natural History, of which he was secretary, had elected Thoreau a corresponding member, "with all the *honores, privilegia, etc., ad gradum tuum pertinentia*, without the formality of paying any entrance fee, or annual subscription. Your duties in return are to advance the interests of the Society by communications or otherwise, as shall seem good." This is believed to be the only learned body which honored itself by electing Thoreau. The immediate occasion of this election was the present, by Thoreau, to the Society, of a fine specimen of the American goshawk, caught or shot by Jacob Farmer, which Mr. Cabot acknowledged, December 18, 1849, saying: "It was first described by Wilson; lately Audubon has identified it with the European goshawk, thereby committing a very flagrant blunder. It is usually a very rare species with us. The European bird is used in hawking; and doubtless ours would be equally *game*. If Mr. Farmer skins him now, he will have to take second cut; for his skin is already off and stuffed,—his remains dissected, measured, and deposited in alcohol."

TO T. W. HIGGINSON (AT BOSTON).

CONCORD, April 2-3, 1852.

DEAR SIR,—I do not see that I can refuse to read another lecture, but what makes me hesitate is the fear that I have not another available which will *entertain* a large audience, though I have thoughts to offer which I think will be quite as worthy of their attention. However, I will try; for the prospect of earning a few dollars is alluring. As far as I can foresee, my subject would be "Reality" rather transcendentally treated. It lies still in "Walden, or Life in the Woods." Since you are kind enough to undertake the arrangements, I will leave it to you to name an evening of next week, decide on the most suitable room, and advertise,—if this is not taking you too literally at your word.

If you still think it worth the while to attend to this, will you let me know as soon as may be what evening will be most convenient? I certainly do not feel prepared to offer myself as a lecturer to the Boston *public*, and hardly know whether more to dread a small audience or a large one. Nevertheless, I will repress this squeamishness, and propose no alteration in your arrangements. I shall be glad to accept your invitation to tea.

This lecture was given, says Colonel Higginson, "at the Mechanics' Apprentices Library in Boston, with the snow outside, and the young boys rustling their newspapers among the Alcotts and Blakes." Or, possibly, this remark may apply to a former lecture in the same year, which was that in which Thoreau first lectured habitually away from Concord. He commenced by accepting an invitation to speak at Leyden Hall, in Plymouth, where his friends the Watsons had organized Sunday services, that the Transcendentalists and Abolitionists might have a chance to be heard at a time when they were generally excluded from the popular "Lyceum courses" throughout New England. Mr. B. M. Watson says:—

"I have found two letters from Thoreau in answer to my invitation in 1852 to address our congregation at Leyden Hall on Sunday mornings,—an enterprise I undertook about that time. I find among the distinguished men who addressed us the names of Thoreau, Emerson, Ellery Channing, Alcott, Higginson, Remond, S. Johnson, F. J. Appleton, Edmund Quincy, Garrison, Phillips, J. P. Lesley, Shackford, W. F. Channing, N. H. Whiting, Adin Ballou, Abby K. Foster and her husband, J. T. Sargent, T. T. Stone, Jones Very, Wasson, Hurlbut, F. W. Holland, and Scherb; so you may depend we had some fun."

These letters were mere notes. The first, dated February 17, 1852, says: "I have not yet seen Mr. Channing, though I believe he is in town,—having decided to come to Plymouth myself,—but I will let him know that he is expected. Mr. Daniel Foster wishes me to say that he accepts your invitation, and that he would like to come Sunday after next. I will take the Saturday afternoon train. I shall be glad to get a winter view of Plymouth Harbor, and see where your garden lies under the snow."

The second letter follows:—

TO MARSTON WATSON (AT PLYMOUTH).

Concord, December 31, 1852.

Mr. Watson,—I would be glad to visit Plymouth again, but at present I have nothing to read which is not severely heathenish, or at least secular,—which the dictionary defines as "relating to affairs of the present world, not holy,"—though not necessarily unholy; nor have I any leisure to prepare it. My writing at present is profane, yet in a good sense, and, as it were, sacredly, I may say; for, finding the air of the temple too close, I sat outside. Don't think I say this to get off; no, no! It will not do to read such things to hungry ears. "If they ask for bread, will you give them a stone?" When I have something of the right kind, depend upon it I will let you know.

Up to 1848, when he was invited to lecture before the Salem Lyceum by Nathaniel Hawthorne, then its secretary, Thoreau seems to have spoken publicly very little except in Concord; nor did he extend the circuit of his lectures much until his two books had made him known as a thinker. There was little to attract a popular audience in his manner or his matter; but it was the era of lectures, and if one could once gain admission to the circle of "lyceum lecturers," it did not so much matter what he said; a lecture was a lecture, as a sermon was a sermon, good, bad, or indifferent. But it was common to exclude the antislavery speakers from the lyceums, even those of more eloquence than Thoreau; this led to invitations from the small band of reformers scattered about New England and New York, so that the most unlikely of platform speakers (Ellery Channing, for example) sometimes gave lectures at Plymouth, Greenfield, Newburyport, or elsewhere. The present fashion of parlor lectures had not come in; yet at Worcester Thoreau's friends early organized for him something of that kind, as his letters to Mr. Blake show. In default of an audience of numbers, Thoreau fell into the habit of lecturing in his letters to this friend; the most marked instance being the thoughtful essay on Love and Chastity which makes the bulk of his epistle dated September, 1852. Like most of his serious writing, this was made up from his daily journal, and hardly comes under the head of "familiar letters;" the didactic purpose is rather too apparent. Yet it cannot be spared from any collection of his epistles,—none of which flowed more directly from the quickened moral nature of the man.

TO SOPHIA THOREAU (AT BANGOR).

Concord, July 13, 1852.

Dear Sophia,—I am a miserable letter-writer, but perhaps if I should say this at length and with sufficient emphasis and regret it would make a letter. I am sorry that nothing transpires here of much moment; or, I should rather say, that I am so slackened and rusty, like the telegraph wire this season, that no wind that blows can extract music from me.

I am not on the trail of any elephants or mastodons, but have succeeded in trapping only a few ridiculous mice, which cannot feed my imagination. I have become sadly scientific. I would rather come upon the vast valley-like "spoor" only of some celestial beast which this world's woods can no longer sustain, than spring my net over a bushel of moles. You must do better in those woods where you are. You must have some adventures to relate and repeat for years to come, which will eclipse even mother's voyage to Goldsborough and Sissiboo.

They say that Mr. Pierce, the presidential candidate, was in town last 5th of July, visiting Hawthorne, whose college chum he was; and that Hawthorne is writing a life of him, for electioneering purposes.

Concord is just as idiotic as ever in relation to the spirits and their knockings. Most people here believe in a spiritual world which no respectable junk bottle, which had not met with a slip, would condescend to contain even a portion of for a moment,—whose atmosphere would extinguish a candle let down into it, like a well that wants airing; in spirits which the very bullfrogs in our meadows would blackball. Their evil genius is seeing how low it can degrade them. The hooting of owls, the croaking of frogs, is celestial wisdom in comparison. If I could be brought to believe in the things which they believe, I should make haste to get rid of my certificate of stock in this and the next world's enterprises, and buy a share in the first Immediate Annihilation Company that offered. I would exchange my immortality for a glass of small beer this hot weather. Where *are* the heathen? Was there ever any superstition before? And yet I suppose there may be a vessel this very moment setting sail from the coast of North America to that of Africa with a missionary on board! Consider the dawn and the sunrise,—the rainbow and the evening,—the words of Christ and the aspiration of all the saints! Hear music! see, smell, taste, feel, hear,—anything,—and then hear these idiots, inspired by the cracking of a restless board, humbly asking, "Please, Spirit, if you cannot answer by knocks, answer by tips of the table." ! ! ! ! ! ! !

TO HARRISON BLAKE (AT WORCESTER).

Concord, July 21, 1852.

Mr. Blake,—I am too stupidly well these days to write to you. My life is almost altogether outward,—all shell and no tender kernel; so that I fear the report of it would be only a nut for you to crack, with no meat in it for you to eat. Moreover, you have not cornered me up, and I enjoy such large liberty in writing to you, that I feel as vague as the air. However, I rejoice to hear that you have attended so patiently to anything which I have said heretofore, and have detected any truth in it. It encourages me to say more,—not in this letter, I fear, but in some book which I may write one day. I am glad to know that I am as much to any mortal as a persistent and consistent scarecrow is to a farmer,—such a bundle of straw in a man's clothing as I am, with a few bits of tin to sparkle in the sun dangling about me, as if I were hard at work there in the field. However, if this kind of life saves any man's corn,—why, he is the gainer. I am not afraid that you will flatter me as long as you know what I am, as well as what I think, or aim to be, and distinguish between these two, for then it will commonly happen that if you praise the last you will condemn the first.

I remember that walk to Asnebumskit very well,—a fit place to go to on a Sunday; one of the true temples of the earth. A temple, you know, was anciently "an open place without a roof," whose walls served merely to shut out the world and direct the mind toward heaven; but a modern *meeting-house* shuts out the heavens, while it crowds the world into still closer quarters. Best of all is it when, as on a mountain-top, you have for all walls your own elevation and deeps of surrounding ether. The partridge-berries, watered with mountain dews which are gathered there, are more memorable to me than the words which I last heard from the pulpit at least; and for my part, I would rather look toward Rutland than Jerusalem. Rutland,—modern town,—land of ruts,—trivial and worn,—not too sacred,—with no holy sepulchre, but profane green fields and dusty roads, and opportunity to live as holy a life as you can,—where the sacredness, if there is any, is all in yourself and not in the place.

I fear that your Worcester people do not often enough go to the hilltops, though, as I am told, the springs lie nearer to the surface on your hills than in your valleys. They have the reputation of being Free-Soilers.[44] Do they insist on a free atmosphere, too, that is, on freedom for the head or brain as well as the feet? If I were consciously to join any party, it would be that which is the most free to entertain thought.

All the world complain nowadays of a press of trivial duties and engagements, which prevents their employing themselves on some higher ground they know of; but, undoubtedly, if they were made of the right stuff to work on that higher ground, provided they were released from all those engagements, they would now at once fulfill the superior engagement, and neglect all the rest, as naturally as they breathe. They would never be caught saying that they had no time for this, when the dullest man knows that this is all that he has time for. No man who acts from a sense of duty ever puts the lesser duty above the greater. No man has the desire and the ability to work on high things, but he has also the ability to build himself a high staging.

As for passing *through* any great and glorious experience, and rising *above* it, as an eagle might fly athwart the evening sky to rise into still brighter and fairer regions of the heavens, I cannot say that I ever sailed so creditably; but my bark ever seemed thwarted by some side wind, and went off over the edge, and now only occasionally tacks back toward the centre of that sea again. I have outgrown nothing good, but, I do not fear to say, fallen behind by whole continents of virtue, which should have been passed as islands in my course; but I trust—what else can I trust? that, with a stiff wind, some Friday, when I have thrown some of my cargo overboard, I may make up for all that distance lost.

Perchance the time will come when we shall not be content to go back and forth upon a raft to some huge Homeric or Shakespearean Indiaman that lies upon the reef, but build a bark out of that wreck and others that are buried in the sands of this desolate island, and such new timber as may be required, in which to sail away to whole new worlds of light and life, where our friends are.

Write again. There is one respect in which you did not finish your letter: you did not write it with ink, and it is not so good, therefore, against or for you in the eye of the law, nor in the eye of

H. D. T.

TO HARRISON BLAKE (AT WORCESTER).

September, 1852.

Mr. Blake,—Here come the sentences which I promised you. You may keep them, if you will regard and use them as the disconnected fragments of what I may find to be a completer essay, on looking over my journal, at last, and may claim again.

I send you the thoughts on Chastity and Sensuality with diffidence and shame, not knowing how far I speak to the condition of men generally, or how far I betray my peculiar defects. Pray enlighten me on this point if you can.

LOVE.

What the essential difference between man and woman is, that they should be thus attracted to one another, no one has satisfactorily answered. Perhaps we must acknowledge the justness of the distinction which assigns to man the sphere of wisdom, and to woman that of love, though neither belongs exclusively to either. Man is continually saying to woman, Why will you not be more wise? Woman is continually saying to man, Why will you not be more loving? It is not in their wills to be wise or to be loving; but, unless each is both wise and loving, there can be neither wisdom nor love.

All transcendent goodness is one, though appreciated in different ways, or by different senses. In beauty we see it, in music we hear it, in fragrance we scent it, in the palatable the pure palate tastes it, and in rare health the whole body feels it. The variety is in the surface or manifestation; but the radical identity we fail to express. The lover sees in the glance of his beloved the same beauty that in the sunset paints the western skies. It is the same daimon, here lurking under a human eyelid, and there under the closing eyelids of the day. Here, in small compass, is the ancient and natural beauty of evening and morning. What loving astronomer has ever fathomed the ethereal depths of the eye?

The maiden conceals a fairer flower and sweeter fruit than any calyx in the field; and, if she goes with averted face, confiding in her purity and high resolves, she will make the heavens retrospective, and all nature humbly confess its queen.

Under the influence of this sentiment, man is a string of an æolian harp, which vibrates with the zephyrs of the eternal morning.

There is at first thought something trivial in the commonness of love. So many Indian youths and maidens along these banks have in ages past yielded to the influence of this great civilizer. Nevertheless, this generation is not disgusted nor discouraged, for love is no individual's experience; and though we are imperfect mediums, it does not partake of our imperfection; though we are finite, it is infinite and eternal; and the same divine influence broods over these banks, whatever race may inhabit them, and perchance still would, even if the human race did not dwell here.

Perhaps an instinct survives through the intensest actual love, which prevents entire abandonment and devotion, and makes the most ardent lover a little reserved. It is the anticipation of change. For the most ardent lover is not the less practically wise, and seeks a love which will last forever.

Considering how few poetical friendships there are, it is remarkable that so many are married. It would seem as if men yielded too easy an obedience to nature without consulting their genius. One may be drunk with love without being any nearer to finding his mate. There is more of good nature than of good sense at the bottom of most marriages. But the good nature must have the counsel of the good spirit or Intelligence. If common sense had been consulted, how many marriages would never have taken place; if uncommon or divine sense, how few marriages such as we witness would ever have taken place!

Our love may be ascending or descending. What is its character, if it may be said of it,—

We must *respect* the souls above,

But only *those below we love*."

Love is a severe critic. Hate can pardon more than love. They who aspire to love worthily, subject themselves to an ordeal more rigid than any other.

Is your friend such a one that an increase of worth on your part will surely make her more your friend? Is she retained—is she attracted by more nobleness in you,—by more of that virtue which is peculiarly yours; or is she indifferent and blind to that? Is she to be flattered and won by your meeting her on any other than the ascending path? Then duty requires that you separate from her.

Love must be as much a light as a flame.

Where there is not discernment, the behavior even of the purest soul may in effect amount to coarseness.

A man of fine perceptions is more truly feminine than a merely sentimental woman. The heart is blind; but love is not blind. None of the gods is so discriminating.

In love and friendship the imagination is as much exercised as the heart; and if either is outraged the other will be estranged. It is commonly the imagination which is wounded first, rather than the heart,—it is so much the more sensitive.

Comparatively, we can excuse any offense against the heart, but not against the imagination. The imagination knows—nothing escapes its glance from out its eyry—and it controls the breast. My heart may still yearn toward the valley, but my imagination will not permit me to jump off the precipice that debars me from it, for it is wounded, its wings are clipt, and it cannot fly, even descendingly. Our "blundering hearts!" some poet says. The imagination never forgets; it is a re-membering. It is not foundationless, but most reasonable, and it alone uses all the knowledge of the intellect.

Love is the profoundest of secrets. Divulged, even to the beloved, it is no longer Love. As if it were merely I that loved you. When love ceases, then it is divulged.

In our intercourse with one we love, we wish to have answered those questions at the end of which we do not raise our voice; against which we put no interrogation-mark,—answered with the same unfailing, universal aim toward every point of the compass.

I require that thou knowest everything without being told anything. I parted from my beloved because there was one thing which I had to tell her. She *questioned* me. She should have known all by sympathy. That I had to tell it her was the difference between us,—the misunderstanding.

A lover never hears anything that he is *told*, for that is commonly either false or stale; but he hears things taking place, as the sentinels heard Trenck[45] mining in the ground, and thought it was moles.

The relation may be profaned in many ways. The parties may not regard it with equal sacredness. What if the lover should learn that his beloved dealt in incantations and philters! What if he should hear that she consulted a clairvoyant! The spell would be instantly broken.

If to chaffer and higgle are bad in trade, they are much worse in Love. It demands directness as of an arrow.

There is danger that we lose sight of what our friend is absolutely, while considering what she is to us alone.

The lover wants no partiality. He says, Be so kind as to be just.

Canst thou love with thy mind,

And reason with thy heart?

Canst thou be kind,

And from thy darling part?

Canst thou range earth, sea, and air,

And so meet me everywhere?

Through all events I will pursue thee,

Through all persons I will woo thee.

I need thy hate as much as thy love. Thou wilt not repel me entirely when thou repellest what is evil in me.

Indeed, indeed, I cannot tell,

Though I ponder on it well,

Which were easier to state,

All my love or all my hate.

Surely, surely, thou wilt trust me

When I say thou doth disgust me.

O, I hate thee with a hate

That would fain annihilate;

Yet, sometimes, against my will,

My dear Friend, I love thee still.

It were treason to our love,

And a sin to God above,

One iota to abate

Of a pure, impartial hate.

It is not enough that we are truthful; we must cherish and carry out high purposes to be truthful about.

It must be rare, indeed, that we meet with one to whom we are prepared to be quite ideally related, as she to us. We should have no reserve; we should give the whole of ourselves to that society; we should have no duty aside from that. One who could bear to be so wonderfully and beautifully exaggerated every day. I would take my friend out of her low self and set her higher, infinitely higher, and *there* know her. But, commonly, men are as much afraid of love as of hate. They have lower engagements. They have near ends to serve. They have not imagination enough to be thus employed about a human being, but must be coopering a barrel, forsooth.

What a difference, whether, in all your walks, you meet only strangers, or in one house is one who knows you, and whom you know. To have a brother or a sister! To have a gold mine on your farm! To find diamonds in the gravel heaps before your door! How rare these things are! To share the day with you, —to people the earth. Whether to have a god or a goddess for companion in your walks, or to walk alone with hinds and villains and carles. Would not a friend enhance the beauty of the landscape as much as a deer or hare? Everything would acknowledge and serve such a relation; the corn in the field, and the cranberries in the meadow. The flowers would bloom, and the birds sing, with a new impulse. There would be more fair days in the year.

The object of love expands and grows before us to eternity, until it includes all that is lovely, and we become all that can love.

CHASTITY AND SENSUALITY.

The subject of sex is a remarkable one, since, though its phenomena concern us so much, both directly and indirectly, and, sooner or later, it occupies the thoughts of all, yet all mankind, as it were, agree to be silent about it, at least the sexes commonly one to another. One of the most interesting of all human facts is veiled more completely than any mystery. It is treated with such secrecy and awe as surely do not go to any religion. I believe that it is unusual even for the most intimate friends to communicate the pleasures and anxieties connected with this fact,—much as the external affair of love, its comings and goings, are bruited. The Shakers do not exaggerate it so much by their manner of speaking of it as all mankind by their manner of keeping silence about it. Not that men should speak on this or any subject without having anything worthy to say; but it is plain that the education of man has hardly commenced, —there is so little genuine intercommunication.

In a pure society, the subject of marriage would not be so often avoided,—from shame and not from reverence, winked out of sight, and hinted at only; but treated naturally and simply,—perhaps simply avoided, like the kindred mysteries. If it cannot be spoken of for shame, how can it be acted of? But, doubtless, there is far more purity, as well as more impurity, than is apparent.

Men commonly couple with their idea of marriage a slight degree at least of sensuality; but every lover, the world over, believes in its inconceivable purity.

If it is the result of a pure love, there can be nothing sensual in marriage. Chastity is something positive, not negative. It is the virtue of the married especially. All lusts or base pleasures must give place to loftier delights. They who meet as superior beings cannot perform the deeds of inferior ones. The deeds of love are less questionable than any action of an individual can be, for, it being founded on the rarest mutual respect, the parties incessantly stimulate each other to a loftier and purer life, and the act in which they are associated must be pure and noble indeed, for innocence and purity can have no equal. In this relation we deal with one whom we respect more religiously even than we respect our better selves, and we shall necessarily conduct as in the presence of God. What presence can be more awful to the lover than the presence of his beloved?

If you seek the warmth even of affection from a similar motive to that from which cats and dogs and slothful persons hug the fire,—because your temperature is low through sloth,—you are on the downward road, and it is but to plunge yet deeper into sloth. Better the cold affection of the sun, reflected from fields of ice and snow, or his warmth in some still, wintry dell. The warmth of celestial love does not relax, but nerves and braces its enjoyer. Warm your body by healthful exercise, not by cowering over a stove. Warm your spirit by performing independently noble deeds, not by ignobly seeking the sympathy of your fellows who are no better than yourself. A man's social and spiritual discipline must answer to his corporeal. He must lean on a friend who has a hard breast, as he would lie on a hard bed. He must drink cold water for his only beverage. So he must not hear sweetened and colored words, but pure and refreshing truths. He must daily bathe in truth cold as spring water, not warmed by the sympathy of friends.

Can love be in aught allied to dissipation? Let us love by refusing, not accepting one another. Love and lust are far asunder. The one is good, the other bad. When the affectionate sympathize by their higher natures, there is love; but there is danger that they will sympathize by their lower natures, and then there is lust. It is not necessary that this be deliberate, hardly even conscious; but, in the close contact of affection, there is danger that we may stain and pollute one another; for we cannot embrace but with an entire embrace.

We must love our friend so much that she shall be associated with our purest and holiest thoughts alone. When there is impurity, we have "descended to meet," though we knew it not.

The *luxury* of affection,—there's the danger. There must be some nerve and heroism in our love, as of a winter morning. In the religion of all nations a purity is hinted at, which, I fear, men never attain to. We may love and not elevate one another. The love that takes us as it finds us degrades us. What watch we must keep over the fairest and purest of our affections, lest there be some taint about them! May we so love as never to have occasion to repent of our love!

There is to be attributed to sensuality the loss to language of how many pregnant symbols! Flowers, which, by their infinite hues and fragrance, celebrate the marriage of the plants, are intended for a symbol of the open and unsuspected beauty of all true marriage, when man's flowering season arrives.

Virginity, too, is a budding flower, and by an impure marriage the virgin is deflowered. Whoever loves flowers, loves virgins and chastity. Love and lust are as far asunder as a flower-garden is from a brothel.

J. Biberg, in the "Amoenitates Botanicae," edited by Linnæus, observes (I translate from the Latin): "The organs of generation, which, in the animal kingdom, are for the most part concealed by nature, as if they were to be ashamed of, in the vegetable kingdom are exposed to the eyes of all; and, when the nuptials of plants are celebrated, it is wonderful what delight they afford to the beholder, refreshing the senses with the most agreeable color and the sweetest odor; and, at the same time, bees and other insects, not to mention the hummingbird, extract honey from their nectaries, and gather wax from their effete pollen." Linnæus himself calls the calyx the *thalamus*, or bridal chamber; and the corolla the *aulaeum*, or tapestry of it, and proceeds to explain thus every part of the flower.

Who knows but evil spirits might corrupt the flowers themselves, rob them of their fragrance and their fair hues, and turn their marriage into a secret shame and defilement? Already they are of various qualities, and there is one whose nuptials fill the lowlands in June with the odor of carrion.

The intercourse of the sexes, I have dreamed, is incredibly beautiful, too fair to be remembered. I have had thoughts about it, but they are among the most fleeting and irrecoverable in my experience. It is strange that men will talk of miracles, revelation, inspiration, and the like, as things past, while love remains.

A true marriage will differ in no wise from illumination. In all perception of the truth there is a divine ecstasy, an inexpressible delirium of joy, as when a youth embraces his betrothed virgin. The ultimate delights of a true marriage are one with this.

No wonder that, out of such a union, not as end, but as accompaniment, comes the undying race of man. The womb is a most fertile soil.

Some have asked if the stock of men could not be improved,—if they could not be bred as cattle. Let Love be purified, and all the rest will follow. A pure love is thus, indeed, the panacea for all the ills of the world.

The only excuse for reproduction is improvement. Nature abhors repetition. Beasts merely propagate their kind; but the offspring of noble men and women will be superior to themselves, as their aspirations are. By their fruits ye shall know them.

TO HARRISON BLAKE (AT WORCESTER).

Concord, February 27, 1853.

Mr. Blake,—I have not answered your letter before, because I have been almost constantly in the fields surveying of late. It is long since I have spent many days so profitably in a pecuniary sense; so unprofitably, it seems to me, in a more important sense. I have earned just a dollar a day for seventy-six days past; for, though I charge at a higher rate for the days which are seen to be spent, yet so many more are spent than appears. This is instead of lecturing, which has not offered, to pay for that book which I printed.[46] I have not only cheap hours, but cheap weeks and months; that is, weeks which are bought at the rate I have named. Not that they are quite lost to me, or make me very melancholy, alas! for I too often take a cheap satisfaction in so spending them,—weeks of pasturing and browsing, like beeves and deer,—which give me animal health, it may be, but create a tough skin over the soul and intellectual part. Yet, if men should offer my body a maintenance for the work of my head alone, I feel that it would be a dangerous temptation.

As to whether what you speak of as the "world's way" (which for themost part is my way), or that which is shown me, is the better, the former is imposture, the latter is truth. I have the coldest confidence in the last. There is only such hesitation as the appetites feel in following the aspirations. The clod hesitates because it is inert, wants *animation*. The one is the way of death, the other of life everlasting. My hours are not "cheap in such a way that *I* doubt whether the world's way would not have been better," but cheap in such a way that I doubt whether the world's way, which I have adopted for the time, could be worse. The whole enterprise of this nation, which is not an upward, but a westward one, toward Oregon, California, Japan, etc., is totally devoid of interest to me, whether performed on foot, or by a Pacific railroad. It is not illustrated by a thought; it is not warmed by a sentiment; there is nothing in it which one should lay down his life for, nor even his gloves,—hardly which one should take up a newspaper for. It is perfectly heathenish,—a filibustering *toward* heaven by the great western route. No; they may go their way to their manifest destiny, which I trust is not mine. May my seventy-six dollars, whenever I get them, help to carry me in the other direction! I see them on their winding way, but no music is wafted from their host,—only the rattling of change in their pockets. I would rather be a captive knight, and let them all pass by, than be free only to go whither they are bound. What end do they propose to themselves beyond Japan? What aims more lofty have they than the prairie dogs?

As it respects these things, I have not changed an opinion one iota from the first. As the stars looked to me when I was a shepherd in Assyria, they look to me now, a New-Englander. The higher the mountain on which you stand, the less change in the prospect from year to year, from age to age. Above a certain height there is no change. I am a Switzer on the edge of the glacier, with his advantages and disadvantages, goitre, or what not. (You may suspect it to be some kind of swelling at any rate.) I have had but one *spiritual* birth (excuse the word), and now whether it rains or snows, whether I laugh or cry, fall farther below or approach nearer to my standard; whether Pierce or Scott is elected,—not a new scintillation of light flashes on me, but ever and anon, though with longer intervals, the same surprising and everlastingly new light dawns to me, with only such variations as in the coming of the natural day, with which, indeed, it is often coincident.

As to how to preserve potatoes from rotting, your opinion may change from year to year; but as to how to preserve your soul from rotting, I have nothing to learn, but something to practice.

Thus I declaim against them; but I in my folly am the world I condemn.

I very rarely, indeed, if ever, "feel any itching to be what is called useful to my fellow-men." Sometimes—it may be when my thoughts for want of employment fall into a beaten path or humdrum—I have dreamed idly of stopping a man's horse that was running away; but, perchance, I wished that he might run, in order that I might stop him;—or of putting out a fire; but then, of course, it must have got well a-going. Now, to tell the truth, I do not dream much of acting upon horses before they run, or of preventing fires which are not yet kindled. What a foul subject is this of doing good! instead of minding one's life, which should be his business; doing good as a dead carcass, which is only fit for manure, instead of as a living man,—instead of taking care to flourish, and smell and taste sweet, and refresh all mankind to the extent of our capacity and quality. People will sometimes try to persuade you that you have done something from that motive, as if you did not already know enough about it. If I ever *did* a man any good, in their sense, of course it was something exceptional and insignificant compared with the good or evil which I am constantly doing by being what I am. As if you were to preach to ice to shape itself into burning-glasses, which are sometimes useful, and so the peculiar properties of ice be lost. Ice that merely performs the office of a burning-glass does not do its duty.

The problem of life becomes, one cannot say by how many degrees, more complicated as our material wealth is increased,—whether that needle they tell of was a gateway or not,—since the problem is not merely nor mainly to get life for our bodies, but by this or a similar discipline to get life for our souls; by cultivating the lowland farm on right principles, that is, with this view, to turn it into an upland farm. You have so many more talents to account for. If I accomplish as much more in spiritual work as I am richer in worldly goods, then I am just as worthy, or worth just as much, as I was before, and no more. I see that, in my own case, money *might* be of great service to me, but probably it would not be; for the difficulty now is, that I do not improve my opportunities, and therefore I am not prepared to have my opportunities increased. Now, I warn you, if it be as you say, you have got to put on the pack of an upland farmer in good earnest the coming spring, the lowland farm being cared for; ay, you must be selecting your seeds forthwith, and doing what winter work you can; and, while others are raising potatoes and Baldwin apples for you, you must be raising apples of the Hesperides for them. (Only hear how he preaches!) No man can suspect that he is the proprietor of an upland farm,—upland in the sense that it will produce nobler crops, and better repay cultivation in the long run,—but he will be perfectly sure that he ought to cultivate it.

Though we are desirous to earn our bread, we need not be anxious to *satisfy* men for it,—though we shall take care to pay them,—but God, who alone gave it to us. Men may in effect put us in the debtors' jail for that matter, simply for paying our whole debt to God, which includes our debt to them, and though we have His receipt for it,—for His paper is dishonored. The cashier will tell you that He has no stock in his bank.

How prompt we are to satisfy the hunger and thirst of our bodies; how slow to satisfy the hunger and thirst of our *souls*! Indeed, we would-be practical folks cannot use this word without blushing because of our infidelity, having starved this substance almost to a shadow. We feel it to be as absurd as if a man were to break forth into a eulogy on *his dog*, who has n't any. An ordinary man will work every day for a year at shoveling dirt to support his body, or a family of bodies; but he is an extraordinary man who will work a whole day in a year for the support of his soul. Even the priests, the men of God, so called, for the most part confess that they work for the support of the body. But he alone is the truly enterprising and practical man who succeeds in *maintaining* his soul here. Have not we our everlasting life to get? and is not that the only excuse at last for eating, drinking, sleeping, or even carrying an umbrella when it rains? A man might as well devote himself to raising pork as to fattening the bodies, or temporal part merely, of the whole human family. If we made the true distinction we should almost all of us be seen to be in the almshouse for souls.

I am much indebted to you because you look so steadily at the better side, or rather the true centre of me (for our true centre may, and perhaps oftenest does, lie entirely aside from us, and we are in fact eccentric), and, as I have elsewhere said, "give me an opportunity to live." You speak as if the image or idea which I see were reflected from me to you; and I see it again reflected from you to me, because we stand at the right angle to one another; and so it goes zigzag to what successive reflecting surfaces, before it is all dissipated or absorbed by the more unreflecting, or differently reflecting,—who knows? Or, perhaps, what you see directly, you refer to me. What a little shelf is required, by which we may impinge upon another, and build there our eyry in the clouds, and all the heavens we see above us we refer to the crags around and beneath us. Some piece of mica, as it were, in the face or eyes of one, as on the Delectable Mountains, slanted at the right angle, reflects the heavens to us. But, in the slow geological upheavals and depressions, these mutual angles are disturbed, these suns set, and new ones rise to us. That ideal which I worshiped was a greater stranger to the mica than to me. It was not the hero I admired, but the reflection from his epaulet or helmet. It is nothing (for us) permanently inherent in another, but his attitude or relation to what we prize, that we admire. The meanest man may glitter with micacious particles to his fellow's eye. These are the spangles that adorn a man. The highest union,—the only *un*-ion (don't laugh), or central oneness, is the coincidence of visual rays. Our club-room was an apartment in a constellation where our visual rays met (and there was no debate about the restaurant). The way between us is over the mount.

Your words make me think of a man of my acquaintance whom I occasionally meet, whom you, too, appear to have met, one Myself, as he is called. Yet, why not call him *Your*self? If you have met with him and know him, it is all I have done; and surely, where there is a mutual acquaintance, the *my* and *thy* make a distinction without a difference.

I do not wonder that you do not like my Canada story. It concerns me but little, and probably is not worth the time it took to tell it. Yet I had absolutely no design whatever in my mind, but simply to report what I saw. I have inserted all of myself that was implicated, or made the excursion. It has come to an end, at any rate; they will print no more, but return me my MS. when it is but little more than half done, as well as another I had sent them, because the editor[47] requires the liberty to omit the heresies without consulting me,—a privilege California is not rich enough to bid for.

I thank you again and again for attending to me; that is to say, I am glad that you hear me and that you also are glad. Hold fast to your most indefinite, waking dream. The very green dust on the walls is an organized vegetable; the atmosphere has its fauna and flora floating in it; and shall we think that dreams are but dust and ashes, are always disintegrated and crumbling thoughts, and not dust-like thoughts trooping to their standard with music,—systems beginning to be organized? These expectations,—these are roots, these are nuts, which even the poorest man has in his bin, and roasts or cracks them occasionally in winter evenings,—which even the poor debtor retains with his bed and his pig, i. e., his idleness and sensuality. Men go to the opera because they hear there a faint expression in sound of this news which is never quite distinctly proclaimed. Suppose a man were to sell the hue, the least amount of coloring matter in the superficies of his thought, for a farm,—were to exchange an absolute and infinite value for a relative and finite one, —to gain the whole world and lose his own soul!

Do not wait as long as I have before you write. If you will look at another star, I will try to supply my side of the triangle.

Tell Mr. Brown that I remember him, and trust that he remembers me.

P. S.—Excuse this rather flippant preaching, which does not cost me enough; and do not think that I mean you *always*, though your letter *requested* the subjects.

TO HARRISON BLAKE (AT WORCESTER).

Concord, April 10, 1853.

Mr. Blake,—Another singular kind of spiritual football,—really nameless, handleless, homeless, like myself,—a mere arena for thoughts and feelings; definite enough outwardly, indefinite more than enough inwardly. But I do not know why we should be styled "misters" or "masters:" we come so near to being anything or nothing, and seeing that we are mastered, and not wholly sorry to be mastered, by the least phenomenon. It seems to me that we are the mere creatures of thought,—one of the lowest forms of intellectual life, we men,—as the sunfish is of animal life. As yet our thoughts have acquired no definiteness nor solidity; they are purely molluscous, not vertebrate; and the height of our existence is to float upward in an ocean where the sun shines,—appearing only like a vast soup or chowder to the eyes of the immortal navigators. It is wonderful that I can be here, and you there, and that we can correspond, and do many other things, when, in fact, there is so little of us, either or both, anywhere. In a few minutes, I expect, this slight film or dash of vapor that I am will be what is called asleep,—resting! forsooth from what? Hard work? and thought? The hard work of the dandelion down, which floats over the meadow all day; the hard work of a pismire that labors to raise a hillock all day, and even by moonlight. Suddenly I can come forward into the utmost apparent distinctness, and speak with a sort of emphasis to you; and the next moment I am so faint an entity, and make so slight an impression, that nobody can find the traces of me. I try to hunt myself up, and find the little of me that is discoverable is falling asleep, and then I assist and tuck it up. It is getting late. How can *I* starve or feed? Can *I* be said to sleep? There is not enough of me even for that. If you hear a noise,—'t ain't I,—'t ain't I,— as the dog says with a tin kettle tied to his tail. I read of something happening to another the other day: how happens it that nothing ever happens to me? A dandelion down that never alights,—settles,—blown off by a boy to see if his mother wanted him,—some divine boy in the upper pastures.

Well, if there really is another such a meteor sojourning in these spaces, I would like to ask you if you know whose estate this is that we are on? For my part I enjoy it well enough, what with the wild apples and the scenery; but I should n't wonder if the owner set his dog on me next. I could remember something not much to the purpose, probably; but if I stick to what I do know, then—

It is worth the while to live respectably unto ourselves. We can possibly *get along* with a neighbor, even with a bedfellow, whom we respect but very little; but as soon as it comes to this, that we do not respect ourselves, then we do not get along at all, no matter how much money we are paid for halting. There are old heads in the world who cannot help me by their example or advice to live worthily and satisfactorily to myself; but I believe that it is in my power to elevate myself this very hour above the common level of my life. It is better to have your head in the clouds, and know where you are, if indeed you cannot get it above them, than to breathe the clearer atmosphere below them, and think that you are in paradise.

Once you were in Milton[48] doubting what to do. To live a better life,—this surely can be done. Dot and carry one. Wait not for a clear sight, for that you are to get. What you see clearly you may omit to do. Milton and Worcester? It is all Blake, Blake. Never mind the rats in the wall; the cat will take care of them. All that men have said or are is a very faint rumor, and it is not worth the while to remember or refer to that. If you are to meet God, will you refer to anybody out of that court? How shall men know how I succeed, unless they are in at the life? I did not see the *Times* reporter there.

Is it not delightful to provide one's self with the necessaries of life,—to collect dry wood for the fire when the weather grows cool, or fruits when we grow hungry?—not till then. And then we have all the time left for thought!

Of what use were it, pray, to get a little wood to burn, to warm your body this cold weather, if there were not a divine fire kindled at the same time to warm your spirit?

"Unless above himself he can

Erect himself, how poor a thing is man!"

I cuddle up by my stove, and there I get up another fire which warms fire itself. Life is so short that it is not wise to take roundabout ways, nor can we spend much time in waiting. Is it absolutely necessary, then, that we should do as we are doing? Are we chiefly under obligations to the devil, like Tom Walker? Though it is late to leave off this wrong way, it will seem early the moment we begin in the right way; instead of mid-afternoon, it will be early morning with us. We have not got half-way to dawn yet.

As for the lectures, I feel that I have something to say, especially on Traveling, Vagueness, and Poverty; but I cannot come now. I will wait till I am fuller, and have fewer engagements. Your suggestions will help me much to write them when I am ready. I am going to Haverhill[49] to-morrow, surveying, for a week or more. You met me on my last errand thither.

I trust that you realize what an exaggerator I am,—that I lay myself out to exaggerate whenever I have an opportunity,—pile Pelion upon Ossa, to reach heaven so. Expect no trivial truth from me, unless I am on the witness-stand. I will come as near to lying as you can drive a coach and four. If it is n't thus and so with me, it is with something. I am not particular whether I get the shells or meat, in view of the latter's worth.

I see that I have not at all answered your letter, but there is time enough for that.

TO HARRISON BLAKE (AT WORCESTER).

CONCORD, December 19, 1853.

MR. BLAKE,—My debt has accumulated so that I should have answered your last letter at once, if I had not been the subject of what is called a press of engagements, having a lecture to write for last Wednesday, and surveying more than usual besides. It has been a kind of running fight with me,—the enemy not always behind me I trust.

True, a man cannot lift himself by his own waistbands, because he cannot get out of himself; but he can expand himself (which is better, there being no up nor down in nature), and so split his waistbands, being already within himself.

You speak of doing and being, and the vanity, real or apparent, of much doing. The suckers—I think it is they—make nests in our river in the spring of more than a cart-load of small stones, amid which to deposit their ova. The other day I opened a muskrat's house. It was made of weeds, five feet broad at base, and three feet high, and far and low within it was a little cavity, only a foot in diameter, where the rat dwelt. It may seem trivial, this piling up of weeds, but so the race of muskrats is preserved. We must heap up a great pile of doing, for a small diameter of being. Is it not imperative on us that we *do* something, if we only work in a treadmill? And, indeed, some sort of revolving is necessary to produce a centre and nucleus of being. What exercise is to the body, employment is to the mind and morals. Consider what an amount of drudgery must be performed,—how much humdrum and prosaic labor goes to any work of the least value. There are so many layers of mere white lime in every shell to that thin inner one so beautifully tinted. Let not the shellfish think to build his house of that alone; and pray, what are its tints to him? Is it not his smooth, close-fitting shirt merely, whose tints *are not* to him, being in the dark, but only when he is gone or dead, and his shell is heaved up to light, a wreck upon the beach, do they appear. With him, too, it is a Song of the Shirt, "Work,—work,—work!" And the work is not merely a police in the gross sense, but in the higher sense a discipline. If it is surely the means to the highest end we know, can any work be humble or disgusting? Will it not rather be elevating as a ladder, the means by which we are translated?

How admirably the artist is made to accomplish his self-culture by devotion to his art! The wood-sawyer, through his effort to do his work well, becomes not merely a better wood-sawyer, but measurably a better *man*. Few are the men that can work on their navels,—only some Brahmins that I have heard of. To the painter is given some paint and canvas instead; to the Irishman a hog, typical of himself. In a thousand apparently humble ways men busy themselves to make some right take the place of some wrong,—if it is only to make a better paste blacking,—and they are themselves *so much* the better morally for it.

You say that you do not succeed much. Does it concern you enough that you do not? Do you work hard enough at it? Do you get the benefit of discipline out of it? If so, persevere. Is it a more serious thing than to walk a thousand miles in a thousand successive hours? Do you get any corns by it? Do you ever think of hanging yourself on account of failure?

If you are going into that line,—going to besiege the city of God,—you must not only be strong in engines, but prepared with provisions to starve out the garrison. An Irishman came to see me to-day, who is endeavoring to get his family out to this New World. He rises at half past four, milks twenty-eight cows (which has swollen the joints of his fingers), and eats his breakfast, without any milk in his tea or coffee, before six; and so on, day after day, for six and a half dollars a month; and thus he keeps his virtue in him, if he does not add to it; and he regards me as a gentleman able to assist him; but if I ever get to be a gentleman, it will be by working after my fashion harder than he does. If my joints are not swollen, it must be because I deal with the teats of celestial cows before breakfast (and the milker in this case is always allowed some of the milk for his breakfast), to say nothing of the flocks and herds of Admetus afterward.

It is the art of mankind to polish the world, and every one who works is scrubbing in some part.

If the work is high and far,

You must not only aim aright,

But draw the bow with all your might.

You must qualify yourself to use a bow which no humbler archer can bend.

"Work,—work,—work!"

Who shall know it for a bow? It is not of yew tree. It is straighter than a ray of light; flexibility is not known for one of its qualities.

December 22.

So far I had got when I was called off to survey. Pray read the life of Haydon the painter, if you have not. It is a small revelation for these latter days; a great satisfaction to know that he has lived, though he is now dead. Have you met with the letter of a Turkish cadi at the end of Layard's "Ancient Babylon"? that also is refreshing, and a capital comment on the whole book which precedes it,—the Oriental genius speaking through him.

Those Brahmins "put it through." They come off, or rather stand still, conquerors, with some withered arms or legs at least to show; and they are said to have cultivated the faculty of abstraction to a degree unknown to Europeans. If we cannot sing of faith and triumph, we will sing our despair. We will be that kind of bird. There are day owls, and there are night owls, and each is beautiful and even musical while about its business.

Might you not find some positive work to do with your back to Church and State, letting your back do all the rejection of them? Can you not *go* upon your pilgrimage, Peter, along the winding mountain path whither you face? A step more will make those funereal church bells over your shoulder sound far and sweet as a natural sound.

"Work,—work,—work!"

Why not make a *very large* mud pie and bake it in the sun! Only put no Church nor State into it, nor upset any other pepper-box that way. Dig out a woodchuck,—for that has nothing to do with rotting institutions. Go ahead.

Whether a man spends his day in an ecstasy or despondency, he must do some work to show for it, even as there are flesh and bones to show for him. We are superior to the joy we experience.

Your last two letters, methinks, have more nerve and will in them than usual, as if you had erected yourself more. Why are not they good work, if you only had a hundred correspondents to tax you?

Make your failure tragical by the earnestness and steadfastness of your endeavor, and then it will not differ from success. Prove it to be the inevitable fate of mortals,—of one mortal,—if you can.

You said that you were writing on Immortality. I wish you would communicate to me what you know about that. You are sure to live while that is your theme.

Thus I write on some text which a sentence of your letters may have furnished.

I think of coming to see you as soon as I get a new coat, if I have money enough left. I will write to you again about it.

TO HARRISON BLAKE (AT WORCESTER).

CONCORD, January 21, 1854.

MR. BLAKE,—My coat is at last done, and my mother and sister allow that I am *so far* in a condition to go abroad. I feel as if I had gone abroad the moment I put it on. It is, as usual, a production strange to me, the wearer,—invented by some Count D'Orsay; and the maker of it was not acquainted with any of my real depressions or elevations. He only measured a peg to hang it on, and might have made the loop big enough to go over my head. It requires a not quite innocent indifference, not to say insolence, to wear it. Ah! the process by which we get our coats is not what it should be. Though the Church declares it righteous, and its priest pardons me, my own good genius tells me that it is hasty, and coarse, and false. I expect a time when, or rather an integrity by which, a man will get his coat as honestly and as perfectly fitting as a tree its bark. Now our garments are typical of our conformity to the ways of the world, *i. e.*, of the devil, and to some extent react on us and poison us, like that shirt which Hercules put on.

I think to come and see you next week, on Monday, if nothing hinders. I have just returned from court at Cambridge, whither I was called as a witness, having surveyed a water-privilege, about which there is a dispute, since you were here.

Ah! what foreign countries there are, greater in extent than the United States or Russia, and with no more souls to a square mile, stretching away on every side from every human being with whom you have no sympathy. Their humanity affects me as simply monstrous. Rocks, earth, brute beasts, comparatively are not so strange to me. When I sit in the parlors and kitchens of some with whom my business brings me—I was going to say in contact—(business, like misery, makes strange bedfellows), I feel a sort of awe, and as forlorn as if I were cast away on a desolate shore. I think of Riley's Narrative[50] and his sufferings. You, who soared like a merlin with your mate through the realms of æther, in the presence of the unlike, drop at once to earth, a mere amorphous squab, divested of your air-inflated pinions. (By the way, excuse this writing, for I am using the stub of the last feather I chance to possess.) You travel on, however, through this dark and desert world; you see in the distance an intelligent and sympathizing lineament; stars come forth in the dark, and oases appear in the desert.

But (to return to the subject of coats), we are well-nigh smothered under yet more fatal coats, which do not fit us, our whole lives long. Consider the cloak that our employment or station is; how rarely men treat each other for what in their true and naked characters they are; how we use and tolerate pretension; how the judge is clothed with dignity which does not belong to him, and the trembling witness with humility that does not belong to him, and the criminal, perchance, with shame or impudence which no more belong to him. It does not matter so much, then, what is the fashion of the cloak with which we cloak these cloaks. Change the coat; put the judge in the criminal-box, and the criminal on the bench, and you might think that you had changed the men.

No doubt the thinnest of all cloaks is conscious deception or lies; it is sleazy and frays out; it is not close-woven like cloth; but its meshes are a coarse network. A man can afford to lie only at the intersection of the threads; but truth puts in the filling, and makes a consistent stuff.

I mean merely to suggest how much the station affects the demeanor and self-respectability of the parties, and that the difference between the judge's coat of cloth and the criminal's is insignificant compared with, or only partially significant of, the difference between the coats which their respective stations permit them to wear. What airs the judge may put on over his coat which the criminal may not! The judge's opinion (*sententia*) of the criminal *sentences* him, and is read by the clerk of the court, and published to the world, and executed by the sheriff; but the criminal's opinion of the judge has the weight of a sentence, and is published and executed only in the supreme court of the universe,—a court not of common pleas. How much juster is the one than the other? Men are continually *sentencing* each other; but, whether we be judges or criminals, the sentence is ineffectual unless we continue ourselves.

I am glad to hear that I do not always limit your vision when you look this way; that you sometimes see the light through me; that I am here and there windows, and not all dead wall. Might not the community sometimes petition a man to remove himself as a nuisance, a darkener of the day, a too large mote?

TO HARRISON BLAKE (AT WORCESTER).

Concord, August 8, 1854.

Mr. Blake,—Methinks I have spent a rather unprofitable summer thus far. I have been too much with the world, as the poet might say.[51] The completest performance of the highest duties it imposes would yield me but little satisfaction. Better the neglect of all such, because your life passed on a level where it was impossible to recognize them. Latterly, I have heard the very flies buzz too distinctly, and have accused myself because I did not still this superficial din. We must not be too easily distracted by the crying of children or of dynasties. The Irishman erects his sty, and gets drunk, and jabbers more and more under my eaves, and I am responsible for all that filth and folly. I find it, as ever, very unprofitable to have much to do with men. It is sowing the wind, but not reaping even the whirlwind; only reaping an unprofitable calm and stagnation. Our conversation is a smooth, and civil, and never-ending speculation merely. I take up the thread of it again in the morning, with very much such courage as the invalid takes his prescribed Seidlitz powders. Shall I help you to some of the mackerel? It would be more respectable if men, as has been said before, instead of being such pigmy desperates, were Giant Despairs. Emerson says that his life is so unprofitable and shabby for the most part, that he is driven to all sorts of resources, and, among the rest, to men. I tell him that we differ only in our resources. Mine is to get away from men. They very rarely affect me as grand or beautiful; but I know that there is a sunrise and a sunset every day. In the summer, this world is a mere watering-place,—a Saratoga,—drinking so many tumblers of Congress water; and in the winter, is it any better, with its oratorios? I have seen more men than usual, lately; and, well as I was acquainted with one, I am surprised to find what vulgar fellows they are. They do a little business commonly each day, in order to pay their board, and then they congregate in sitting-rooms and feebly fabulate and paddle in the social slush; and when I think that they have sufficiently relaxed, and am prepared to see them steal away to their shrines, they go unashamed to their beds, and take on a new layer of sloth. They may be single, or have families in their *faineancy*. I do not meet men who can have nothing to do with me because they have so much to do with themselves. However, I trust that a very few cherish purposes which they never declare. Only think, for a moment, of a man about his affairs! How we should respect him! How glorious he would appear! Not working for any corporation, its agent, or president, but fulfilling the end of his being! A man about *his business* would be the cynosure of all eyes.

The other evening I was determined that I would silence this shallow din; that I would walk in various directions and see if there was not to be found any depth of silence around. As Bonaparte sent out his horsemen in the Red Sea on all sides to find shallow water, so I sent forth my mounted thoughts to find deep water. I left the village and paddled up the river to Fair Haven Pond. As the sun went down, I saw a solitary boatman disporting on the smooth lake. The falling dews seemed to strain and purify the air, and I was smoothed with an infinite stillness. I got the world, as it were, by the nape of the neck, and held it under in the tide of its own events, till it was drowned, and then I let it go down-stream like a dead dog. Vast hollow chambers of silence stretched away on every side, and my being expanded in proportion, and filled them. Then first could I appreciate sound, and find it musical.[52]

But now for your news. Tell us of the year. Have you fought the good fight? What is the state of your crops? Will your harvest answer well to the seed-time, and are you cheered by the prospect of stretching cornfields? Is there any blight on your fields, any murrain in your herds? Have you tried the size and quality of your potatoes? It does one good to see their balls dangling in the lowlands. Have you got your meadow hay before the fall rains shall have set in? Is there enough in your barns to keep your cattle over? Are you killing weeds nowadays? or have you earned leisure to go a-fishing? Did you plant any Giant Regrets last spring, such as I saw advertised? It is not a new species, but the result of cultivation and a fertile soil. They are excellent for sauce. How is it with your marrow squashes for winter use? Is there likely to be a sufficiency of fall feed in your neighborhood? What is the state of the springs? I read that in your county there is more water on the hills than in the valleys. Do you find it easy to get all the help you require? Work early and late, and let your men and teams rest at noon. Be careful not to drink too much sweetened water, while at your hoeing, this hot weather. You can bear the heat much better for it.

TO MARSTON WATSON (AT PLYMOUTH).

CONCORD, September 19, 1854.

DEAR SIR,—I am glad to hear from you and the Plymouth men again. The world still holds together between Concord and Plymouth, it seems. I should like to be with you while Mr. Alcott is there, but I cannot come next Sunday. I will come Sunday after next, that is, October 1st, if that will do; and look out for you at the depot. I do not like to promise more than one discourse. Is there a good precedent for two?

The first of Thoreau's many lecturing visits to Worcester, the home of his friend Blake, was in April, 1849, and from that time onward he must have read lectures there at least annually, until his last illness, in 1861-62. By 1854, the lecturing habit, in several places besides Concord, had become established; and there was a constant interchange of visits and excursions with his friends at Worcester, Plymouth, New Bedford, etc. Soon after the publication of "Walden," in the summer of 1854, Thoreau wrote these notes to Mr. Blake, touching on various matters of friendly interest.

TO HARRISON BLAKE (AT WORCESTER).

CONCORD, September 21, 1854.

BLAKE,—I have just read your letter, but do not mean now to answer it, solely for want of time to say what I wish. I directed a copy of "Walden" to you at Ticknor's, on the day of its publication, and it should have reached you before. I am encouraged to know that it interests you as it now stands,—a printed book,—for you apply a very severe test to it,—you make the highest demand on me. As for the excursion you speak of, I should like it right well, —indeed I thought of proposing the same thing to you and Brown, some months ago. Perhaps it would have been better if I had done so then; for in that case I should have been able to enter into it with that infinite margin to my views,—spotless of all engagements,—which I think so necessary. As it is, I have agreed to go a-lecturing to Plymouth, Sunday after next (October 1) and to Philadelphia in November, and thereafter to the West, *if they shall want me*; and, as I have prepared nothing in that shape, I feel as if my hours were spoken for. However, I think that, after having been to Plymouth, I may take a day or two—if that date will suit you and Brown. *At any rate* I will write to you then.

CONCORD, October 5, 1854.

After I wrote to you, Mr. Watson postponed my going to Plymouth one week, *i. e.*, till next Sunday; and now he wishes me to carry my instruments and survey his grounds, to which he has been adding. Since I want a little money, though I contemplate but a short excursion, I do not feel at liberty to decline this work. I do not know exactly how long it will detain me,—but there is plenty of time yet, and I will write to you again—perhaps from Plymouth.

There is a Mr. Thomas Cholmondeley (pronounced Chumly), a young English author, staying at our house at present, who asks me to teach him *botany*—*i. e.*, anything which I know; and also to make an excursion to some mountain with him. He is a well-behaved person, and *possibly* I may propose his taking that run to Wachusett with us—if it will be agreeable to you. Nay, if I do not hear any objection from you, I will consider myself *at liberty* to invite him.

CONCORD, Saturday P. M., October 14, 1854.

I have just returned from Plymouth, where I have been detained surveying much longer than I expected. What do you say to visiting Wachusett next Thursday? I will start at 7¼ A. M. *unless there is a prospect of a stormy day*, go by cars to Westminster, and thence on foot five or six miles to the mountain-top, where I may engage to meet you, at (or before) 12 M. If the weather is unfavorable, I will try again, on Friday,—and again on Monday. If a storm comes on after starting, I will seek you at the tavern at Princeton centre, as soon as circumstances will permit. I shall expect an answer at once, to clinch the bargain.

The year 1854 was a memorable one in Thoreau's life, for it brought out his most successful book, "Walden," and introduced him to the notice of the world, which had paid small attention to his first book, the "Week," published five years earlier. This year also made him acquainted with two friends to whom he wrote much, and who loved to visit and stroll with him around Concord, or in more distant places,—Thomas Cholmondeley, an Englishman from Shropshire, and Daniel Ricketson, a New Bedford Quaker, of liberal mind and cultivated tastes,—an author and poet, and fond of corresponding with poets, as he did with the Howitts and William Barnes of England, and with Bryant, Emerson, Channing, and Thoreau, in America. Few of the letters to Cholmondeley are yet found, being buried temporarily in the mass of family papers at Condover Hall, an old Elizabethan mansion near Shrewsbury, which Thomas Cholmondeley inherited, and which remains in his family's possession since his own death at Florence in 1864. But the letters of the Englishman, recently printed in the *Atlantic Monthly* (December, 1893), show how sincere was the attachment of this ideal friend to the

Concord recluse, and how well he read that character which the rest of England, and a good part of America, have been so slow to recognize for what it really was.

Thomas Cholmondeley was the eldest son of Rev. Charles Cowper Cholmondeley, rector of Overleigh, Cheshire, and of a sister to Reginald Heber, the celebrated bishop of Calcutta. He was born in 1823, and brought up at Hodnet, in Shropshire, where his father, a cousin of Lord Delamere, had succeeded his brother-in-law as rector, on the departure of Bishop Heber for India, in 1823. The son was educated at Oriel College, Oxford,—a friend, and perhaps pupil of Arthur Hugh Clough, who gave him letters to Emerson in 1854. Years before, after leaving Oxford, he had gone with some relatives to New Zealand, and before coming to New England he had published a book, "Ultima Thule," describing that Australasian colony of England, where he lived for part of a year. He had previously studied in Germany, and traveled on the Continent. He landed in America the first time in August, 1854, and soon after went to Concord, where, at the suggestion of Emerson, he became an inmate of Mrs. Thoreau's family. This made him intimate with Henry Thoreau for a month or two, and also brought him into acquaintance with Ellery Channing, then living across the main street of Concord, in the west end of the village, and furnishing to Thoreau a landing-place for his boat under the willows at the foot of Channing's small garden. Alcott was not then in Concord, but Cholmondeley made his acquaintance in Boston, and admired his character and manners.[53]

Thoreau's Boat-landing, Concord River

With Channing and Thoreau the young Englishman visited their nearest mountain, Wachusett, and in some of their walks the artist Rowse, who had made the first portrait of Thoreau, joined, for he was then in Concord, late in 1854, engraving the fine head of Daniel Webster from a painting by Ames, and this engraving he gave both to Thoreau and to Cholmondeley. In December the Englishman, whose patriotism was roused by the delays and calamities of England in her Crimean war, resolved to go home and raise a company, as he did, first spending some weeks in lodgings at Boston (Orange Street) in order to hear Theodore Parker preach and visit Harvard College, of which I was then a student, in the senior class. He visited me and my classmate, Edwin Morton, and called on some of the Cambridge friends of Clough. In January, 1855, he sailed for England, and there received the letter of Thoreau printed on pages 249-251.

The acquaintance with Mr. Ricketson began by letter before Cholmondeley reached Concord, but Thoreau did not visit him until December, 1854. Mr. Ricketson says, "In the summer of 1854 I purchased, in New Bedford, a copy of 'Walden.' I had never heard of its author, but in this admirable and most original book I found so many observations on plants, birds, and natural objects generally in which I was also interested, that I felt at once I had found a congenial spirit. During this season I was rebuilding a house in the country, three miles from New Bedford, and had erected a small building which was called my 'shanty;' and my family being then in my city house, I made this building my temporary home. From it I addressed my first letter to the author of 'Walden.' In reply he wrote, 'I had duly received your very kind and frank letter, but delayed to answer it thus long because I have little skill as a correspondent, and wished to send you something more than my thanks. I was gratified by your prompt and hearty acceptance of my book. Yours is the only word of greeting I am likely to receive from a dweller in the woods like myself,—from where the whip-poor-will and cuckoo are heard, and there are better than moral clouds drifting over, and real breezes blow.' From that year until his death in 1862 we exchanged visits annually, and letters more frequently. He was much interested in the botany of our region, finding here many marine plants he had not before seen. When our friendship began, the admirers of his only two published books were few; most prominent among them were Emerson, Alcott, and Channing of Concord, Messrs. Blake and T. Brown of Worcester, Mr. Marston Watson of Plymouth, and myself. Many accused him of being an imitator of Emerson; others thought him unsocial, impracticable, and ascetic. Now he was none of these; a more original man never lived, nor one more thoroughly personifying civility; no man could hold a finer relationship with his family than he."

In reply to Mr. Ricketson's first letter (August 12, 1854) above mentioned, Thoreau sent, after six weeks' delay, the reply of October 1, the beginning of which was just quoted. Continuing, Thoreau said:—

"Your account excites in me a desire to see the Middleborough ponds, of which I had already heard somewhat; as also some very beautiful ponds on the Cape, in Harwich, I think, near which I once passed. I have sometimes also thought of visiting that remnant of *our* Indians still living near you. But then, you know, there is nothing like one's native fields and lakes. The best news you send me is, not that Nature with you is so fair and genial, but that there is one there who likes her so well. That proves all that was asserted.

"Homer, of course, you include in your list of lovers of Nature; and, by the way, let me mention here—for this is 'my thunder' lately—William Gilpin's long series of books on the Picturesque, with their illustrations. If it chances that you have not met with these, I cannot just now frame a better wish than that you may one day derive as much pleasure from the inspection of them as I have.

"Much as you have told me of yourself, you have still, I think, a little the advantage of me in this correspondence, for I have told you still more in my book. You have therefore the broadest mark to fire at.

"A young English author, Thomas Cholmondeley, is just now waiting for me to take a walk with him; therefore excuse this very barren note from

"Yours, hastily at last."

Between the letter just quoted and Thoreau's next, of December 19, 1854, a letter is obviously missing. Mr. Ricketson had answered (October 12), the first letter, and on December 14 had written again to convey an invitation from Mr. Mitchell that Thoreau should lecture at New Bedford, the 26th, on his way to Nantucket for the 28th. Probably Thoreau had replied to the letter of October 12, and to the invitation to bring Cholmondeley with him in the pleasant October season. In this reply he had said something which called forth from Ricketson an expression of sympathy, as well as the December invitation; for Thoreau thus replied to the letter of December 14:—

TO DANIEL RICKETSON (AT NEW BEDFORD).

CONCORD, December 19, 1854.

DEAR SIR,—I wish to thank you for your sympathy. I had counted on seeing you when I came to New Bedford, though I did not know exactly how near to it you permanently dwelt; therefore I gladly accept your invitation to stop at your house. I am going to lecture at Nantucket the 28th, and as I suppose I must improve the earliest opportunity to get there from New Bedford, I will endeavor to come on Monday, that I may see yourself and New Bedford before my lecture.

I should like right well to see your ponds, but that is hardly to be thought of at present. I fear that it is impossible for me to combine such things with the business of lecturing. You cannot serve God and Mammon. However, perhaps I shall have time to see something of your country. I am aware that you have not so much snow as we; there has been excellent sleighing here since the 5th inst.

Mr. Cholmondeley has left us, so that I shall come alone. Will you be so kind as to warn Mr. Mitchell that I accept at once his invitation to lecture on the 26th of this month, for I do not know that he has got my letter. Excuse this short note.[54]

TO HARRISON BLAKE (AT WORCESTER).

CONCORD, December 19, 1854.

MR. BLAKE,—I suppose you have heard of my truly providential meeting with Mr. [T.] Brown; providential because it saved me from the suspicion that my words had fallen altogether on stony ground, when it turned out that there was some Worcester soil there. You will allow me to consider that I correspond with him through you.

I confess that I am a very bad correspondent, so far as promptness of reply is concerned; but then I am sure to answer sooner or later. The longer I have forgotten you, the more I remember you. For the most part I have not been idle since I saw you. How does the world go with you? or rather, how do you get along without it? I have not yet learned to live, that I can see, and I fear that I shall not very soon. I find, however, that in the long run things correspond to my original idea,—that they correspond to nothing else so much; and thus a man may really be a true prophet without any great exertion. The day is never so dark, nor the night even, but that the laws at least of light still prevail, and so may make it light in our minds if they are open to the truth. There is considerable danger that a man will be crazy between dinner and supper; but it will not directly answer any good purpose that I know of, and it is just as easy to be sane. We have got to know what both life and death are, before we can begin to live after our own fashion. Let us be learning our a-b-c's as soon as possible. I never yet knew the sun to be knocked down and rolled through a mud-puddle; he comes out honor-bright from behind every storm. Let us then take sides with the sun, seeing we have so much leisure. Let us not put all we prize into a football to be kicked, when a bladder will do as well.

When an Indian is burned, his body may be broiled, it may be no more than a beefsteak. What of that? They may broil his *heart*, but they do not therefore broil his *courage*,—his principles. Be of good courage! That is the main thing.

If a man were to place himself in an attitude to bear manfully the greatest evil that can be inflicted on him, he would find suddenly that there was no such evil to bear; his brave back would go a-begging. When Atlas got his back made up, that was all that was required. (In this case *a priv.*, not *pleon.*, and τλῆμι.) The world rests on principles. The wise gods will never make underpinning of a man. But as long as he crouches, and skulks, and shirks his work, every creature that has weight will be treading on his toes, and crushing him; he will himself tread with one foot on the other foot.

The monster is never just there where we think he is. What is truly monstrous is our cowardice and sloth.

Have no idle disciplines like the Catholic Church and others; have only positive and fruitful ones. Do what you know you ought to do. Why should we ever go abroad, even across the way, to ask a neighbor's advice? There is a nearer neighbor within us incessantly telling us how we should behave. But we wait for the neighbor without to tell us of some false, easier way.

They have a census-table in which they put down the number of the insane. Do you believe that they put them all down there? Why, in every one of these houses there is at least one man fighting or squabbling a good part of his time with a dozen pet demons of his own breeding and cherishing, which are relentlessly gnawing at his vitals; and if perchance he resolve at length that he will courageously combat them, he says, "Ay! ay! I will attend to you after dinner!" And, when that time comes, he concludes that he is good for another stage, and reads a column or two about the *Eastern War*! Pray, to be in earnest, where is Sevastopol? Who is Menchikoff? and Nicholas behind there? who the Allies? Did not we fight a little (little enough to be sure, but just enough to make it interesting) at Alma, at Balaclava, at Inkermann? We love to fight far from home. Ah! the Minié musket is the king of weapons. Well, let us get one then.

I just put another stick into my stove,—a pretty large mass of white oak. How many men will do enough this cold winter to pay for the fuel that will be required to warm them? I suppose I have burned up a pretty good-sized tree to-night,—and for what? I settled with Mr. Tarbell for it the other day; but that was n't the final settlement. I got off cheaply from him. At last, one will say, "Let us see, how much wood did you burn, sir?" And I shall shudder to think that the next question will be, "What did you do while you were warm?" Do we think the ashes will pay for it? that God is an ash-man? It is a fact that we have got to render an account for the deeds done in the body.

Who knows but we shall be better the next year than we have been the past? At any rate, I wish you a really *new* year,—commencing from the instant you read this,—and happy or unhappy, according to your deserts.

TO HARRISON BLAKE.

Concord, December 22, 1854.

Mr. Blake,—I will lecture for your Lyceum on the 4th of January next; and I hope that I shall have time for that good day out of doors. Mr. Cholmondeley is in Boston, yet *perhaps* I may invite him to accompany me. I have engaged to lecture at New Bedford on the 26th inst., stopping with Daniel Ricketson, three miles out of town; and at Nantucket on the 28th, so that I shall be gone all next week. They say there is some danger of being weather-bound at Nantucket; but I see that others run the same risk. You had better acknowledge the receipt of this at any rate, though you should write nothing else; otherwise I shall not know whether you get it; but perhaps you will not wait till you have seen me, to answer my letter (of December 19). I will tell you what I think of lecturing when I see you. Did you see the notice of "Walden" in the last *Anti-Slavery Standard*? You will not be surprised if I tell you that it reminded me of you.

On the Christmas Day that Thoreau reached New Bedford, he had left home in the forenoon, as usual in his Cambridge visits, spent some time at Harvard College, and gone on by the train in the afternoon, which accounted for his delay. His host, who then saw him for the first time, says:—

"I had expected him at noon, but as he did not arrive, I had given him up for the day. In the latter part of the afternoon I was clearing off the snow from my front steps, when, looking up, I saw a man walking up the carriage-road, bearing a portmanteau in one hand and an umbrella in the other. He was dressed in a long overcoat of dark color, and wore a dark soft hat. I had no suspicion it was Thoreau, and rather supposed it was a peddler of small wares."

This was a common mistake to make. When Thoreau ran the gantlet of the Cape Cod villages,—"feeling as strange," he says, "as if he were in a town in China,"—one of the old fishermen could not believe that he had not something to sell. Being finally satisfied that it was not a peddler with his pack, the old man said, "Wal, it makes no odds what 't is you carry, so long as you carry Truth along with ye." Mr. Ricketson came to the same conclusion about his visitor, and in the early September of 1855 returned the visit.

On the 4th of January, 1855, Ricketson wrote, saying, "Your visit, short as it was, gave us all at Brooklawn much satisfaction;" adding that he might visit Concord late in January, when he expected to be in Boston. Thoreau replied:—

TO DANIEL RICKETSON (AT NEW BEDFORD).

Concord, January 6, 1855.

Mr. Ricketson,—I am pleased to hear from the shanty, whose inside and occupant I have seen. I had a very pleasant time at Brooklawn, as you know, and thereafter at Nantucket. I was obliged to pay the usual tribute to the sea, but it was more than made up to me by the hospitality of the Nantucketers. Tell Arthur that I can now compare notes with him; for though I went neither before nor behind the mast, since we had n't any, I went with my head hanging over the side all the way.

In spite of all my experience, I persisted in reading to the Nantucket people the lecture which I read at New Bedford, and I found them to be the very audience for me. I got home Friday night, after being lost in the fog off Hyannis.[55] I have not yet found a new jackknife, but I had a glorious skating with Channing the other day, on the skates found long ago.

Mr. Cholmondeley sailed for England direct, in the America, on the 3d, after spending a night with me. He thinks even to go to the East and enlist. Last night I returned from lecturing in Worcester.

I shall be glad to see you when you come to Boston, as will also my mother and sister, who know something about you as an abolitionist. Come directly to our house. Please remember me to Mrs. Ricketson, and also to the young folks.

After writing that he expected to be at the anti-slavery meetings in Boston, January 24 and 25, ill health and a snow-storm detained Ricketson at Brooklawn, whereupon Thoreau wrote:—

TO DANIEL RICKETSON (AT NEW BEDFORD).

CONCORD, February 1, 1855.

DEAR SIR,—I supposed, as I did not see you on the 24th or 25th, that some track or other was obstructed; but the solid earth still holds together between New Bedford and Concord, and I trust that as this time you stayed away, you may live to come another day.

I did not go to Boston, for with regard to that place I sympathize with one of my neighbors, an old man, who has not been there since the last war, when he was compelled to go. No, I have a real genius for staying at home.

I have been looking of late at Bewick's tail-pieces in the "Birds,"—all they have of him at Harvard. Why will he be a little vulgar at times? Yesterday I made an excursion up our river,—skated some thirty miles in a few hours, if you will believe it. So with reading and writing and skating the night comes round again.

The early part of 1855 was spent by Thomas Cholmondeley in a tiresome passage to England, whence he wrote (January 27) to say to Thoreau that he had reached Shropshire, and been commissioned captain in the local militia, in preparation for service at Sevastopol, but reminding his Concord friend of a half promise to visit England some day. To this Thoreau made answer thus:—

TO THOMAS CHOLMONDELEY (AT HODNET).

CONCORD, Mass., February 7, 1855.

DEAR CHOLMONDELEY,—I am glad to hear that you have arrived safely at Hodnet, and that there is a solid piece of ground of that name which can support a man better than a floating plank, in that to me as yet purely historical England. But have I not seen you with my own eyes, a piece of England herself, and was not your letter come out to me thence? I have now reason to believe that Salop is as real a place as Concord; with at least as good an underpinning of granite, floating on liquid fire. I congratulate you on having arrived safely at that floating isle, after your disagreeable passage in the steamer America. So are we not all making a passage, agreeable or disagreeable, in the steamer Earth, trusting to arrive at last at some less undulating Salop and brother's house?

I cannot say that I am surprised to hear that you have joined the militia, after what I have heard from your lips; but I am glad to doubt if there will be occasion for your volunteering into the line. Perhaps I am thinking of the saying that it "is always darkest just before day." I believe it is only necessary that England be fully awakened to a sense of her position, in order that she may right herself, especially as the weather will soon cease to be her foe. I wish I could believe that the cause in which you are embarked is the cause of the people of England. However, I have no sympathy with the idleness that would contrast this fighting with the teachings of the pulpit; for, perchance, more true virtue is being practiced at Sevastopol than in many years of peace. It is a pity that we seem to require a war, from time to time, to assure us that there is any manhood still left in man.

I was much pleased with [J. J. G.] Wilkinson's vigorous and telling assault on Allopathy, though he substitutes another and perhaps no stronger *thy* for that. Something as good on the whole conduct of the war would be of service. Cannot Carlyle supply it? We will not require him to provide the remedy. Every man to his trade. As you know, I am not in any sense a politician. You, who live in that snug and compact isle, may dream of a glorious commonwealth, but I have some doubts whether I and the new king of the Sandwich Islands shall pull together. When I think of the gold-diggers and the Mormons, the slaves and the slaveholders and the flibustiers, I naturally dream of a glorious private life. No, I am not patriotic; I shall not meddle with the Gem of the Antilles. General Quitman[56] cannot count on my aid, alas for him! nor can General Pierce.[57]

I still take my daily walk, or skate over Concord fields or meadows, and on the whole have more to do with nature than with man. We have not had much snow this winter, but have had some remarkably cold weather, the mercury, February 6, not rising above 6° below zero during the day, and the next morning falling to 26°. Some ice is still thirty inches thick about us. A rise in the river has made uncommonly good skating, which I have improved to the extent of some thirty miles a day, fifteen out and fifteen in.

Emerson is off westward, enlightening the Hamiltonians [in Canada] and others, mingling his thunder with that of Niagara. Channing still sits warming his five wits—his sixth, you know, is always limber—over that stove, with the dog down cellar. Lowell has just been appointed Professor of Belles-Lettres in Harvard University, in place of Longfellow, resigned, and will go very soon to spend another year in Europe, before taking his seat.

I am from time to time congratulating myself on my general want of success as a lecturer; apparent want of success, but is it not a real triumph? I do my work clean as I go along, and they will not be likely to want me anywhere again. So there is no danger of my repeating myself, and getting to a barrel of sermons, which you must upset, and begin again with.

My father and mother and sister all desire to be remembered to you, and trust that you will never come within range of Russian bullets. Of course, I would rather think of you as settled down there in Shropshire, in the camp of the English people, making acquaintance with your men, striking at the root of the evil, perhaps assaulting that rampart of cotton bags that you tell of. But it makes no odds where a man goes or stays, if he is only about his business.

Let me hear from you, wherever you are, and believe me yours ever in the good fight, whether before Sevastopol or under the wreken.

While Cholmondeley's first letter from England was on its way to Concord, Thoreau was one day making his occasional call at the Harvard College Library (where he found and was allowed to take away volumes relating to his manifold studies), when it occurred to him to call at my student-chamber in Holworthy Hall, and there leave a copy of his "Week." I had never met him, and was then out; the occasion of his call was a review of his two books that had come out a few weeks earlier in the *Harvard Magazine*, of which I was an editor and might be supposed to have had some share in the criticism. The volume was left with my classmate Lyman, accompanied by a message that it was intended for the critic in the Magazine. Accordingly, I gave it to Edwin Morton, who was the reviewer, and notified Thoreau by letter of that fact, and of my hope to see him soon in Cambridge or Concord.[58] To this he replied in a few days as below:—

TO F. B. SANBORN (AT HAMPTON FALLS, N. H.).

Concord, February 2, 1855.

Dear Sir,—I fear that you did not get the note which I left with the Librarian for you, and so will thank you again for your politeness. I was sorry that I was obliged to go into Boston almost immediately. However, I shall be glad to see you whenever you come to Concord, and I will suggest nothing to discourage your coming, so far as I am concerned; trusting that you know what it is to take a partridge on the wing. You tell me that the author of the criticism is Mr. Morton. I had heard as much,—and indeed guessed more. I have latterly found Concord nearer to Cambridge than I believed I should, when I was leaving my Alma Mater; and hence you will not be surprised if even I feel some interest in the success of the *Harvard Magazine*.

Believe me yours truly,
Henry D. Thoreau.

At this time I was under engagement with Mr. Emerson and others in Concord to take charge of a small school there in March; and did so without again seeing the author of "Walden" in Cambridge. Soon after my settlement at Concord, in the house of Mr. Channing, just opposite Thoreau's, he made an evening call on me and my sister (April 11, 1855), but I had already met him more than once at Mr. Emerson's, and was even beginning to take walks with him, as frequently happened in the next six years. In the following summer I began to dine daily at his mother's table, and thus saw him almost every day for three years.

TO HARRISON BLAKE (AT WORCESTER).

CONCORD, June 27, 1855.

MR. BLAKE,—I have been sick and good for nothing but to lie on my back and wait for something to turn up, for two or three months. This has *compelled me* to postpone several things, among them writing to you, to whom I am so deeply in debt, and inviting you and Brown to Concord,—not having brains adequate to such an exertion. I should feel a little less ashamed if I could give any name to my disorder,—but I cannot, and our doctor cannot help me to it, —and I will not take the name of any disease in vain. However, there is one consolation in being sick; and that is the possibility that you may recover to a better state than you were ever in before. I expected in the winter to be deep in the woods of Maine in my canoe, long before this; but I am so far from this that I can only take a languid walk in Concord streets.

I do not know how the mistake arose about the Cape Cod excursion. The nearest I have come to that with anybody is this: About a month ago Channing proposed to me to go to Truro on Cape Cod with him, and board there a while,—but I declined. For a week past, however, I have been a little inclined to go there and sit on the seashore a week or more; but I do not venture to propose myself as the companion of him or of any peripatetic man. Not that I should not rejoice to have you and Brown or C. sitting there also. I am not sure that C. really wishes to go now; and as I go simply for the medicine of it, I should not think it worth the while to notify him when I am about to take my bitters. Since I began this, or within five minutes, I have begun to think that I will start for Truro next Saturday morning, the 30th. I do not know at what hour the packet leaves Boston, nor exactly what kind of accommodation I shall find at Truro.

I should be singularly favored if you and Brown were there at the same time; and though you speak of the 20th of July, I will be so bold as to suggest your coming to Concord Friday night (when, by the way, Garrison and Phillips hold forth here), and going to the Cape with me. Though we take short walks together there, we can have *long* talks, and you and Brown will have time enough for your own excursions besides.

I received a letter from Cholmondeley last winter, which I should like to show you, as well as his book.[59] He said that he had "accepted the offer of a captaincy in the Salop Militia," and was hoping to take an active part in the war before long.

I thank you again and again for the encouragement your letters are to me. But I must stop this writing, or I shall have to pay for it.

North Truro, July 8, 1855.

There being no packet, I did not leave Boston till last Thursday, though I came down on Wednesday, and Channing with me. There is no public house here; but we are boarding in a little house attached to the Highland Lighthouse with Mr. James Small, the keeper. It is true the table is not so clean as could be desired, but I have found it much superior in that respect to a Provincetown hotel. They are what are called "good livers." Our host has another larger and very good house, within a quarter of a mile, unoccupied, where he says he can accommodate several more. He is a very good man to deal with,—has often been the representative of the town, and is perhaps the most intelligent man in it. I shall probably stay here as much as ten days longer. Board $3.50 per week. So you and Brown had better come down forthwith. You will find either the schooner Melrose or another, or both, leaving Commerce Street, or else T Wharf, at 9 A. M. (it commonly means 10), Tuesdays, Thursdays, and Saturdays,—if not other days. We left about 10
A. M., and reached Provincetown at 5 P. M.,—a very good run. A stage runs up the Cape every morning but Sunday, starting at 4½ A. M., and reaches the post-office in North Truro, seven miles from Provincetown, and one from the lighthouse, about 6 o'clock. If you arrive at P. before night, you can walk over, and leave your baggage to be sent. You can also come by cars from Boston to Yarmouth, and thence by stage forty miles more,—through every day, but it costs much more, and is not so pleasant. Come by all means, for it is the best place to see the ocean in the States.... I *hope* I shall be worth meeting.

July 14.

You say that you hope I will excuse your frequent writing. I trust you will excuse my infrequent and curt writing until I am able to resume my old habits, which for three months I have been compelled to abandon. Methinks I am beginning to be better. I think to leave the Cape next Wednesday, and so shall not see you here; but I shall be glad to meet you in Concord, though I may not be able to go *before the mast*, in a boating excursion. This is an admirable place for coolness and sea-bathing and retirement. You must come prepared for cool weather and fogs.

P. S.—There is no mail up till Monday morning.

During the spring and early summer of 1855, Thoreau was much occupied with his home duties, or was ill,—the earlier approaches of that disease of which he languished, taking medical advice in 1860-61. This must have prevented an earlier visit to Concord by his friend Ricketson than September, 1855, and I find no letters intervening, although there must have been one or two, to arrange the visit. He reached Concord about September 20, and found me living in the lower stories of Channing's house, while the owner chiefly occupied the attic, where, no doubt, as in the old Hunt house, Ricketson smoked with him. They went together to call on Edmund Hosmer, and it was at the sight of this old house that Ricketson formed the plan of occupying a chamber there. It stood a half-mile down the river, a little below where the Assabet runs into the main channel. Writing to Thoreau, Sunday, September 23, Ricketson said:—

"How charmingly you, Channing, and I dovetailed together! Few men smoke such pipes as we did,—the real Calumet; the tobacco that we smoked was free labor produce. I haven't lost sight of Solon Hosmer, the wisest-looking man in Concord, and a real *feelosofer*. I want you to see him, and tell him not to take down the old house where the *feelosofers* met. I think I should like to have the large chamber for an occasional sojourn in Concord. It can be easily tinkered up so as to be a comfortable roost for a *feelosofer*,—a few old chairs, a table, bed, etc., would be all-sufficient; then you and Channing could come over in your punt and rusticate."

The "punt" was Thoreau's boat, in which he sometimes set up a small mast and sail, and which he kept at the foot of Channing's garden, where, that summer, my heavy four-oared boat also lay, when my pupils were not rowing in it. In his letter to Blake of September 26, Thoreau described Ricketson, and the next day he answered Ricketson's letter. Cholmondeley in the meantime, the war being not yet over, was making his way to the Crimea through southern Europe.

TO HARRISON BLAKE (AT WORCESTER).

CONCORD, September 26, 1855.

MR. BLAKE,—The other day I thought that my health must be better,—that I gave at last a sign of vitality,—because I experienced a slight chagrin. But I do not see how strength is to be got into my legs again. These months of feebleness have yielded few, if any, thoughts, though they have not passed without serenity, such as our sluggish Musketaquid suggests. I hope that the harvest is to come. I trust that you have at least warped up the stream a little daily, holding fast by your anchors at night, since I saw you, and have kept my place for me while I have been absent.

Mr. Ricketson of New Bedford has just made me a visit of a day and a half, and I have had a quite good time with him. He and Channing have got on particularly well together. He is a man of very simple tastes, notwithstanding his wealth; a lover of nature; but, above all, singularly frank and plain-spoken. I think that you might enjoy meeting him.

Sincerity is a great but rare virtue, and we pardon to it much complaining, and the betrayal of many weaknesses. R. says of himself, that he sometimes thinks that he has all the infirmities of genius without the genius; is wretched without a hair pillow, etc.; expresses a great and awful uncertainty with regard to "God," "Death," his "immortality;" says, "If I only knew," etc. He loves Cowper's "Task" better than anything else; and thereafter perhaps, Thomson, Gray, and even Howitt. He has evidently suffered for want of sympathizing companions. He says that he sympathizes with much in my books, but much in them is naught to him,—"namby-pamby,"—"stuff,"—"mystical." Why will not I, having common sense, write in plain English always; *teach* men in detail how to live a simpler life, etc.; not go off into ——? But I say that I have no scheme about it,—no designs on men at all; and, if I had, my mode would be to tempt them with the fruit, and not with the manure. To what end do I lead a simple life at all, pray? That I may teach others to simplify their lives?—and so all our lives be *simplified* merely, like an algebraic formula? Or not, rather, that I may make use of the ground I have cleared, to live more worthily and profitably? I would fain lay the most stress forever on that which is the most important,—imports the most to me,—though it were only (what it is likely to be) a vibration in the air. As a preacher, I should be prompted to tell men, not so much how to get their wheat bread cheaper, as of the bread of life compared with which *that* is bran. Let a man only taste these loaves, and he becomes a skillful economist at once. He'll not waste much time in earning those. Don't spend your time in drilling soldiers, who may turn out hirelings after all, but give to undrilled peasantry a *country* to fight for. The schools begin with what they call the elements, and where do they end?

I was glad to hear the other day that Higginson and —— were gone to Ktaadn; it must be so much better to go to than a Woman's Rights or Abolition Convention; better still, to the delectable primitive mounts within you, which you have dreamed of from your youth up, and seen, perhaps, in the horizon, but never climbed.

But how do *you* do? Is the air sweet to you? Do you find anything at which you can work, accomplishing something solid from day to day? Have you put sloth and doubt behind, considerably?—had one redeeming dream this summer? I dreamed, last night, that I could vault over any height it pleased me. That was *something*; and I contemplated myself with a slight satisfaction in the morning for it.

Methinks I will write to you. Methinks you will be glad to hear. We will stand on solid foundations to one another,—I a column planted on this shore, you on that. We meet the same sun in his rising. We were built slowly, and have come to our bearing. We will not mutually fall over that we may meet, but will grandly and eternally guard the straits. Methinks I see an inscription on you, which the architect made, the stucco being worn off to it. The name of that ambitious worldly king is crumbling away. I see it toward sunset in favorable lights. Each must read for the other, as might a sailer-by. Be sure you are star-y-pointing still. How is it on your side? I will not require an answer until you think I have paid my debts to you.

I have just got a letter from Ricketson, urging me to come to New Bedford, which possibly I may do. He says I can wear my old clothes there.

Let me be remembered in your quiet house.

TO DANIEL RICKETSON (AT NEW BEDFORD).

CONCORD, September 27, 1855.

FRIEND RICKETSON,—I am sorry that you were obliged to leave Concord without seeing more of it,—its river and woods, and various pleasant walks, and its worthies. I assure you that I am none the worse for my walk with you, but on all accounts the better. Methinks I am regaining my health; but I would like to know first what it was that ailed me.

I have not yet conveyed your message to Mr. Hosmer,[60] but will not fail to do so. That idea of occupying the old house is a good one,—quite feasible,—and you could bring your hair pillow with you. It is an *inn* in Concord which I had not thought of,—a philosopher's inn. That large chamber might make a man's idea expand proportionately. It would be well to have an interest in some old chamber in a deserted house in every part of the country which attracted us. There would be no such place to receive one's guests as that. If old furniture is fashionable, why not go the whole house at once? I shall endeavor to make Mr. Hosmer believe that the old house is the chief attraction of his farm, and that it is his duty to preserve it by all honest appliances. You might take a lease of it *in perpetuo*, and done with it.

I am so wedded to my way of spending a day,—require such broad margins of leisure, and such a complete wardrobe of old clothes,—that I am ill fitted for going abroad. Pleasant is it sometimes to sit at home, on a single egg all day, in your own nest, though it may prove at last to be an egg of chalk. The old coat that I wear is Concord; it is my morning robe and study gown, my working dress and suit of ceremony, and my nightgown after all. Cleave to the simplest ever. Home,—home,—home. *Cars* sound like *cares* to me.

I am accustomed to think very long of going anywhere,—am slow to move. I hope to hear a response of the oracle first. However, I think that I will try the effect of your talisman on the iron horse next Saturday, and dismount at Tarkiln Hill. Perhaps your sea air will be good for me. I conveyed your invitation to Channing, but he apparently will not come.

Excuse my not writing earlier; but I had not decided.

TO DANIEL RICKETSON (AT NEW BEDFORD).

Concord, October 12, 1855.

Mr. Ricketson,—I fear that you had a lonely and disagreeable ride back to New Bedford through the Carver woods and so on,—perhaps in the rain, too, and I am in part answerable for it. I feel very much in debt to you and your family for the pleasant days I spent at Brooklawn. Tell Arthur and Walton[61] that the shells which they gave me are spread out, and make quite a show to inland eyes. Methinks I still hear the strains of the piano, the violin, and the flageolet blended together. Excuse *me* for the noise which I believe drove you to take refuge in the shanty. That shanty is indeed a favorable place to expand in, which I fear I did not enough improve.

On my way through Boston I inquired for Gilpin's works at Little, Brown & Co.'s, Munroe's, Ticknor's, and Burnham's. They have not got them. They told me at Little, Brown & Co.'s that his works (not complete), in twelve vols., 8vo, were imported and sold in this country five or six years ago for about fifteen dollars. Their terms for importing are ten per cent on the cost. I copied from the "London Catalogue of Books, 1846-51," at their shop, the following list of Gilpin's Works:—

Gilpin (Wm.), Dialogues on Various Subjects. 8vo. 9*s*.	Cadell.
—— Essays on Picturesque Subjects. 8vo. 15*s*.	Cadell.
—— Exposition of the New Testament. 2 vols. 8vo. 16*s*.	Longman.
—— Forest Scenery, by Sir T. D. Lauder. 2 vols. 8vo. 18*s*.	Smith & E.
—— Lectures on the Catechism. 12mo. 3*s*. 6*d*.	Longman.
—— Lives of the Reformers. 2 vols. 12mo. 8*s*.	Rivington.
—— Sermons Illustrative and Practical. 8vo. 12*s*.	Hatchard.
—— Sermons to Country Congregations. 4 vols. 8vo. £1 16*s*.	Longman.

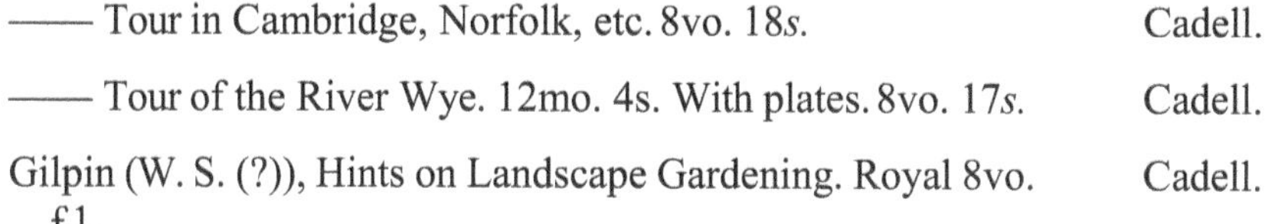

—— Tour in Cambridge, Norfolk, etc. 8vo. 18*s*.	Cadell.
—— Tour of the River Wye. 12mo. 4s. With plates. 8vo. 17*s*.	Cadell.
Gilpin (W. S. (?)), Hints on Landscape Gardening. Royal 8vo. £1.	Cadell.

Beside these, I remember to have read one volume on "Prints;" his "Southern Tour" (1775); "Lakes of Cumberland," two vols.; "Highlands of Scotland and West of England," two vols.—*N. B.* There *must* be plates in every volume.

I still see an image of those Middleborough ponds in my mind's eye,—broad shallow lakes, with an iron mine at the bottom,—comparatively unvexed by sails,—only by Tom Smith and his squaw Sepit's "sharper." I find my map of the State to be the best I have seen of that district. It is a question whether the islands of Long Pond or Great Quitticus offer the greatest attractions to a Lord of the Isles. That plant which I found on the shore of Long Pond chances to be a rare and beautiful flower,—the *Sabbatia chloroides*,—referred to Plymouth.

In a Description of Middleborough in the Hist. Coll., vol. iii, 1810, signed Nehemiah Bennet, Middleborough, 1793, it is said: "There is on the easterly shore of Assawampsitt Pond, on the shore of Betty's Neck, two rocks which have curious marks thereon (supposed to be done by the Indians), which appear like the steppings of a person with naked feet which settled into the rocks; likewise the prints of a hand on several places, with a number of other marks; also there is a rock on a high hill a little to the eastward of the old stone fishing wear, where there is the print of a person's hand in said rock."

It would be well to look at those rocks again more carefully; also at the rock on the hill.

I should think that you would like to explore Snipatuit Pond in Rochester,—it is so large and near. It is an interesting fact that the alewives used to ascend to it,—if they do not still,—both from Mattapoisett and through Great Quitticus.

There will be no trouble about the chamber in the old house, though, as I told you, Mr. Hosmer *may* expect some compensation for it. He says, "Give my respects to Mr. Ricketson, and tell him that I cannot be at a large expense to preserve an antiquity or curiosity. Nature must do its work." "But," says I, "he asks you only not to assist nature."

It was on October 1 that Thoreau made this visit to New Bedford, spending the best part of a week with his friends there. They sailed about the bay and visited the ponds in Middleborough, and on Saturday, October 6, he parted with Ricketson at Plymouth, and returned home. At that time Ricketson proposed to return Thoreau's visit before October 20, but, in a note now lost,

Thoreau sent him word that Channing had left Concord, "perhaps for the winter." The visit was then given up,—which accounts for the tone of Thoreau's next letter, of October 16.

TO DANIEL RICKETSON (AT NEW BEDFORD).

Concord, October 16, 1855.

Friend Ricketson,—I have got both your letters at once. You must not think Concord so barren a place when Channing[62] is away. There are the river and fields left yet; and I, though ordinarily a man of business, should have some afternoons and evenings to spend with you, I trust,—that is, if you could stand so much of me. If you can spend your time profitably here, or without *ennui*, having an occasional ramble or *tête-à-tête* with one of the natives, it will give me pleasure to have you in the neighborhood. You see I am preparing you for our awful unsocial ways,—keeping in our dens a good part of the day,—sucking our claws perhaps. But then we make a religion of it, and that you cannot but respect.

If you know the taste of your own heart, and like it, come to Concord, and I'll warrant you enough here to season the dish with,—aye, even though Channing and Emerson and I were all away. We might paddle quietly up the river. Then there are one or two more ponds to be seen, etc.

I should very much enjoy further rambling with you in your vicinity, but must postpone it for the present. To tell the truth, I am planning to get seriously to work after these long months of inefficiency and idleness. I do not know whether you are haunted by any such demon which puts you on the alert to pluck the fruit of each day as it passes, and store it safely in your bin. True, it is well to live abandonedly from time to time; but to our working hours that must be as the spile to the bung. So for a long season I must enjoy only a low slanting gleam in my mind's eye from the Middleborough ponds faraway.

Methinks I am getting a little more strength into those knees of mine; and, for my part, I believe that God *does* delight in the strength of a man's legs.

TO HARRISON BLAKE (AT WORCESTER).

Concord, December 9, 1855.

Mr. Blake,—Thank you! thank you for going a-wooding with me,—and enjoying it,—for being warmed by my wood fire. I have indeed enjoyed it much alone. I see how I might enjoy it yet more with company,—how we might help each other to live. And to be admitted to Nature's hearth costs nothing. None is excluded, but excludes himself. You have only to push aside the curtain.

I am glad to hear that you were there too. There are many more such voyages, and longer ones, to be made on that river, for it is the water of life. The Ganges is nothing to it. Observe its reflections,—no idea but is familiar to it. That river, though to dull eyes it seems terrestrial wholly, flows through Elysium. What powers bathe in it invisible to villagers! Talk of its shallowness,—that hay-carts can be driven through it at midsummer; its depth passeth my understanding. If, forgetting the allurements of the world, I could drink deeply enough of it; if, cast adrift from the shore, I could with complete integrity float on it, I should never be seen on the Mill-Dam again.[63] If there is any depth in me, there is a corresponding depth in it. It is the cold blood of the gods. I paddle and bathe in their artery.

I do not want a stick of wood for so trivial a use as to burn even, but they get it overnight, and carve and gild it that it may please my eye. What persevering lovers they are! What infinite pains to attract and delight us! They will supply us with fagots wrapped in the daintiest packages, and freight paid; sweet-scented woods, and bursting into flower, and resounding as if Orpheus had just left them,—these shall be our fuel, and we still prefer to chaffer with the wood-merchant!

The jug we found still stands draining bottom up on the bank, on the sunny side of the house. That river,—who shall say exactly whence it came, and whither it goes? Does aught that flows come from a higher source? Many things drift downward on its surface which would enrich a man. If you could only be on the alert all day, and every day! And the nights are as long as the days.

Do you not think you could contrive thus to get woody fibre enough to bake your wheaten bread with? Would you not perchance have tasted the sweet crust of another kind of bread in the meanwhile, which ever hangs ready baked on the bread-fruit trees of the world?

Talk of burning your smoke after the wood has been consumed! There is a far more important and warming heat, commonly lost, which precedes the burning of the wood. It is the smoke of industry, which is incense. I had been so thoroughly warmed in body and spirit, that when at length my fuel was housed, I came near selling it to the ash-man, as if I had extracted all its heat.

You should have been here to help me get in my boat. The last time I used it, November 27th, paddling up the Assabet, I saw a great round pine log sunk deep in the water, and with labor got it aboard. When I was floating this home so gently, it occurred to me why I had found it. It was to make wheels with to roll my boat into winter quarters upon. So I sawed off two thick rollers from one end, pierced them for wheels, and then of a joist which I had found drifting on the river in the summer I made an axletree, and on this I rolled my boat out.

Miss Mary Emerson[64] is here,—the youngest person in Concord, though about eighty,—and the most apprehensive of a genuine thought; earnest to know of your inner life; most stimulating society; and exceedingly witty withal. She says they called her old when she was young, and she has never grown any older. I wish you could see her.

My books[65] did not arrive till November 30th, the cargo of the Asia having been complete when they reached Liverpool. I have arranged them in a case which I made in the meanwhile, partly of river boards. I have not dipped far into the new ones yet. One is splendidly bound and illuminated. They are in English, French, Latin, Greek, and Sanscrit. I have not made out the significance of this godsend yet.

Farewell, and bright dreams to you!

TO DANIEL RICKETSON (AT NEW BEDFORD).

Concord, December 25, 1855.

Friend Ricketson,—Though you have not shown your face here, I trust that you did not interpret my last note to my disadvantage. I remember that, among other things, I wished to break it to you, that, owing to engagements, I should not be able to show you so much attention as I could wish, or as you had shown to me. How we did scour over the country! I hope your horse will live as long as one which I hear just died in the south of France at the age of forty. Yet I had no doubt you would get quite enough of me. Do not give it up so easily. The old house is still empty, and Hosmer is easy to treat with.

Channing was here about ten days ago. I told him of my visit to you, and that he too must go and see you and your country.[66] This may have suggested his writing to you.

That island lodge, especially for some weeks in a summer, and new explorations in your vicinity, are certainly very alluring; but *such are my engagements to myself*, that I dare not promise to wend your way, but will for the present only heartily thank you for your kind and generous offer. When my vacation comes, then look out.

My legs have grown considerably stronger, and that is all that ails me.

But I wish now above all to inform you,—though I suppose you will not be particularly interested,—that Cholmondeley has gone to the Crimea, "a complete soldier," with a design, when he returns, if he ever returns, to buy a cottage in the South of England, and tempt me over; but that, before going, he busied himself in buying, and has caused to be forwarded to me by Chapman, a royal gift, in the shape of twenty-one distinct works (one in nine volumes,—forty-four volumes in all), almost exclusively relating to ancient Hindoo literature, and scarcely one of them to be bought in America.[67] I am familiar with many of them, and know how to prize them. I send you information of this as I might of the birth of a child.

Please remember me to all your family.

On the date of Thoreau's letter of December 25, 1855, another event occurred, of some note in these annals of friendship. Channing, from his Dorchester abode, suddenly showed himself at Ricketson's door. "I had just written his name when old Ranger announced him.... He arrived on Christmas day" (as Thoreau had done the year before) "and his first salutation on meeting me at the front door of my house was, 'That's your shanty,' pointing towards it. He is engaged with the editor of the N. B. *Mercury*, and boards in town, but whereabout I have not yet [February 26, 1856] discovered. He usually spends Saturday and a part of Sunday with me." In replying to this information, Thoreau gives that admirable character of his poet neighbor which has often been quoted.

TO DANIEL RICKETSON (AT NEW BEDFORD).

Concord, March 5, 1856.

Friend Ricketson,—I have been out of town, else I should have acknowledged your letter before. Though not in the best mood for writing, I will say what I can now. You plainly have a rare, though a cheap, resource in your shanty. Perhaps the time will come when every country-seat will have one,—when every country-seat will *be one*. I would advise you to see that shanty business out, though you go shanty-mad. Work your vein till it is exhausted, or conducts you to a broader one; so that Channing shall stand before your shanty, and say, "That is your house."

This has indeed been a grand winter for me, and for all of us. I am not considering how much I have enjoyed it. What matters it how happy or unhappy we have been, if we have minded our business and advanced our affairs? I have made it a part of my business to wade in the snow and take the measure of the ice. The ice on one of our ponds was just two feet thick on the first of March; and I have to-day been surveying a wood-lot, where I sank about two feet at every step.

It is high time that you, fanned by the warm breezes of the Gulf Stream, had begun to "*lay*" for even the Concord hens have, though one wonders where they find the raw material of egg-shell here. Beware how you put off your laying to any later spring, else your cackling will not have the inspiring early spring sound.

I was surprised to hear the other day that Channing was in New Bedford. When he was here last (in December, I think), he said, like himself, in answer to my inquiry where he lived, “that he did not know the name of the place;” so it has remained in a degree of obscurity to me. As you have made it certain to me that he is in New Bedford, perhaps I can return the favor by putting you on the track to his boarding-house there. Mrs. Arnold told Mrs. Emerson where it was; and the latter thinks, though she may be mistaken, that it was at a Mrs. Lindsay’s.

I am rejoiced to hear that you are getting on so bravely with him and his verses. He and I, as you know, have been old cronies,[68] —

Fed the same flock, by fountain, shade, and rill,

Together both, ere the high lawns appeared

Under the opening eyelids of the morn,

We drove afield, and both together heared," etc.

"But O, the heavy change," now he is gone. The Channing you have seen and described is the real Simon Pure. You have seen him. Many a good ramble may you have together! You will see in him still more of the same kind to attract and to puzzle you. How to serve him most effectually has long been a problem with his friends. Perhaps it is left for you to solve it. I suspect that the most that you or any one can do for him is to appreciate his genius,—to buy and read, and cause others to buy and read, his poems. That is the hand which he has put forth to the world,—take hold of that. Review them if you can,—perhaps take the risk of publishing something more which he may write. Your knowledge of Cowper will help you to know Channing. He will accept sympathy and aid, but he will not bear questioning, unless the aspects of the sky are particularly auspicious. He will ever be "reserved and enigmatic," and you must deal with him at arm's length.

I have no secrets to tell you concerning him, and do not wish to call obvious excellences and defects by far-fetched names. I think I have already spoken to you more, and more to the purpose, on this theme, than I am likely to write now; nor need I suggest how witty and poetic he is, and what an inexhaustible fund of good fellowship you will find in him.

As for visiting you in April, though I am inclined enough to take some more rambles in your neighborhood, especially by the seaside, I dare not engage myself, nor allow you to expect me. The truth is, I have my enterprises now as ever, at which I tug with ridiculous feebleness, but admirable perseverance, and cannot say when I shall be sufficiently fancy-free for such an excursion.

You have done well to write a lecture on Cowper. In the expectation of getting you to read it here, I applied to the curators of our Lyceum;[69] but, alas, our Lyceum has been a failure this winter for want of funds. It ceased some weeks since, with a debt, they tell me, to be carried over to the next year's account. Only one more lecture is to be read by a Signor Somebody, an Italian, paid for by private subscription, as a deed of charity to the lecturer. They are not rich enough to offer you your expenses even, though probably a month or two ago they would have been glad of the chance.

However, the old house has not failed yet. That offers you lodging for an indefinite time after you get into it; and in the meanwhile I offer you bed and board in my father's house,—always excepting hair pillows and new-fangled bedding.

Remember me to your family.

TO HARRISON BLAKE (AT WORCESTER).

CONCORD, March 13, 1856.

MR. BLAKE,—It is high time I sent you a word. I have not heard from Harrisburg since offering to go there, and have not been invited to lecture anywhere else the past winter. So you see I am fast growing rich. This is quite right, for such is my relation to the lecture-goers, I should be surprised and alarmed if there were any great call for me. I confess that I am considerably alarmed even when I hear that an individual wishes to meet me, for my experience teaches me that we shall thus only be made certain of a mutual strangeness, which otherwise we might never have been aware of.

I have not yet recovered strength enough for such a walk as you propose, though pretty well again for circumscribed rambles and chamber work. Even now, I am probably the greatest walker in Concord,—to its disgrace be it said. I remember our walks and talks and sailing in the past with great satisfaction, and trust that we shall have more of them ere long,—have more woodings-up, —for even in the spring we must still seek "fuel to maintain our fires."

As you suggest, we would fain value one another for what we are absolutely, rather than relatively. How will this do for a symbol of sympathy?

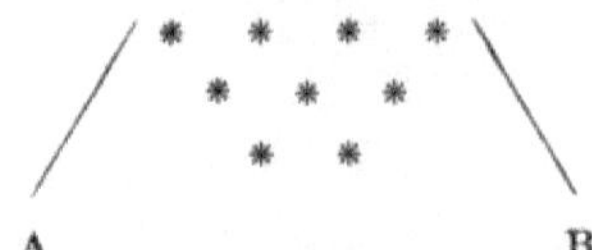

As for compliments, even the stars praise me, and I praise them. They and I sometimes belong to a mutual admiration society. Is it not so with you? I know you of old. Are you not tough and earnest to be talked at, praised, or blamed? Must *you* go out of the room because you are the subject of conversation? Where will you go to, pray? Shall we look into the "Letter Writer" to see what compliments are admissible? I am not afraid of praise, for I have practiced it on myself. As for my deserts, I never took an account of that stock, and in this connection care not whether I am deserving or not. When I hear praise coming, do I not elevate and arch myself to hear it like the sky, and as impersonally? Think I appropriate any of it to my weak legs? No. Praise away *till all is blue.*

I see by the newspapers that the season for making sugar is at hand. Now is the time, whether you be rock, or white maple, or hickory. I trust that you have prepared a store of sap-tubs and sumach spouts, and invested largely in kettles. Early the first frosty morning, tap your maples,—the sap will not run in summer, you know. It matters not how little juice you get, if you get all you can, and boil it down. I made just one crystal of sugar once, one twentieth of an inch cube, out of a pumpkin, and it sufficed. Though the yield be no greater than that, this is not less the season for it, and it will be not the less sweet, nay, it will be infinitely the sweeter.

Shall, then, the maple yield sugar, and not man? Shall the farmer be thus active, and surely have so much sugar to show for it, before this very March is gone,—while I read the newspaper? While he works in his sugar-camp let me work in mine,—for sweetness is in me, and to sugar it shall come,—it shall not all go to leaves and wood. Am I not a *sugar maple* man, then? Boil down the sweet sap which the spring causes to flow within you. Stop not at syrup,—go on to sugar, though you present the world with but a single crystal,—a crystal not made from trees in your yard, but from the new life that stirs in your pores. Cheerfully skim your kettle, and watch it set and crystallize, making a holiday of it if you will. Heaven will be propitious to you as to him.

Say to the farmer: There is your crop; here is mine. Mine is a sugar to sweeten sugar with. If you will listen to me, I will sweeten your whole load,—your whole life.

Then will the callers ask, Where is Blake? He is in his sugar-camp on the mountainside. Let the world await him. Then will the little boys bless you, and the great boys too, for such sugar is the origin of many condiments,—Blakians in the shops of Worcester, of new form, with their mottoes wrapped up in them. Shall men taste only the sweetness of the maple and the cane the coming year?

A walk over the crust to Asnebumskit, standing there in its inviting simplicity, is tempting to think of,—making a fire on the snow under some rock! The very poverty of outward nature implies an inward wealth in the walker. What a Golconda is he conversant with, thawing his fingers over such a blaze! But—but—

Have you read the new poem, "The Angel in the House"? Perhaps you will find it good for you.

TO HARRISON BLAKE (AT WORCESTER).

CONCORD, May 21, 1856.

MR. BLAKE,—I have not for a long time been *putting such thoughts together* as I should like to read to the company you speak of. I have enough of that sort to say, or even read, but not time now to arrange it. Something I have prepared might prove for their entertainment or refreshment perchance; but I would not like to have a hat carried round for it. I have just been reading some papers to see if they would do for your company; but though I thought pretty well of them as long as I read them to myself, when I got an auditor to try them on, I felt that they would not answer. How could I let you drum up a company to hear them? In fine, what I have is either too scattered or loosely arranged, or too light, or else is too scientific and matter-of-fact (I run a good deal into that of late) for so hungry a company.

I am still a learner, not a teacher, feeding somewhat omnivorously, browsing both stalk and leaves; but I shall perhaps be enabled to speak with the more precision and authority by and by,—if philosophy and sentiment are not buried under a multitude of details.

I do not refuse, but accept your invitation, only changing the time. I consider myself invited to Worcester once for all, and many thanks to the inviter. As for the Harvard excursion,[70] will you let me suggest another? Do you and Brown come to Concord on Saturday, if the weather promises well, and spend the Sunday here on the river or hills, or both. So we shall save some of our money (which is of next importance to our souls), and lose—I do not know what. You say you *talked* of coming here before; now *do* it. I do not propose this because I think that I am worth your spending time with, but because I hope that we may prove flint and steel to one another. It is at most only an hour's ride farther, and you can at any rate do what you please when you get here.

Then we will see if we have any apology to offer for our existence. So come to Concord,—come to Concord,—come to Concord! or—your suit shall be defaulted.

As for the dispute about solitude and society, any comparison is impertinent. It is an idling down on the plane at the base of a mountain, instead of climbing steadily to its top. Of course you will be glad of all the society you can get to go up with. Will you go to glory with me? is the burden of the song. I love society so much that I swallowed it all at a gulp,—that is, all that came in my way. It is not that we love to be alone, but that we love to soar, and when we do soar, the company grows thinner and thinner till there is none at all. It is either the *Tribune*[71] on the plain, a sermon on the mount, or a very private ecstasy still higher up. We are not the less to aim at the summits, though the multitude does not ascend them. Use all the society that will abet you. But perhaps I do not enter into the spirit of your talk.

In the spring of 1856, Mr. Alcott, then living in Walpole, N. H., visited Concord, and while there suggested to Thoreau that the upper valley of the Connecticut, in which Walpole lies, was good walking-ground, and that he would be glad to see him there. When autumn began to hover in the distance,

Thoreau recalled this invitation, and sent the letter below.

TO BRONSON ALCOTT (AT WALPOLE, N. H.).

CONCORD, September 1, 1856.

MR. ALCOTT,—I remember that, in the spring, you invited me to visit you. I feel inclined to spend a day or two with you and on your hills at this season, returning, perhaps, by way of Brattleboro. What if I should take the cars for Walpole next Friday morning? Are you at home? And will it be convenient and agreeable to you to see me then? I will await an answer.

I am but poor company, and it will not be worth the while to put yourself out on my account; yet from time to time I have some thoughts which would be the better for an airing. I also wish to get some hints from September on the Connecticut to help me understand that season on the Concord; to snuff the musty fragrance of the decaying year in the primitive woods. There is considerable cellar-room in my nature for such stores; a whole row of bins waiting to be filled, before I can celebrate my Thanksgiving. Mould is the richest of soils, yet *I* am not mould. It will always be found that one flourishing institution exists and battens on another mouldering one. The Present itself is parasitic to this extent.

Your fellow-traveler,
HENRY D. THOREAU.

As fortune would have it, Mr. Alcott was then making his arrangements for a conversational tour in the vicinity of New York; but he renewed the invitation for himself, while repeating it in the name of Mrs. Alcott and his daughters. Thoreau made the visit, I believe, and some weeks later, at the suggestion of Mr. Alcott, he was asked by Marcus Spring of New York to give lectures and survey their estate for a community at Perth Amboy, N. J., in which Mr. Spring and his friends, the Birneys, Welds, Grimkés, etc., had united for social and educational purposes. It was a colony of radical opinions and old-fashioned culture; the Grimkés having been bred in Charleston, S. C., which they left by reason of their opposition to negro slavery, and the elder Birney having held slaves in Alabama until his conscience bade him emancipate them, after which he, too, could have no secure home among slaveholders. He was the first presidential candidate of the voting Abolitionists, as Lincoln was the last; and his friend, Theodore Weld, who married Miss Grimké, had been one of the early apostles of emancipation in Ohio. Their circle at Eagleswood appealed to Thoreau's sense of humor, and is described by him in a letter soon to be given.

In June, 1856, Thoreau made a long visit at Brooklawn. In August, Mr. Ricketson, who had proposed a summer visit to Concord, found himself prevented by feeble health, and received the two following letters from Thoreau:—

TO DANIEL RICKETSON (AT NEW BEDFORD).

CONCORD, September 2, 1856.

FRIEND RICKETSON,—My father and mother regret that your indisposition is likely to prevent your coming to Concord at present. It is as well that you do not, if you depend on seeing me, for I expect to go to New Hampshire the latter part of the week. I shall be glad to see you afterward, if you are prepared for and can endure my unsocial habits.

I would suggest that you have one or two of the teeth which you can best spare extracted at once, for the sake of your general, no less than particular health. This is the advice of one who has had quite his share of toothache in this world. I am a trifle stouter than when I saw you last, yet far, far short of my best estate.

I thank you for two newspapers which you have sent me; am glad to see that you have studied out the history of the ponds, got the Indian names straightened,—which means made more crooked,—etc., etc. I remember them with great satisfaction. They are all the more interesting to me for the lean and sandy soil that surrounds them. Heaven is not one of your fertile Ohio bottoms, you may depend on it. Ah, the Middleborough ponds!—Great Platte lakes. Remember me to the perch in them. I trust that I may have some better craft than that oarless pumpkin-seed[72] the next time I navigate them.

From the size of your family I infer that Mrs. Ricketson and your daughters have returned from Franconia. Please remember me to them, and also to Arthur and Walton; and tell the latter that if, in the course of his fishing, he should chance to come across the shell of a terrapin, and will save it for me, I shall be exceedingly obliged to him.

Channing dropped in on us the other day, but soon dropped out again.

CONCORD, September 23, 1856.

FRIEND RICKETSON,—I have returned from New Hampshire, and find myself *in statu quo*. My journey proved one of business purely. As you suspected, I saw Alcott, and I spoke to him of you, and your good will toward him; so now you may consider yourself introduced. He would be glad to hear from you about a conversation in New Bedford. He was about setting out on a conversing tour to Fitchburg, Worcester, and, three or four weeks hence, Waterbury, Ct., New York, Newport (?) or Providence (?). You may be sure that you will not have occasion to repent of any exertions which you may make to secure an audience for him. I send you one of his programmes, lest he should not have done so himself.

You propose to me teaching the following winter. I find that I cannot entertain the idea. It would require such a revolution of all my habits, I think, and would sap the very foundations of me. I am engaged to Concord and my own private pursuits by 10,000 ties, and it would be suicide to rend them. If I were weaker, and not somewhat stronger, physically, I should be more tempted. I am so busy that I cannot even think of visiting you. The days are not long enough, or I am not strong enough to do the work of the day, before bedtime.

Excuse my paper. It chances to be the best I have.

In October, 1856, Mr. Spring, whom Mr. Alcott was then visiting, wrote to Thoreau inviting him to come to Eagleswood, give lectures, and survey two hundred acres of land belonging to the community, laying out streets and making a map of the proposed village. Thoreau accepted the proposal, and soon after wrote the following letter, which Miss Thoreau submitted to Mr. Emerson for publication, with other letters, in the volume of 1865; but he returned it, inscribed, "Not printable at present." The lapse of time has removed this objection.

TO SOPHIA THOREAU.

[Direct] Eagleswood, Perth Amboy, N. J.,

Saturday eve, November 1, 1856.

Dear Sophia,—I have hardly had time and repose enough to write to you before. I spent the afternoon of Friday (it seems some months ago) in Worcester, but failed to see [Harrison] Blake, he having "gone to the horse-race" in Boston; to atone for which I have just received a letter from him, asking me to stop at Worcester and lecture on my return. I called on [Theo.] Brown and [T. W.] Higginson; in the evening came by way of Norwich to New York in the steamer Commonwealth, and, though it was so windy inland, had a perfectly smooth passage, and about as good a sleep as usually at home. Reached New York about seven A. M., too late for the John Potter (there was n't any Jonas), so I spent the forenoon there, called on Greeley (who was not in), met [F. A. T.] Bellew in Broadway and walked into his workshop, read at the Astor Library, etc. I arrived here, about thirty miles from New York, about five P. M. Saturday, in company with Miss E. Peabody, who was returning in the same covered wagon from the Landing to Eagleswood, which last place she has just left for the winter.

This is a queer place. There is one large long stone building, which cost some forty thousand dollars, in which I do not know exactly who or how many work (one or two familiar places and more familiar names have turned up), a few shops and offices, an old farmhouse, and Mr. Spring's perfectly private residence, within twenty rods of the main building. The city of Perth Amboy is about as big as Concord, and Eagleswood is one and a quarter miles southwest of it, on the Bay side. The central fact here is evidently Mr. [Theodore] Weld's school, recently established, around which various other things revolve. Saturday evening I went to the schoolroom, hall, or what not, to see the children and their teachers and patrons dance. Mr. Weld, a kind-looking man with a long white beard, danced with them, and Mr. [E. J.] Cutler, his assistant (lately from Cambridge, who is acquainted with Sanborn), Mr. Spring, and others. This Saturday evening dance is a regular thing, and it is thought something strange if you don't attend. They take it for granted that you want society!

Sunday forenoon I attended a sort of Quaker meeting at the same place (the Quaker aspect and spirit prevail here,—Mrs. Spring says, "Does thee not?"), where it was expected that the Spirit would move me (I having been previously spoken to about it); and it, or something else, did,—an inch or so. I said just enough to set them a little by the ears and make it lively. I had excused myself by saying that I could not adapt myself to a particular audience; for all the speaking and lecturing here have reference to the children, who are far the greater part of the audience, and they are not so bright as New England children. Imagine them sitting close to the wall, all around a hall, with old Quaker-looking men and women here and there. There sat Mrs. Weld [Grimké] and her sister, two elderly gray-headed ladies, the former in extreme Bloomer costume, which was what you may call remarkable; Mr. Arnold Buffum, with broad face and a great white beard, looking like a pier-head made of the cork-tree with the bark on, as if he could buffet a considerable wave; James G. Birney, formerly candidate for the presidency, with another particularly white head and beard; Edward Palmer, the anti-money man (for whom communities were made), with his ample beard somewhat grayish. Some of them, I suspect, are very worthy people. Of course you are wondering to what extent all these make one family, and to what extent twenty. Mrs. Kirkland[73] (and this a name only to me) I saw. She has just bought a lot here. They all know more about your neighbors and acquaintances than you suspected.

On Monday evening I read the moose story to the children, to their satisfaction. Ever since I have been constantly engaged in surveying Eagleswood,—through woods, salt marshes, and along the shore, dodging the tide, through bushes, mud, and beggar-ticks, having no time to look up or think where I am. (It takes ten or fifteen minutes before each meal to pick the beggar-ticks out of my clothes; burs and the rest are left, and rents mended at the first convenient opportunity.) I shall be engaged perhaps as much longer. Mr. Spring wants me to help him about setting out an orchard and vineyard,

Mr. Birney asks me to survey a small piece for him, and Mr. Alcott, who has just come down here for the third Sunday, says that Greeley (I left my name for him) invites him and me to go to his home with him next Saturday morning and spend the Sunday.

It seems a twelvemonth since I was not here, but I hope to get settled deep into my den again ere long. The hardest thing to find here is solitude—and Concord. I am at Mr. Spring's house. Both he and she and their family are quite agreeable.

I want you to write to me immediately (just left off to talk French with the servant man), and let father and mother put in a word. To them and to Aunts, love from

HENRY.

The date of this visit to Eagleswood is worthy of note, because in that November Thoreau made the acquaintance of the late Walt Whitman, in whom he ever after took a deep interest. Accompanied by Mr. Alcott, he called on Whitman, then living at Brooklyn; and I remember the calm enthusiasm with which they both spoke of Whitman upon their return to Concord. "Three men," said Emerson, in his funeral eulogy of Thoreau, "have of late years strongly impressed Mr. Thoreau,—John Brown, his Indian guide in Maine, Joe Polis, and a third person, not known to this audience." This last was Whitman, who has since become well known to a largeraudience.

TO HARRISON BLAKE (AT WORCESTER).

EAGLESWOOD, N. J., November 19, 1856.

MR. BLAKE,—I have been here much longer than I expected, but have deferred answering you, because I could not foresee when I should return. I do not know yet within three or four days. This uncertainty makes it impossible for me to appoint a day to meet you, until it should be too late to hear from you again. I think, therefore, that I must go straight home. I feel some objection to reading that "What shall it profit" lecture again in Worcester; but if you are quite sure that it will be worth the while (it is a grave consideration), I will even make an independent journey from Concord for that purpose. I have read three of my old lectures (that included) to the Eagleswood people, and, unexpectedly, with rare success,—*i. e.*, I was aware that what I was saying was silently taken in by their ears.

You must excuse me if I write mainly a business letter now, for I am sold for the time,—am merely Thoreau the surveyor here,—and solitude is scarcely obtainable in these parts.

Alcott has been here three times, and, Saturday before last, I went with him and Greeley, by invitation of the last, to G.'s farm, thirty-six miles north of New York. The next day A. and I heard Beecher preach; and what was more, we visited Whitman the next morning (A. had already seen him), and were much interested and provoked. He is apparently the greatest democrat the world has seen. Kings and aristocracy go by the board at once, as they have long deserved to. A remarkably strong though coarse nature, of a sweet disposition, and much prized by his friends. Though peculiar and rough in his exterior, his skin (all over (?)) red, he is essentially a gentleman. I am still somewhat in a quandary about him,—feel that he is essentially strange to me, at any rate; but I am surprised by the sight of him. He is very broad, but, as I have said, not fine. He said that I misapprehended him. I am not quite sure that I do. He told us that he loved to ride up and down Broadway all day on an omnibus, sitting beside the driver, listening to the roar of the carts, and sometimes gesticulating and declaiming Homer at the top of his voice. He has long been an editor and writer for the newspapers,—was editor of the *New Orleans Crescent* once; but now has no employment but to read and write in the forenoon, and walk in the afternoon, like all the rest of the scribbling gentry.

I shall probably be in Concord next week; so you can direct to methere.

TO HARRISON BLAKE (AT WORCESTER).

CONCORD, December 6, 1853.

MR. BLAKE,—I trust that you got a note from me at Eagleswood, about a fortnight ago. I passed through Worcester on the morning of the 25th of November, and spent several hours (from 3.30 to 6.20) in the travelers' room at the depot, as in a dream, it now seems. As the first Harlem train unexpectedly connected with the first from Fitchburg, I did not spend the forenoon with you as I had anticipated, on account of baggage, etc. If it had been a seasonable hour, I should have seen you,—*i. e.*, if you had not gone to a horse-race. But think of making a call at half past three in the morning! (would it not have implied a three-o'clock-in-the-morning courage in both you and me?) as it were, ignoring the fact that mankind are really not at home, —are not out, but so deeply in that they cannot be seen,—nearly half their hours at this season of the year.

I walked up and down the main street, at half past five, in the dark, and paused long in front of Brown's store, trying to distinguish its features; considering whether I might safely leave his *Putnam* in the door-handle, but concluded not to risk it. Meanwhile a watchman (?) seemed to be watching me, and I moved off. Took another turn around there, and had the very earliest offer of the *Transcript*[74] from an urchin behind, whom I actually could not see, it was so dark. So I withdrew, wondering if you and B. would know if I had been there. You little dream who is occupying Worcester when you are all asleep. Several things occurred there that night which I will venture to say were not put into the *Transcript*. A cat caught a mouse at the depot, and gave it to her kitten to play with. So that world-famous tragedy goes on by night as well as by day, and nature is *emphatically* wrong. Also I saw a young Irishman kneel before his mother, as if in prayer, while she wiped a cinder out of his eye with her tongue; and I found that it was never too late (or early?) to learn something. These things transpired while you and B. were, to all practical purposes, nowhere, and good for nothing,—not even for society,—not for horse-races,—nor the taking back of a *Putnam's Magazine*. It is true, I might have recalled you to life, but it would have been a cruel act, considering the kind of life you would have come back to.

However, I would fain write to you now by broad daylight, and report to you some of my life, such as it is, and recall you to your life, which is not always lived by you, even by daylight. Blake! Brown! are you awake? are you aware what an ever-glorious morning this is,—what long-expected, never-to-be-repeated opportunity is now offered to get life and knowledge?

For my part, I am trying to wake up,—to wring slumber out of my pores; for, generally, I take events as unconcernedly as a fence-post,—absorb wet and cold like it, and am pleasantly tickled with lichens slowly spreading over me. Could I not be content, then, to be a cedar post, which lasts twenty-five years? Would I not rather be that than the farmer that set it? or he that preaches to the farmer? and go to the heaven of posts at last? I think I should like that as well as any would like it. But I should not care if I sprouted into a living tree, put forth leaves and flowers, and bore fruit.

I am grateful for what I am and have. My thanksgiving is perpetual. It is surprising how contented one can be with nothing definite,—only a sense of existence. Well, anything for variety. I am ready to try this for the next ten thousand years, and exhaust it. How sweet to think of! my extremities well charred, and my intellectual part too, so that there is no danger of worm or rot for a long while. My breath is sweet to me. O how I laugh when I think of my vague, indefinite riches. No run on my bank can drain it, for my wealth is not possession but enjoyment.

What are all these years made for? and now another winter comes, so much like the last? Can't we satisfy the beggars once for all?

Have you got in your wood for this winter? What else have you got in? Of what use a great fire on the hearth, and a confounded little fire in the heart? Are you prepared to make a decisive campaign,—to pay for your costly tuition,—to pay for the suns of past summers,—for happiness and unhappiness lavished upon you?

Does not Time go by swifter than the swiftest equine trotter or racker?

Stir up Brown. Remind him of his duties, which outrun the date and span of Worcester's years past and to come. Tell him to be sure that he is on the main street, however narrow it may be, and to have a lit sign, visible by night as well as by day.

Are they not patient waiters,—they who wait for us? But even they shall not be losers.

December 7.

That Walt Whitman, of whom I wrote to you, is the most interesting fact to me at present. I have just read his second edition (which he gave me), and it has done me more good than any reading for a long time. Perhaps I remember best the poem of Walt Whitman, an American, and the Sun-Down Poem. There are two or three pieces in the book which are disagreeable, to say the least; simply sensual. He does not celebrate love at all. It is as if the beasts spoke. I think that men have not been ashamed of themselves without reason. No doubt there have always been dens where such deeds were unblushingly recited, and it is no merit to compete with their inhabitants. But even on this side he has spoken more truth than any American or modern that I know. I have found his poem exhilarating, encouraging. As for its sensuality,—and it may turn out to be less sensual than it appears,—I do not so much wish that those parts were not written, as that men and women were so pure that they could read them without harm, that is, without understanding them. One woman told me that no woman could read it,—as if a man could read what a woman could not. Of course Walt Whitman can communicate to us no experience, and if we are shocked, whose experience is it that we are reminded of?

On the whole, it sounds to me very brave and American, after whatever deductions. I do not believe that all the sermons, so called, that have been preached in this land put together are equal to it for preaching.

We ought to rejoice greatly in him. He occasionally suggests something a little more than human. You can't confound him with the other inhabitants of Brooklyn or New York. How they must shudder when they read him! He is awfully good.

To be sure I sometimes feel a little imposed on. By his heartiness and broad generalities he puts me into a liberal frame of mind prepared to see wonders, —as it were, sets me upon a hill or in the midst of a plain,—stirs me well up, and then—throws in a thousand of brick. Though rude, and sometimes ineffectual, it is a great primitive poem,—an alarum or trumpet-note ringing through the American camp. Wonderfully like the Orientals, too, considering that when I asked him if he had read them, he answered, "No: tell me about them."

I did not get far in conversation with him,—two more being present,—and among the few things which I chanced to say, I remember that one was, in answer to him as representing America, that I did not think much of America or of politics, and so on, which may have been somewhat of a damper to him.

Since I have seen him, I find that I am not disturbed by any brag or egoism in his book. He may turn out the least of a braggart of all, having a better right to be confident.

He is a great fellow.

There is in Alcott's diary an account of this interview with Whitman, and the Sunday morning in Ward Beecher's Brooklyn church, from which a few passages may be taken. Hardly any person met by either of these Concord friends in their later years made so deep an impression on both as did this then almost unknown poet and thinker, concerning whom Cholmondeley wrote to Thoreau in 1857: "Is there actually such a man as Whitman? Has any one seen or handled him? His is a tongue 'not understanded' of the English people. I find *the gentleman* altogether left out of the book. It is the first book I have ever seen which I should call a 'new book.'"

Mr. Alcott writes under date of November 7, 1856, in New York: "Henry Thoreau arrives from Eagleswood, and sees Swinton, a wise young Scotchman, and Walt Whitman's friend, at my room (15 Laight Street),—Thoreau declining to accompany me to Mrs. Botta's parlors, as invited by her. He sleeps here. (November 8.) We find Greeley at the Harlem station, and ride with him to his farm, where we pass the day, and return to sleep in the city,—Greeley coming in with us; Alice Cary, the authoress, accompanying us also. (Sunday, November 9.) We cross the ferry to Brooklyn, and hear Ward Beecher at the Plymouth Church. It was a spectacle,—and himself the preacher, if preacher there be anywhere now in pulpits. His auditors had to weep, had to laugh, under his potent magnetism, while his doctrine of justice to all men, bond and free, was grand. House, entries, aisles, galleries, all were crowded. Thoreau called it pagan, but I pronounced it good, very good,—the best I had witnessed for many a day, and hopeful for the coming time. At dinner at Mrs. Manning's. Miss M. S. was there, curious to see Thoreau. After dinner we called on Walt Whitman (Thoreau and I), but finding him out, we got all we could from his mother, a stately, sensible matron, believing absolutely in Walter, and telling us how good he was, and how wise when a boy; and how his four brothers and two sisters loved him, and still take counsel of the great man he has grown to be. We engaged to call again early in the morning, when she said Walt would be glad to see us. (Monday, 10th.) Mrs. Tyndale of Philadelphia goes with us to see Walt,—Walt the satyr, the Bacchus, the very god Pan. We sat with him for two hours, and much to our delight; he promising to call on us at the International at ten in the morning to-morrow, and there have the rest of it." Whitman failed to call at his hour the next day.

TO B. B. WILEY (AT CHICAGO).

Concord, December 12, 1856.

Mr. Wiley,[75] —It is refreshing to hear of your earnest purpose with respect to your culture, and I can send you no better wish than that you may not be thwarted by the cares and temptations of life. Depend on it, *now* is the accepted time, and probably you will never find yourself better disposed or freer to attend to your culture than at this moment. When *They* who inspire us with the idea are ready, shall not we be ready also?

I do not remember anything which Confucius has said directly respecting man's "origin, purpose, and destiny." He was more practical than that. He is full of wisdom applied to human relations,—to the private life,—the family, —government, etc. It is remarkable that, according to his own account, the sum and substance of his teaching is, as you know, to do as you would be done by.

He also said (I translate from the French), "Conduct yourself suitably towards the persons of your family, then you will be able to instruct and to direct a nation of men."

"To nourish one's self with a little rice, to drink water, to have only his bended arm to support his head, is a state which has also its satisfaction. To be rich and honored by iniquitous means is for me as the floating cloud which passes."

"As soon as a child is born he must respect its faculties: the knowledge which will come to it by and by does not resemble at all its present state. If it arrive at the age of forty or fifty years without having learned anything, it is no more worthy of any respect." This last, I think, will speak to yourcondition.

But at this rate I might fill many letters.

Our acquaintance with the ancient Hindoos is not at all personal. The full names that can be relied upon are very shadowy. It is, however, tangible works that we know. The best I think of are the Bhagvat Geeta (an episode in an ancient heroic poem called the Mahabarat), the Vedas, the Vishnu Purana, the Institutes of Menu, etc.

I cannot say that Swedenborg has been directly and practically valuable to me, for I have not been a reader of him, except to a slight extent; but I have the highest regard for him, and trust that I shall read his works in some world or other. He had a wonderful knowledge of our interior and spiritual life, though his illuminations are occasionally blurred by trivialities. He comes nearer to answering, or attempting to answer, literally, your questions concerning man's origin, purpose, and destiny, than any of the worthies I have referred to. But I think that that is not *altogether* a recommendation; since such an answer to these questions cannot be discovered any more than perpetual motion, for which no reward is now offered. The noblest man it is, methinks, that knows, and by his life suggests, the most about these things. Crack away at these nuts, however, as long as you can,—the very exercise will ennoble you, and you may get something better than the answer you expect.

TO B. B. WILEY (AT CHICAGO).

CONCORD, April 26, 1857.

MR. WILEY,—I see that you are turning a broad furrow among the books, but I trust that some very private journal all the while holds its own through their midst. Books can only reveal us to ourselves, and as often as they do us this service we lay them aside. I should say, read Goethe's autobiography, by all means, also Gibbon's, Haydon the painter's, and our Franklin's of course; perhaps also Alfieri's, Benvenuto Cellini's, and De Quincey's "Confessions of an Opium-Eater,"—since you like autobiography. I think you must read Coleridge again, and further, skipping all his theology, *i. e.*, if you value precise definitions and a discriminating use of language. By the way, read De Quincey's Reminiscences of Coleridge and Wordsworth.

How shall we account for our pursuits, if they are original? We get the language with which to describe our various lives out of a common mint. If others have their losses which they are busy repairing, so have I mine, and their hound and horse may *perhaps* be the symbols of some of them.[76] But also I have lost, or am in danger of losing, a far finer and more ethereal treasure which commonly no loss, of which they are conscious, will symbolize. This I answer hastily and with some hesitation, according as I now understand my words....

Methinks a certain polygamy with its troubles is the fate of almost all men. They are married to two wives: their genius (a celestial muse), and also to some fair daughter of the earth. Unless these two were fast friends before marriage, and so are afterward, there will be but little peace in the house.

TO HARRISON BLAKE (AT WORCESTER).

CONCORD, December 31, 1856.

Mr. Blake,—I think it will not be worth the while for me to come to Worcester to lecture at all this year. It will be better to wait till I am—perhaps unfortunately—more in that line. My writing has not taken the shape of lectures, and therefore I should be obliged to read one of three or four old lectures, the best of which I have read to some of your auditors before. I carried that one which I call "Walking, or the Wild," to Amherst, N. H., the evening of that cold Thursday,[77] and I am to read another at Fitchburg, February 3. I am simply their hired man. This will probably be the extent of my lecturing hereabouts.

I must depend on meeting Mr. Wasson some other time.

Perhaps it always costs me more than it comes to to lecture before a promiscuous audience. It is an irreparable injury done to my modesty even,—I become so indurated.

O solitude! obscurity! meanness! I never triumph so as when I have the least success in my neighbor's eyes. The lecturer gets fifty dollars a night; but what becomes of his winter? What consolation will it be hereafter to have fifty thousand dollars for living in the world? I should like not to exchange *any* of my life for money.

These, you may think, are reasons for not lecturing, when you have no great opportunity. It is even so, perhaps. I could lecture on dry oak leaves; I could, but who could hear me? If I were to try it on any large audience, I fear it would be no gain to them, and a positive loss to me. I should have behaved rudely toward my rustling friends.[78]

I am surveying, instead of lecturing, at present. Let me have a skimming from your "pan of unwrinkled cream."

The proposition about Mr. Alcott in Thoreau's letter of September 23, 1856, to Mr. Ricketson took effect in the spring of 1857, and early in April he went to visit the Ricketsons in New Bedford, going down from Walpole, and there met his younger friends Channing and Thoreau. Anticipating Mr. Alcott's visit, Thoreau wrote thus:—

TO DANIEL RICKETSON (AT NEW BEDFORD).

Concord, March 28, 1857.

Friend Ricketson,—If it chances to be perfectly agreeable and convenient to you, I will make you a visit next week (say Wednesday or Thursday), and we will have some more rides to Assawampset and the seashore. Have you got a boat on the former yet? Who knows but we may camp out on the island? I propose this now, because it will be more novel to me at this season, and I should like to see your early birds, etc.

Your historical papers have all come safely to hand, and I thank you for them. I see that they will be indispensable *mémoires pour servir*. By the way, have you read Church's "History of Philip's War," and looked up the localities? It should make part of a chapter.

I had a long letter from Cholmondeley lately, which I should like to show you,

I will expect an answer to this straightway,—but be sure you let your own convenience and inclinations rule it. Please remember me to your family.

He was welcomed, of course, and went down April 2, as indicated in the letter of the day before. But he had not been informed that Alcott was already there, writing in his Diary of April 1, this sketch of Brooklawn and its occupants:—

"A neat country residence, surrounded by wild pastures and low woods,—the little stream Acushnet flowing east of the house, and into Fairhaven Bay. The hamlet of Acushnet at the 'Head of the River' lies within half a mile of Ricketson's house. His tastes are pastoral, simple even to wildness; and he passes a good part of his day in the fields and woods,—or in his rude 'Shanty' near his house, where he writes and reads his favorite authors, Cowper having the first place. He is in easy circumstances, and has the manners of an English gentleman,—frank, hospitable, and with positive persuasions of his own; mercurial, perhaps, and wayward a little sometimes, but full of kindness and sensibility to suffering."

TO DANIEL RICKETSON (AT NEW BEDFORD).

Concord, April 1, 1857.

Dear Ricketson,—I got your note of welcome night before last. Channing is not here; at least I have not seen nor heard of him, but depend on meeting him in New Bedford. I expect, if the weather is favorable, to take the 4.30 train from Boston to-morrow, Thursday, P. M., for I hear of no noon train, and shall be glad to find your wagon at Tarkiln Hill, for I see it will be rather late for going across lots.

Alcott was here last week, and will probably visit New Bedford within a week or two.

I have seen all the spring signs you mention, and a few more, even here. Nay, I heard one frog peep nearly a week ago,—methinks the very first one in all this region. I wish that there were a few more signs of spring in myself; however, I take it that there *are* as many within us as we think we hear *without* us. I am decent for a steady pace, but not yet for a race. I have a little cold at present, and you speak of rheumatism about the head and shoulders. Your frost is not quite out. I suppose that the earth itself has a little cold and rheumatism about these times; but all these things together produce a very fair general result. In a concert, you know, we must sing our parts feebly sometimes, that we may not injure the general effect. I should n't wonder if my two-year-old invalidity had been a positively charming feature to some amateurs favorably located. Why not a blasted man as well as a blasted tree, on your lawn?

If you should happen not to see me by the train named, do not go again, but wait at home for me, or a note from

Yours,
Henry D. Thoreau.

On that Thursday, April 2, Alcott wrote in his Diary, "Henry Thoreau comes to tea, also Ellery Channing, and we talk till into the evening late." This visit of Thoreau was his longest, lasting until April 15, and it was during the fortnight that he sang "Tom Bowling" and danced with vigor in the Brooklawn drawing-room, a scene which Alcott loved to describe. Sophia Thoreau, writing in 1862, said: "I have so often witnessed the like that I can easily imagine how it was, and I remember that Henry gave me some account. I recollect he said that he did not scruple to tread on Mr. Alcott'stoes."

TO HARRISON BLAKE (AT WORCESTER).

Concord, April 17, 1857.

Mr. Blake,—I returned from New Bedford night before last. I met Alcott there, and learned from him that probably you had gone to Concord. I am very sorry that I missed you. I had expected you earlier, and at last thought that I should get back before you came; but I ought to have notified you of my absence. However, it would have been too late, after I had made up my mind to go. I hope you lost nothing by going a little round.

I took out the celtis seeds at your request, at the time we spoke of them, and left them in the chamber on some shelf or other. If you have found them, very well; if you have not found them, very well; but tell Hale[79] of it, if you see him. My mother says that you and Brown and Rogers and Wasson (titles left behind) talk of coming down on me some day. Do not fail to come, one and all, and within a week or two, if possible; else I may be gone again. Give me a short notice, and then come and spend a day on Concord River,—or say that you will come if it is fair, unless you are confident of bringing fair weather with you. Come and be Concord, as I have been Worcestered.

Perhaps you came nearer to me for not finding me at home; for trains of thought the more connect when trains of cars do not. If I had actually met you, you would have gone again; but now I have not yet dismissed you. I hear what you say about personal relations with joy. It is as if you had said: "I value the best and finest part of you, and not the worst. I can even endure your very near and real approach, and prefer it to a shake of the hand." This intercourse is not subject to time or distance.

I have a very long new and faithful letter from Cholmondeley which I wish to show you. He speaks of sending me more books!!

If I were with you now, I could tell you much of Ricketson, and my visit to New Bedford; but I do not know how it will be by and by. I should like to have you meet R., who is the frankest man I know. Alcott and he get along very well together. Channing has returned to Concord with me,—probably for a short visit only.

Consider this a business letter, which you know *counts* nothing in the game we play. Remember me particularly to Brown.

TO HARRISON BLAKE (AT WORCESTER).

Concord, June 6, 1857, 3 P. M.

Mr. Blake,—I have just got your note, but I am sorry to say that I this very morning sent a note to Channing, stating that I would go with him to Cape Cod next week on an excursion which we have been talking of for some time. If there were time to communicate with you, I should ask you to come to Concord on Monday, before I go; but as it is, I must wait till I come back, which I think will be about ten days hence. I do not like this delay, but there seems to be a fate in it. Perhaps Mr. Wasson will be well enough to come by that time. I will notify you of my return, and shall depend on seeing you all.

June 23d. I returned from Cape Cod last evening, and now take the first opportunity to invite you men of Worcester to this quiet *Mediterranean* shore. Can you come this week on Friday, or next Monday? I mention the earliest days on which I suppose you can be ready. If more convenient, name some other time *within ten days*. I shall be rejoiced to see you, and to act the part of skipper in the contemplated voyage. I have just got another letter from Cholmondeley, which may interest you somewhat.

TO MARSTON WATSON (AT PLYMOUTH).

Concord, August 17, 1857.

Mr. Watson,—I am much indebted to you for your glowing communication of July 20th. I had that very day left Concord for the wilds of Maine; but when I returned, August 8th, two out of the six worms remained nearly, if not quite, as bright as at first, I was assured. In their best estate they had excited the admiration of many of the inhabitants of Concord. It was a singular coincidence that I should find these worms awaiting me, for my mind was full of a phosphorescence which I had seen in the woods. I have waited to learn something more about them before acknowledging the receipt of them. I have frequently met with glow-worms in my night walks, but am not sure they were the same kind with these. Dr. Harris once described to me a larger kind than I had found, "nearly as big as your little finger;" but he does not name them in his report.

The only authorities on Glow-worms which I chance to have (and I am pretty well provided) are Kirby and Spence (the fullest), Knapp ("Journal of a Naturalist"), "The Library of Entertaining Knowledge" (Rennie), a French work, etc., etc.; but there is no minute, scientific description of any of these. This is apparently a female of the genus *Lampyris*; but Kirby and Spence say that there are nearly two hundred species of this genus alone. The one commonly referred to by English writers is the *Lampyris noctiluca*; but judging from Kirby and Spence's description, and from the description and plate in the French work, this is not that one, for, besides other differences, both say that the light proceeds from the abdomen. Perhaps the worms exhibited by Durkee (whose statement to the Boston Society of Natural History, second July meeting, in the *Traveller* of August 12, 1857, I send you) were the same with these. I do not see how they could be the *L. noctiluca*, as he states.

I expect to go to Cambridge before long, and if I get any more light on this subject I will inform you. The two worms are still alive.

I shall be glad to receive the drosera at any time, if you chance to come across it. I am looking over Loudon's "Arboretum," which we have added to our library, and it occurs to me that it was written expressly for you, and that you cannot avoid placing it on your own shelves.

I should have been glad to see the whale, and might perhaps have done so, if I had not at that time been seeing "the elephant" (or moose) in the Maine woods. I have been associating for about a month with one Joseph Polis, the chief man of the Penobscot tribe of Indians, and have learned a great deal from him, which I should like to tell you some time.

TO DANIEL RICKETSON (AT NEW BEDFORD).

Concord, August 18, 1857.

Dear Sir,—Your Wilson Flagg[80] seems a serious person, and it is encouraging to hear of a contemporary who recognizes Nature so squarely, and selects such a theme as "Barns." (I would rather "Mount Auburn" were omitted.) But he is not alert enough. He wants stirring up with a pole. He should practice turning a series of somersets rapidly or jump up and see how many times he can strike his feet together before coming down. Let him make the earth turn round now the other way, and whet his wits on it, whichever way it goes, as on a grindstone; in short, see how many ideas he can entertain at once.

His style, as I remember, is singularly vague (I refer to the book), and, before I got to the end of the sentences, I was off the track. If you indulge in long periods, you must be sure to have a snapper at the end. As for style of writing, if one has anything to say, it drops from him simply and directly, as a stone falls to the ground. There are no two ways about it, but down it comes, and he may stick in the points and stops wherever he can get a chance. New ideas come into this world somewhat like falling meteors, with a flash and an explosion, and perhaps somebody's castle-roof perforated. To try to polish the stone in its descent, to give it a peculiar turn, and make it whistle a tune, perchance, would be of no use, if it were possible. Your polished stuff turns out not to be meteoric, but of this earth. However, there is plenty of time, and Nature is an admirable schoolmistress.

Speaking of correspondence, you ask me if I "cannot turn over a new leaf in that line." I certainly could if I were to receive it; but just then I looked up and saw that your page was dated "May 10," though mailed in August, and it occurred to me that I had seen you since that date this year. Looking again, it appeared that your note was written in '56!! However, it was a *new* leaf to me, and I *turned it over* with as much interest as if it had been written the day before. Perhaps you kept it so long in order that the manuscript and subject-matter might be more in keeping with the old-fashioned paper on which it was written.

I traveled the length of Cape Cod on foot, soon after you were here, and, within a few days, have returned from the wilds of Maine, where I have made a journey of three hundred and twenty-five miles with a canoe and an Indian, and a single white companion,—Edward Hoar, Esq., of this town, lately from California,—traversing the head waters of the Kennebec, Penobscot, and St. John.

Can't you extract any advantage out of that depression of spirits you refer to? It suggests to me cider-mills, wine-presses, etc., etc. All kinds of pressure or power should be used and made to turn some kind of machinery.

Channing was just leaving Concord for Plymouth when I arrived, but said he should be here again in two or three days.

Please remember me to your family, and say that I have at length learned to sing "Tom Bowlin" according to the notes.

TO DANIEL RICKETSON (AT NEW BEDFORD).

CONCORD, September 9, 1857.

Friend Ricketson,—I thank you for your kind invitation to visit you, but I have taken so many vacations this year,—at New Bedford, Cape Cod, and Maine,—that any more relaxation—call it rather dissipation—will cover me with shame and disgrace. I have not earned what I have already enjoyed. As some heads cannot carry much wine, so it would seem that I cannot bear so much society as you can. I have an immense appetite for solitude, like an infant for sleep, and if I don't get enough of it this year, I shall cry all the next.

My mother's house is full at present; but if it were not, I would have no right to invite you hither, while entertaining such designs as I have hintedat. However, if you care to storm the town, I will engage to take some afternoon walks with you,—retiring into profoundest solitude the most sacred part of the day.

Ricketson had written to invite Thoreau to visit him again, saying among other things, "Walton's small sailboat is now on Assawampset Pond." After visiting Concord that autumn, he proposed another visit in December, saying (December 11, 1857), "I long to see your long beard. Channing says it is terrible to behold, but improves you mightily." This fixes the date, late in that year, when Thoreau first wore his full beard, as shown in his latest portraits.

TO HARRISON BLAKE (AT WORCESTER).

Concord, August 18, 1857.

Mr. Blake,—Fifteenthly. It seems to me that you need some absorbing pursuit. It does not matter much what it is, so it be honest. Such employment will be favorable to your development in more characteristic and important directions. You know there must be impulse enough for steerageway, though it be not toward your port, to prevent your drifting helplessly on to rocks or shoals. Some sails are set for this purpose only. There is the large fleet of scholars and men of science, for instance, always to be seen standing off and on every coast, and saved thus from running on to reefs, who will at last run into their proper haven, we trust.

It is a pity you were not here with Brown and Wiley. I think that in this case, *for a rarity*, the more the merrier.

You perceived that I did not entertain the idea of our going together to Maine on such an excursion as I had planned. The more I thought of it, the more imprudent it appeared to me. I did think to have written you before going, though not to propose your going also; but I went at last very suddenly, and could only have written a business letter, if I had tried, when there was no business to be accomplished. I have now returned, and think I have had a quite profitable journey, chiefly from associating with an intelligent Indian.

My companion, Edward Hoar, also found his account in it, though he suffered considerably from being obliged to carry unusual loads over wet and rough "carries,"—in one instance five miles through a swamp, where the water was frequently up to our knees, and the fallen timber higher than our heads. He went over the ground three times, not being able to carry all his load at once. This prevented his ascending Ktaadn. Our best nights were those when it rained the hardest, on account of the mosquitoes. I speak of these things, which were not unexpected, merely to account for my not inviting you.

Having returned, I flatter myself that the world appears in some respects a little larger, and not, as usual, smaller and shallower, for having extended my range. I have made a short excursion into the new world which the Indian dwells in, or is. He begins where we leave off. It is worth the while to detect new faculties in man,—he is so much the more divine; and anything that fairly excites our admiration expands us. The Indian, who can find his way so wonderfully in the woods, possesses so much intelligence which the white man does not,—and it increases my own capacity, as well as faith, to observe it. I rejoice to find that intelligence flows in other channels than I knew. It redeems for me portions of what seemed brutish before.

It is a great satisfaction to find that your oldest convictions are permanent. With regard to essentials, I have never had occasion to change my mind. The aspect of the world varies from year to year, as the landscape is differently clothed, but I find that the *truth* is still *true*, and I never regret any emphasis which it may have inspired. Ktaadn is there still, but much more surely my old conviction is there, resting with more than mountain breadth and weight on the world, the source still of fertilizing streams, and affording glorious views from its summit, if I can get up to it again. As the mountains still stand on the plain, and far more unchangeable and permanent,—stand still grouped around, farther or nearer to my maturer eye, the ideas which I have entertained,—the everlasting teats from which we draw our nourishment.

TO HARRISON BLAKE (AT WORCESTER).

Concord, November 16, 1857.

Mr. Blake,—You have got the start again. It was I that owed you a letter or two, if I mistake not.

They make a great ado nowadays about hard times;[81] but I think that the community generally, ministers and all, take a wrong view of the matter, though some of the ministers preaching according to a formula may pretend to take a right one. This general failure, both private and public, is rather occasion for rejoicing, as reminding us whom we have at the helm,—that justice is always done. If our merchants did not most of them fail, and the banks too, my faith in the old laws of the world would be staggered. The statement that ninety-six in a hundred doing such business surely break down is perhaps the sweetest fact that statistics have revealed,—exhilarating as the fragrance of sallows in spring. Does it not say somewhere, “The Lord reigneth, let the earth rejoice”? If thousands are thrown out of employment, it suggests that they were not well employed. Why don’t they take the hint? It is not enough to be industrious; so are the ants. What are you industrious about?

The merchants and company have long laughed at transcendentalism, higher laws, etc., crying, “None of your moonshine,” as if they were anchored to something not only definite, but sure and permanent. If there was any institution which was presumed to rest on a solid and secure basis, and more than any other represented this boasted common sense, prudence, and practical talent, it was the bank; and now those very banks are found to be mere reeds shaken by the wind. Scarcely one in the land has kept its promise…. It would seem as if you only need live forty years in any age of this world, to see its most promising government become the government of Kansas, and banks nowhere. Not merely the Brook Farm and Fourierite communities, but now the community generally has failed. But there is the moonshine still, serene, beneficent, and unchanged. Hard times, I say, have this value, among others, that they show us what such promises are worth,—where the *sure* banks are. I heard some Mr. Eliot praised the other day because he had paid some of his debts, though it took nearly all he had (why, I’ve done as much as that myself many times, and a little more), and then gone to board. What if he has? I hope he’s got a good boarding-place, and can pay for it. It’s not everybody that can. However, in my opinion, it is cheaper to keep house,—*i. e.*, if you don’t keep too big a one.

Men will tell you sometimes that “money’s hard.” That shows it was not made to eat, I say. Only think of a man in this new world, in his log cabin, in the midst of a corn and potato patch, with a sheepfold on one side, talking about money being hard! So are flints hard; there is no alloy in them. What has that got to do with his raising his food, cutting his wood (or breaking it), keeping indoors when it rains, and, if need be, spinning and weaving his clothes? Some of those who sank with the steamer the other day found out that money was *heavy* too. Think of a man’s priding himself on this kind of wealth, as if it greatly enriched him. As if one struggling in mid-ocean with a bag of gold on his back should gasp out, “I am worth a hundred thousand dollars.” I see them struggling just as ineffectually on dry land, nay, even more hopelessly, for, in the former case, rather than sink, they will finally let the bag go; but in the latter they are pretty sure to hold and go down with it. I see them swimming about in their greatcoats, collecting their rents, really *getting their dues*, drinking bitter draughts which only increase their thirst, becoming more and more water-logged, till finally they sink plumb down to the bottom. But enough of this.

Have you ever read Ruskin's books? If not, I would recommend [you] to try the second and third volumes (not parts) of his "Modern Painters." I am now reading the fourth, and have read most of his other books lately. They are singularly good and encouraging, though not without crudeness and bigotry. The themes in the volumes referred to are Infinity, Beauty, Imagination, Love of Nature, etc.,—all treated in a very living manner. I am rather surprised by them. It is remarkable that these things should be said with reference to painting chiefly, rather than literature. The "Seven Lamps of Architecture," too, is made of good stuff; but, as I remember, there is too much about art in it for me and the Hottentots. We want to know about matters and things in general. Our house is as yet a hut.

You must have been enriched by your solitary walk over the mountains. I suppose that I feel the same awe when on their summits that many do on entering a church. To see what kind of earth that is on which you have a house and garden somewhere, perchance! It is equal to the lapse of many years. You must ascend a mountain to learn your relation to matter, and so to your own body, for *it* is at home there, though *you* are not. It might have been composed there, and will have no farther to go to return to dust there, than in your garden; but your spirit inevitably comes away, and brings your body with it, if it lives. Just as awful really, and as glorious, is your garden. See how I can play with my fingers! They are the funniest companions I have ever found. Where did they come from? What strange control I have over them! *Who* am I? What are they?—those little peaks—call them Madison, Jefferson, Lafayette. What is *the matter*? *My* fingers, do I say? Why, ere long, they may form the topmost crystal of Mount Washington. I go up there to see my body's cousins. There are some fingers, toes, bowels, etc., that I take an interest in, and therefore I am interested in all their relations.

Let me suggest a theme for you: to state to yourself precisely and completely what that walk over the mountains amounted to for you,—returning to this essay again and again, until you are satisfied that all that was important in your experience is in it. Give this good reason to yourself for having gone over the mountains, for mankind is ever going over a mountain. Don't suppose that you can tell it precisely the first dozen times you try, but at 'em again, especially where, after a sufficient pause, you suspect that you are touching the heart or summit of the matter, reiterate your blows there, and account for the mountain to yourself. Not that the story need be long, but it will take a long while to make it short. It did not take very long to get over the mountain, you thought; but have you got over it indeed? If you have been to the top of Mount Washington, let me ask, what did you find there? That is the way they prove witnesses, you know. Going up there and being blown on is nothing. We never do much climbing while we are there, but we eat our luncheon, etc., very much as at home. It is after we get home that we really go over the mountain, if ever. What did the mountain say? What did the mountain do?

I keep a mountain anchored off eastward a little way, which I ascend in my dreams both awake and asleep. Its broad base spreads over a village or two, which does not know it; neither does it know them, nor do I when I ascend it. I can see its general outline as plainly now in my mind as that of Wachusett. I do not invent in the least, but state exactly what I see. I find that I go up it when I am light-footed and earnest. It ever smokes like an altar with its sacrifice. I am not aware that a single villager frequents it or knows of it. I keep this mountain to ride instead of a horse.

Do you not mistake about seeing Moosehead Lake from Mount Washington? That must be about one hundred and twenty miles distant, or nearly twice as far as the Atlantic, which last some doubt if they can see thence. Was it not Umbagog?

Dr. Solger[82] has been lecturing in the vestry in this town on Geography, to Sanborn's scholars, for several months past, at five P. M. Emerson and Alcott have been to hear him. I was surprised when the former asked me, the other day, if I was not going to hear Dr. Solger. What, to be sitting in a meeting-house cellar at that time of day, when you might possibly be outdoors! I never thought of such a thing. What was the sun made for? If he does not prize daylight, I do. Let him lecture to owls and dormice. He must be a wonderful lecturer indeed who can keep me indoors at such an hour, when the night is coming in which no man can walk.

Are you in want of amusement nowadays? Then play a little at the game of getting a living. There never was anything equal to it. Do it temperately, though, and don't sweat. Don't let this secret out, for I have a design against the Opera. OPERA!! Pass along the exclamations, devil.[83]

Now is the time to become conversant with your wood-pile (this comes under Work for the Month), and be sure you put some warmth into it by your mode of getting it. Do not consent to be passively warmed. An intense degree of that is the hotness that is threatened. But a positive warmth within can withstand the fiery furnace, as the vital heat of a living man can withstand the heat that cooks meat.

After returning from the last of his three expeditions to the Maine woods (in 1846, 1853, and 1857), Thoreau was appealed to by his friend Higginson, then living in Worcester, for information concerning a proposed excursion from Worcester into Maine and Canada, then but little visited by tourists, who now go there in droves. He replied in this long letter, with its minute instructions and historical references. The Arnold mentioned is General Benedict Arnold, who in 1775-76 made a toilsome march through the Maine forest with a small New England army for the conquest of Canada, while young John Thoreau, Henry's grandfather, was establishing himself as a merchant in Boston (not yet evacuated by British troops), previous to his marriage with Jane Burns.

TO T. W. HIGGINSON (AT WORCESTER).

CONCORD, January 28, 1858.

DEAR SIR,—It would be perfectly practicable to go to the Madawaska the way you propose. As for the route to Quebec, I do not find the Sugar Loaf Mountains on my maps. The most direct and regular way, as you know, is substantially Montresor's and Arnold's and the younger John Smith's—by the Chaudière; but this is less wild. If your object is to see the St. Lawrence River below Quebec, you will probably strike it at the Rivière du Loup. (*Vide* Hodge's account of his excursion thither *via* the Allegash,—I believe it is the second Report on the Geology of the Public Lands of Maine and Massachusetts in '37.) I think that our Indian last summer, when we talked of going to the St. Lawrence, named another route, near the Madawaska,—perhaps the St. Francis,—which would save the long portage which Hodge made.

I do not know whether you think of ascending the St. Lawrence in a canoe; but if you should, you might be delayed not only by the current, but by the waves, which frequently run too high for a canoe on such a mighty stream. It would be a grand excursion to go to Quebec by the Chaudière, descend the St. Lawrence to the Rivière du Loup, and return by the Madawaska and St. John to Fredericton, or farther,—almost all the way *down-stream*—a very important consideration.

I went to Moosehead in company with a party of four who were going a-hunting down the Allegash and St. John, and thence by some other stream over into the Restigouche, and down that to the Bay of Chaleur,—to be gone six weeks. Our northern terminus was an island in Heron Lake on the Allegash. (*Vide* Colton's railroad and township map of Maine.)

The Indian proposed that we should return to Bangor by the St. John and Great Schoodic Lake, which we had thought of ourselves; and he showed us on the map where we should be each night. It was then noon, and the next day night, continuing down the Allegash, we should have been at the Madawaska settlements, having made only one or two portages; and thereafter, on the St. John there would be but one or two more falls, with short carries; and if there was not too much wind, we could go down that stream one hundred miles a day. It is settled all the way below Madawaska. He knew the route well. He even said that this was easier, and would take but little more time, though much farther, than the route we decided on,—*i. e.*, by Webster Stream, the East Branch, and main Penobscot to Oldtown; but he may have wanted a longer job. We preferred the latter, not only because it was shorter, but because, as he said, it was wilder.

We went about three hundred and twenty-five miles with the canoe (including sixty miles of stage between Bangor and Oldtown); were out twelve nights, and spent about $40 apiece,—which was more than was necessary. We paid the Indian, who was a very good one, $1.50 per day and 50 cents a week for his canoe. This is enough in ordinary seasons. I had formerly paid $2 for an Indian and for white batteau-men.

If you go to Madawaska in a leisurely manner, supposing no delay on account of rain or the violence of the wind, you may reach Mt. Kineo by noon, and have the afternoon to explore it. The next day you may get to the head of the lake before noon, make the portage of two and a half miles over a wooden railroad, and drop down the Penobscot half a dozen miles. The third morning you will perhaps walk half a mile about Pine Stream Falls, while the Indian runs down,—cross the head of Chesuncook, reach the junction of the Caucomgomock and Umbazookskus by noon, and ascend the latter to Umbazookskus Lake that night. If it is low water, you may have to walk and carry a little on the Umbazookskus before entering the lake. The fourth morning you will make the carry of two miles to Mud Pond (Allegash water),—and a very wet carry it is,—and reach Chamberlain Lake by noon, and Heron Lake, perhaps, that night, after a couple of very short carries at the outlet of Chamberlain. At the end of two days more you will probably be at Madawaska. Of course the Indian *can* paddle twice as far in a day as he commonly does.

Perhaps you would like a few more details. We used (three of us) exactly twenty-six pounds of hard bread, fourteen pounds of pork, three pounds of coffee, twelve pounds of sugar (and could have used more), besides a little tea, Indian meal, and rice,—and plenty of berries and moose-meat. This was faring very luxuriously. I had not formerly carried coffee, sugar, or rice. But for solid food, I decide that it is not worth the while to carry anything but hard bread and pork, whatever your tastes and habits may be. These wear best, and you have no time nor dishes in which to cook anything else. Of course you will take a little Indian meal to fry fish in; and half a dozen lemons also, if you have sugar, will be very refreshing,—for the water is warm.[84]

To save time, the sugar, coffee, tea, salt, etc., should be in separate water-tight bags, labeled, and tied with a leathern string; and all the provisions and blankets should be put into two large india-rubber bags, if you can find them water-tight. Ours were not. A four-quart tin pail makes a good kettle for all purposes, and tin plates are portable and convenient. Don't forget an india-rubber knapsack, with a large flap,—plenty of dish-cloths, old newspapers, strings, and twenty-five feet of strong cord. Of india-rubber clothing, the most you can wear, if any, is a very light coat,—and that you cannot work in. I could be more particular,—but perhaps have been too much so already.

TO MARSTON WATSON (AT PLYMOUTH).

CONCORD, April 25, 1858.

DEAR SIR,—Your unexpected gift of pear trees reached me yesterday in good condition, and I spent the afternoon in giving them a good setting out; but I fear that this cold weather may hurt them. However, I am inclined to think they are insured, since you have looked on them. It makes one's mouth water to read their names only. From what I hear of the extent of your bounty, if a reasonable part of the trees succeed, this transplanting will make a new era for Concord to date from.

Mine must be a lucky star, for day before yesterday I received a box of mayflowers from Brattleboro, and yesterday morning your pear trees, and at evening a hummingbird's nest from Worcester. This looks like fairy housekeeping.

I discovered two new plants in Concord last winter, the Labrador tea (*Ledum latifolium*), and yew (*Taxis baccata*).

By the way, in January I communicated with Dr. Durkee, whose report on glow-worms I sent you, and it appeared, as I expected, that he (and by his account Agassiz, Gould, Jackson, and others to whom he showed them) did not consider them a distinct species, but a variety of the common, or *Lampyris noctiluca*, some of which you got in Lincoln. Durkee, at least, has never seen the last. I told him that I had no doubt about their being a distinct species. His, however, were luminous throughout every part of the body, as those which you sent me were not, while I had them.

Is nature as full of vigor to your eyes as ever, or do you detect some falling off at last? Is the mystery of the hog's bristle cleared up, and with it that of our life? It is the question, to the exclusion of every other interest.

I am sorry to hear of the burning of your woods, but, thank Heaven, your great ponds and your sea cannot be burnt. I love to think of your warm, sandy wood-roads, and your breezy island out in the sea. What a prospect you can get every morning from the hilltop east of your house![85] I think that even the heathen that I am could say, or sing, or dance, morning prayers there of some kind.

Please remember me to Mrs. Watson, and to the rest of your family who are helping the sun shine yonder.

Of his habits in mountain-climbing, Channing says:[86] "He ascended such hills as Monadnoc by his own path; would lay down his map on the summit and draw a line to the point he proposed to visit below,—perhaps forty miles away on the landscape, and set off bravely to make the 'short-cut.' The lowland people wondered to see him scaling the heights as if he had lost his way, or at his jumping over their cow-yard fences,—asking if he had fallen from the clouds. In a walk like this he always carried his umbrella; and on this Monadnoc trip, when about a mile from the station [in Troy, N. H.], a torrent of rain came down; without the umbrella his books, blankets, maps, and provisions would all have been spoiled, or the morning lost by delay. On the mountain there being a thick, soaking fog, the first object was to camp and make tea. He spent five nights in camp, having built another hut, to get varied views. Flowers, birds, lichens, and the rocks were carefully examined, all parts of the mountain were visited, and as accurate a map as could be made by pocket compass was carefully sketched and drawn out, in the five days spent there,—with notes of the striking aerial phenomena, incidents of travel and natural history. The outlook across the valley over to Wachusett, with its thunder-storms and battles in the cloud; the farmers' back-yards in Jaffrey, where the family cotton can be seen bleaching on the grass, but no trace of the pigmy family; the dry, soft air all night, the lack of dew in the morning; the want of water,—a pint being a good deal,—these, and similar things make up some part of such an excursion."

The Monadnock excursion above mentioned began June 3d, and continued three days. It inspired Thoreau to take a longer mountain tour with his neighbor and friend Edward Hoar, to which these letters relate, giving the ways and means of the journey,—a memorable one to all concerned.

TO HARRISON BLAKE (AT WORCESTER).

CONCORD, June 29, 1858, 8 A. M.

MR. BLAKE,—Edward Hoar and I propose to start for the White Mountains in a covered wagon, with one horse, on the morning of Thursday the 1st of July, intending to explore the mountain-tops botanically, and camp on them at least several times. Will you take a seat in the wagon with us? Mr. Hoar prefers to hire the horse and wagon himself. Let us hear by express, as soon as you can, whether you will join us here by the earliest train on Thursday morning, or Wednesday night. Bring your map of the mountains, and as much *provision* for the road as you can,—hard bread, sugar, tea, meat, etc.,—for we intend to live like gipsies; also, a blanket and some thick clothes for the mountain-top.

July 1st. Last Monday evening Mr. Edward Hoar said that he thought of going to the White Mountains. I remarked casually that I should like to go well enough if I could afford it. Whereupon he declared that if I would go with him, he would hire a horse and wagon, so that the ride would cost me nothing, and we would explore the mountain-tops *botanically*, camping on them many nights. The next morning I suggested you and Brown's accompanying us in another wagon, and we could all camp and cook, gipsy-like, along the way,—or, perhaps, if the horse could draw us, you would like to bear half the expense of the horse and wagon, and take a seat with us. He liked either proposition, but said that if you would take a seat with us, he would prefer to hire the horse and wagon himself. You could contribute something else if you pleased. Supposing that Brown would be confined, I wrote to you accordingly, by *express* on Tuesday morning, *via* Boston, stating that we should start to-day, suggesting provision, thick clothes, etc., and asking for an answer; but I have not received one. I have just heard that you *may* be at Sterling, and now write to say that we shall still be glad if you will join us at Senter Harbor, where we expect to be next Monday morning. In any case, will you please direct a letter to us there *at once*?

TO DANIEL RICKETSON (AT NEW BEDFORD).

CONCORD, June 30, 1858.

FRIEND RICKETSON,—I am on the point of starting for the White Mountains in a wagon with my neighbor Edward Hoar, and I write to you now rather to apologize for not writing, than to answer worthily your three notes. I thank you heartily for them. You will not care for a little delay in acknowledging them, since your date shows that you can afford to wait. Indeed, my head has been so full of company, etc., that I could not reply to you fitly before, nor can I now.

As for preaching to men these days in the Walden strain, is it of any consequence to preach to an audience of men who *can* fail, or who can be *revived*? There are few beside. Is it any success to interest these parties? If a man has *speculated* and *failed*, he will probably do these things again, in spite of you or me. I confess that it is rare that I rise to sentiment in my relations to men,—ordinarily to a mere patient, or may be wholesome, good-will. I can imagine something more, but the truth compels me to regard the ideal and the actual as two things.

Channing has come, and as suddenly gone, and left a short poem, "Near Home," published (?) or printed by Munroe, which I have hardly had time to glance at. As you may guess, I learn nothing of you from him.

You already foresee my answer to your invitation to make you a summer visit: I am bound for the mountains. But I trust that you have vanquished, ere this, those dusky demons that seem to lurk around the Head of the River.[87] You know that this warfare is nothing but a kind of nightmare, and it is our thoughts alone which give those *un*worthies any body or existence.

I made an excursion with Blake, of Worcester, to Monadnock, a few weeks since. We took our blankets and food, spent two nights on the mountain, and did not go into a house.

Alcott has been very busy for a long time repairing an old shell of a house, and I have seen very little of him.[88] I have looked more at the houses which birds build. Watson made us all very generous presents from his nursery in the spring. Especially did he remember Alcott.

Excuse me for not writing any more at present, and remember me to your family.

In explanation of the next letter (October 31, 1858), it may be said that Ricketson had formed a plan for visiting Europe, which he gave up, and had recommended an "English Australian" who proposed to see Concord. In Thoreau's reply, he mentions Mr. Hoar, who was not only his companion in later journeys, but, while in college or the Harvard Law School, had assisted Thoreau in that accidental forest fire, mentioned in the Journal, which brought both the young men into much disrepute among the Concord farmers and owners of wood-lots. At the date of the letter, Channing was flitting between New Bedford and Concord, and soon returned to spend the rest of his days in Thoreau's town, where he died, December 23, 1901, the last survivor of the group of friends to whom these letters relate.

In July, 1858, as mentioned in this letter to Mr. Ricketson, Thoreau journeyed from Concord to the White Mountains, first visited with his brother John in 1839. His later companion was Edward Hoar, a botanist and lover of nature, who had been a magistrate in California, and in boyhood a comrade of Thoreau in shooting excursions on the Concord meadows. They journeyed in a wagon and Thoreau disliked the loss of independence in choice of camping-places involved in the care of a horse. He complained also of the magnificent inns ("mountain houses") that had sprung up in the passes and on the plateaus since his first visit. "Give me," he said, "a spruce house made in the rain," such as he and Channing afterward (1860) made on Monadnock in his last trip to that mountain. The chief exploit in the White Mountain trip was a visit to Tuckerman's Ravine on Mt. Washington, of which Mr. Hoar, some years before his death (in 1893), gave me an account, containing the true anecdote of Thoreau's finding the arnica plant when he needed it.

On their way to this rather inaccessible chasm, Thoreau and his comrade went first to what was then but a small tavern on the "tip-top" of Mt. Washington. It was a foggy day; and when the landlord was asked if he could furnish a guide to Tuckerman's Ravine, he replied, "Yes, my brother is the guide; but if he went to-day he could never find his way back in this fog." "Well," said Thoreau, "if we cannot have a guide we will find it ourselves;" and he at once produced a map he had made the day before at a roadside inn, where he had found a wall map of the mountain region, and climbed on a table to copy that portion he needed. With this map and his pocket compass he "struck a bee-line," said Mr. Hoar, for the ravine, and soon came to it, about a mile away. They went safely down the steep stairs into the chasm, where they found the midsummer iceberg they wished to see. But as they walked down the bed of the Peabody River, flowing from this ravine, over boulders five or six feet high, the heavy packs on their shoulders weighed them down, and finally, Thoreau's foot slipping, he fell and sprained his ankle. He rose, but had not limped five steps from the place where he fell, when he said, "Here is the arnica, anyhow,"—reached out his hand and plucked the *Arnica mollis*, which he had not before found anywhere. Before reaching the mountains they had marked in their botany books forty-six species of plants they hoped to find there, and before they came away they had found forty-two of them.

When they reached their camping-place, farther down, Thoreau was so lame he could not move about, and lay there in the camp several days, eating the pork and other supplies they had in their packs, Mr. Hoar going each day to the inn at the mountain summit. This camp was in a thicket of dwarf firs at the foot of the ravine, where, just before his accident, by carelessness in lighting a fire, some acres of the mountain woodland had been set on fire; but this proved to be the signal for which Thoreau had told his Worcester friends to watch, if they wished to join him on the mountain. "I had told Blake," says Thoreau in his Journal, "to look out for a smoke and a white tent. We had made a smoke sure enough. We slept five in the tent that night, and found it quite warm." Mr. Hoar added: "In this journey Thoreau insisted on our carrying heavy packs, and rather despised persons who complained of the burden. He was chagrined, in the Maine woods, to find his Indian, Joe Polis (whom, on the whole, he admired), excited and tremulous at sight of a moose, so that he could scarcely load his gun properly. Joe, who was a good Catholic, wanted us to stop traveling on Sunday and hold a meeting; and when we insisted on going forward, the Indian withdrew into the woods to say his prayers,—then came back and picked up the breakfast things, and we paddled on. As to Thoreau's courage and manliness, nobody who had seen him among the Penobscot rocks and rapids—the Indian trusting his life and his canoe to Henry's skill, promptitude, and nerve—would ever doubt it."

Channing says:[89] "In his later journeys, if his companion was footsore or loitered, he steadily pursued his road. Once, when a follower was done up with headache and incapable of motion, hoping his associate would comfort him and perhaps afford him a sip of tea, he said, 'There are people who are sick in that way every morning, and go about their affairs,' and then marched off about his. In such limits, so inevitable, was he compacted.... This tone of mind grew out of no insensibility; or, if he sometimes looked coldly on the suffering of more tender natures, he sympathized with their afflictions, but could do nothing to admire them. He would not injure a plant unnecessarily. At the time of the John Brown tragedy, Thoreau was driven sick. So the country's misfortunes in the Union war acted on his feelings with great force: he used to say he 'could never recover while the war lasted.'" Hawthorne had an experience somewhat similar, though he, too, was of stern stuff when need was, and had much of the old Salem sea-captains in his sensitive nature.

TO DANIEL RICKETSON (AT NEW BEDFORD).

Concord, October 31, 1858.

Friend Ricketson,—I have not seen anything of your English author yet. Edward Hoar, my companion in Maine and at the White Mountains, his sister Elizabeth, and a Miss Prichard, another neighbor of ours, went to Europe in the Niagara on the 6th. I told them to look out for you under the Yardley Oak, but it seems they will not find you there.

I had a pleasant time in Tuckerman's Ravine at the White Mountains in July, entertaining four beside myself under my little tent through some soaking rains; and more recently I have taken an interesting walk with Channing about Cape Ann. We were obliged to "dipper it" a good way, on account of the scarcity of fresh water, for we got most of our meals by the shore. Channing is understood to be here for the winter, but I rarely see him.

I should be pleased to see your face here in the course of the Indian summer, which may still be expected, if any authority can tell us when that phenomenon *does* occur. We would like to hear the story of your travels; for if you have not been fairly intoxicated with Europe, you have been half-seas-over, and so can probably tell more about it.

This alludes to the fact that Ricketson got as far as Halifax in his attempt at Europe; and in his reply (November 3, 1858) he gave Thoreau an account of his short voyage, on which the next letter comments.

TO DANIEL RICKETSON (AT NEW BEDFORD).

Concord, November 6, 1858.

Friend Ricketson,—I was much pleased with your lively and lifelike account of your voyage. You were more than repaid for your trouble after all. The coast of Nova Scotia, which you sailed along from Windsor westward, is particularly interesting to the historian of this country, having been settled earlier than Plymouth. Your "Isle of Haut" is properly "Isle Haute," or the High Island of Champlain's map. There is another off the coast of Maine. By the way, the American elk of *American authors* (*Cervus Canadensis*) is a distinct animal from the moose (*Cervus alces*), though the latter is called elk by many.

You drew a very vivid portrait of the Australian,—short and stout, with a pipe in his mouth, and his book inspired by beer, Pot First, Pot Second, etc. I suspect that he must be potbellied withal. Methinks I see the smoke going up from him as from a cottage on the moor. If he does not quench his genius with his beer, it may burst into a clear flame at last. However, perhaps he intentionally adopts the low style.

What do you mean by that ado about smoking, and my "purer tastes"? I should like his pipe as well as his beer at least. Neither of them is so bad as to be "highly connected," which you say he is, unfortunately. No! I expect nothing but pleasure in "smoke from *your* pipe."

You and the Australian must have put your heads together when you concocted those titles,—with pipes in your mouths over a pot of beer. I suppose that your chapters are, Whiff the First, Whiff the Second, etc. But of course it is a more modest expression for "Fire from my Genius."

You must have been very busy since you came back, or before you sailed, to have brought out your History, of whose publication I had not heard. I suppose that I have read it in the *Mercury*. Yet I am curious to see how it looks in a volume, with your name on the title-page.

I am more curious still about the poems. Pray put some sketches into the book: your shanty for frontispiece; Arthur and Walton's boat (if you can) running for Cuttyhunk in a tremendous gale; not forgetting "Be honest boys," etc., near by; the Middleborough ponds with a certain island looming in the distance; the Quaker meeting-house, and the Brady house, if you like; the villagers catching smelts with dip-nets in the twilight, at the Head of the River, etc., etc. Let it be a local and villageous book as much as possible. Let some one make a characteristic selection of mottoes from your shanty walls, and sprinkle them in an irregular manner, at all angles, over the fly-leaves and margins, as a man stamps his name in a hurry; and also canes, pipes, and jackknives, of all your patterns, about the frontispiece. I can think of plenty of devices for tail-pieces. Indeed, I should like to see a hair pillow, accurately drawn, for one; a cat, with a bell on, for another; the old horse, with his age printed in the hollow of his back; half a cocoanut-shell by a spring; a sheet of blotted paper; a settle occupied by a settler at full length, etc., etc., etc. Call all the arts to your aid.

Don't wait for the Indian summer, but bring it with you.

P. S.—Let me ask a favor. I am trying to write something about the autumnal tints, and I wish to know how much our trees differ from English and European ones in this respect. Will you observe, or learn for me, what English or European trees, if any, still retain their leaves in Mr. Arnold's garden (the gardener will supply the true names); and also if the foliage of any (and what) European or foreign trees there have been brilliant the past month. If you will do this you will greatly oblige me. I return the newspaper with this.

TO DANIEL RICKETSON (AT NEW BEDFORD).

Concord, November 22, 1858.

Friend Ricketson,—I thank you for your "History."[90] Though I have not yet read it again, I have looked far enough to see that I like the homeliness of it; that is, the good, old-fashioned way of writing, as if you actually lived where you wrote. A man's interest in a single bluebird is worth more than a complete but dry list of the fauna and flora of a town. It is also a considerable advantage to be able to say at any time, "If D. R. is not here, here is his book." Alcott being here, and inquiring after you (whom he has been expecting), I lent the book to him almost immediately. He talks of going West the latter part of this week. Channing is here again, as I am told, but I have not seen him.

I thank you also for the account of the trees. It was to my purpose, and I hope you got something out of it too. I suppose that the cold weather prevented your coming here. Suppose you try a winter walk on skates. Please remember me to your family.

Late in November, 1858, Cholmondeley, who had not written for a year and six months, suddenly notified Thoreau from Montreal that he was in Canada, and would visit Concord the next week. Accordingly he arrived early in December, and urged his friend to go with him to the West Indies. John Thoreau, the father, was then in his last illness, and for that and other reasons Thoreau could not accept the invitation; but he detained Cholmondeley in Concord some days, and took him to New Bedford, December 8th, having first written this note to Mr. Ricketson:—

"Thomas Cholmondeley, my English acquaintance, is here, on his way to the West Indies. He wants to see New Bedford, a whaling town. I tell him I would like to introduce him to you there,—thinking more of his seeing you than New Bedford. So we propose to come your way to-morrow. Excuse this short notice, for the time is short. If on any account it is inconvenient to see us, you will treat us accordingly."

Of this visit and his English visitor, Mr. Ricketson wrote in his journal the next day:—

"We were all much pleased with Mr. Cholmondeley. He is a tall spare man, thirty-five years of age, of fair and fresh complexion, blue eyes, light-brown and fine hair, nose small and Roman, beard light and worn full, with a mustache. A man of fine culture and refinement of manners, educated at Oriel College, Oxford, of an old Cheshire family by his father, a clergyman. He wore a black velvet sack coat, and lighter-colored trousers,—a sort of genteel traveling suit; perhaps a cap, but by no means a fashionable 'castor.' He reminded me of our dear friend, George William Curtis." Few greater compliments could this diarist give than to compare a visitor to Curtis, the lamented.

Mr. Cholmondeley left Concord for the South, going as far as to Virginia, in December and January; then came back to Concord the 20th of January, 1859, and after a few days returned to Canada, and thence to England by way of Jamaica. He was in London when Theodore Parker reached there from Santa Cruz, in June, and called on him, with offers of service; but does not seem to have heard of Parker's death till I wrote him in May, 1861. At my parting with him in Concord, he gave me money with which to buy grapes for the invalid father of Thoreau,—an instance of his constant consideration for others; the Thoreaus hardly affording such luxuries as hothouse grapes for the sick. Sophia Thoreau, who perhaps was more appreciative of him than her more stoical brother, said after his death, "We have always had the truest regard for him, as a person of rare integrity, great benevolence, and the sincerest friendliness." This well describes the man whose every-day guise was literally set down by Mr. Ricketson.

TO HARRISON BLAKE (AT WORCESTER).

CONCORD, January 1, 1859.

MR. BLAKE,—It may interest you to hear that Cholmondeley has been this way again, *via* Montreal and Lake Huron, going to the West Indies, or rather to Weiss-nicht-wo, whither he urges me to accompany him. He is rather more demonstrative than before, and, on the whole, what would be called "a good fellow,"—is a man of principle, and quite reliable, but very peculiar. I have been to New Bedford with him, to show him a whaling town and Ricketson. I was glad to hear that you had called on R. How did you like him? I suspect that you did not see one another fairly.

I have lately got back to that glorious society called Solitude, where we meet our friends continually, and can imagine the outside world also to be peopled. Yet some of my acquaintance would fain hustle me into the almshouse for *the sake of society*, as if I were pining for that diet, when I seem to myself a most befriended man, and find constant employment. However, they do not believe a word I say. They have got a club, the handle of which is in the Parker House at Boston, and with this they beat me from time to time, expecting to make me tender or minced meat, so fit for a club to dine off.

Hercules with his club

The Dragon did drub;

But More of More Hall

With nothing at all,

He slew the Dragon of Wantley."

Ah! that More of More Hall knew what fair play was. Channing, who wrote to me about it once, brandishing the club vigorously (being set on by another, probably), says *now*, seriously, that he is sorry to find by my letters that I am "absorbed in politics," and adds, begging my pardon for his plainness, "Beware of an extraneous life!" and so he does his duty, and washes his hands of me. I tell him that it is as if he should say to the sloth, that fellow that creeps so slowly along a tree, and cries *ai* from time to time, "Beware of dancing!"

The doctors are all agreed that I am suffering for want of society. Was never a case like it. First, I did not know that I was suffering at all. Secondly, as an Irishman might say, I had thought it was indigestion of the society I got.

As for the Parker House, I went there once, when the Club[91] was away, but I found it hard to see through the cigar smoke, and men were deposited about in chairs over the marble floor, as thick as legs of bacon in a smoke-house. It was all smoke, and no salt, Attic or other. The only room in Boston which I visit with alacrity is the Gentlemen's Room at the Fitchburg Depot, where I wait for the cars, sometimes for two hours, in order to get out of town. It is a paradise to the Parker House, for no smoking is allowed, and there is far more retirement. A large and respectable club of us hire it (Town and Country Club), and I am pretty sure to find some one there whose face is set the same way as my own.

My last essay, on which I am still engaged, is called "Autumnal Tints." I do not know how readable (*i. e.*, by me to others) it will be.

I met Mr. James the other night at Emerson's, at an Alcottian conversation, at which, however, Alcott did not talk much, being disturbed by James's opposition. The latter is a hearty man enough, with whom you can differ very satisfactorily, on account of both his doctrines and his good temper. He utters *quasi* philanthropic dogmas in a metaphysic dress; but they are for all practical purposes very crude. He charges society with all the crime committed, and praises the criminal for committing it. But I think that all the remedies he suggests out of his head—for he goes no farther, hearty as he is—would leave us about where we are now. For, of course, it is not by a gift of turkeys on Thanksgiving Day that he proposes to convert the criminal, but by a true sympathy with each one,—with him, among the rest, who lyingly tells the world from the gallows that he has never been treated kindly by a single mortal since he was born. But it is not so easy a thing to sympathize with another, though you may have the best disposition to do it. There is Dobson over the hill. Have not you and I and all the world been trying, ever since he was born, to sympathize with him? (as doubtless he with us), and yet we have got no farther than to send him to the house of correction once at least; and he, on the other hand, as I hear, has sent us to another place several times. This is the real state of things, as I understand it, at least so far as James's remedies go. We are now, alas! exercising what charity we actually have, and new laws would not give us any more. But, perchance, we might make some improvements in the house of correction. You and I are Dobson; what will James do for us?

Have you found at last in your wanderings a place where the solitude is sweet?

What mountain are you camping on nowadays? Though I had a good time at the mountains, I confess that the journey did not bear any fruit that I know of. I did not expect it would. The mode of it was not simple and adventurous enough. You must first have made an infinite demand, and not unreasonably, but after a corresponding outlay, have an all-absorbing purpose, and at the same time that your feet bear you hither and thither, travel much more in imagination.

To let the mountains slide,—live at home like a traveler. It should not be in vain that these things are shown us from day to day. Is not each withered leaf that I see in my walks something which I have traveled to find?—traveled, who can tell how far? What a fool he must be who thinks that his El Dorado is anywhere but where he lives!

We are always, methinks, in some kind of ravine, though our bodies may walk the smooth streets of Worcester. Our souls (I use this word for want of a better) are ever perched on its rocky sides, overlooking that lowland. (What a more than Tuckerman's Ravine is the body itself, in which the "soul" is encamped, when you come to look into it! However, eagles always have chosen such places for their eyries.)

Thus is it ever with your fair cities of the plain. Their streets may be paved with silver and gold, and six carriages roll abreast in them, but the real *homes* of the citizens are in the Tuckerman's Ravines which ray out from that centre into the mountains round about, one from each man, woman, and child. The masters of life have so ordered it. That is their *beau-ideal* of a country-seat. There is no danger of being *tuckered* out before you get to it.

So we live in Worcester and in Concord, each man taking his exercise regularly in his ravine, like a lion in his cage, and sometimes spraining his ankle there. We have very few clear days, and a great many small plagues which keep us busy. Sometimes, I suppose, you hear a neighbor halloo (Brown, maybe) and think it is a bear. Nevertheless, on the whole, we think it very grand and exhilarating, this ravine life. It is a capital advantage withal, living so high, the excellent drainage of that city of God. Routine is but a shallow and insignificant sort of ravine, such as the ruts are, the conduits of puddles. But these ravines are the source of mighty streams, precipitous, icy, savage, as they are, haunted by bears and loup-cerviers; there are born not only Sacos and Amazons, but prophets who will redeem the world. The at last smooth and fertilizing water at which nations drink and navies supply themselves begins with melted glaciers, and burst thunder-spouts. Let us pray that, if we are not flowing through some Mississippi valley which we fertilize, —and it is not likely we are,—we may know ourselves shut in between grim and mighty mountain walls amid the clouds, falling a thousand feet in a mile, through dwarfed fir and spruce, over the rocky insteps of slides, being exercised in our minds, and so developed.

Concord, January 19, 1859.

Mr. Blake,—If I could have given a favorable report as to the skating, I should have answered you earlier. About a week before you wrote there was good skating; there is now none. As for the lecture, I shall be glad to come. I cannot now say when, but I will let you know, I think within a week or ten days at most, and will then leave you a week clear to make the arrangements in. I will bring something else than "What shall it profit a Man?" My father is very sick, and has been for a long time, so that there is the more need of me at home. This occurs to me, even when contemplating so short an excursion as to Worcester.

I want very much to see or hear your account of your adventures in the Ravine,[92] and I trust I shall do so when I come to Worcester. Cholmondeley has been here again, returning from Virginia (for he went no farther south) to Canada; and will go thence to Europe, he thinks, in the spring, and never ramble any more. (January 29.) I am expecting daily that my father will die, therefore I cannot leave home at present. I will write you again within ten days.

The death of John Thoreau (who was born October 8, 1787) occurred February 3d, and Thoreau gave his lecture on "Autumnal Tints" at Worcester, February 22, 1859. Mrs. Thoreau survived all her children except Sophia, and died in 1872.

At his fathers death, Thoreau sent a newspaper announcement of it to Ricketson, who had already seen it mentioned by Channing in the *Mercury*. Ricketson at once wrote, to pay his tribute to the character of the elder Thoreau, saying: "I have rarely met a man who inspired me with more respect. I remember with pleasure a ramble I took with him about Concord some two or three years ago, at a time when you were away from home; on which occasion I was much impressed with his good sense, his fine social nature, and his genuine hospitality." Of this remark Thoreau took notice in his interesting reply.

TO DANIEL RICKETSON (AT NEW BEDFORD).

Concord, 12th February, 1859.

Friend Ricketson,—I thank you for your kind letter. I sent you the notice of my father's death as much because you knew him as because you knew me. I can hardly realize that he is dead. He had been sick about two years, and at last declined rather rapidly, though steadily. Till within a week or ten days before he died he was hoping to see another spring, but he then discovered that this was a vain expectation, and, thinking that he was dying, he took his leave of us several times within a week before his departure. Once or twice he expressed a slight impatience at the delay. He was quite conscious to the last, and his death was so easy that, though we had all been sitting around the bed for an hour or more expecting that event (as we had sat before), he was gone at last, almost before we were aware of it.

I am glad to read what you say of his social nature. I think I may say that he was wholly unpretending; and there was this peculiarity in his aim, that though he had pecuniary difficulties to contend with the greater part of his life, he always studied how to make a *good* article, pencil or other (for he practiced various arts), and was never satisfied with what he had produced. Nor was he ever disposed in the least to put off a poor one for the sake of pecuniary gain,—as if he labored for a higher end.

Though he was not very old, and was not a native of Concord, I think that he was, on the whole, more identified with Concord street than any man now alive, having come here when he was about twelve years old, and set up for himself as a merchant here, at the age of twenty-one, fifty years ago. As I sat in a circle the other evening with my mother and sister, my mother's two sisters, and my father's two sisters, it occurred to me that my father, though seventy-one, belonged to the youngest four of the eight who recently composed our family.

How swiftly at last, but unnoticed, a generation passes away! Three years ago I was called with my father to be a witness to the signing of our neighbor Mr. Frost's will. Mr. Samuel Hoar, who was there writing it, also signed it. I was lately required to go to Cambridge to testify to the genuineness of the will, being the only one of the four who could be there, and now I am the only one alive.

My mother and sister thank you heartily for your sympathy. The latter, in particular, agrees with you in thinking that it is communion with still living and healthy nature alone which can restore to sane and cheerful views. I thank you for your invitation to New Bedford, but I feel somewhat confined here for the present.

I did not know but we should see you the day after Alger was here. It is not too late for a winter walk in Concord. It does me good to hear of spring birds, and singing ones too,—for spring seems far away from Concord yet. I am going to Worcester to read a parlor lecture on the 22d, and shall see Blake and Brown. What if you were to meet me there, or go with me from here? You would see them to good advantage. Cholmondeley has been here again, after going as far south as Virginia, and left for Canada about three weeks ago. He is a good soul, and I am afraid I did not sufficiently recognize him.

Please remember me to Mrs. Ricketson, and to the rest of your family.

A long silence had passed on Thoreau's part before he wrote again to Ricketson,—nearly two years, in fact,—and his friend complained of it. He had followed the public utterances of Thoreau with entire sympathy, although much in advance, in 1859-60, of public opinion respecting John Brown and slavery, and he had sent him letters and complimentary verses. Finally, he almost implored Thoreau to renew the bond of friendship. This will explain the tenor of Thoreau's reply.

TO DANIEL RICKETSON, (AT NEW BEDFORD).

CONCORD, November 4, 1860.

FRIEND RICKETSON,—I thank you for the verses. They are quite too good to apply to me. However, I know what a poet's license is, and will not get in the way.

But what do you mean by that prose? Why will you waste so many regards on me, and not know what to think of my silence? Infer from it what you might from the silence of a dense pine wood. It is its natural condition, except when the winds blow, and the jays scream, and the chickadee winds up his clock. My silence is just as inhuman as that, and no more. You know that I never promised to correspond with you, and so, when I do, I do more than I promised.

Such are my pursuits and habits that I rarely go abroad; and it is quite a habit with me to decline invitations to do so. Not that I could not enjoy such visits, if I were not otherwise occupied. I have enjoyed very much my visits to you, and my rides in your neighborhood, and am sorry that I cannot enjoy such things oftener; but life is short, and there are other things also to be done. I admit that you are more social than I am and far more attentive to "the common courtesies of life;" but this is partly for the reason that you have fewer or less exacting private pursuits.

Not to have written a note for a year is with me a very venial offense. I think that I do not correspond with any one so often as once in six months.

I have a faint recollection of your invitation referred to; but I suppose that I had no new nor particular reason for declining, and so made no new statement. I have felt that you would be glad to see me almost whenever I got ready to come; but I only offer myself as a rare visitor, and a still rarer correspondent.

I am very busy, after my fashion, little as there is to show for it, and feel as if I could not spend many days nor dollars in traveling; for the shortest visit must have a fair margin to it, and the days thus affect the weeks, you know. Nevertheless, we cannot forego these luxuries altogether. You must not regard me as a regular diet, but at most only as acorns, which, too, are not to be despised,—which, at least, we love to think are edible in a bracing walk. We have got along pretty well together in several directions, though we are such strangers in others.

I hardly know what to say in answer to your letter. Some are accustomed to write many letters, others very few. I am one of the last. At any rate, we are pretty sure, if we write at all, to send those thoughts which we cherish, to that one who, we believe, will most religiously attend to them.

This life is not for complaint, but for satisfaction. I do not feel addressed by this letter of yours. It suggests only misunderstanding. Intercourse may be good; but of what use are complaints and apologies? Any complaint *I* have to make is too serious to be uttered, for the evil cannot be mended.

Turn over a new leaf.

My outdoor harvest this fall has been one Canada lynx, a fierce-looking fellow, which, it seems, we have hereabouts; eleven barrels of apples from trees of my own planting; and a large crop of white oak acorns, which I did not raise.

Please remember me to your family. I have a very pleasant recollection of your fireside, and I trust that I shall revisit it;—also of your shanty and the surrounding regions.

TO HARRISON BLAKE (AT WORCESTER).

Concord, September 26, 1859.

Mr. Blake,—I am not sure that I am in a fit mood to write to you, for I feel and think rather too much like a business man, having some very irksome affairs to attend to these months and years on account of my family.[93] This is the way I am serving King Admetus, confound him! If it were not for my relations, I would let the wolves prey on his flocks to their bellies' content. Such fellows you have to deal with! herdsmen of some other king, or of the same, who tell no tale, but in the sense of counting their flocks, and then lie drunk under a hedge. How is your grist ground? Not by some murmuring stream, while you lie dreaming on the bank; but, it seems, you must take hold with your hands, and shove the wheel round. You can't depend on streams, poor feeble things! You can't depend on worlds, left to themselves; but you've got to oil them and goad them along. In short, you've got to carry on two farms at once,—the farm on the earth and the farm in your mind. Those Crimean and Italian battles were mere boys' play,—they are the scrapes into which truants get. But what a battle a man must fight everywhere to maintain his standing army of thoughts, and march with them in orderly array through the always hostile country! How many enemies there are to sane thinking! Every soldier has succumbed to them before he enlists for those other battles. Men may sit in chambers, seemingly safe and sound, and yet despair, and turn out at last only hollowness and dust within, like a Dead Sea apple. A standing army of numerous, brave, and well-disciplined thoughts, and you at the head of them, marching straight to your goal,—how to bring this about is the problem, and Scott's Tactics will not help you to it. Think of a poor fellow begirt only with a sword-belt, and no such staff of athletic thoughts! his brains rattling as he walks and *talks*! These are your prætorian guard. It is easy enough to maintain a family, or a state, but it is hard to maintain these children of your brain (or say, rather, these guests that trust to enjoy your hospitality), they make such great demands; and yet, he who does only the former, and loses the power to *think* originally, or as only he ever can, fails miserably. Keep up the fires of thought, and all will go well.

Zouaves?—pish! How you can overrun a country, climb any rampart, and carry any fortress, with an army of *alert* thoughts!—thoughts that send their bullets home to heaven's door,—with which you can *take* the whole world, without paying for it, or robbing anybody. See, the conquering hero comes! You *fail* in your thoughts, or you *prevail* in your thoughts only. Provided you *think* well, the heavens falling, or the earth gaping, will be the music for you to march by. No foe can ever see you, or you him; you cannot so much as *think* of him. Swords have no edges, bullets no penetration, for such a contest. In your mind must be a liquor which will dissolve the world whenever it is dropt in it. There is no universal solvent but this, and all things together cannot saturate it. It will hold the universe in solution, and yet be as translucent as ever. The vast machine may indeed roll over our toes, and we not know it, but it would rebound and be staved to pieces like an empty barrel, if it should strike fair and square on the smallest and least angular of a man's thoughts.

You seem not to have taken Cape Cod the right way. I think that you should have persevered in walking on the beach and on the bank, even to the land's end, however soft, and so, by long knocking at Ocean's gate, have gained admittance at last,—better, if separately, and in a storm, not knowing where you would sleep by night, or eat by day. Then you should have given a day to the sand behind Provincetown, and ascended the hills there, and been blown on considerably. I hope that you like to remember the journey better than you did to make it.

I have been confined at home all this year, but I am not aware that I have grown any rustier than was to be expected. One while I explored the bottom of the river pretty extensively. I have engaged to read a lecture to Parker's society on the 9th of October next.

I am off—a-barberrying.

TO HARRISON BLAKE (AT WORCESTER).

CONCORD, October 31, 1859.

MR. BLAKE,—I spoke to my townsmen last evening on "The Character of Captain Brown, now in the Clutches of the Slaveholder." I should like to speak to any company at Worcester who may wish to hear me; and will come if only my expenses are paid. I think we should express ourselves at once, while Brown is alive. The sooner the better. Perhaps Higginson may like to have a meeting. Wednesday evening would be a good time. The people here are deeply interested in the matter. Let me have an answer as soon as may be.

P. S.—I may be engaged toward the end of the week.

HENRY D. THOREAU.

This address on John Brown was one of the first public utterances in favor of that hero; it was made up mainly from the entries in Thoreau's journals, since I had introduced Brown to him, and he to Emerson, in March, 1857; and especially from those pages that Thoreau had written after the news of Brown's capture in Virginia had reached him. It was first given in the vestry of the old parish church in Concord (where, in 1774, the Provincial Congress of Massachusetts had met to prepare for armed resistance to British tyranny); was repeated at Worcester the same week, and before a great audience in Boston, the following Sunday,—after which it was published in the newspapers, and had a wide reading. Mr. Alcott in his diary mentions it under date of Sunday, October 30, thus: "Thoreau reads a paper on John Brown, his virtues, spirit, and deeds, this evening, and to the delight of his company,—the best that could be gathered at short notice,—and among them Emerson. (November 4.) Thoreau calls and reports about the reading of his lecture on Brown at Boston and Worcester. He has been the first to speak and celebrate the hero's courage and magnanimity; it is these that he discerns and praises. The men have much in common,—the sturdy manliness, straightforwardness, and independence. (November 5.) Ricketson from New Bedford arrives; he and Thoreau take supper with us. Thoreau talks freely and enthusiastically about Brown,—denouncing the Union, the President, the States, and Virginia particularly; wishes to publish his late speech, and has seen Boston publishers, but failed to find any to print it for him." It was soon after published, along with Emerson's two speeches in favor of Brown, by a new Boston publishing house (Thayer & Eldridge), in a volume called "Echoes of Harper's Ferry," edited by the late James Redpath, Brown's first biographer. In the following summer, Thoreau sent a second paper on Brown (written soon after his execution) to be read at a commemoration of the martyr, beside his grave among the Adirondack Mountains. This is mentioned in his letter to Sophia Thoreau, July 8, 1860. He took an active part in arranging for the funeral service in honor of Brown, at Concord, the day of his death,

December 2, 1859.

TO HARRISON BLAKE (AT WORCESTER).

CONCORD, May 20, 1860.

MR. BLAKE,—I must endeavor to pay some of my debts to you. To begin where we left off, then.

The presumption is that *we* are always the same; our opportunities, and Nature herself, fluctuating. Look at mankind. No great difference between two, apparently; perhaps the same height, and breadth, and weight; and yet, to the man who sits most east, this life is a weariness, routine, dust and ashes, and he drowns his imaginary *cares* (!) (a sort of friction among his vital organs) in a bowl. But to the man who sits most west, his *contemporary* (!), it is a field for all noble endeavors, an elysium, the dwelling-place of heroes and demigods. The former complains that he has a thousand affairs to attend to; but he does not realize that his affairs (though they may be a thousand) and he are one.

Men and boys are learning all kinds of trades but how to make *men* of themselves. They learn to make houses; but they are not so well housed, they are not so contented in their houses, as the woodchucks in their holes. What is the use of a house if you haven't got a tolerable planet to put it on?—if you cannot tolerate the planet it is on? Grade the ground first. If a man believes and expects great things of himself, it makes no odds where you put him, or what you show him (of course *you* cannot put him anywhere, nor show him anything), he will be surrounded by grandeur. He is in the condition of a healthy and hungry man, who says to himself,—How sweet this crust is! If he despairs of himself, then Tophet is his dwelling-place, and he is in the condition of a sick man who is disgusted with the fruits of finest flavor.

Whether he sleeps or wakes,—whether he runs or walks,—whether he uses a microscope or a telescope, or his naked eye,—a man never discovers anything, never overtakes anything, or leaves anything behind, but himself. Whatever he says or does, he merely reports himself. If he is in love, he *loves*; if he is in heaven, he *enjoys*; if he is in hell, he *suffers*. It is his condition that determines his locality.

The principal, the only, thing a man makes, is his condition of fate. Though commonly he does not know it, nor put up a sign to this effect, "My own destiny made and mended here." (Not *yours*.) He is a master workman in the business. He works twenty-four hours a day at it, and gets it done. Whatever else he neglects or botches, no man was ever known to neglect this work. A great many pretend to make *shoes* chiefly, and would scout the idea that they make the hard times which they experience.

Each reaching and aspiration is an instinct with which all nature consists and coöperates, and therefore it is not in vain. But alas! each relaxing and desperation is an instinct too. To be active, well, happy, implies rare courage. To be ready to fight in a duel or a battle implies desperation, or that you hold your life cheap.

If you take this life to be simply what old religious folks pretend (I mean the effete, gone to seed in a drought, mere human galls stung by the devil once), then all your joy and serenity is reduced to grinning and bearing it. The fact is, you have got to take the world on your shoulders like Atlas, and "put along" with it. You will do this for an idea's sake, and your success will be in proportion to your devotion to ideas. It may make your back ache occasionally, but you will have the satisfaction of hanging it or twirling it to suit yourself. Cowards suffer, heroes enjoy. After a long day's walk with it, pitch it into a hollow place, sit down and eat your luncheon. Unexpectedly, by some immortal thoughts, you will be compensated. The bank whereon you sit will be a fragrant and flowery one, and your world in the hollow a sleek and light gazelle.

Where is the "unexplored land" but in our own untried enterprises? To an adventurous spirit any place—London, New York, Worcester, or his own yard—is "unexplored land," to seek which Frémont and Kane travel so far. To a sluggish and defeated spirit even the Great Basin and the Polaris are trivial places. If they can get there (and, indeed, they are there now), they will want to sleep, and give it up, just as they always do. These are the regions of the Known and of the Unknown. What is the use of going right over the old track again? There is an adder in the path which your own feet have worn. You must make tracks into the Unknown. That is what you have your board and clothes for. Why do you ever mend your clothes, unless that, wearing them, you may mend your ways? Let us sing.

TO SOPHIA THOREAU (AT CAMPTON, N. H.).

CONCORD, July 8, 1860.

DEAR SOPHIA,—Mother reminds me that I must write to you, if only a few lines, though I have sprained my thumb, so that it is questionable whether I can write legibly, if at all. I can't "bear on" much. What is worse, I believe that I have sprained my brain too—that is, it sympathizes with my thumb. But that is no excuse, I suppose, for writing a letter in such a case is like sending a newspaper, only a hint to let you know that "all is well,"—but my thumb.

I hope that you begin to derive some benefit from that more mountainous air which you are breathing. Have you had a distinct view of the Franconia Notch Mountains (blue peaks in the northern horizon)? which I told you you could get from the road in Campton, probably from some other points nearer. Such a view of the mountains is more memorable than any other. Have you been to Squam Lake or overlooked it? I should think that you could make an excursion to some mountain in that direction from which you could see the lake and mountains generally. Is there no friend of N. P. Rogers who can tell you where the "lions" are?

Of course I did not go to North Elba,[94] but I sent some reminiscences of last fall. I hear that John Brown, Jr., has now come to Boston for a few days. Mr. Sanborn's case, it is said, will come on after some murder cases have been disposed of here.

I have just been invited formally to be present at the annual picnic of Theodore Parker's society (that was), at Waverley, next Wednesday, and to make some remarks. But that is wholly out of my line. I do not go to picnics, even in Concord, you know.

Mother and Aunt Sophia rode to Acton in time yesterday. I suppose that you have heard that Mr. Hawthorne has come home. I went to meet him the other evening and found that he has not altered, except that he was looking quite brown after his voyage. He is as simple and childlike as ever.

I believe that I have fairly scared the kittens away, at last, by my pretended fierceness, which was. I will consider my thumb—and your eyes.

Henry.

TO HARRISON BLAKE (AT WORCESTER).

Concord, August 3, 1860.

Mr. Blake,—I some time ago asked Channing if he would not spend a week with me on Monadnock; but he did not answer decidedly. Lately he has talked of an excursion somewhere, but I said that *now* I must wait till my sister returned from Plymouth, N. H. She has returned,—and accordingly, on receiving your note this morning, I made known its contents to Channing, in order to see how far I was engaged with him. The result is that he decides to go to Monadnock to-morrow morning;[95] so I must defer making an excursion with you and Brown to another season. Perhaps you will call as you pass the mountain. I send this by the earliest mail.

P. S.—That was a very insufficient visit which you made here the last time. My mother is better, though far from well; and if you should chance along here any time after your journey, I trust that we shall all do better.

The mention by Thoreau of John Brown and my "case" recalls to me an incident of those excited days which followed the attack by Brown on slavery in Virginia. The day after Brown's death, but before the execution of his comrades, I received a message from the late Dr. David Thayer of Boston, implying, as I thought, that a son of Brown was at his house, whither I hurried to meet him. Instead, I found young F. J. Merriam of Boston, who had escaped with Owen Brown from Harper's Ferry, and was now in Boston to raise another party against the slaveholders. He was unfit to lead or even join in such a desperate undertaking, and we insisted he should return to safety in Canada,—a large reward being offered for his seizure. He agreed to go back to Canada that night by the Fitchburg Railroad; but in his hot-headed way he took the wrong train, which ran no farther than Concord,—and found himself in the early evening at my house, where my sister received him, but insisted that I should not see him, lest I might be questioned about my guest. While he had supper and went to bed, I posted down to Mr. Emerson's and engaged his horse and covered wagon, to be ready at sunrise,—he asking no questions. In the same way I engaged Mr. Thoreau to drive his friend's horse to South Acton the next morning, and there put on board the first Canadian train a Mr. Lockwood, whom he would find at my house. Thoreau readily consented, asked no questions, walked to the Emerson stable the next morning, found the horse ready, drove him to my door, and took up Merriam, under the name of Lockwood,—neither knowing who the other was. Merriam was so flighty that, though he had agreed to go to Montreal, and knew that his life might depend on getting there early, he declared he must see Mr. Emerson, to lay before him his plan for invading the South, and consult him about some moral questions that troubled his mind. His companion listened gravely,—and hurried the horse towards Acton. Merriam grew more positive and suspicious, —"Perhaps YOU are Mr. Emerson; you look somewhat like him."[96] "No, I am not," said Thoreau, and drove steadily away from Concord. "Well, then, I am going back," said the youth, and flung himself out of the wagon. How Thoreau got him in again, he never told me; but I suspected some judicious force, accompanying the grave persuasive speech natural to our friend. At any rate, he took his man to Acton, saw him safe on the train, and reported to me that "Mr. Lockwood had taken passage for Canada," where he arrived that night. Nothing more passed between us until, more than two years after, he inquired one day, in his last illness, who my fugitive was. Merriam was then out of danger in that way, and had been for months a soldier in the Union army, where he died. I therefore said that "Lockwood" was the grandson of his mother's old friend, Francis Jackson, and had escaped from Maryland. In return he gave me the odd incidents of their drive, and mentioned that he had spoken of the affair to his mother only since his illness. So reticent and practically useful could he be; as Channing says, "He made no useless professions, never asked one of those questions which destroy all relation; but he was on the spot at the time, he meant friendship, and meant nothing else, and stood by it without the slightest abatement."

TO HARRISON BLAKE (AT WORCESTER).

Concord, November 4, 1860.

Mr. Blake,—I am glad to hear any particulars of your excursion. As for myself, I looked out for you somewhat on that Monday, when, it appears, you passed Monadnock; turned my glass upon several parties that were ascending the mountain half a mile on one side of us. In short, I came as near to seeing you as you to seeing me. I have no doubt that we should have had a good time if you had come, for I had, all ready, two good spruce houses, in which you could stand up, complete in all respects, half a mile apart, and you and B. could have lodged by yourselves in one, if not with us.

We made an excellent beginning of our mountain life.[97] You may remember that the Saturday previous was a stormy day. Well, we went up in the rain,—wet through,—and found ourselves in a cloud there at mid-afternoon, in no situation to look about for the best place for a camp. So I proceeded at once, through the cloud, to that memorable stone, "chunk yard," in which we made our humble camp once, and there, after putting our packs under a rock, having a good hatchet, I proceeded to build a substantial house, which Channing declared the handsomest he ever saw. (He never camped out before, and was, no doubt, prejudiced in its favor.) This was done about dark, and by that time we were nearly as wet as if we had stood in a hogshead of water. We then built a fire before the door, directly on the site of our little camp of two years ago, and it took a long time to burn through its remains to the earth beneath. Standing before this, and turning round slowly, like meat that is roasting, we were as dry, if not drier, than ever, after a few hours, and so at last we "turned in."

This was a great deal better than going up there in fair weather, and having no adventure (not knowing how to appreciate either fair weather or foul) but dull, commonplace sleep in a useless house, and before a comparatively useless fire,—such as we get every night. Of course we thanked our stars, when we saw them, which was about midnight, that they had seemingly withdrawn for a season. We had the mountain all to ourselves that afternoon and night. There was nobody going up that day to engrave his name on the summit, nor to gather blueberries. The genius of the mountains saw us starting from Concord, and it said, There come two of our folks. Let us get ready for them. Get up a serious storm, that will send a-packing these holiday guests. (They may have their say another time.) Let us receive them with true mountain hospitality,—kill the fatted cloud. Let them know the value of a spruce roof, and of a fire of dead spruce stumps. Every bush dripped tears of joy at our advent. Fire did its best, and received our thanks. What could fire have done in fair weather? Spruce roof got its share of our blessings. And then, such a view of the wet rocks, with the wet lichens on them, as we had the next morning, but did not get again!

We and the mountain had a sound season, as the saying is. How glad we were to be wet, in order that we might be dried! How glad we were of the storm which made our house seem like a new home to us! This day's experience was indeed lucky, for we did not have a thunder-shower during all our stay. Perhaps our host reserved this attention in order to tempt us to come again.

Our next house was more substantial still. One side was rock, good for durability; the floor the same; and the roof which I made would have upheld a horse. I stood on it to do the shingling.

I noticed, when I was at the White Mountains last, several nuisances which render traveling thereabouts unpleasant. The chief of these was the mountain houses. I might have supposed that the main attraction of that region, even to citizens, lay in its wildness and unlikeness to the city, and yet they make it as much like the city as they can afford to. I heard that the Crawford House was lighted with gas, and had a large saloon, with its band of music, for dancing. But give me a spruce house made in the rain.

From the Summit of Monadnock

An old Concord farmer tells me that he ascended Monadnock once, and danced on the top. How did that happen? Why, he being up there, a party of young men and women came up, bringing boards and a fiddler; and, having laid down the boards, they made a level floor, on which they danced to the music of the fiddle. I suppose the tune was "Excelsior." This reminds me of the fellow who climbed to the top of a very high spire, stood upright on the ball, and hurrahed for—what? Why, for Harrison and Tyler. That's the kind of sound which most ambitious people emit when they culminate. They are wont to be singularly frivolous in the thin atmosphere; they can't contain themselves, though our comfort and their safety require it; it takes the pressure of many atmospheres to do this; and hence they helplessly evaporate there. It would seem that as they ascend, they breathe shorter and shorter, and, at each *expiration*, some of their wits leave them, till, when they reach the pinnacle, they are so light-headed as to be fit only to show how the wind sits. I suspect that Emerson's criticism called "Monadnoc" was inspired, not by remembering the inhabitants of New Hampshire as they are in the valleys, so much as by meeting some of them on the mountain-top.

After several nights' experience, Channing came to the conclusion that he was "lying outdoors," and inquired what was the largest beast that might nibble his legs there. I fear that he did not improve all the night, as he might have done, to sleep. I had asked him to go and spend a week there. We spent five nights, being gone six days, for C. suggested that six working days made a week, and I saw that he was ready to *decamp*. However, he found his account in it as well as I.

We were seen to go up in the rain, grim and silent, like two genii of the storm, by Fassett's men or boys; but we were never identified afterward, though we were the subject of some conversation which we overheard. Five hundred persons at least came on to the mountain while we were there, but not one found our camp. We saw one party of three ladies and two gentlemen spread their blankets and spend the night on the top, and heard them converse; but they did not know that they had neighbors who were comparatively old settlers. We spared them the chagrin which that knowledge would have caused them, and let them print their story in a newspaper accordingly.

Yes, to meet men on an honest and simple footing, meet with rebuffs, suffer from sore feet, as you did,—ay, and from a sore heart, as perhaps you also did,—all that is excellent. What a pity that that young prince[98] could not enjoy a little of the legitimate experience of traveling—be dealt with simply and truly, though rudely. He might have been invited to some hospitable house in the country, had his bowl of bread and milk set before him, with a clean pinafore; been told that there were the punt and the fishing-rod, and he could amuse himself as he chose; might have swung a few birches, dug out a woodchuck, and had a regular good time, and finally been sent to bed with the boys,—and so never have been introduced to Mr. Everett at all. I have no doubt that this would have been a far more memorable and valuable experience than he got.

The snow-clad summit of Mt. Washington must have been a very interesting sight from Wachusett. How wholesome winter is, seen far or near; how good, above all mere sentimental, warm-blooded, short-lived, soft-hearted, *moral* goodness, commonly so called. Give me the goodness which has forgotten its own deeds,—which God has seen to be good, and let be. None of your *just made perfect*,—pickled eels! All that will save them will be their picturesqueness, as with blasted trees. Whatever is, and is not ashamed to be, is good. I value no moral goodness or greatness unless it is good or great, even as that snowy peak is. Pray, how could thirty feet of bowels improve it? Nature is goodness crystallized. You looked into the land of promise. Whatever beauty we behold, the more it is distant, serene, and cold, the purer and more durable it is. It is better to warm ourselves with ice than with fire.

Tell Brown that he sent me more than the price of the book, viz., a word from himself, for which I am greatly his debtor.

Thoreau began to be more seriously ill than he had been for some years, early in December, 1860. He exposed himself unduly in one of his walks, while counting the rings on stumps of trees, amid snow. He ceased much of his small activity of letter-writing; but, in addressing Ricketson the next spring, he took the unusual pains of writing him a letter of some length which he never sent. It was found among his papers after death,—the first draft of it, which ran as follows, but was left a fragment:—

TO DANIEL RICKETSON (AT NEW BEDFORD).

Concord, March 19, 1861.

Friend R,—Your letter reached me in due time, but I had already heard the bluebirds. They were here on the 26th of February at least,—but not yet do the larks sing or the flickers call, with us. The bluebirds come again, as does the same spring, but it does not find the same mortals here to greet it. You remember Minott's cottage on the hillside,—well, it finds some change there, for instance. The little gray hip-roofed cottage was occupied at the beginning of February, this year, by George Minott and his sister Mary, respectively 78 and 80 years old, and Miss Potter, 74. These had been its permanent occupants for many years. Minott had been on his last legs for some time,—at last off his legs, expecting weekly to take his departure,—a burden to himself and friends,—yet dry and natural as ever. His sister took care of him, and supported herself and family with her needle, as usual. He lately willed his little property to her, as a slight compensation for her care. Feb. 13 their sister, 86 or 87, who lived across the way, died. Miss Minott had taken cold in visiting her, and was so sick that she could not go to her funeral. She herself died of lung fever[99] on the 18th (which was said to be the same disease that her sister had),—having just willed her property back to George, and added her own mite to it. Miss Potter, too, had now become ill,—too ill to attend the funeral,—and she died of the same disease on the 23d. All departed as gently as the sun goes down, leaving George alone.

I called to see him the other day,—the 27th of February, a remarkably pleasant spring day,—and as I was climbing the sunny slope to his strangely deserted house, I heard the first bluebirds upon the elm that hangs over it. They had come as usual, though some who used to hear them were gone. Even Minott had not heard them, though the door was open,—for he was thinking of other things. Perhaps there will be a time when the bluebirds themselves will not return any more.

I hear that George, a few days after this, called out to his niece, who had come to take care of him, and was in the next room, to know if she did not feel lonely? "Yes, I do," said she. "So do I," added he. He said he was like an old oak, all shattered and decaying. "I am sure, Uncle," said his niece, "you are not much like an oak!" "I mean," said he, "that I am like an oak or any other tree, inasmuch as I cannot stir from where I am."

Either this topic was too pathetic for Thoreau to finish the letter, or perchance he thought it not likely to interest his friend; for he threw aside this draft for three days, and then, with the same beginning, wrote a very different letter. The Minotts were old familiar acquaintance, and related to that Captain Minott whom Thoreau's grandmother married as a second husband. George was his "old man of Verona," who had not left Concord for more than forty years, except to stray over the town bounds in hunting or wood-ranging; and Mary was the "tailoress" who for years made Thoreau's garments.

TO DANIEL RICKETSON (AT NEW BEDFORD).

CONCORD, March 22, 1861.

FRIEND RICKETSON,—The bluebird was here the 26th of February, at least, which is one day earlier than you date; but I have not heard of larks nor pigeon woodpeckers. To tell the truth, I am not on the alert for the signs of spring, not having had any winter yet. I took a severe cold about the 3d of December, which at length resulted in a kind of bronchitis, so that I have been confined to the house ever since, excepting a very few experimental trips as far as the post-office in some particularly fine noons. My health otherwise has not been affected in the least, nor my spirits. I have simply been imprisoned for so long, and it has not prevented my doing a good deal of reading and the like.

Channing has looked after me very faithfully; says he has made a study of my case, and knows me better than I know myself, etc., etc. Of course, if I knew how it began, I should know better how it would end. I trust that when warm weather comes I shall begin to pick up my crumbs. I thank you for your invitation to come to New Bedford, and will bear it in mind; but at present my health will not permit my leaving home.

The day I received your letter, Blake and Brown arrived here, having walked from Worcester in two days, though Alcott, who happened in soon after, could not understand what pleasure they found in walking across the country in this season, when the ways were so unsettled. I had a solid talk with them for a day and a half—though my pipes were not in good order—and they went their way again.

You may be interested to hear that Alcott is at present, perhaps, the most successful man in the town. He had his second annual exhibition of all the schools in the town, at the Town Hall last Saturday; at which all the masters and misses did themselves great credit, as I hear, and of course reflected some on their teachers and parents. They were making their little speeches from one till six o'clock P. M., to a large audience, which patiently listened to the end. In the meanwhile, the children made Mr. Alcott an unexpected present of a fine edition of "Pilgrim's Progress" and Herbert's Poems, which, of course, overcame all parties. I inclose an order of exercises.[100]

We had, last night, an old-fashioned northeast snow-storm, far worse than anything in the winter; and the drifts are now very high above the fences. The inhabitants are pretty much confined to their houses, as I was already. All houses are one color, white, with the snow plastered over them, and you cannot tell whether they have blinds or not. Our pump has another pump, its ghost, as thick as itself, sticking to one side of it. The town has sent out teams of eight oxen each, to break out the roads; and the train due from Boston at 8½ A. M. has not arrived yet (4 P. M.). All the passing has been a train from above at 12 M., which also was due at 8½ A. M. Where are the bluebirds now, think you? I suppose that you have not so much snow at New Bedford, if any.

TO PARKER PILLSBURY (AT CONCORD N. H.).

Concord, April 10, 1861.

Friend Pillsbury,—I am sorry to say that I have not a copy of "Walden" which I can spare; and know of none, unless possibly Ticknor & Fields may have one. I send, nevertheless, a copy of "The Week," the price of which is one dollar and twenty-five cents, which you can pay at your convenience.

As for your friend, my prospective reader, I hope he ignores Fort Sumter, and "Old Abe," and all that; for that is just the most fatal, and, indeed, the only fatal weapon you can direct against evil, ever; for, as long as you *know of it*, you are *particeps criminis*. What business have you, if you are an "angel of light," to be pondering over the deeds of darkness, reading the *New York*

Herald, and the like?

I do not so much regret the present condition of things in this country (provided I regret it at all), as I do that I ever heard of it. I know one or two, who have this year, for the first time, read a President's Message; but they do not see that this implies a *fall* in themselves, rather than a *rise* in the President. Blessed were the days before you read a President's Message. Blessed are the young, for they do not read the President's Message. Blessed are they who never read a newspaper, for they shall see Nature, and, through her, God.

But, alas! *I* have heard of Sumter and Pickens, and even of Buchanan (though I did not read his Message). I also read the *New York Tribune*; but then, I am reading Herodotus and Strabo, and Blodget's "Climatology," and "Six Years in the Desert of North America," as hard as I can, to counterbalance it.

By the way, Alcott is at present our most popular and successful man, and has just published a volume in size, in the shape of the Annual School Report, which I presume he has sent to you.

Yours, for remembering all good things,

HENRY D. THOREAU.

Parker Pillsbury, to whom this letter went, was an old friend of the Thoreau family, with whom he became intimate in the antislavery agitation, wherein they took part, while he was a famous orator, celebrated by Emerson in one of his essays. Mr. Pillsbury visited Thoreau in his last illness, when he could scarcely speak above a whisper, and, having made to him some remark concerning the future life, Thoreau replied, "My friend, one world at a time." His petulant words in this letter concerning national affairs would hardly have been said a few days later, when, at the call of Abraham Lincoln, the people rose to protect their government, and every President's Message became of thrilling interest, even to Thoreau.

Arrangements were now making for the invalid, about whose health his friends had been anxious for some years, to travel for a better climate than the New England spring affords, and early in May Thoreau set out for the upper Mississippi. He thus missed the last letter sent to him by his English friend Cholmondeley, which I answered, then forwarded to him at Redwing, in Minnesota. It is of interest enough to be given here.

T. CHOLMONDELEY TO THOREAU (IN MINNESOTA).

SHREWSBURY [England], April 23, 1861.

MY DEAR THOREAU,—It is now some time since I wrote to you or heard from you, but do not suppose that I have forgotten you, or shall ever cease to cherish in my mind those days at dear old Concord. The last I heard about you all was from Morton,[101] who was in England about a year ago; and I hope that he has got over his difficulties and is now in his own country again. I think he has seen rather more of English country life than most Yankee tourists; and appeared to find it *curious*, though I fear he was dulled by our ways; for he was too full of ceremony and compliments and bows, which is a mistake here; though very well in Spain. I am afraid he was rather on pins and needles; but he made a splendid speech at a volunteer supper, and indeed the *very best*, some said, ever heard in this part of the country.

We are here in a state of alarm and apprehension, the world being so troubled in East and West and everywhere. Last year the harvest was bad and scanty. This year our trade is beginning to feel the events in America. In reply to the northern tariff, of course we are going to smuggle as much as we can. The supply of cotton being such a necessity to us, we must work up India and South Africa a little better. There is war even in old New Zealand, but not in the same island where my people are! Besides, we are certainly on the eve of a continental blaze, *so we are making merry and living while we can*; not being sure where we shall be this time a year.

Give my affectionate regards to your father, mother, and sister, and to Mr. Emerson and his family, and to Channing, Sanborn, Ricketson, Blake, and Morton and Alcott and Parker. A thought arises in my mind whether I may not be enumerating some dead men! Perhaps Parker is!

These rumors of wars make me wish that we had got done with this brutal stupidity of war altogether; and I believe, Thoreau, that the human race will at last get rid of it, though perhaps not in a creditable way; but such *powers* will be brought to bear that it will become monstrous even to the French. Dundonald declared to the last that he possessed secrets which from their tremendous character would make war impossible. So peace may be begotten from the machinations of evil.

Have you heard of any good books lately? I think "Burnt Njal" good, and believe it to be genuine. "Hast thou not heard" (says Steinrora to Thangbrand) "how Thor challenged Christ to single combat, and how he did not dare to fight with Thor?" When Gunnar brandishes his sword, three swords are seen in air. The account of Ospah and Brodir and Brian's battle is the only historical account of that engagement, which the Irish talk so much of; for I place little trust in O'Halloran's authority, though the outline is the same in both.

Darwin's "Origin of Species" may be fanciful, but it is a move in theright direction. Emerson's "Conduct of Life" has done me good; but it will not go down in England for a generation or so. But *these* are some of them already a year or two old. The book of the season is Du Chaillu's "Central Africa," with accounts of the Gorilla, of which you are aware that you have had a skeleton at Boston for many years. There is also one in the British Museum; but they have now several stuffed specimens at the Geographical Society's rooms in Town. I suppose you will have seen Sir Emerson Tennent's "Ceylon," which is perhaps as complete a book as ever was published; and a better monument to a governor's residence in a great province was never made.

We have been lately astonished by a foreign Hamlet, a supposed impossibility; but Mr. Fechter does real wonders. No doubt he will visit America, and then you may see the best actor in the world. He has carried out Goethe's idea of Hamlet as given in the "Wilhelm Meister," showing him forth as a fair-haired and fat man. I suppose you are not got fat yet?

Yours ever truly,

THOS. CHOLMONDELEY.[102]

TO HARRISON BLAKE (AT WORCESTER).

CONCORD, May 3, 1861.

MR. BLAKE,—I am still as much an invalid as when you and Brown were here, if not more of one, and at this rate there is danger that the cold weather may come again, before I get over my bronchitis. The doctor accordingly tells me that I must "clear out" to the West Indies, or elsewhere,—he does not seem to care much where. But I decide against the West Indies, on account of their muggy heat in the summer, and the South of Europe, on account of the expense of time and money, and have at last concluded that it will be most expedient for me to try the air of Minnesota, say somewhere about St. Paul's. I am only waiting to be well enough to start. Hope to get off within a week or ten days.

The inland air may help me at once, or it may not. At any rate, I am so much of an invalid that I shall have to study my comfort in traveling to a remarkable degree,—stopping to rest, etc., etc., if need be. I think to get a through ticket to Chicago, with liberty to stop frequently on the way, making my first stop of consequence at Niagara Falls, several days or a week, at a private boarding-house; then a night or day at Detroit; and as much at Chicago as my health may require. At Chicago I can decide at what point (Fulton, Dunleith, or another) to strike the Mississippi, and take a boat to St. Paul's.

I trust to find a private boarding-house in one or various agreeable places in that region, and spend my time there. I expect, and shall be prepared, to be gone three months; and I would like to return by a different route,—perhaps

Mackinaw and Montreal.

I have thought of finding a companion, of course, yet not seriously, because I had no right to offer myself as a companion to anybody, having such a peculiarly private and all-absorbing but miserable business as *my* health, and not altogether *his*, to attend to, causing me to stop here and go there, etc., etc., unaccountably.

Nevertheless, I have just now decided to let you know of my intention, thinking it barely possible that you might like to make a part or the whole of this journey at the same time, and that perhaps your own health may be such as to be benefited by it.

Pray let me know if such a statement offers any temptations to you. I write in great haste for the mail, and must omit all the moral.

TO F. B. SANBORN (AT CONCORD).

REDWING, MINNESOTA, June 26, 1861.

MR. SANBORN,—I was very glad to find awaiting me, on my arrival here on Sunday afternoon, a letter from you. I have performed this journey in a very dead and alive manner, but nothing has come so near waking me up as the receipt of letters from Concord. I read yours, and one from my sister (and Horace Mann, his four), near the top of a remarkable isolated bluff here, called Barn Bluff, or the Grange, or Redwing Bluff, some four hundred and fifty feet high, and half a mile long,—a bit of the main bluff or bank standing alone. The top, as you know, rises to the general level of the surrounding country, the river having eaten out so much. Yet the valley just above and below this (we are at the head of Lake Pepin) must be three or four miles wide.

I am not even so well informed as to the progress of the war as you suppose. I have seen but one Eastern paper (that, by the way, *was* the *Tribune*) for five weeks. I have not taken much pains to get them; but, necessarily, I have not seen any paper at all for more than a week at a time. The people of Minnesota have *seemed* to me more cold,—to feel less implicated in this war than the people of Massachusetts. It is apparent that Massachusetts, for one State at least, is doing much more than her share in carrying it on. However, I have dealt partly with those of Southern birth, and have seen but little way beneath the surface. I was glad to be told yesterday that there was a good deal of weeping here at Redwing the other day, when the volunteers stationed at Fort Snelling followed the regulars to the seat of the war. They do not weep when their children go *up* the river to occupy the deserted forts, though they *may* have to fight the Indians there.

I do not even know what the attitude of England is at present.

The grand feature hereabouts is, of course, the Mississippi River. Too much can hardly be said of its grandeur, and of the beauty of this portion of it (from Dunleith, and probably from Rock Island to this place). St. Paul is a dozen miles below the Falls of St. Anthony, or near the head of uninterrupted navigation on the main stream, about two thousand miles from its mouth. There is not a "rip" below that, and the river is almost as wide in the upper as the lower part of its course. Steamers go up the Sauk Rapids, above the Falls, near a hundred miles farther, and then you are fairly in the pine woods and lumbering country. Thus it flows from the pine to the palm.

The lumber, as you know, is sawed chiefly at the Falls of St. Anthony (what is not rafted in the log to ports far below), having given rise to the towns of St. Anthony, Minneapolis, etc., etc. In coming up the river from Dunleith, you meet with great rafts of sawed lumber and of logs, twenty rods or more in length, by five or six wide, floating down, all from the pine region above the Falls. An old Maine lumberer, who has followed the same business here, tells me that the sources of the Mississippi were comparatively free from rocks and rapids, making easy work for them; but he thought that the timber was more knotty here than in Maine.

It has chanced that about half the men whom I have spoken with in Minnesota, whether travelers or settlers, were from Massachusetts.

After spending some three weeks in and about St. Paul, St. Anthony, and Minneapolis, we made an excursion in a steamer, some three hundred or more miles up the Minnesota (St. Peter's) River, to Redwood, or the Lower Sioux Agency, in order to see the plains, and the Sioux, who were to receive their annual payment there. This is eminently *the* river of Minnesota (for she shares the Mississippi with Wisconsin), and it is of incalculable value to her. It flows through a very fertile country destined to be famous for its wheat; but it is a remarkably winding stream, so that Redwood is only half as far from its mouth by land as by water. There was not a straight reach a mile in length as far as we went,—generally you could not see a quarter of a mile of water, and the boat was steadily turning this way or that. At the greater bends, as the Traverse des Sioux, some of the passengers were landed, and walked across to be taken in on the other side. Two or three times you could have thrown a stone across the neck of the isthmus, while it was from one to three miles around it. It was a very novel kind of navigation to me. The boat was perhaps the largest that had been up so high, and the water was rather low (it had been about fifteen feet higher). In making a short turn, we repeatedly and designedly ran square into the steep and soft bank, taking in a cart-load of earth,—this being more effectual than the rudder to fetch us about again; or the deeper water was so narrow and close to the shore, that we were obliged to run into and break down at least fifty trees which overhung the water, when we did not cut them off, repeatedly losing a part of our outworks, though the most exposed had been taken in. I could pluck almost any plant on the bank from the boat. We very frequently got aground, and then drew ourselves along with a windlass and a cable fastened to a tree, or we swung round in the current, and completely blocked up and blockaded the river, one end of the boat resting on each shore. And yet we would haul ourselves round again with the windlass and cable in an hour or two, though the boat was about one hundred and sixty feet long, and drew some three feet of water, or, often, water and sand. It was one consolation to know that in such a case we were all the while damming the river, and so raising it. We once ran fairly on to a concealed rock, with a shock that aroused all the passengers, and rested there, and the mate went below with a lamp, expecting to find a hole, but he did not. Snags and sawyers were so common that I forgot to mention them. The sound of the boat rumbling over one was the ordinary music. However, as long as the boiler did not burst, we knew that no serious accident was likely to happen. Yet this was a singularly navigable river, more so than the Mississippi above the Falls, and it is owing to its very crookedness. Ditch it straight, and it would not only be very swift, but soon run out. It was from ten to fifteen rods wide near the mouth, and from eight to ten or twelve at Redwood. Though the current was swift, I did not see a "rip" on it, and only three or four rocks. For three months in the year I am told that it can be navigated by small steamers about twice as far as we went, or to its source in Big Stone Lake; and a former Indian agent told me that at high water it was thought that such a steamer might pass into the Red River.

In short, this river proved so very *long* and navigable, that I was reminded of the last letter or two in the voyage of the Baron la Hontan (written near the end of the seventeenth century, I *think*), in which he states, that, after reaching the Mississippi (by the Illinois or Wisconsin), the limit of previous exploration westward, he voyaged up it with his Indians, and at length turned up a great river coming in from the west, which he called "La Rivière Longue;" and he relates various improbable things about the country and its inhabitants, so that this letter has been regarded as pure fiction, or, more properly speaking, a lie. But I am somewhat inclined now to reconsider the matter.

The Governor of Minnesota (Ramsay), the superintendent of Indian affairs in this quarter, and the newly appointed Indian agent were on board; also a German band from St. Paul, a small cannon for salutes, and the money for the Indians (ay, and the gamblers, it was said, who were to bring it back in another boat). There were about one hundred passengers, chiefly from St.

Paul, and more or less recently from the northeastern States; also half a dozen young educated Englishmen. Chancing to speak with one who sat next to me, when the voyage was nearly half over, I found that he was the son of the Rev. Samuel May,[103] and a classmate of yours, and had been looking for us at St. Anthony.

The last of the little settlements on the river was New Ulm, about one hundred miles this side of Redwood. It consists wholly of Germans. We left them one hundred barrels of salt, which will be worth something more when the water is lowest than at present.

Redwood is a mere locality,—scarcely an Indian village,—where there is a store, and some houses have been built for them. We were now fairly on the great plains, and looking south; and, after walking that way three miles, could see no tree in that horizon. The buffalo were said to be feeding within twenty-five or thirty miles.

A regular council was held with the Indians, who had come in on their ponies, and speeches were made on both sides through an interpreter, quite in the described mode,—the Indians, as usual, having the advantage in point of truth and earnestness, and therefore of eloquence. The most prominent chief was named Little Crow. They were quite dissatisfied with the white man's treatment of them, and probably have reason to be so. This council was to be continued for two or three days,—the payment to be made the second day; and another payment to other bands a little higher up, on the Yellow Medicine (a tributary of the Minnesota), a few days thereafter.

In the afternoon, the half-naked Indians performed a dance, at the request of the Governor, for our amusement and their own benefit; and then we took leave of them, and of the officials who had come to treat with them.

Excuse these pencil marks, but my inkstand is *unscrewable*, and I can only direct my letter at the bar. I could tell you more, and perhaps more interesting things, if I had time. I am considerably better than when I left home, but still far from well.

Our faces are already set toward home. Will you please let my sister know that we shall *probably* start for Milwaukee and Mackinaw in a day or two (or as soon as we hear from home) *via* Prairie du Chien, and not La Crosse.

I am glad to hear that you have written Cholmondeley,[104] as it relieves me of some *responsibility*.

The tour described in this long letter was the first and last that Thoreau ever made west of the Mohawk Valley, though his friend Channing had early visited the great prairies, and lived in log cabins of Illinois, or sailed on the chain of great lakes, by which Thoreau made a part of this journey. It was proposed that Channing should accompany him this time, as he had in the tour through Lower Canada, and along Cape Cod, as well as in the journeys through the Berkshire and Catskill mountains, and down the Hudson; but some misunderstanding or temporary inconvenience prevented. The actual comrade was young Horace Mann, eldest son of the school-reformer and statesman of that name,—a silent, earnest, devoted naturalist, who died early. The place where his party met the Indians—only a few months before the Minnesota massacre of 1862—was in the county of Redwood, in the southwest of the State, where now is a thriving village of 1500 people, and no buffaloes within five hundred miles. Red Wing, whence the letter was written, is below St. Paul, on the Mississippi, and was even then a considerable town, —now a city of 7000 people. The Civil War had lately begun, and the whole North was in the first flush of its uprising in defense of the Union,—for which Thoreau, in spite of his earlier defiance of government (for its alliance with slavery), was as zealous as any soldier. He returned in July, little benefited by the journey, of which he did not take his usual sufficiency of notes, and to which there is little allusion in his books. Nor does it seem that he visited on the way his correspondent since January, 1856,—C. H. Greene, of Rochester, Michigan, who had never seen him in Concord. The opinion of Thoreau himself concerning this journey will be found in his next letter to Daniel Ricketson.

TO DANIEL RICKETSON (AT NEW BEDFORD).

Concord, August 15, 1861.

Friend Ricketson,—When your last letter was written I was away in the far Northwest, in search of health. My cold turned to bronchitis, which made me a close prisoner almost up to the moment of my starting on that journey, early in May. As I had an incessant cough, my doctor told me that I must "clear out,"—to the West Indies, or elsewhere,—so I selected Minnesota. I returned a few weeks ago, after a good deal of steady traveling, considerably, yet not essentially, better; my cough still continuing. If I don't mend very quickly, I shall be obliged to go to another climate again very soon.

My ordinary pursuits, both indoors and out, have been for the most part omitted, or seriously interrupted,—walking, boating, scribbling, etc. Indeed, I have been sick so long that I have almost forgotten what it is to be well; and yet I feel that it is in all respects only my envelope. Channing and Emerson are as well as usual; but Alcott, I am sorry to say, has for some time been more or less confined by a lameness, perhaps of a neuralgic character, occasioned by carrying too great a weight on his back while gardening.

On returning home, I found various letters awaiting me; among others, one from Cholmondeley, and one from yourself.

Of course I am sufficiently surprised to hear of your conversion;[105] yet I scarcely know what to say about it, unless that, judging by your account, it appears to me a change which concerns yourself peculiarly, and will not make you more valuable to mankind. However, perhaps I must see you before I can judge.

Remembering your numerous invitations, I write this short note now, chiefly to say that, if you are to be at home, and it will be quite agreeable to you, I will pay you a visit next week, and take such rides or sauntering walks with you as an invalid may.

The visit was made, and we owe to it the preservation of the latest portraiture of Thoreau, who, at his friend's urgency, sat to a photographer in New Bedford; and thus we have the full-bearded likeness of August, 1861; from which, also, and from personal recollection, Mr. Walton Ricketson made the fine profile medallion reproduced in photogravure for this volume.

TO DANIEL RICKETSON (AT NEW BEDFORD).

Concord, October 14, 1861.

Friend Ricketson,—I think that, on the whole, my health is better than when you were here; but my faith in the doctors has not increased. I thank you all for your invitation to come to New Bedford, but I suspect that it must still be warmer here than there; that, indeed, New Bedford is warmer than Concord only in the winter, and so I abide by Concord.

September was pleasanter and much better for me than August, and October has thus far been quite tolerable. Instead of riding on horseback, I ride in a wagon about every other day. My neighbor, Mr. E. R. Hoar, has two horses, and he, being away for the most part this fall, has generously offered me the use of one of them; and, as I notice, the dog throws himself in, and does scouting duty.

I am glad to hear that you no longer chew, but eschew, sugar-plums. One of the worst effects of sickness is, that it may get one into the *habit* of taking a little something—his bitters, or sweets, as if for his bodily good—from time to time, when he does not need it. However, there is no danger of this if you do not dose even when you are sick.

I went with a Mr. Rodman, a young man of your town, here the other day, or week, looking at farms for sale, and rumor says that he is inclined to buy a particular one. Channing says that he received his book, but has not got any of yours.

It is easy to talk, but hard to write.

From the worst of all correspondents,

Henry D. Thoreau.

No later letter than this was written by Thoreau's own hand; for he was occupied all the winter of 1861-62, when he could write, in preparing his manuscripts for the press. Nothing appeared before his death, but in June, 1862, Mr. Fields, then editing the *Atlantic*, printed "Walking,"—the first of three essays which came out in that magazine the same year. Nothing of Thoreau's had been accepted for the *Atlantic* since 1858, when he withdrew the rest of "Chesuncook," then coming out in its pages, because the editor (Mr. Lowell) had made alterations in the manuscript. In April, just before his death, the *Atlantic* printed a short and characteristic sketch of Thoreau by Bronson Alcott, and in August, Emerson's funeral oration, given in the parish church of Concord. During the last six months of his illness, his sister and his friends wrote letters for him, as will be seen by the two that follow.

SOPHIA THOREAU TO DANIEL RICKETSON (AT NEW BEDFORD).

Concord, December 19, 1861.

Mr. Ricketson:

Dear Sir,—Thank you for your friendly interest in my dear brother. I wish that I could report more favorably in regard to his health. Soon after your visit to Concord, Henry commenced riding, and almost every day he introduced me to some of his familiar haunts, far away in the thick woods, or by the ponds; all very new and delightful to me. The air and exercise which he enjoyed during the fine autumn days were a benefit to him; he seemed stronger, had a good appetite, and was able to attend somewhat to his writing; but since the cold weather has come, his cough has increased, and he is able to go out but seldom. Just now he is suffering from an attack of pleurisy, which confines him wholly to the house. His spirits do not fail him; he continues in his usual serene mood, which is very pleasant for his friends as well as himself. I am hoping for a short winter and early spring, that the invalid may again be out of doors.

I am sorry to hear of your indisposition, and trust that you will be well again soon. It would give me pleasure to see some of your newspaper articles, since you possess a hopeful spirit. My patience is nearly exhausted. The times look *very* dark. I think the next soldier who is shot for sleeping on his post should be Gen. McClellan. Why does he not do something in the way of fighting? I despair of ever living under the reign of Sumner or Phillips.

BRONSON ALCOTT TO DANIEL RICKETSON (AT NEW BEDFORD).

Concord, January 10, 1862.

Dear Friend,—You have not been informed of Henry's condition this winter, and will be sorry to hear that he grows feebler day by day, and is evidently failing and fading from our sight. He gets some sleep, has a pretty good appetite, reads at intervals, takes notes of his readings, and likes to see his friends, conversing, however, with difficulty, as his voice partakes of his general debility. We had thought this oldest inhabitant of our Planet would have chosen to stay and see it fairly dismissed into the Chaos (out of which he has brought such precious jewels,—gifts to friends, to mankind generally, diadems for fame to coming followers, forgetful of his own claims to the honors) before he chose simply to withdraw from the spaces and times he has adorned with the truth of his genius. But the masterly work is nearly done for us here. And our woods and fields are sorrowing, though not in sombre, but in robes of white, so becoming to the piety and probity they have known so long, and soon are to miss. There has been none such since Pliny, and it will be long before there comes his like; the most sagacious and wonderful Worthy of his time, and a marvel to coming ones.

I write at the suggestion of his sister, who thought his friends would like to be informed of his condition to the latest date.

Ever yours and respectfully,

A. Bronson Alcott.

The last letter of Henry Thoreau, written by the hand of his sister, was sent to Myron Benton, a young literary man then living in Dutchess County, New York, who had written a grateful letter to the author of "Walden" (January 6, 1862), though quite unacquainted with him. Mr. Benton said that the news of Thoreau's illness had affected him as if it were that "of a personal friend whom I had known a long time," and added: "The secret of the influence by which your writings charm me is altogether as intangible, though real, as the attraction of Nature herself. I read and reread your books with ever fresh delight. Nor is it pleasure alone; there is a singular spiritual healthiness with which they seem imbued,—the expression of a soul essentially sound, so free from any morbid tendency." After mentioning that his own home was in a pleasant valley, once the hunting-ground of the Indians, Mr. Benton said:—

"I was in hope to read something more from your pen in Mr. Conway's *Dial*, [106] but only recognized that fine pair of Walden twinlets. Of your two books, I perhaps prefer the 'Week'—but after all, 'Walden' is but little less a favorite. In the former, I like especially those little snatches of poetry interspersed throughout. I would like to ask what progress you have made in a work some way connected with natural history,—I think it was on Botany,—which Mr. Emerson told me something about in a short interview I had with him two years ago at Poughkeepsie.... If you should feel perfectly able at any time to drop me a few lines, I would like much to know what your state of health is, and if there is, as I cannot but hope, a prospect of your speedy recovery."

Two months and more passed before Thoreau replied; but his habit of performing every duty, whether of business or courtesy, would not excuse him from an answer, which was this:—

TO MYRON B. BENTON (AT LEEDSVILLE, N. Y.).

CONCORD, March 21, 1862.

DEAR SIR,—I thank you for your very kind letter, which, ever since I received it, I have intended to answer before I died, however briefly. I am encouraged to know, that, so far as you are concerned, I have not written my books in vain. I was particularly gratified, some years ago, when one of my friends and neighbors said, "I wish you would write another book,—write it for me." He is actually more familiar with what I have written than I am myself.

The verses you refer to in Conway's *Dial* were written by F. B. Sanborn of this town. I never wrote for that journal.

I am pleased when you say that in the "Week" you like especially "those little snatches of poetry interspersed through the book," for these, I suppose, are the least attractive to most readers. I have not been engaged in any particular work on Botany, or the like, though, if I were to live, I should have much to report on Natural History generally.

You ask particularly after my health. I *suppose* that I have not many months to live; but, of course, I know nothing about it. I may add that I am enjoying existence as much as ever, and regret nothing.

Yours truly,
HENRY D. THOREAU,
bySOPHIA E. THOREAU.

He died May 6, 1862; his mother died March 12, 1872, and his sister Sophia, October, 1876. With the death of his aunt, Maria Thoreau, nearly twenty years after her beloved nephew, the last person of the name in America (or perhaps in England) passed away.

APPENDIX

The letters of Thoreau, early or late, which did not reach me in time to be used in the original edition of this book, and have since appeared in print here and there, are included either in order of their date in the preceding pages (in the case of the additional Ricketson letters) or in this Appendix. I owe the right to use the following correspondence to Mr. E. H. Russell of Worcester and to Dr. S. A. Jones of Ann Arbor, Michigan, who first obtained from the family of Calvin H. Greene of Rochester, Michigan, the Greene letters, five in number, all short, but characteristic. Dr. Jones printed these in a small edition at Jamaica, N. Y., and along with them some letters of Miss Sophia Thoreau to Mr. Greene, and portions of Greene's Diary during his two visits to Concord in September, 1863, and August, 1874. In these papers he left initials, or letters commonly used for unknown quantities, to stand for certain names occurring there. "X." and "X. Y. Z." in this Diary, and in Miss Thoreau's letters, signify Ellery Channing, to whom in March, 1863, Mr. Greene had sent the manzanita cane, headed with buffalo-horn and tipped with silver, which he had made with his own hands and intended for Thoreau, and which Mr. Channing gave to me, as the mutual friend of the two Concord poets. In the Diary I am "Mr. S." This Diary and the letters of Miss Thoreau supply some useful facts for a Thoreau biography, which this collection of Familiar Letters was meant to be,—a biography largely in the words of its subject. Notice is taken of such facts in footnotes.

The earlier letters to Isaac Hecker, afterwards known as Father Hecker of New York, grew out of an acquaintance formed with him while he was living at Mrs. Thoreau's, and taking lessons of the late George Bradford, brother of Mrs. Ripley. They were subsequent to Hecker's brief stay at Brook Farm and Fruitlands, and when he was studying to be a Catholic priest. He cherished the vain hope of converting Thoreau to his own newly acquired faith, amid the influences of Catholic Europe. The brief correspondence is printed in the *Atlantic Monthly* for September, 1902.

Isaac Hecker, born in December, 1819, two and a half years after Thoreau, was the son of a German baker in New York city, and of little education until he came to Massachusetts at the age of twenty-three, as the disciple and friend of Dr. Brownson, then a Protestant preacher and social democrat. In January, 1843, he entered the Brook Farm community, not as a member, but as a worker and student, making the bread for the family and taking lessons of George Ripley, George Bradford, Charles Dana, and John S. Dwight,—all friends of the Concord circle of authors. But he was restless, and yearned for a more ascetic life, and before he had been at Brook Farm a month he was writing to Bronson Alcott about entering the as yet unopened Fruitlands convent, between which and Brook Farm Concord was a half-way station, both physically and spiritually. Hecker tried all three; was at Brook Farm, off and on, for six months, at Fruitlands two weeks (from July 11 to July 25, 1843), and at Concord two months (from April 22 to June 20, 1844). Then, August 1, he was baptized in the Catholic faith at New York. The day before this final step, towards which he had been tending for a year, he wrote to Thoreau, proposing a journey through Europe on foot and without money. During his brief Concord life he had been a lodger at the house of John Thoreau (the Parkman house, where now the Public Library stands), and had seen Henry Thoreau daily. Hecker thus describes his room, his rent, and his landlady, who was Thoreau's mother:

"All that is needed for my comfort is here,—a room of good size, very good people, furnished and to be kept in order for 75 cents a week, including lights, —wood is extra pay; a good straw bed, a large table, carpet, wash-stand, bookcase, stove, chairs, looking-glass,—all, all that is needful. The lady of the house, Mrs. Thoreau, is a *woman*. The only fear I have about her is that she is too much like dear mother,—she will take too much care of me. If you were to see her, Mother, you would be perfectly satisfied that I have fallen into good hands, and met a second mother, if that is possible. I have just finished my dinner,—unleavened bread from home, maple-sugar, and apples which I purchased this morning. Previous to taking dinner I said my first lesson to Mr. Bradford in Greek and Latin."

Hecker "boarded himself," but no doubt often partook of Mrs. Thoreau's hospitality, and took long walks with Thoreau. Writing to him three months after the first meeting at Concord, Hecker said: "I have formed a certain project which your influence has no slight share in forming. It is, to work our passage to Europe, and to walk, work, and beg, if need be, as far, when there, as we are inclined to do."

TO ISAAC HECKER (AT NEW YORK).

Concord, August 14, 1844.

Friend Hecker,—I am glad to hear your voice from that populous city, and the more so for the tenor of its discourse. I have but just returned from a pedestrian excursion somewhat similar to that you propose, *parvis componere magna*, to the Catskill Mountains, over the principal mountains of this State, subsisting mainly on bread and berries, and slumbering on the mountain-tops. As usually happens, I now feel a slight sense of dissipation. Still, I am strongly tempted by your proposal, and experience a decided schism between my outward and inward tendencies. Your method of traveling, especially,—to live along the road, citizens of the world, without haste or petty plans,—I have often proposed this to my dreams, and still do. But the fact is, I cannot so decidedly postpone exploring the *Farther Indies*, which are to be reached, you know, by other routes and other methods of travel. I mean that I constantly return from every external enterprise with disgust, to fresh faith in a kind of Brahminical, Artesian, Inner Temple life. All my experience, as yours probably, proves only this reality. Channing wonders how I can resist your invitation, I, a single man—unfettered—and so do I. Why, there are Roncesvalles, the Cape de Finisterre, and the Three Kings of Cologne; Rome, Athens, and the rest, to be visited in serene, untemporal hours, and all history to revive in one's memory, as he went by the way, with splendors too bright for this world,—I know how it is. But is not here, too, Roncesvalles with greater lustre? Unfortunately, it may prove dull and desultory weather enough here, but better trivial days with faith than the fairest ones lighted by sunshine alone. Perchance, my *Wanderjahr* has not arrived, but you cannot wait for that. I hope you will find a companion who will enter as heartily into your schemes as I should have done.

I remember you, as it were, with the whole Catholic Church at your skirts. And the other day, for a moment, I think I understood your relation to that body; but the thought was gone again in a twinkling, as when a dry leaf falls from its stem over our heads, but is instantly lost in the rustling mass at our feet.

I am really sorry that the Genius will not let me go with you, but I trust that it will conduct to other adventures, and so, if nothing prevents, we will compare notes at last.

When this invitation reached Concord, Thoreau was absent on a tour with Channing to the Berkshire Mountains and the Catskills,—Channing coming up the Hudson from New York (where he then lived, aiding Horace Greeley in the *Tribune* office), and meeting his friend at the foot of the Hoosac Mountain. On its summit Thoreau had spent the night, sleeping under a board near the observatory tower built by the Williams College students, as related by him in the *Week*. They then crossed the Hudson and journeyed on to the Catskills, returning together to Concord.[107] Meantime Hecker had got impatient, and wrote again, to which Thoreau replied, August 17, thus briefly:—

TO ISAAC HECKER (AT NEW YORK).

I improve the occasion of my mother's sending to acknowledge the receipt of your stirring letter. You have probably received mine by this time. I thank you for not anticipating any vulgar objections on my part. *Far* travel, very *far* travel, or travail, comes near to the worth of staying at home. Who knows whence his education is to come! Perhaps I may drag my anchor at length, or rather, when the *winds* which blow *over* the deep fill my sails, may stand away for distant parts,—for now I seem to have a firm *ground* anchorage, though the harbor is low-shored enough, and the traffic with the natives inconsiderable. I may be away to Singapore by the next tide.

I like well the ring of your last maxim, "It is only the fear of death makes us reason of impossibilities." And but for fear, death itself is an impossibility.

Believe me, I can hardly let it end so. If you do not go soon, let me hear from you again.

Yrs. in great haste,
HENRY D. THOREAU.

Hecker did not in fact go to Europe till a year later, and when he walked over a part of central Europe, it was in company with one or two young Catholic priests,—men very unlike Thoreau.

The short correspondence with Calvin Greene (longer than that with Hecker) occurred at intervals, a dozen years and more after the Fruitlands period, when the Walden experience had been lived through and recorded, and the friendship with the Ricketson family was in its earlier stages. Mr. Greene, when he called on me at his first visit to the Thoreau family in 1863, mentioned that he had just read Thoreau's poem, "The Departure," which at Sophia's request I had lately printed in the Boston *Commonwealth*, a weekly that I had been editing since Moncure Conway had left Concord for London, in the winter of 1862-63. Greene was a plain, sincere man, never in New England before, who amused Channing by saying he had "taken a boat-ride on the Atlantic." He came once more in 1874, and spent an evening with me in the house where Thoreau lived and died,—Mrs. Thoreau then being dead, and Sophia at Bangor, where she died in 1876.

TO CALVIN H. GREENE (AT ROCHESTER, MICH.).

CONCORD, January 18, 1856.

DEAR SIR,—I am glad to hear that my "Walden" has interested you,—that perchance it holds some truth still as far off as Michigan. I thank you for your note.

The "Week" had so poor a publisher that it is quite uncertain whether you will find it in any shop. I am not sure but authors must turn booksellers themselves. The price is $1.25. If you care enough for it to send me that sum by mail (stamps will do for change), I will forward you a copy by the same conveyance.

As for the "more" that is to come, I cannot speak definitely at present, but I trust that the mine—be it silver or lead—is not yet exhausted. At any rate, I shall be encouraged by the fact that you are interested in its yield.

Yours respectfully,
HENRY D. THOREAU.

CONCORD, February 10, 1856.

DEAR SIR,—I forwarded to you by mail on the 31st of January a copy of my "Week," post paid, which I trust that you have received. I thank you heartily for the expression of your interest in "Walden" and hope that you will not be disappointed by the "Week." You ask how the former has been received. It has found an audience of excellent character, and quite numerous, some 2000 copies having been dispersed.[108] I should consider it a greater success to interest one wise and earnest soul, than a million unwise and frivolous.

You may rely on it that you have the best of me in my books, and that I am not worth seeing personally, the stuttering, blundering clod-hopper that I am. Even poetry, you know, is in one sense an infinite brag and exaggeration. Not that I do not stand on all that I have written,—but what am I to the truth I feebly utter?

I like the name of your county.[109] May it grow men as sturdy as its trees! Methinks I hear your flute echo amid the oaks. Is not yours, too, a good place to study theology? I hope that you will ere long recover your turtle-dove, and that it may bring you glad tidings out of that heaven in which it disappeared.

Yours sincerely,
HENRY D. THOREAU.

CONCORD, May 31, 1856.

DEAR SIR,—I forwarded by mail a copy of my "Week," post paid to James Newberry, Merchant, Rochester, Oakland Co., Mich., according to your order, about ten days ago, or on the receipt of your note.

I will obtain and forward a copy of "Walden" and also of the "Week" to California, to your order, post paid, for $2.60. The postage will be between 60 and 70 cents.

I thank you heartily for your kind intentions respecting me. The West has many attractions for me, particularly the lake country and the Indians, yet I do [not] foresee what my engagements may be in the fall. I have once or twice come near going West a-lecturing, and perhaps some winter may bring me into your neighborhood, in which case I should probably see you. Yet lecturing has commonly proved so foreign and irksome to me, that I think I could only use it to acquire the means with which to make an independent tour another time.

As for my pen, I can say that it is not altogether idle, though I have finished nothing new in the book form. I am drawing a rather long bow, though it may be a feeble one, but I pray that the archer may receive new strength before the arrow is shot.

With many thanks, yours truly,
HENRY D. THOREAU.

CONCORD, Saturday, June 21, 1856.

DEAR SIR,—On the 12th I forwarded the two books to California, observing your directions in every particular, and I trust that Uncle Sam will discharge his duty faithfully. While in Worcester this week I obtained the accompanying daguerreotype,[110] which my friends think is pretty good, though better-looking than I.

Books and postage	$2.64
Daguerreotype	.50
Postage	.16
	3.30
5.00	You will accordingly
3.30	

find 1.70 enclosed with my shadow.

Yrs.,
HENRY D. THOREAU.

CONCORD, July 8, 1857.

DEAR SIR,—You are right in supposing that I have not been Westward. I am very little of a traveler. I am gratified to hear of the interest you take in my books; it is additional encouragement to write more of them. Though my pen is not idle, I have not published anything for a couple of years at least. I like a private life, and cannot bear to have the public in my mind.

You will excuse me for not responding more heartily to your notes, since I realize what an interval there always is between the actual and imagined author and feel that it would not be just for *me* to appropriate the sympathy and good will of my unseen readers.

Nevertheless, I should like to meet you, and if I ever come into your neighborhood shall endeavor to do so. Can't you tell the world of your life also? Then I shall know you, at least as well as you me.

Yours truly,
HENRY D. THOREAU.

CONCORD, November 24, 1859.

DEAR SIR,—The lectures which you refer to were reported in the newspapers, *after a fashion*,—the last one in some half-dozen of them,—and if I possessed one, or all, I would send them to you, bad as they are. The best, or at least longest one of the Boston lectures was in the Boston *Atlas and Bee* of November 2d,—maybe half the whole. There were others in the *Traveller*, the *Journal*, etc., of the same date.

I am glad to know that you are interested to see my things, and I wish I had them in printed form to send to you. I exerted myself considerably to get the last discourse printed and sold for the benefit of Brown's family, but the publishers are afraid of pamphlets, and it is now too late.[111]

I return the stamps which I have not used.

I shall be glad to see you if I ever come your way.

Yours truly,
HENRY D. THOREAU.

The Riverside Press
H. O. HOUGHTON AND COMPANY
CAMBRIDGE
MASSACHUSETTS

FOOTNOTES

[1] These, written to Thomas Cholmondeley, are still (1906) lacking; but a few other letters have been published since 1894.

[2] He was named David for this uncle; Dr. Ripley was the minister of the whole town in 1817. The Red House stood near the Emerson house on the Lexington road; the Woodwards were a wealthy family, afterwards in Quincy, to which town Dr. Woodward left a large bequest.

[3] John Thoreau, grandfather of Henry, born at St. Helier's, Jersey, April, 1754, was a sailor on board the American privateer General Lincoln, November, 1779, and recognized La Sensible, French frigate, which carried John Adams from Boston to France. See *Journal*, vol. v, June 11, 1853. This John Thoreau, son of Philip, died in Concord, 1800.

[4] This had been the abode of old Deacon Parkman, a granduncle of the late Francis Parkman, the historian, and son of the Westborough clergyman from whom this distinguished family descends. Deacon Parkman was a merchant in Concord, and lived in what was then a good house. It stood in the middle of the village, where the Public Library now is. The "Texas" house was built by Henry Thoreau and his father John; it was named from a section of the village then called "Texas," because a little remote from the churches and schools; perhaps the same odd fancy that had bestowed the name of "Virginia" on the road of Thoreau's birthplace. The "Yellow House reformed" was a small cottage rebuilt and enlarged by the Thoreaus in 1850; in this, on the main street, Henry and his father and mother died.

[5] During the greater part of his college course he signed himself D. H. Thoreau, as he was christened (David Henry); but being constantly called "Henry," he put this name first about the time he left college, and was seldom afterwards known by the former initials.

[6] The impression made on one classmate and former room-mate ("chum") of Thoreau, by this utterance, will be seen by this fragment of a letter from James Richardson of Dedham (afterwards Reverend J. Richardson), dated Dedham, September 7, 1837:—

"Friend Thoreau,—After you had finished your part in the Performances of Commencement (the tone and sentiment of which, by the way, I liked much, as being of a sound philosophy), I hardly saw you again at all. Neither at Mr. Quincy's levee, neither at any of our classmates' evening entertainments, did I find you; though for the purpose of taking a farewell, and leaving you some memento of an old chum, as well as on matters of business, I much wished to see your face once more. Of course you must be present at our October meeting,—notice of the time and place for which will be given in the newspapers. I hear that you are comfortably located, in your native town, as the guardian of its children, in the immediate vicinity, I suppose, of one of our most distinguished apostles of the future, R. W. Emerson, and situated under the ministry of our old friend Reverend Barzillai Frost, to whom please make my remembrances. I heard from you, also, that Concord Academy, lately under the care of Mr. Phineas Allen of Northfield, is now vacant of a preceptor; should Mr. Hoar find it difficult to get a scholar college-distinguished, perhaps he would take up with one, who, though in many respects a critical thinker, and a careful philosopher of language among other things, has never distinguished himself in his class as a regular attendant on college studies and rules. If so, could you do me the kindness to mention my name to him as of one intending to make teaching his profession, at least for a part of his life. If recommendations are necessary, President Quincy has offered me one, and I can easily get others."

[7] This eldest of the children of John Thoreau and Cynthia Dunbar was born October 22, 1812, and died June 14, 1849. Her grandmother, Mary Jones of Weston, Mass., belonged to a Tory family, and several of the Jones brothers served as officers in the British army against General Washington.

[8] White Pond, in the district called "Nine-Acre Corner," is here meant; the "Lee-vites" were a family then living on Lee's Hill. Naushawtuck is another name for this hill, where the old Tahatawan lived at times, before the English settled in Concord in September, 1635. The real date of this letter is November 11-14, 1837, and between its two dates the Massachusetts State election was held. The "great council-house" was the Boston State-House, to which the Concord people were electing deputies; the "Eagle-Beak" named on the next page was doubtless Samuel Hoar, the first citizen of the town, and for a time Member of Congress from Middlesex County. He was the father of Rockwood and Frisbie Hoar, afterwards judge and senator respectively.

[9] A delicate sarcasm on young B., who could not finish his speech in town-meeting without looking at his notes. The allusion to the "Medicine whose words are like the music of the mockingbird" is hard to explain; it may mean Edward Everett, then Governor of Massachusetts, or, possibly, Emerson, whose lectures began to attract notice in Boston and Cambridge. It can hardly mean Wendell Phillips, though his melodious eloquence had lately been heard in attacks upon slavery.

[10] *Americana*, in this note, is the old *Encyclopedia Americana*, which had been edited from the German *Conversations-Lexicon*, and other sources, by Dr. Francis Lieber, T. G. Bradford, and other Boston scholars, ten years earlier, and was the only convenient book of reference at Thoreau's hand. The inquiry of John Thoreau is another evidence of the interest he took, like his brother, in the Indians and their flint arrowheads. The relics mentioned in the next letter were doubtless Indian weapons and utensils, very common about Taunton in the region formerly controlled by King Philip.

[11] Dr. Edward Jarvis, born in Concord (1803), had gone to Louisville, Ky., in April, 1837, and was thriving there as a physician. He knew the Thoreaus well, and gave them good hopes of success in Ohio or Kentucky as teachers. The plan was soon abandoned, and Henry went to Maine to find a school, but without success. See Sanborn's *Thoreau*, p. 57.

[12] This was the old monument of the Fight in 1775, for the dedication of which Emerson wrote his hymn, "By the rude bridge." This was sung by Thoreau, among others, to the tune of Old Hundred.

[13] For twenty-five years (1866-91) the house of Ellery Channing, and now of Charles Emerson, nephew of Waldo Emerson.

[14] The steamer Lexington lately burnt on Long Island Sound, with Dr. Follen on board.

[15] Mrs. Brown was the elder sister of Mrs. R. W. Emerson and of the eminent chemist and geologist, Dr. Charles T. Jackson, of Plymouth and Boston. She lived for a time in Mrs. Thoreau's family, and Thoreau's early verses, "Sic Vita," were thrown into her window there by the young poet, wrapped round a cluster of violets.

[16] This business of pencil-making had become the family bread-winner, and Henry Thoreau worked at it and kindred arts by intervals for the next twenty years.

[17] I. T. Williams, who had lived in Concord, but now wrote from Buffalo, N. Y.

[18] Mrs. Brown, to whom this letter and several others of the years 1841-43 were written, lived by turns in Plymouth, her native place, and in Concord, where she often visited Mrs. Emerson at the time when Thoreau was an inmate of the

Emerson household. In the early part of 1843 she was in Plymouth, and her sister was sending her newspapers and other things, from time to time. The incident of the music-box, mentioned above, occurred at the Old Manse, where Hawthorne was living from the summer of 1842 until the spring of 1845, and was often visited by Thoreau and Ellery Channing. In the letter following, this incident is recalled, and with it the agreeable gift by Richard Fuller (a younger brother of Margaret Fuller and of Ellen, the wife of Ellery Channing, who came to reside in Concord about these years, and soon became Thoreau's most intimate friend), which was a music-box for the Thoreaus. They were all fond of music, and enjoyed it even in this mechanical form,—one evidence of the simple conditions of life in Concord then. The note of thanks to young Fuller, who had been, perhaps, a pupil of Thoreau, follows this letter to Mrs. Brown, though earlier in date. Mary Russell afterwards became Mrs. Marston Watson.

[19] Editor of the *Democratic Review*, for which Hawthorne, Emerson, Thoreau, and Whittier all wrote, more or less.

[20] An interesting fact in connection with Thoreau and Wheeler (whose home was in Lincoln, four miles southeast of Concord) is related by Ellery Channing in a note to me. It seems that Wheeler had built for himself, or hired from a farmer, a rough woodland study near Flint's Pond, half-way from Lincoln to Concord, which he occupied for a short time in 1841-42, and where Thoreau and Channing visited him. Mr. Channing wrote me in 1883: "Stearns Wheeler built a 'shanty' on Flint's Pond for the purpose of economy, for purchasing Greek books and going abroad to study. Whether Mr. Thoreau assisted him to build this shanty I cannot say, but I think he may have; also that he spent six weeks with him there. As Mr. Thoreau was not too original and inventive to follow the example of others, if good to him, it is very probable this undertaking of Stearns Wheeler, whom he regarded (as I think I have heard him say) a heroic character, suggested his own experiment on Walden. I believe I visited this shanty with Mr. Thoreau. It was very plain, with bunks of straw, and built in the Irish manner. I think Mr. Wheeler was as good a mechanic as Mr. Thoreau, and built this shanty for his own use. The object of these two experiments was quite unlike, except in the common purpose of economy. It seems to me highly probable that Mr. Wheeler's experiment suggested Mr. Thoreau's, as he was a man he almost worshiped. But I could not understand what relation Mr. Lowell had to this fact, if it be one. Students, in all parts of the earth, have pursued a similar course from motives of economy, and to carry out some special study. Mr. Thoreau wished to study birds, flowers, and the stone age, just as Mr. Wheeler wished to study Greek. And Mr. Hotham came next from just the same motive of economy (necessity) and to study the Bible. The prudential sides of all three were the same." Mr. Hotham was the young theological student who dwelt in a cabin by Walden in 1869-70.

[21] An English critic and poetaster. See *Memoir of Bronson Alcott*, pp. 292-318.

[22] *Thoreau, the Poet-Naturalist.* With Memorial Verses. By William Ellery Channing, New Edition, enlarged, edited by F. B. Sanborn (Boston: Charles Goodspeed, 1902). This volume, in some respects the best biography of Thoreau, is no longer rare. Among the Verses are those written by Channing for his friend's funeral; at which, also, Mr. Alcott read Thoreau's poem of Sympathy.

[23] Headley died at the age of twenty-three, in 1788. His posthumous book was edited in 1810 by Rev. Henry Kett, and published in London by John Sharp.

[24] An allusion to the strange and painful death of John Thoreau, by lockjaw. He had slightly wounded himself in shaving, and the cut became inflamed and brought on that hideous and deforming malady, of which, by sympathy, Henry also partook, though he recovered.

[25] Past and Present.

[26] Of the publishing house of Bradbury & Soden, in Boston, which had taken Nathan Hale's *Boston Miscellany* off his hands, and had published in it, with promise of payment, Thoreau's "Walk to Wachusett." But much time had passed, and the debt was not paid; hence the lack of a "shower of shillings" which the letter laments. Emerson's reply gives the first news of the actual beginning of Alcott's short-lived paradise at Fruitlands, and dwells with interest on the affairs of the rural and lettered circle at Concord.

[27] At Fruitlands with the Alcotts. See Sanborn's *Thoreau*, p. 137, for this letter.

[28] Emerson also was satisfied with it for once, and wrote to Thoreau: "Our *Dial* thrives well enough in these weeks. I print W. E. Channing's 'Letters,' or the first ones, but he does not care to have them named as his for a while. They are very agreeable reading."

[29] Afterwards Senator Hoar of Massachusetts, but then in Harvard College.

[30] Henry James, Senior.

[31] Emerson had written, July 20: "I am sorry to say that when I called on Bradbury & Soden, nearly a month ago, their partner, in their absence, informed me that they should not pay you, at present, any part of their debt on account of the *Boston Miscellany*. After much talking, all the promise he could offer was 'that within a year it would probably be paid,'—a probability which certainly looks very slender. The very worst thing he said was the proposition that you should take your payment in the form of *Boston Miscellanies*! I shall not fail to refresh their memory at intervals."

[32] It may need to be said that these were New York weeklies—the *Mirror*, edited in part by N. P. Willis, and the *New World* by Park Benjamin, formerly of Boston, whose distinction it is to have first named Hawthorne as a writer of genius. "Miss Fuller" was Margaret,—not yet resident in New York, whither she went to live in 1844.

[33] The allusion here is to Ellery Channing's "Youth of the Poet and Painter," in the *Dial*,—an unfinished autobiography. The *Present* of W. H. Channing, his cousin, named above, was a short-lived periodical, begun September 15, 1843, and ended in April, 1844. "McKean" was Henry Swasey McKean, who was a classmate of Charles Emerson at Harvard in 1828, a tutor there in 1830-35, and who died in 1857.

[34] This inkstand was presented by Miss Hoar, with a note dated "Boston, May 2, 1843," which deserves to be copied:—

Dear Henry,—The rain prevented me from seeing you the night before I came away, to leave with you a parting assurance of good will and good hope. We have become better acquainted within the two past years than in our whole life as schoolmates and neighbors before; and I am unwilling to let you go away without telling you that I, among your other friends, shall miss you much, and follow you with remembrance and all best wishes and confidence. Will you take this little inkstand and try if it will carry ink safely from Concord to Staten Island? and the pen, which, if you can write with steel, may be made sometimes the interpreter of friendly thoughts to those whom you leave beyond the reach of your voice,—or record the inspirations of Nature, who, I doubt not, will be as faithful to you who trust her in the sea-girt Staten Island as in Concord woods and meadows. Good-by, and εὖ πράττειν, which, a wise man says, is the only salutation fit for the wise.

Truly your friend, E. Hoar.

[35] Where Agassiz was giving a course of Lowell lectures.

[36] The town almshouse was across the field from the Emerson house.

[37] At this date Alcott had passed his forty-eighth year, while Channing and

Thoreau were still in the latitude of thirty. Hawthorne had left Concord, and was in the Salem custom-house, the Old Manse having gone back into the occupancy of Emerson's cousins, the Ripleys, who owned it.

[38] See Sanborn's *Thoreau*, p. 214, and Channing's *Thoreau*, New Edition, pp. 207-210, for this poem.

[39] This is the political neighbor mentioned in a former letter.

[40] From England Emerson wrote: "I am not of opinion that your book should be delayed a month. I should print it at once, nor do I think that you would incur any risk in doing so that you cannot well afford. It is very certain to have readers and debtors, here as well as there. The Dial is absurdly well known here. We at home, I think, are always a little ashamed of it,—I am,—and yet here it is spoken of with the utmost gravity, and I do not laugh."

[41] This letter was addressed, "R. Waldo Emerson, care of Alexander Ireland, Esq., Manchester, England, *via* New York and Steamer Cambria, March 25." It was mailed in Boston, March 24, and received in Manchester, April 19.

[42] It will readily be seen that this letter relates to the shipwreck on Fire Island, near New York, in which Margaret Fuller, Countess Ossoli, with her husband and child, was lost. A letter with no date of the year, but probably written February 15, 1840, from Emerson to Thoreau, represents them both as taking much trouble about a house in Concord for Mrs. Fuller, the mother of Margaret, who had just sold her Groton house, and wished to live with her daughter near Emerson.

[43] Rev. A. B. Fuller, then of Manchester, N. H., afterward of Boston; a brother of Margaret, who died a chaplain in the Civil War.

[44] The name of a political party, afterwards called "Republicans."

[45] Baron Trenck, the famous prisoner.

[46] The *Week*.

[47] Of *Putnam's Magazine*.

[48] A town near Boston.

[49] A Massachusetts town, the birthplace of Whittier.

[50] An American seaman, wrecked on the coast of Arabia,—once a popular book.

[51] "The world is too much with us."—*Wordsworth*.

[52] A lady who made such a night voyage with Thoreau, years before, says: "How wise he was to ask the elderly lady with a younger one for a row on the Concord River one moonlit night! The river that night was as deep as the heavens above; serene stars shone from its depths, as far off as the stars above. Deep answered unto deep in our souls, as the boat glided swiftly along, past low-lying fields, under overhanging trees. A neighbor's cow waded into the cool water,—she became at once a Behemoth, a river-horse, hippopotamus, or river-god. A dog barked,—he was Diana's hound, he waked Endymion. Suddenly we were landed on a little isle; our boatman, our boat glided far off in the flood. We were left alone, in the power of the river-god; like two white birds we stood on this bit of ground, the river flowing about us; only the eternal powers of nature around us. Time for a prayer, perchance,—and back came the boat and oarsman; we were ferried to our homes, —no question asked or answered. We had drank of the cup of the night,—had left the silence and the stars."

[53] See Memoir of Bronson Alcott, pp. 485-494. The remark of Emerson quoted on p. 486, that Cholmondeley was "the son of a Shropshire squire," was not strictly correct, his father being a Cheshire clergyman of a younger branch of the ancient race of Cholmondeley. But he was the *grandson* of a Shropshire squire (owner of land), for his mother was daughter and sister of such gentlemen, and it was her

brother Richard who presented Reginald Heber and Charles Cholmondeley to the living of Hodnet, near Market Drayton.

[54] Mr. Ricketson's immediate reply was received by Thoreau before he wrote to Blake on the 22d. He set out from Concord for Cambridge on Christmas Day, and reached Brooklawn, the country-house of his friend, towards evening of that short day, on foot, with his umbrella and traveling-bag, and he made so striking a figure in the eyes of Ricketson that he sketched it roughly in his shanty-book. His children have engraved it in their pleasing volume *Daniel Ricketson and his Friends*, from the pages of which several of these letters are taken. It is by no means a bad likeness of the plain and upright Thoreau.

[55] Hyannis was once a port for the sailing of the steamers to Nantucket, where probably Thoreau was to land on his return. He had visited the Cape before, but never Nantucket. Thomas Cholmondeley went home with the distinct purpose of going to the Crimean war, and did so. The subject of the New Bedford lecture was "Getting a Living."

Channing, his wife and children having left him, was living by himself in his house opposite to Thoreau. Late in 1855 he rejoined Mrs. Channing, in a household near Dorchester, and became one of the editors of the New Bedford *Mercury*, residing in that city in 1856-57, after the death of Mrs. Channing.

[56] Quitman, aided perhaps by Laurence Oliphant, was aiming to capture Cuba with "filibusters" (flibustiers).

[57] Then President of the United States, whose life Hawthorne had written in 1852.

[58] I had been visiting Emerson occasionally for a year or two, and knew Alcott well at this time; was also intimate with Cholmondeley in the autumn of 1854, but had never seen Thoreau, a fact which shows how recluse were then his habits. The letter below, and the long one describing his trip to Minnesota, were the only ones I received from him in a friendship of seven years. See Sanborn's *Thoreau*, pp. 195-200. Edwin Morton was my classmate. See pp. 286, 353, 440.

[59] The book was *Ultima Thule*, describing New Zealand.

[60] This was Edmund Hosmer, a Concord farmer, before mentioned as a friend of Emerson, who was fond of quoting his sagacious and often cynical remarks. He had entertained George Curtis and the Alcotts at his farm on the "Turnpike," southeast of Emerson's; but now was living on a part of the old manor of Governor Winthrop, which soon passed to the ownership of the Hunts; and this house which Mr. Ricketson proposed to lease was the "old Hunt farmhouse,"—in truth built for the Winthrops two centuries before. It was soon after torn down.

[61] Sons of Mr. Ricketson; the second, a sculptor, modeled the medallion head of Thoreau reproduced in photogravure for the frontispiece of this volume.

[62] Mr. Channing had gone, October, 1855, to live in New Bedford, and help edit the *Mercury* there.

[63] The centre of Concord village, where the post-office and shops are,—so called from an old mill-dam where now is a street.

[64] The aunt of R. W. Emerson, then eighty-one years old, an admirer of Thoreau, as her notes to him show. For an account of her see Emerson's *Lectures and Biographical Sketches*, Centenary Ed., pp. 397-433; Riverside Ed., pp. 371-404.

[65] The books on India, Egypt, etc., sent by Cholmondeley. See p. 271. They were divided between the Concord Public Library and the libraries of Alcott, Blake, Emerson, Sanborn, etc.

[66] Mr. Channing became a frequent visitor at Brooklawn in the years of his

residence at New Bedford, 1856-58. See p. 274.

[67] These books were ordered by Cholmondeley in London, and sent to Boston just as he was starting for the Crimean War, in October, 1855, calling them "a nest of Indian books." They included Mill's *History of British India*, several translations of the sacred books of India, and one of them in Sanscrit; the works of Bunsen, so far as then published, and other valuable books. In the note accompanying this gift, Cholmondeley said, "I think I never found so much kindness in all my travels as in your country of New England." In return, Thoreau sent his English friend, in 1857, his own *Week*, Emerson's Poems, Walt Whitman's *Leaves of Grass*, and F. L. Olmsted's book on the Southern States (then preparing for the secession which they attempted four years later). This was perhaps the first copy of Whitman seen in England, and when Cholmondeley began to read it to his stepfather, Rev. Z. Macaulay, at Hodnet, that clergyman declared he would not hear it, and threatened to throw it in the fire. On reading the *Week* (he had received *Walden* from Thoreau when first in America), Cholmondeley wrote me, "Would you tell dear Thoreau that the lines I admire so much in his *Week* begin thus:—

> 'Low-anchored cloud,
> Newfoundland air,' etc.

In my mind the best thing he ever wrote."

[68] Ellery Channing is mentioned, though not by name, in the *Week* (pp. 169, 378), and in *Walden* (p. 295). He was the comrade of Thoreau in Berkshire, and on the Hudson, in New Hampshire, Canada, and Cape Cod, and in many rambles nearer Concord. He was also a companion of Hawthorne in his river voyages, as mentioned in the *Mosses*.

[69] The Concord Lyceum, founded in 1829, and still extant, though not performing its original function of lectures and debates. See pp. 51, 154, etc.

[70] This was the town of Harvard, not the college. Perhaps the excursion was to visit Fruitlands, where Alcott and Lane had established their short-lived community, in a beautiful spot near Still River, an affluent of the Nashua, and half-way from Concord to Wachusett. "Asnebumskit," mentioned in a former letter, is the highest hill near Worcester, as "Nobscot" is the highest near Concord. Both have Indian names.

[71] The New York newspaper.

[72] An odd boat.

[73] Mrs. Caroline Kirkland, wife of Prof. William Kirkland, then of New York,—a writer of wit and fame at that time.

[74] A Worcester newspaper.

[75] B. B. Wiley, then of Providence, since of Chicago (deceased), had written to Thoreau, September 4, for the *Week*, which the author was then selling on his own account, having bought back the unsalable first edition from his publisher, Munroe. In a letter of October 31, to which the above is a reply, he mentions taking a walk with Charles Newcomb, then of Providence, since of London and Paris, now dead, —a *Dial* contributor, and a special friend of Emerson; then inquires about Confucius, the Hindoo philosophers, and Swedenborg.

[76] When, in 1855 or 1856, Thoreau started to wade across from Duxbury to Clark's Island, and was picked up by a fishing-boat in the deep water, and landed on the "back side" of the island (see letter to Mr. Watson of April 25, 1858), Edward Watson ("Uncle Ed") was "saggin' round" to see that everything was right alongshore, and encountered the unexpected visitor. "How did *you* come here?" "Oh, from Duxbury," said Thoreau, and they walked to the old Watson house together. "You say in one of your books," said Uncle Ed, "that you once lost a

horse and a hound and a dove,—now I should like to know what you meant by that?" "Why, everybody has met with losses, haven't they?" "H'm,—pretty way to answer a fellow!" said Mr. Watson; but it seems this was the usual answer. In the long dining-room of the old house that night he sat by the window and told the story of the Norse voyagers to New England,—perhaps to that very island and the Gurnet near by,—as Morton fancies in his review of Thoreau in the *Harvard Magazine* (January, 1855).

[77] This was when he spoke in the vestry of the Calvinistic church, and said, on his return to Concord, "that he hoped he had done something to upheave and demolish the structure above,"—the vestry being beneath the church.

[78] Notwithstanding this unwillingness to lecture, Thoreau did speak at Worcester, February 13, 1857, on "Walking," but scrupulously added to his consent (February 6), "I told Brown it had not been much altered since I read it in Worcester; but now I think of it, much of it must have been new to you, because, having since divided it into two, I am able to read what before I omitted. Nevertheless, I should like to have it understood by those whom it concerns, that I am invited to read in public (if it be so) what I have already read, in part, to a private audience." This throws some light on his method of preparing lectures, which were afterwards published as essays; they were made up from his journals, and new entries expanded them.

[79] Rev. Edward E. Hale, then pastor at Worcester. Others mentioned in the letter are Rev. David A. Wasson and Dr. Seth Rogers,—the latter a physician with whom Mr. Wasson was living in Worcester.

[80] A writer on scenery and natural history, who outlived Thoreau, and never forgave him for the remark about "stirring up with a pole," which really might have been less graphic.

[81] The panic of 1857,—the worst since 1837.

[82] Reinhold Solger, Ph. D.,—a very intellectual and well-taught Prussian, who was one of the lecturers for a year or two at my "Concord School," the successor of the Concord "Academy," in which the children of the Emerson, Alcott, Hawthorne, Hoar, and Ripley families were taught. At this date the lectures were given in the vestry of the parish church, which Thoreau playfully termed "a meeting-house cellar." It was there that Louisa Alcott acted plays.

[83] Exclamation points and printer's devil.

[84] Channing says (*Thoreau, the Poet-Naturalist*, new ed., pp. 41, 42): "He made for himself a knapsack, with partitions for his books and papers,—india-rubber cloth (strong and large and spaced, the common knapsacks being unspaced).... After trying the merit of cocoa, coffee, water, and the like, tea was put down as the felicity of a walking '*travail*,'—tea plenty, strong, with enough sugar, made in a tin pint cup.... He commended every party to carry 'a junk of heavy cake' with plums in it, having found by long experience that after toil it was a capital refreshment."

[85] Marston Watson, whose uncle, Edward Watson, with his nephews, owned the "breezy island" where Thoreau had visited his friends (Clark's Island, the only one in Plymouth Bay), had built his own house, "Hillside," on the slope of one of the hills above Plymouth town, and there laid out a fine park and garden, which Thoreau surveyed for him in the autumn of 1854, Alcott and Mr. Watson carrying the chain. For a description of Hillside, see Channing's *Wanderer* (Boston, 1871) and Alcott's *Sonnets and Canzonets* (Boston: Roberts, 1882). It was a villa much visited by Emerson, Alcott, Channing, Thoreau, George Bradford, and the Transcendentalists generally. Mr. Watson graduated at Harvard two years after Thoreau, and in an old diary says, "I remember Thoreau in the college yard (1836) with downcast thoughtful look intent, as if he were searching for something; always in a green coat,—green because the authorities required black, I suppose." In a letter he says: "I have always heard the 'Maiden in the East' was Mrs. Watson,

—Mary Russell Watson,—and I suppose there is no doubt of it. I may be prejudiced, but I have always thought it one of his best things,—and I have highly valued his lines. I find in my *Dial*, No. 6, I have written six new stanzas in the margin of Friendship, and they are numbered to show how they should run. I think Mrs. Brown gave them to me."

[86] *Thoreau, the Poet-Naturalist*, new ed., pp. 42-45.

[87] Near which, at New Bedford, Mr. Ricketson lived.

[88] This was the "Orchard House," near Hawthorne's "Wayside." The estate on which it stands, now owned by Mrs. Lothrop, who also owns the "Wayside," was surveyed for Mr. Alcott by Thoreau in October, 1857.

[89] Channing's *Thoreau, the Poet-Naturalist*, new ed., pp. 6, 15, 16. Channing himself was, no doubt, the "follower" and "companion" here mentioned; no person so frequently walked with Thoreau in his long excursions. They were together in New Boston, N. H., when the minister mentioned in the *Week* reproved Thoreau for not going to meeting on Sunday. When I first lived in Concord (March, 1855), and asked the innkeeper what Sunday services the village held, he replied, "There's the Orthodox, an' the Unitarian, an' th' Walden Pond Association,"—meaning by the last what Emerson called "the Walkers,"—those who rambled in the Walden woods on Sundays.

[90] Of New Bedford, first published in the *Mercury* of that city, while Channing was one of the editors, and afterwards in a volume.

[91] The club with which Thoreau here makes merry was the Saturday Club, meeting at Parker's Hotel in Boston the last Saturday in each month, of which Emerson, Agassiz, Longfellow, Holmes, Lowell, Henry James, and other men of letters were members. Thoreau, though invited, never seems to have met with them, as Channing did, on one memorable occasion, at least, described by Mr. James in a letter cited in the *Memoir of Bronson Alcott*, who also occasionally dined with this club. The conversation at Emerson's next mentioned was also memorable for the vigor with which Miss Mary Emerson, then eighty-four years old, rebuked Mr. James for what she thought his dangerous Antinomian views concerning the moral law.

[92] This was Tuckerman's Ravine at the White Mountains, where Thoreau met with his mishap in the preceding July.

[93] He was looking after the manufacture of fine plumbago for the electrotypers, which was the family business after pencil-making grew unprofitable. The Thoreaus had a grinding-mill in Acton, and a packing-shop attached to their Concord house. "Parker's society," mentioned at the close of the letter, was the congregation of Theodore Parker, then in Italy, where he died in May, 1860.

[94] He was invited to a gathering of John Brown's friends at the grave in the Adirondack woods. "Mr. Sanborn's case" was an indictment and civil suit against Silas Carleton *et als.* for an attempt to kidnap F. B. Sanborn, who had refused to accept the invitation of the Senate at Washington to testify in the John Brown investigation.

[95] This is the excursion described by Thoreau in a subsequent letter,—lasting six days, and the first that Channing had made which involved "camping out." It was also Thoreau's last visit to this favorite mountain; but Channing continued to go there after the death of his friend; and some of these visits are recorded in his poem "The Wanderer." The last one was in September, 1869, when I accompanied him, and we again spent five nights on the plateau where he had camped with Thoreau. At that time, one of the "two good spruce houses, half a mile apart," mentioned by Thoreau, was still standing, in ruins,—the place called by Channing "Henry's Camp," and thus described:—

We built our fortress where you see
Yon group of spruce-trees, sidewise on the line
Where the horizon to the eastward bounds,—
A point selected by sagacious art,
Where all at once we viewed the Vermont hills,
And the long outline of the mountain-ridge,
Ever renewing, changeful every hour.
See *The Wanderer* (Boston, 1871), p. 61.

[96] See Thoreau's *Journal*, Dec. 3, 1859. Merriam mentioned Thoreau's name to him, but never guessed who his companion was.

[97] This was Thoreau's last visit to Monadnock, and the one mentioned in the note of August 3, and in Channing's *Wanderer*.

[98] The Prince of Wales (now King Edward VII), then visiting America with the Duke of Newcastle.

[99] Now termed pneumonia.

[100] In April, 1859, Mr. Alcott was chosen superintendent of the public schools of Concord, by a school committee of which Mr. Bull, the creator of the Concord grape, and Mr. Sanborn, were members, and for some years he directed the studies of the younger pupils, to their great benefit and delight. At the yearly "exhibitions," songs were sung composed by Louisa Alcott and others, and the whole town assembled to see and hear. The stress of civil war gradually checked this idyllic movement, and Mr. Alcott returned to his garden and library. It was two years after this that Miss Alcott had her severe experience as hospital nurse at Washington.

[101] Edwin Morton of Plymouth, Mass., a friend of John Brown and Gerrit Smith, who went to England in October, 1859, to avoid testifying against his friends.

[102] A word may be said of the after life of this magnanimous Englishman, who did not long survive his Concord correspondent. In March, 1863, being then in command of a battalion of Shropshire Volunteers, which he had raised, he inherited Condover Hall and the large estate adjacent, and took the name of Owen as a condition of the inheritance. A year later he married Miss Victoria Cotes, daughter of John and Lady Louisa Cotes (Co. Salop), a godchild of the Queen, and went to Italy for his wedding tour. In Florence he was seized with a malignant fever, April 10, 1864, and died there April 20,—not quite two years after Thoreau's death. His brother Reginald, who had met him in Florence, carried back his remains to England, and he is buried in Condover churchyard. Writing to an American friend, Mr. R. Cholmondeley said: "The whole county mourned for one who had made himself greatly beloved. During his illness his thoughts went back very much to America and her great sufferings. His large heart felt for your country as if it were his own." It seems that he did not go to New Zealand with the "Canterbury Pilgrims," as suggested in the *Atlantic Monthly* (December, 1893), but in the first of Lord Lyttelton's ships (the Charlotte Jane), having joined in Lord L.'s scheme for colonizing the island, where he remained only six months, near Christchurch.

[103] Rev. Joseph May, a cousin of Louisa Alcott.

[104] I had answered T. Cholmondeley's last letter, explaining that Thoreau was ill and absent.

[105] A return to religious Quakerism, of which his friend had written enthusiastically.

[106] This was a short-lived monthly, edited at Cincinnati (1861-62) by Moncure D. Conway, since distinguished as an author, who had resided for a time in Concord, after leaving his native Virginia. He wrote asking Thoreau and all his Concord friends to contribute to this new *Dial*, and several of them did so.

[107] Channing more than once described to me Thoreau's disheveled appearance as he came down the mountain the next morning, after rather a comfortless night. He was carrying for valise a green leather satchel that had been Charles Emerson's, having but recently been the guest of both William and Waldo Emerson. In depicting the scene from the Berkshire mountain, he recurred (in the *Week*) to the homesteads of the Huguenots on Staten Island, where he had rambled the year before this Berkshire experience, while living at William Emerson's and giving lessons to his sons.

[108] This was ten times as many in eighteen months as the *Week* sold in five years.

[109] Mr. Greene lived in Oakland County.

[110] This fixes the date of the Worcester portrait,—June, 1856, two years after the Rowse crayon.

[111] This "last discourse" was the long one on John Brown, now included in Thoreau's *Miscellanies*, and formerly in the volume beginning with "A Yankee in Canada."

www.ingramcontent.com/pod-product-compliance
Lightning Source LLC
Chambersburg PA
CBHW060805310726
48980CB00002B/245

9783732630363